Patrick's DILEMMA

To Brandon,
Thank you for your work to provide permission to use the photo on the back cover of this book. It looks great.
Enjoy!
John W. Fosnaught
12/1/19

JOHN W. FOSNAUGHT

First Edition

PAGE PUBLISHING, INC.
New York, NY

First originally published by Page Publishing, Inc. 2019

ISBN 978-1-64584-641-3 (Paperback)
ISBN 978-1-64584-941-4 (Hardcover)
ISBN 978-1-64584-642-0 (Digital)

Printed in the United States of America

Dedication

THIS BOOK IS dedicated to my friend Mary Blair, who lived a full and prosperous life but had to battle lung cancer in that long, long final year. Still, she shared with me her contagious smile in the last moment I saw her.

In Loving Memory

Sara Fosnaught Darling
Robert Fosnaught
Eugene Ierace

ACKNOWLEDGMENTS

I WISH TO ACKNOWLEDGE the following individuals for their invaluable contributions to this work. Without their ideas, comments, criticisms, and encouragement, this book would never have happened.

Kathy Acton
Mark Acton
Charles "Pete" Aldenderfer
Christine Calderwood
Katrina Calderwood
Robert Calderwood
Dr. Steven Dryden
Pam Dryden
Ellen Fosnaught
Erik Fosnaught
Marian Fosnaught
Joan Gray
Dr. Gil Herod
Helen Hofmann
Indiana Blood Center
Dr. Erica Leazenby
Lynn Lorton
Carla Monroe
Yvette Robinson
Sandi Slavin
Alicia Wojciechowski

Chapter One

I ALWAYS DID WELL on binary tests. With just two choices, the answer was easy. True or false, yes or no, go or no go. Pick one. You are either right or wrong. Get on to the next question. My instincts were pretty good, and I picked the correct answer more often than I had any right to expect. That was before the two choices were life or death.

Back in high school we had a lot of binary exams. My Spanish teacher, Miss Rosen, gave us true-or-false quizzes after every reading assignment. Most of the time, I didn't do the reading. I did great on these tests, though. That's because I cheated. Miss Rosen knew I cheated because I could never answer questions during class discussion, but she couldn't figure out how I did it. She confronted me once, and I gave her a story about being able to read the tone of her voice and determine whether she was telling the truth or not. Of course, she didn't believe me, but she had no proof otherwise.

She began to administer the tests from right in front of my desk so she could watch me closely. I didn't mind that. She was the reason I took Spanish in the first place. She was the most beautiful teacher in the school, the most beautiful woman I had ever seen. She held the questions and answers close to her chest so I could not see. She asked the questions in the most monotonic voice her Spanish accent would allow, even though she knew that was not my secret. She watched my every movement to be sure I wasn't using cribbed notes or referencing the reading. Since the readings were in Spanish and the test was in Spanish, this method of cheating would have been just as educational as doing the assignment in the first place, but I didn't point that out.

She watched my eyes closely to be sure I wasn't looking on someone else's paper. My eyes always looked directly at her. She was a sight to behold. Dazzling black hair hung to her shoulders then swept inward under her chin. Her sea-green eyes shone next to her fair complexion. Her nose was short, straight, and rounded at the end. Her lips always looked slightly moist even though she didn't appear to use lipstick. Although she dressed conservatively, her jackets could not conceal her breasts from my vivid imagination. I tried not to stare, but sometimes I couldn't help it. She was straight out of college, which would have placed her at four or five years my senior. Not that big an age gap in my opinion. I loved to gaze at her as she scrutinized my expression and my motions, looking for any hint as to how I came up with the right answers when I didn't even understand the questions.

In these tests, we were to answer yes, if true, and no, if false. Of course, we were to answer in Spanish. The Spanish for "yes" is *sí*, with an accent over the *í*. Making an accent requires such a dramatic pencil flick that peripheral vision is sufficient to pick it up without the slightest movement of the eye. The only thing necessary was to have the smartest girl in the class sitting just to my right. When her pencil flicked, the answer was "*sí*," and when it did not, the answer was "*no*." It was that simple.

I wish all my "yes or no" tests were as simple. Now, as I face the ultimate binary question—to be or not to be. I have no answer. If only I had the smartest girl in the class sitting next to me right now, I would know what to do. But I don't.

Chapter Two

WHY IS IT that in movies, the day and the weather always fit the situation? If the mood is gloomy, the day is overcast. If the circumstances are damp and dreary, the weather is the same. If the vampire is on the prowl, the night is dark, the wind howls eerily, and the moon gets clouded over. In real life, this doesn't happen.

From my hospital bed I could see that this January day was cheery and bright, though my mood was far removed from that. Sunshine streamed into the room on golden beams through the open curtains. The wide blue sky was occasionally broken by a billowing cumulous cloud but was otherwise clear and clean. Those few clouds floated gently across that blue field in no hurry to get to wherever clouds go. I was in no hurry to get to where I was going either.

I wasn't born yesterday. I knew I would have to go there eventually. We all make that journey. But at twenty-six, it was not only too soon to go; it was way too soon to even think about going. And unlike most of the people in these hospital beds, I had a choice. I could go now, or I could go later. Later is better, right?

My little sister, Corinne, was fussing with the stuff that cluttered my side table. There was a package of breath mints and a box of Kleenex and a slew of empty cracker wrappers and a pitcher of water with a water glass and a bunch of other muddle I couldn't identify. She needed room to sit the vase of winter roses she had brought, so the cracker wrappers had to go. She efficiently swept them into the wastebasket with one hand while holding the flowers in the other.

She was practiced at this sort of thing and managed to clean up the table without spilling the water or tipping the flower vase.

I say "little sister," but that's only because she's two years younger than me. She is not little at all. She stands a full six feet without shoes and has the strength of most men and more stamina than any woman. She needs every bit of that strength and stamina—she's a nurse.

In spite of her size and strength, she is still feminine. She was second runner-up for homecoming queen in high school, and the phone never quit ringing with guys wanting to take her out. As she matured from her adolescent beauty, she became even more lovely. Her auburn hair burns bright, and her smile lightens even my dark moods. It elicits a grin in return. Corinne Maloney is one tall, cool drink of water.

"Have you called Brian yet?" she asked.

"He doesn't speak to me," I replied. "Does he speak to you?"

"Of course, he does," she said. "He just needs to hear you say you're sorry, Paddy. Can't you just do that for him? It's not much to do before you…"

She didn't finish. As a nurse, one would think she would be used to talking about death. But she could not bring herself to say it. Perhaps her area of nursing didn't deal with death as often as other specialties. The Indiana Heart Institute, where she worked, was one hospital where people actually came out better than when they went in. Their pacemaker implants, valve replacements, coronary bypasses, angioplasties, and heart transplants were successful the vast majority of the time. Nearly all her patients were fundamentally stronger after treatment than before.

That was not the case here in the cancer ward at Community Hospital East. Most of these patients were going to die. The only question was how long they had. They faced that truth day in and day out, treatment after treatment, fighting against the inevitable. If the disease didn't get them, the treatment would. When you fight an invader with poison, it's often the poison that kills you.

Corinne rearranged the roses mixed with baby's breath.

"There, that's better."

I couldn't tell the difference.

"These flowers are from Daddy," she said. "He wanted me to tell you that he hopes you're feeling better."

"I suppose he picked them himself," I said. Dad spoke to me about as often as my brother did.

Corinne's smile faded. Her eyes bedimmed as she turned toward me and tears glistened in them. She was just as pretty with a sad face as with a smile.

"Paddy, you need to make things right with Daddy and Brian," she said. "You can't let things go on like this. Family and friends are all you ever have in this world, and I don't see many friends lining up outside the door here."

She didn't say that to be nasty. She didn't have that kind of streak in her. She just wanted me to come back to the fold. She was merely stating the obvious. But it stung all the same.

Truth hurts. There were no friends waiting at the door of Patrick Maloney, and there would never be friends at his door. Any friends I may have had were long gone. But that had not always been the case.

You won't have a nickname if you have no friends, for friends are the ones who bestow it on you. I had a nickname. I earned it in the eighth grade.

My family lived in Braeburn Village from 1984, the year I was born, until 1998, while my mom and dad saved money for a down payment on a house. That process took a long time since Dad didn't make much as a night security guard, and Mother had her hands full, first with Brian, then with me, then with Corinne.

Mother insisted we have a hot breakfast. Many a morning I came barreling down the steps, running late, eager to dash out and join the other kids at the bus stop, when she would block my way and send me to the table for my bowl of hot oatmeal. On more relaxed mornings my dad might join the four of us for bacon and eggs and fried potatoes before he went off to bed. For years I thought he didn't have a job. He was always asleep into the late afternoon and with us through the evening. I didn't realize that after we went to bed, he went to work.

Braeburn Village was a vast apartment complex on the far east side of Indianapolis. It had a swimming pool in the center of the complex filled with kids every summer day. Two-story red brick townhouses surrounded the pool and spread out for several blocks in all directions. The streets within the complex were all named Braeburn something. We lived on Braeburn Court Drive East. Brian's friend Gino Martinelli lived on Braeburn Terrace Drive East. It was almost like a Homer Price story. The mail carriers were the only ones who could figure out the addresses. Everyone else just referenced the clubhouse, as in, "I live two blocks over from the clubhouse, and then turn right, number 2334."

I went to Lakeside Elementary School from kindergarten through fifth grade. Then I went to Brookview Middle School for sixth and seventh grades. There were plenty of kids at school and in Braeburn Village, but I didn't connect with any of them. I was a late bloomer and was exceptionally small. I couldn't compete in sports or games with the other boys my age. I wasn't the last kid chosen in the pickup basketball game; I was the kid who was never chosen. I was the one they told to go home and come back when I grew up. I was the one they threatened to use as a football or as second base, depending on the season. Unlike my athletic and popular older brother, I had no friends.

But things can change fast in the life of a thirteen-year-old.

During the summer of 1998, between seventh and eighth grade, three things happened that transformed my life for the better: I grew six inches, I added seventy-five pounds, and my family moved to Center Township.

We bought a three-bedroom house on Wallace Avenue. Dad used to tell people we lived in Irvington, but we were actually a few blocks to the west of that famous neighborhood. Grandma Maloney's house on Julian Avenue was smack in the heart of Irvington, but we couldn't afford a house in that neighborhood on Dad's meager income. Wallace Avenue was fine with me. With the change of size and the change of scenery, I also got a change of schools. Brian wasn't happy to move from Warren Central High School to Howe High School, but I was thrilled. My reputation as a squirt was behind me, and I now had a body that could compete. I didn't want to be a star. I just wanted to be on the team. I just wanted to play.

Soccer was being introduced to Howe that year. None of the kids had any experience in the sport, so my lack of familiarity with the techniques was not a hindrance for me. We all learned the moves and the plays and the strategies together. I was a little awkward with my new size, but I noticed the other kids were struggling with the same issues. I began to fit in.

We lost every game but one that year. That one win was where I earned my nickname. It was against Arsenal Tech, which normally excelled in sports, but with a heavy focus on football and basketball, had few resources for soccer. We won the match three to nothing, and I scored all three goals in the second half. That's known as the Hat Trick. Since my name is Patrick, it was only natural to start calling me Patrick the Hat Trick after that.

Chapter Three

PATRICK THE HAT Trick was an excellent nickname. It sure beat Needle Nose or Football Head, which were a couple of other nicknames kids were saddled with in school, and there were some that were much worse. How would you like to be called Wetter? Billy Setter wet the bed at Boy Scout camp and got stuck with that handle to the end of his high school years. My nickname suited me fine.

It wasn't long before Patrick the Hat Trick was shortened to Hat for ease of delivery. It's funny how things evolve. I knew a kid who was called Stink Pot by his older brothers and sisters because of his dirty diapers. Their mother forbade them to use that nickname for fear it would damage his psyche, so they started calling him Ink Spot, which meant the same thing. This evolved to Inky, which his mother calls him to this day. I don't think she realizes the origin of the name. My mother would have known the origin of a nickname before she used it. She knew where my nickname came from, and she was proud of its source, but she never called me Hat. I was always Paddy to her and to my father, brother, and sister as well.

My name evolution came in handy several years later.

Each September, the senior and junior classes conducted campaigns and elections for the class officers: president, vice president, secretary, and treasurer. My senior year, my gorgeous Spanish teacher, Miss Rosen, was assigned faculty sponsor for the elections. Naturally, I decided to run. This way I could be close to her after school.

I remember walking into the gym for the organizational meeting, quaking like an aspen leaf in a gentle breeze, butterflies having a field day in my stomach. I saw her every day in Spanish class, but this was different; this was up close and personal.

"*Señor* Maloney," she greeted me, "you are running for office?"

"I think so," I said.

She was beautiful. Her cheeks had a hint of blush, but not from makeup, a natural flush that came and went with her smile. Her skin looked soft as a petal on a freshly cut wildflower. She was a rose, just as her name declared. I yearned to touch her face, brush my cheek against hers, press her lips to mine, and hold her in my arms. I caught a whiff of her scent, lemon, as in soap, clean and fresh. Her eyes beckoned me.

"What office are you running for?" She had a form in her hand, all business. Her eyes searched mine, not for signs of attraction, but for a response to her question.

"Yes," I said. I looked at the bleachers. They were empty. I didn't know what to do with my hands. I stuffed them in my pants pockets.

"*Señor* Maloney? Are you running for an office?"

"I think so."

I became very conscious of my own appearance. Was I attractive to her? Was my hair orderly or in a mess? I brushed my front locks across my forehead with my fingers. I certainly didn't smell like lemons, but was I acceptable? I'd had a shower after gym class that afternoon, but it was hurried, and I couldn't recall whether I'd used deodorant or not. I took the form from her hand without making contact with her skin and slunk away to the bleachers to complete it.

Unaffected by my lost composure, she moved on to the next student entering the gym.

I'd blown my first opportunity for personal connection with her. I was totally unprepared, and as a result, I reacted without control. I didn't understand my reaction. I had never been uncomfortable with a girl before. I never had to plan a meeting or a conversation; it had always just come naturally. Of course, she was not a girl; she was a woman. She was a teacher, my teacher.

Was that the explanation? Or was there more to it? I felt there was more. She was special.

I took a quick sniff of my armpits and determined that my deodorant was working well in spite of the strain I'd just put it through. I decided that my hair had always been fine before and was still fine now. My clothes were the best I could do. My only hope was that I would get a second chance.

And I did.

The form asked mostly for identifying information, but the school administration had a policy that the faculty sponsor had to preapprove any campaign signs, slogans, or posters. The form had space to write in any slogan that would be used in the campaign. I quickly decided to run for treasurer and just as quickly came up with my slogan: "When it comes to the class treasury, Don't Pass the Hat!"

I sat in the bleachers while the other candidates turned in their forms. Miss Rosen reviewed them briefly before adding them to the stack. As she read each form with her head bent forward, her hair would fall around her face. Every so often she would give her head a jerk and fling her hair back behind her ear. In the same motion she would brush the loose strands into place with her hand using her ear as a catch. This was not done in the flippant manner of some airhead junior girl trying to look sexy, but with a professional, get-the-job-done approach. This was sexy, and I loved to watch.

It didn't seem like the other guys were affected by her or even noticed her. They just wanted to get their forms approved and move on. I couldn't understand why they weren't struck by her beauty, why they didn't want to linger near her. I was glad they didn't. I had seen boys contend for a girl's attention before, and it is not a pretty sight. Sometimes it would even erupt into a fight or other violence. I was never involved in anything like that because I was never involved with a girl.

The girl candidates did not tarry either, and before long I was the only one left.

"*Señor* Maloney? Have you decided whether you will run or not?"

"Yes, I will, *Señorita* Rosen," I said as I walked across the gym floor to her table. I handed her my form and watched as she flipped her hair back behind her ear. She wore a simple ring of silver in her ear that shone brightly against the contrast of her black hair. She read intently then smiled as she finished examining my form.

"That's a great slogan, Patrick. I've heard your friends call you Hat. It's a good idea to work a friendly nickname into your campaign, and you've done it very cleverly. I wish you success."

"Thanks." I didn't know what else to say. I looked around trying to come up with something, but the gym was as empty of ideas as it was of people. "Do you need help taking this stuff to your car?" I finally asked.

"No, thank you. I need to stay for a while longer in case another candidate shows up at the last minute. The notice said the signup would go for an hour."

"I'll stay with you to keep you company," I blurted, realizing I sounded too eager. She didn't notice, though, and smiled in appreciation. I sat in the empty folding chair next to hers and felt the exhilaration of being close to her. I was speechless as we sat for several silent moments.

She finally broke the silence. "You're a senior, Patrick, yet you are just taking Spanish 1 this year. Usually students take at least two years of language for college entrance requirements. Are you planning on going to college?"

"Oh, sure," I said. "I'm going to major in engineering, and that doesn't require a foreign language."

"So why did you decide to take Spanish this year?"

She caught me. I couldn't say I took it to be in her class. That didn't seem appropriate. I was stuck. What could I say? I shrugged my shoulders and looked at the door. It seemed like hours before I answered, but I guess it was only seconds.

"I noticed that there are a bunch of countries that speak Spanish and a ton of people coming to the United States that speak Spanish, so maybe I should learn some. It could turn out to be useful."

She accepted my answer with a nod and didn't comment on my hesitation.

"Why did you decide to teach Spanish?" I asked.

"I don't really know." She looked off toward the door just as I had looked a moment ago. "I guess…" she started, then hesitated, then sighed, "I guess I don't really know."

"Is this your first year teaching?"

"Yes. I graduated last spring. Just four months ago."

"You're not much older than me then."

"No, I'm not. I'm twenty-one, and I'm not yet sure what I want to do with my life. Maybe I want to teach Spanish, but I don't know for sure yet."

I was flabbergasted. I was eighteen, and she was twenty-one. Only three years separated us. That's nothing. When she turned thirty, I would be twenty-seven. When she turned forty, I would be thirty-seven. We could have a life together. I needed to say something to break the silence. With her seemingly in a philosophical mood, I needed to say something wise.

"When you're fifty, I'll be forty-seven," I said.

She laughed, and when she laughed, she was even prettier than before. Her eyes sparkled like polished emeralds, and her teeth shone like the full moon. Her cheeks rounded with the upward curve of her mouth as she blushed ever so lightly. I flushed with embarrassment.

"*¡Estoy embarazada!*" I said.

She laughed even louder, and tears came to her eyes as I turned crimson.

"*Señor* Maloney, *usted no está embarazada.*"

"What do you mean? I'm very embarrassed."

"You said you are pregnant." She laughed again, and tears streamed down those wonderful rosy cheeks.

I also laughed aloud at my mistake. Seeing her cry with laughter made me lose it.

Once we settled down, I managed to say, "I guess a little Spanish can be a dangerous thing." This set us off again, and neither of us could speak for several moments.

This was when I recognized that I was in love. I had never felt this way about any girl before. Did I know what love was? Probably not. But I knew that I was destined to love her. I would give my life for her if she asked. But why would she ask?

Chapter Four

"The flowers are very pretty, Corinne," I said. "Thank you for arranging them for me."

I meant what I said. In spite of the dazzling sunshine streaming in through the window and the fluffy white clouds in the bright blue sky outside, the hospital room was depressing. The sterile tang of disinfecting alcohol permeated the air. The reek of silent death seeped into the room from the quiet hall. Corinne's roses brought a small ray of cheer into both the room and my life.

She turned toward me and smiled.

"And tell Dad I said thanks."

"You can tell him that yourself, Paddy. All you need to do is take one small step toward him, and he'll come to you. One small step."

"I will."

"When will you? You always say you will, but you don't. Just like with everything else." Her face flushed as she flashed angry eyes and tossed her auburn hair with a flick of her head.

"I will, Corinne."

"Sure you will." She then dismissed my comment with a wave of her hand and busied herself with stacking magazines on the windowsill.

I knew what she was thinking. I had let her down before.

My mind raced back to high school again. I was a senior, and Corinne was a sophomore. The school had a Y-Teens dance where the girl asked the guy rather than the other way around. Corinne went to the dance with Bobby Mays, a sharp young kid who played guard on the basketball team.

No one asked me to go.

Since I was free that night, I told her I would drive her and her date to and from the dance if she got the okay from Dad to use the car. I knew she'd be able to get the car. Dad gave her anything she wanted. She went for the idea. She would have a chauffeured date, and I would have the car while they were at the dance.

Everything went fine at first.

"Remember to pick us up at eleven fifteen," she said. "We'll meet the rest of the kids at Steak 'n' Shake for about an hour or so then get home by 1:00. Okay?"

I mumbled incoherently as I lifted the car keys off the hook in the kitchen.

"Okay, Paddy?" She poked me in the stomach to get my full attention.

"Yeah, I got it."

"Don't forget now. Don't leave us stranded."

"I got it—high school, eleven thirty—no problem."

"Eleven fifteen! Not eleven thirty!"

"Yeah, okay, that's what I meant. Eleven fifteen."

I chauffeured her to Bobby Mays's house. She sat in the back and said "Onward, Percival" with a giggle. She was having a time. I sang "Sure It's the Same Old Shillelagh" to her as I drove. Her giggle still makes me want to sing. She floated up to his door and knocked.

Corinne and Bobby made a fine-looking couple. She was dressed to the nines. She wore a brand-new silk dress with eddies of red and blue and green cascading from her bare shoulders. She had her hair done up in curls on top of her head. With her hair up, her emerald earrings were very visible, dangling and bouncing against the creamy skin of her neck. He was all spruced up in a blue blazer with a red-and-blue-striped tie. They blended as they strolled together down the walk to the car. They looked like they could set the world on fire. He held the car door for her as she got in the back seat. His parents were standing at the door, waving as we drove off. It seemed a little bit backward to me. But what did I know? I never went to a Y-Teens dance in my life.

At the high school, kids were streaming into the commons area, girls in long multicolored gowns, hair freshly done up in curls and waves, sequins lightly sprinkled across their eyes and cheeks, guys in sharp jackets and shined shoes and pressed slacks, grins splashed across their faces. The flow of teenagers was like bees to a hive, and the buzz of their chatter filled the air. When Bobby opened the door for Corinne, she exited the car with such grace that it looked practiced. She drew notice just by being there. It was friendly, not competitive, attention. Several girls gathered around, and the murmur centered on her while the guys stood off and admired the girls from a short distance away. It was clear that in a couple of years, she would be in contention for homecoming queen. All was right with the world. The arrangement no longer seemed backward to me.

After I dropped them off at the high school, I drove over to Joe DeMarco's house on Butler Avenue. Joe was a buddy from the soccer team. His family owned a five-bedroom house with landscaped gardens and vast yards all around the house. Joe was their only child, but they still felt like they needed all those bedrooms. Joe told me there were two living rooms, a family room, a library, an office, and a playroom in the house, but I never saw them. Joe's parents didn't allow him to bring friends into the house.

When I drove up the curved driveway, Joe was on the front porch with a guy I had never seen before. They trotted down the several steps and across the front yard to the car. The new guy was a couple of inches shorter than Joe's six feet, but he was stocky and muscular. He looked like a wrestler except that he stooped as he walked. His five o'clock shadow indicated that he was older than we were. I placed him at about twenty-five.

"Hey there, Hat," Joe said. "Meet Tony Palomino."

Tony took my extended hand with too firm of a grip. It was as though someone had advised him that he needed to have a firm handshake in order to impress people, so he made a point of gripping firmly. It didn't impress me. It made me wonder if the guy was real.

"Where are you from, Tony? I don't think I've seen you around."

"I live up in Broad Ripple. I'm not around this area much."

"He cut the grass for one of my dad's rental houses," Joe said.

"Three houses," Tony said, holding up three fingers. He did this by pulling his index finger down with his thumb, leaving the other three fingers pointing up. The gesture also formed a circle with his thumb and index finger.

"Be careful how you do that," I said, nodding toward his hand, "or Joe's dad will pay you for zero."

Joe chuckled at the joke, but Tony just gazed at his hand in bewilderment. With his face still turned down toward his open hand, he looked at me through bushy eyebrows and crinkled his forehead. The left side of his lip raised and ran a curved wrinkle from the corner of his lip to the edge of his nostril. I nearly laughed aloud at his expression. It's good that I didn't.

"What?" Tony said.

"Your three also looks like a zero," Joe explained.

Tony's expression did not reveal any enlightenment.

"Never mind," I said. "What do you want to do? I've only got the car for a couple of hours."

"I lifted a bottle of whiskey from my dad's bar," Joe said. "Let's pick up Mary and go somewhere and drink it."

Mary Kelly was a junior at Howe High School, and she was a very popular girl, if you know what I mean. A little on the wild side, she liked booze and boys, and not necessarily in that order. Joe liked to visit with her every chance he got.

"Let's get some beer to go with it," Tony said, forgetting about his hand.

"I don't know. I've got to pick up Corinne at eleven fifteen. I can't be drinking."

"One drink won't hurt," Joe said. "Come on, Hat."

I gave in too easily.

I drove over to Mary's house on Dequincy Street. I was careful not to drive on Wallace Avenue. Our house was one block over and one block up from Mary's, and I was afraid that if Mother or Dad was out and about, they would see me with a bunch of kids in the car. That would not go over well. I was pretty sure that they would not be away from the house, and by avoiding Wallace Avenue, I felt reasonably safe, but I was uncomfortable all the same.

Mary was waiting for us at the corner, half a block up from her house. Apparently, she didn't want her mother to see her jump into a car full of boys. That was fine with me because my parents knew her mother from PTO, and the less the parents knew about this adventure, the better. She jumped in the back seat with Joe but gave me the biggest come-on smile she could muster.

"Hello, Hat," she purred, "nice to see you."

"Nice to see you too, Mary," I said innocently.

Joe shot me a "don't mess around with my girl" look, and I concentrated on the driving.

I drove over to Hilltop Tavern on Tenth Street, and Joe, Mary, and I waited in the car while Tony went in and bought two six-packs of Budweiser. It turns out that Tony was only nineteen, but his heavy whiskers made him look older, and he never got carded for beer. I parked the car along Pleasant Run Parkway, a two-lane back road that ran along a small stream. It followed a green belt, so it was dark and not heavily traveled. We walked down to the creek side, plunked down in the grass under a big old oak tree, and surveyed our goods.

Tony produced four plastic glasses from who knows where.

"Do you have any ice in your magic bag?" I asked.

"The beer's cold, and that whiskey don't need no ice," he answered.

"So be it," I said as I poured myself half a glass. Tony, Joe, and Mary did the same. I had never drunk whiskey before, but I had seen older men drink it. I knew you could drink it on ice or straight. When they drank it on ice, they usually sipped it. But when they drank it straight, they normally shot it down in one huge gulp. I wanted to show them that I knew what I was doing, so I decided that was how it would go.

"May the road rise up to meet you on your journey," I said. I put the glass to my lips and tipped my head back as I had seen it done at weddings and wakes. What happened next I had never seen or known. My throat burned, and the fire coursed down my esophagus and into my stomach. My choke mechanism kicked in, and I almost threw up the whiskey immediately. Instead, I swallowed it back and then coughed heavily. My eyes filled with tears that flowed freely down my cheeks. The burning did not subside but spread into my ribs. I placed my hand on my chest as though that might settle the blaze. I could feel my heart pounding. Again I felt nauseated. My stomach churned. It was good that I was not standing. I leaned back against the oak tree and closed my eyes.

"Man, that's some great whiskey!" Tony said.

I opened my eyes. Things had calmed down a little. My vision was blurry, but nothing was spinning. The fire had settled into my stomach, and it was slowly dying out. As my vision cleared, I realized that Joe and Tony had emptied their glasses at the same time as I did, and they had no comprehension of my severe reaction. Actually they both looked a little stunned themselves.

Mary, on the other hand, had taken just a sip, and she was fully aware of the whiskey's effect on the three of us. She gave me a knowing glance, and when I looked her in the eye, she winked.

"Excellent," I said. The word reverberated in my ears, and I decided not to say anything else for a while. I closed my eyes and let the echoes die and contemplated that wink. It was obvious that I could have Mary if I wanted her. I thought of Miss Rosen and realized I wanted no one else. I didn't even know her first name.

"Here we go, Hat," Joe said.

I opened my eyes. My glass was again half full. Joe and Tony and Mary were holding their cups up in a toast, waiting for me to join them. I lifted mine in acknowledgment.

"Cheers," Joe said, and we downed them in unison.

I suppose you have to develop a taste for whiskey. I also figure it will take some getting used to. I could tell it was going to take a long, long time and many tries before I came to grips with the stuff. My reaction to the second drink was pretty much the same as to the first, except that I was slower to recover. The burn was more intense. The spin was faster. I broke out into a cold sweat. My mouth began to salivate, and I knew I was going to throw up. My stomach heaved, but I didn't puke.

Joe, Mary, and Tony talked on, but I could not follow the run of the conversation. I could not focus. It was dark and I could not see the water, but I could hear the stream bubbling by, churning over the rocks. I watched the tree branches sway in the breeze, their leaves whispering secrets. The voices were in some faraway place where I could not go.

My hand felt cold. I looked down and found I was holding a can of beer. I drank. The fire was out. It was good that it was gone. I didn't want it to ever return. I drank again. Coolness swept down my throat. Welcome coolness.

I said something to Joe, but I couldn't understand what I said. He and Mary kept talking as though I had said nothing. Tony was silent. I looked down by my side and saw four empty beer cans. There were several more lying by Joe and several lying by Mary. Tony was stretched out on his back in the grass. I leaned back against the tree and rested.

Chapter Five

WHEN I AWOKE, Mary, Joe, and the car were gone. Tony lay still on his back in the grass among the empty beer cans just as I had last seen him, soundlessly sleeping off his inebriation.

My eyes were clogged with sleep and were not focusing properly, but I still could see that Joe and Mary were nowhere about. My head pounded brutally as I tried to rise. I lost my balance and fell back against the tree. I sat back for a moment.

My mouth was dry. It felt like someone had walked across my tongue in their stockinged feet. It tasted like that too. I was weary. I could not move. I had to rest.

My stomach roiled. I rolled over onto my side and threw up in the grass. I just wanted to lie there and wait for it all to go away. It would have to go away eventually. It would have to go away by the time Joe and Mary returned with the car. I had to pick up Corinne.

Now my mouth had a bitter taste. I crawled over to the creek and stuck my face in the cool water. Welcome coolness. I drank a small bit of it. It felt good going down. It felt bad coming back up.

I threw up until I had nothing left in me. Then I dry heaved for about five more minutes. My moaning and groaning must have been heard for miles around, but no one came to check on me. Tony did not stir. My back and stomach muscles began to ache from all the retching. I splashed cold water on my face and sprawled in the grass among the littered beer cans.

My mind started to clear as the fog behind my eyes slowly lifted, although my body was still in agony. I checked my watch. It was 2:30.

Corinne! I had left her stranded.

Chapter Six

CORINNE. I HAD left her standing by the hospital windowsill. All the magazines were straightened, and she had nothing to do with her hands. She silently stared out the window as though she too were remembering that terrible night in high school eight years ago.

"I'm truly sorry I ruined the Y-Teens dance, Corinne. I was wrong to go drinking with those guys when I'd made a promise to you."

"I know you are, Paddy." She turned and stepped over to my bedside. "You've apologized before, and I know you mean it. That's why I've forgiven you. But you've got to do the same with Daddy and with Brian."

"I will."

"It's time you decided what's important in your life. You can't allow what little time you have left to be wasted. I won't allow it."

"I said I will, Corinne. I will."

She walked over to the shelf on the wall opposite my bed. Yesterday she brought in a crucifix that had been Mother's and placed it on that shelf for me. She now adjusted the crucifix so that I would have a better view of it from my bed. The silver Jesus on the cross gleamed in the sunlight as she turned it more fully toward me.

"Paddy, when was the last time you prayed?"

I gave no reply. I just looked blankly at the door, hoping that someone would come in and change the direction of this conversation. I didn't want to tell her that I didn't pray, that I didn't go to church, that I didn't really believe in God. She was a devout Catholic, and hearing me say anything like that would break her heart.

"If you pray to God and ask for His guidance, He'll help you through this terrible ordeal."

"I pray all the time, Corinne."

"You don't need to humor me, Paddy. I know you don't go to church. I know you don't pray. But you do know how. You learned from Mother and from Daddy just as I did. Talk to God about this affliction. It will give you strength and direction."

"I will," I said.

"God has a purpose in all of this. You have a purpose in life. If you talk to Him about it, He may help you understand His plan for you."

"I have a purpose? Right! I'm a joke. My purpose is to go on living—or just die. Hamlet had it right. 'To be or not to be? That is the question.' Except that for me, it doesn't matter either way, does it?"

"Paddy! Don't you talk like that! Of course it matters—life always matters. Life is precious and purposeful. You just have to find your purpose."

"I'm too little, too late. That's exactly what I am. Dr. Blumenthal calls me *Nessa*. Do you know what that means? It means miracle. Some gift I've got. It's more like a curse."

"It is a gift," she said, but I could see in her eyes that she had her doubts. I could hear the hesitation in her voice. She too wondered about God's plan. I hated that I was the source of that doubt, and I hated God for making it so.

"You need to ask God's help to understand this thing," she continued.

"If I have this malady for a reason, then why couldn't I help Mother?"

She didn't answer.

Chapter Seven

OH, GOD, WHY have You forsaken me? Why did You give me this terrible malady when I had my whole life before me? I never had a chance to achieve my full potential before You took it all away from me. And the only redeeming value of this illness was not revealed to me until after it was too late to save Mother. How could You stand silently by and let Mother suffer and die while I held the cure?

The silver Jesus hung on the cross, unresponsive to my pleadings. I thought of the times I had argued the validity of His claim of godliness and wondered at my arrogance. I had been confident of my veracity and debated the issue eloquently. Now I was not so self-assured.

I hated God and I hated Jesus. I had become the source of Corinne's doubt, and I hated myself for that.

Corinne meant only the best for me, and yet, I repeatedly returned her favors with rudeness. She visited me when others had forgotten me. She encouraged me, brought me flowers, read to me, talked to me, and I did nothing for her in return but give her grief. I argued with her, lied to her, refused to listen. She forgave me my most heinous offenses, and I turned around and committed worse. I denied the truth, and ultimately, I shook her faith. I didn't deserve to have her as a sister.

I should never have thrown Mother's pain up to her as I did. It was my failure, my cross to bear, not hers. Corinne did everything humanly possible to ease Mother's pain. She cared for her just as she now cares for me. She learned the value of kindness and compassion at Mother's sick bed and became a professional nurse as a result. But she could not cure Mother's disease any more than she can cure mine.

Only I had the power to cure Mother. I just didn't know it. God, if He exists at all, in His infinite wisdom, chose not to reveal this power to me. He left me to grieve for Mother instead of showing me the way to save her. He allowed me to stand by thinking I was useless when I was the only one who could be helpful. He let me wallow in despair when I could have acted clearly and decisively, if I had only known the power that was within me. He permitted me to do nothing when I could have done everything. I hated Him for that. And I hated myself as well.

Chapter Eight

CORINNE WAS A strong woman. She recovered quickly from my retort, more quickly than I did, in fact.

"Mother was so proud of you, Paddy, when you got your soccer scholarship," she said.

"Yes, she was, but I let her down in the end. Not you though. Both you and Brian earned your scholarships, and in the end you both justified them."

"But you earned yours too."

"Brian got me mine."

Brian was the best athlete in our family. He was the star running back on the Howe High School football team, three-year letterman, two-year all-state. He helped Howe go two years in a row without a loss and win the Indiana state high school football championship both of those years. His senior year, the *Indianapolis Star* named him Mr. Football, the state's best high school football player for that year. He received scholarship offers from Indiana, Purdue, Notre Dame, Michigan State, Ohio State, Miami of Ohio, and Louisville, and he accepted the offer from Ball State University in Muncie, Indiana, because he wanted to be a teacher and he wanted to stay close to home.

Our soccer team did not win any state championships. We barely won any games, eight wins in five years, including three my senior year. That's not the kind of record that catches a college recruiter's eye. Neither did our coach have contacts in the college soccer recruiting programs. As a result, we did not have a student receive a soccer scholarship in the entire five years that I went to Howe.

Except for me, that is, and I nearly blew my opportunity.

Brian started classes at Ball State University the summer after high school. That way he could use their training facilities and go to the unofficial summer football practices before the regular practice sessions started. That summer he met the Ball State soccer coach, Rizzoto Petricola, and talked me up as a possible recruit for the next year. Apparently, soccer coaches listen to superstar football players, because the coach came to observe our first two matches that year. We lost both matches, and he lost interest in me.

He must have seen something he liked, though, because he told the coach from IUPUI about me. IUPUI is a joint venture of Indiana University and Purdue University at Indianapolis with a large campus just west of the downtown area. Without my knowledge, nor that of either my parents or my high school coach, Frank Harrison, the IUPUI head soccer coach, attended several of our matches during that season and was favorably impressed.

But as I said, I nearly blew it. If not for my fascination with my Spanish teacher, Miss Rosen, I never would have ventured over to a construction site one Saturday morning late in the season.

I awoke on the morning of our penultimate soccer match to the unrhythmic pounding of hammers emanating from across the street. After a hearty Saturday breakfast of sausage, eggs, home fries, and wheat toast with blackberry jam, I went out to the front porch to investigate. The Van Landingham family who lived in the one-and-a-half-story bungalow across from us was having the roof replaced. This was not a mere reshingling job but was a full tear off and replacement of shingles and decking. A crew of six or seven Mexicans was hard at work removing the old material and tossing it down to the ground around the house. Another Mexican stood on the ground supervising the removal. At first the men looked like they were scurrying about in a disorganized frenzy like ants that had just had their hill destroyed, but on closer observation, I could see the pattern in their movements and discern the productive objectives in their seemingly random bustle, just like those ants unwearyingly rebuilding their home.

I had been studying Spanish in Miss Rosen's class for about two and a half months and had recently discovered that I was secretly, and silently, in love with her. Feeling sure that a rousing conversation in Spanish with a genuine Mexican from Mexico would go a long way toward providing talking points with my new love, I crossed the street.

"*Buenos días,*" I said, brandishing my best Spanish accent.

"*Buenos días, Señor,*" he replied. "*¿Habla español?*"

"*Yo hablo español un poco,*" I stated slowly and clearly.

"*Está bien, Señor. Pienso que es un día perfecto para hablar y trabajar. ¿Es la verdad?*"

"*Repita usted por favor, más despacio.*" I didn't follow a word of what he said after "*señor.*" The conversation in Spanish idea maybe wasn't so bright after all.

"*Es un día perfecto,*" he repeated, more slowly.

"*Oh, sí,*" I said, even more slowly. "*¿Cómo está usted?*"

"*¿Estoy bien, y usted?*"

"*¿Stoiby yeniu sted?*" I knew this was a simple phrase, one I had learned on day one, but I couldn't place it. I began to feel lost, and my expression must have shown it.

"*Habla pocito, pienso,*" he said. "Thank you for trying to speak my language, *amigo*. You study Spanish in school?"

"Yes. I thought a little practice with a real Spanish speaker would be helpful, but I guess I need to learn a few more things beyond 'hello' to really have a conversation."

"You mean like 'How are you?'" I knew he was laughing at me, but his laugh was not a threatening one. It was friendly and encouraging.

"*Sí,*" I said. I knew that word very well. It had already done its magic on several of those reading quizzes in Spanish class.

"You study hard and learn, amigo, because Spanish is a very important language. It's the second most spoken language in the United States today."

"*¡Mira!*" shouted a worker from the rooftop. I looked up as a cluster of torn shingles descended from the sky, blotting out the light like a swarm of bats exiting their cave at dusk. I barely saw the young worker land on his feet with a thump in a cloud of dirt in the flowerbed. The shingles hit me square in the face and knocked me hard to the grass with a swirl of shingle dust engulfing my head. My face stung with a score of cuts, and my eyes burned and grated from the dust and grit. I choked on the debris but quickly cleared my mouth and caught my breath. I sat up and instinctively rubbed my eyes with dirty knuckles.

"*¡Cuidado, Señor!*" My new friend pulled my hands away from my eyes. "Do not rub your eyes. You might damage them. Here, try these eyedrops. Wash out your eyes."

He struggled to put some drops in my eyes while I fought against him, trying to keep them closed to avoid the pain. He was persistent and finally got a few drops in each eye. The fire still raged, but the scratch of the cinders was diminished. After several applications, the stinging started to subside. I still could not open my eyes, but at least they felt better while closed. My face was swollen both from the impact of the shingles and from the irritation to my eyes. The swelling seemed greatest over the tops of my cheeks and along the line of my eyebrows. I sat in the grass, head bowed, hands folded in my lap, awaiting a return to normalcy.

"*Lo siento mucho, señor.*"

I didn't recognize the voice. I tried to look at the speaker, but I still could not open my eyes.

"What's that?" I asked.

"He says he is very sorry. He tripped and fell with a load of old shingles and dropped them on you. He's very afraid that you are injured. Are you injured?"

"Tell him I'm okay. How is he? He fell from the roof!"

"*Está bien, Carlos. Vuelve a trabajo.*"

He continued in English. "He is fine. He knows how to fall. It's a good thing, too, because he falls from the roof at least once on every job."

I couldn't help but laugh, and my laughter set everyone at ease. Spanish chatter rose in the air like the chirping of crickets. It was a harmonious mix of sound in which I could distinguish no single words, just the "aba aba" of the vowel-oriented language. I felt better as they felt better. Their relief was my relief. I listened to the chorus of uninhibited patter and wished that I were fluent in this rich tongue.

Finally, I mustered the will to open my eyes. It was a slow, laborious process. My amigo gave me the eyedrops to use as I could manage, and I used them liberally. At last, my eyes were clear enough to navigate the terrain. I carefully rose and slowly began the walk across the street.

"Perhaps you should see a doctor."

"Yes, I will," I said, and I did.

Mother panicked when she saw my face. Dad chuckled. The scrapes and scratches on my cheeks and forehead had stopped bleeding almost immediately while I sat in the grass across the street, but red streaks and blotches remained as evidence of their existence. This was what Mother reacted to. Somehow Dad immediately discerned that the cuts and bruises were superficial and merely needed a good cleaning.

"You look like you ran face-first through a raspberry patch, son," he said. Mother watched nervously as Dad ran lukewarm water over my face then lathered up a washcloth and gave me a gentle but thorough scrubbing. I looked a lot better when he finished, and Mother calmed down.

My eyes were still swollen and my vision was blurred, so we went to the immediate care facility at Sixteenth Street and Ritter Avenue for an examination. The eye doctor determined that there was no permanent damage but that my eyes were severely irritated and enflamed. She gave me a prescription eyedrop that contained a steroid called prednisolone acetate and promised that my eyes would be in good health in a few days. They were fine by Monday, but I couldn't play in the soccer match that afternoon.

I sat alone on the bench, and Mother sat in the stands with the other parents. Unlike the football games, soccer matches did not attract big crowds. It was mostly parents and siblings of the guys on the team. This time Dad stayed home since I could not play. At home after the match, Mother told us of a man who inquired about me. She had noticed him at several previous matches but had given him no further thought. Now that he had approached her, she began to wonder. He asked for details of my injury. How did it happen? Was it serious? Would I play the final match of the season on Tuesday? Mother thought he was a concerned parent at first, but as he inquired further, she began to think there was more to it than that. She didn't see any harm in his questions, so she filled him in with all the details, including the presumption that I would indeed play on Tuesday.

I may have played the best game of my life on Tuesday. I didn't pull off a hat trick as I had back in eighth grade, but I did score two of our three goals, and I virtually smothered my man defensively. He barely saw the ball, and when he did, he had to dump it off quickly since I allowed him no play. I intercepted a number of passes and stole the ball several times. We won the match 3 to 2 for our third and final win of the year.

As we carried our coach off the field in celebration, I saw a man talking with Mother and Dad. He was a large man who sat straight in the bleacher seats in spite of there being no back support. His smile was big, and he flashed it readily. He was obviously an athlete. I suddenly realized who it must be: Rizzoto Petricola, the Ball State soccer coach, must have sent an assistant to observe me. I was glad that I had extra energy that day and was fully recovered from my eye inflammation. I had just finished playing a crackerjack game, and a college scout had seen me do it.

I had pretty much given up on the idea of going to college right out of high school. My family had no money for that sort of thing even though they strongly supported us getting as much education as possible. Brian had his expenses covered by his football scholarship, but a scholarship didn't seem likely for me. Since it appeared that Ball State had given up on me, I figured that I would probably go into the military service and then go to college on the GI Bill after I finished my hitch. This sudden appearance of a college scout at my soccer match canceled all that military service speculation and launched a fresh round of expectations of scholarship possibilities. My mind churned with excitement. Envisioning the newly surfaced soccer field at the BSU campus in Muncie, I imagined myself gliding swiftly from side to side, breaking clear at midfield, chasing down the forward pass from an equally animated teammate, gently nudging the ball forward without breaking stride, and then booting it with a powerful sideways kick that left me sliding across the grass and the ball streaking toward the corner of the net. Of course, the Penn State goalie could not get to the ball, and it slammed into the net just out of reach of his outstretched hand.

I broke away early from the victory celebration to join my parents in the stands. The man was still sitting with them, and he rose to greet me as I approached.

"Nice game, young man," he said as he extended his hand. "You were a one-man team out there."

"We all have our roles to play," I answered.

"I'm glad to hear you say that, because that's exactly our philosophy at IUPUI. If everyone fulfills their own specific role, we will have a successful team. If any one of us fails, including the coaches, we will all fail."

He watched my face to see if that sank in while he pumped my hand in a firm handshake. This handshake did not ring false as Tony Palomino's had the night I got drunk and left Corinne stranded. His greeting seemed natural and unforced. I immediately felt at ease with this man with the wide grin.

"My name is Frank Harrison, and I'm the soccer coach at IUPUI," he said.

I was speechless. It wasn't Ball State. I didn't even know that IUPUI had a soccer team even though the school was right here in the city. I don't know whether the disappointment I felt in my heart showed on my face, but something prompted Dad to speak up.

"He's quite taken by surprise, Mr. Harrison," Dad said. "He has been hoping for some attention from a college recruiter, but with the team's poor record, it hasn't been happening."

"That's right, sir," I said, recovering my composure in the brief respite Dad had afforded me. "Earlier this season, Coach Petricola came to a couple of matches, but there hasn't been any interest in me since then."

"I have interest in you, son. If you are interested in going to college at IUPUI, we have interest in offering you a soccer scholarship."

He smiled his broad smile, his eyes glistened, and he extended his hand once again. I felt comfortable in his grasp. It wasn't Ball State, but it wasn't the Army either. It was college, and it was the only offer around.

Chapter Nine

WE MET AT O'Donnell's Irish Pub in Linwood Square that evening. This was Dad's favorite place because they always had shepherd's pie and corned beef and cabbage and Irish beef stew available. Prices were reasonable, and the pub was only a few blocks from the house, so we could walk there as a family. We didn't go out to eat very often, but when we did, it was a grand family outing. We invariably returned walking and singing Irish songs.

That evening we went by car because Coach Harrison picked us up in his fancy red Cadillac Sedan Deville. He was treating.

Dad ordered the beef stew, while Mother and Corinne both had their usual corned beef and cabbage. I liked fish and chips, and although I'd never been to Ireland, I was sure O'Donnell's fish and chips were authentic. You could even get it wrapped in newspaper if you wanted. You didn't have to ask for vinegar for the chips. This was undeniably Irish.

Coach Harrison was not used to this kind of place. I guess his recruits and their families usually wanted to go to fancier, more expensive restaurants since it was a free meal, but we knew what we liked, and we preferred simple pleasures. Good food and good company were all we needed. In spite of his lack of familiarity, Coach Harrison fit in fine. You would have thought his name was Finnegan.

Discussion during dinner revolved around the afternoon's soccer match, Mother's troublesome, persistent cough, and Corinne's upcoming PSAT exam. Coach did not bring up the scholarship until we had finished eating and were relaxing with after-dinner coffee and soft drinks.

"I understand that your brother is on a full scholarship at Ball State University," he said while holding his coffee mug directly over his dinner plate so that a drop of coffee fell onto the few scraps of cabbage left there. When I nodded my head in concurrence, he continued. "The scholarships that we have available at IUPUI are a little different from those at Ball State. We will cover your tuition, books, and any fees, but we don't provide room and board."

"Can he live at home while he goes to school?" Mother asked.

"Yes, he can," Coach answered. "In fact, many of our scholarship recipients are local kids that continue to live at home. Others are from out of town and have rented apartments close to campus. We will provide a twenty-four-hour metro pass so you can get to and from campus at any time at no cost to you. We'll provide a lunch pass for noontime meals in the cafeteria, and we sometimes have meals as a team. If you need tutoring in any subjects, we will provide tutors and study rooms at no cost to you."

He paused to let this information soak in.

"What other expenses are there?" Mother asked. "We have Brian off at Ball State, but everything is covered by the football team. I have no idea what things they are paying for."

Coach took a long sip of his coffee and then continued.

"Living at home, Patrick would have no room expenses. I assume he would have breakfast at home, and we will provide for lunch. Dinner would be an expense for him if he doesn't come home for that. Much of the time he'll be able to come home, but he may have an evening class or he may want to stay on campus for library study or group work or something like that. If he has to stay because of soccer team business, we will have dinner as a team at our expense. He will also have the normal expenses of a young man his age—clothes, snacks, dates, snacks, dates, snacks…"

Corinne poked me in the ribs with her elbow and said, "Paddy's never had a date."

"Yes, I have," I said as I flinched sideways and pushed her elbow out of striking distance. My response was automatic, but I realized what she said was true.

"Well, then that's some expenses you won't need to be concerned about," Coach replied. "Essentially, we will cover all costs specifically associated with school or with soccer. You will need to cover most costs associated with living expenses. In other words, we will launder the soccer uniforms, but you will launder your street clothes."

"That sounds wonderful," Mother said. "Paddy had given up on going straight to college, but now he can go without any extra cost. Is this scholarship for sure?"

"Your grades are pretty good, aren't they?" Coach asked.

I nodded.

"You still have to complete all your high school graduation requirements. You will have to apply for admission to the university, just as any other student would, and be accepted on your own merits. The athletic department will not have any influence on that process. We can provide assistance to you in completing the application forms, but we will not exert any pressure on the admissions committee in their decision to admit you or to deny admission. Do you know what you want to study? What major field are you interested in pursuing?"

"Civil engineering," I said.

"That would be offered by the Purdue University staff at IUPUI. You would actually apply to Purdue University for admission, attend classes that Purdue deems necessary, that are taught by Purdue professors, and you will receive a degree conferred by the Purdue University School of Engineering."

"That sounds fine," Mother said. "Tell me about after he finishes school. Do you find him a job?"

"We won't actually find him a job, no, but he will have full access to the university's job placement services just as all graduating students would have. His scholarship will cover any fees associated with that service. A Purdue graduate in civil engineering seldom has trouble finding a job."

Corinne then got into the act. "What about help making decisions?"

Warily I looked at her, the memory of the Y-Teens dance debacle fresh in my mind. She was smiling. She had forgiven me my failing, but she also knew my life decisions were not always appropriate.

"Ah, now there's a girl that's looking out for her brother. Yes, he will be assigned an academic adviser. All students are assigned an academic adviser whether they are athletes or not. This adviser will make sure that Patrick continues to advance toward his degree. He'll make sure the classes taken will apply toward the degree, and he'll also advise us of any deficiencies in credits or grades. Patrick will have to maintain a 2.0 grade average in order to continue to receive scholarship benefits. As far as other decisions go, we have guidelines and counselors for student athletes to help them adjust to college life and to help them handle situations as they arise. The student athlete is subject to pressures and circumstances that don't confront the average student. We are well aware of this, and we apply our resources as best we can to assist them and support them in any way we can. My guess is he'll get excellent counseling from the three of you sitting at this table."

Corinne was satisfied with that answer. She obviously felt that I would be in good hands.

"To finally answer your question, Mrs. Maloney, as of today, yes, this scholarship is for sure. As long as Patrick is accepted for admission, and as long as he satisfies high school graduation requirements, he has the scholarship."

To this point, Dad had listened quietly to the discussion, nodding approvingly as each aspect was raised and addressed and resolved. But now, with his brow creased and his eyes stern, he leaned forward and addressed the coach. "You said, 'as of today.' If Paddy had not played well today, would this scholarship have gone away?"

"I want to be 100 percent honest with you, Mr. Maloney. There was some concern about Patrick's injury on Saturday. Even though IUPUI doesn't cover every incidental expense the way Ball State does, we are still investing quite a lot of money in your son. It is critical that he be able to play and play well in order to justify that investment. His performance today showed that the injury did not affect his ability to play soccer. That was our concern. Now we can rest assured that he will be a highly productive member of our team, and you can rest assured that his college expenses will be covered."

Dad nodded and sat back in his chair, but the crease did not leave his brow.

I had nearly lost my opportunity for a college scholarship without even knowing that the opportunity existed. There was nothing wrong in what I did last Saturday morning. I was merely trying to improve my Spanish and trying to impress a girl, a woman. It was as innocent as innocence could possibly be. But innocence or guilt has nothing to do with it. It just happens. There is no grand plan, no design. It just happens, and if it works, it works.

Chapter Ten

DR. BLUMENTHAL CAME into my hospital room. He stood six feet two with broad shoulders and gangly arms. At about forty, he was starting to get a touch of gray around his temples, but he still had a head full of thick, dark hair. His green hospital scrubs were crisp and clean as though he had just come on shift, but I knew he had been in the hospital for hours.

"My, you look all fresh and done up," I said before he had a chance to address me. He usually greeted me with the word *Nessa*, meaning "miracle," to which I had come to have an aversion.

"Oh," he glanced down at his greens. "I just changed into fresh scrubs a few minutes ago. My wife always calls me when I've been working for more than four hours and tells me to change into clean clothes. She wants me to make a good impression on my patients, and she knows how hard I am on the scrubs." His face turned pink with embarrassment. This was supposed to be about me, not him.

He nodded toward Corinne. "Hello, Corinne. Nice flowers."

"Thank you, Doctor," she said.

He looked over my chart. "How are you feeling?"

"Tired," I said.

"That's to be expected. Your blood is not carrying enough oxygen to sustain much physical activity." He furrowed his brow as he placed my chart on its clip. He apparently had something on his mind but was slow to express it. "I know you gave blood when you were a freshman in college, *Nessa*. That was the donation that I tracked back to you after Joan Gray's recovery. But did you donate blood any other times?"

"Yes, I did," I replied, "several times."

I thought back to high school. Howe High School had an arrangement with the Indiana Blood Center to encourage giving blood and promote good citizenship. Early every December, the Blood Center would set up shop in the girls' gym so that students could conveniently donate their blood. It not only encouraged good citizenship, engendered vast amounts of goodwill for the high school, and generated many pints of blood for the Blood Center, but for the boys, it also became a rite of passage.

Students under sixteen years old could not give blood. At the age of sixteen, a student needed a parental permission slip. Once you turned seventeen, you were a man; no permission slip was necessary. The girls weren't concerned about this all-important transition into adulthood. They had significant events of their own, but for the boys, it was big-time.

Most kids didn't reach sixteen until late in their sophomore year or until their junior year, but I turned sixteen in September of my sophomore year.

I remember standing in line, early in the morning, outside the gym, permission slip in hand, along with juniors and seniors, while other guys in my sophomore class walked by, envious looks in their eyes. It was a glorious feeling to be moving forward in life ahead of my peers. I was careful to wear a short-sleeve shirt that day, in spite of the temperatures dipping into the twenties, so I could show off the bandage on my arm to all the girls all day long.

Giving held such an honorable place in the school that everyone gave. Therefore, the line was long. It extended from inside the gym, through the double doors, down the corridor, and around the corner toward the cafeteria. When I finally entered the gym, the line still stretched far behind me.

I began to get nervous when I saw the row of four recliner chairs along the far wall. A person rested in each chair, with a tube running from one arm to a bright-red plastic bag hanging from a chrome stand next to the chair. Upon closer inspection, I saw that the bags were not red but were clear, for some of them were not yet full. Men and women in pale-blue scrubs sat on short stools next to the donors, checking that all was going as planned. As one bag filled, the attendant reached to close off the blood flow. I was a little queasy with the sight of blood and the sight of needles, so I looked the other way. When I looked back, the attendant was applying a bandage to the donor's arm and securing it with medical tape. She gave the donor a small glass of orange juice and a cookie. The donor remained seated for several minutes after the procedure then rose and left the gym to be replaced by the next donor.

When at last I arrived at the sign-in table, I exchanged my permission slip for a short questionnaire. The form was easy. I didn't know what Accutane was, but when I was informed that it was a medication for acute acne, I was able to check "never used" and proceed to the physical appraisal. A blood pressure cuff and an in-mouth thermometer followed the questionnaire. Once I passed the tests, I went to the recliner waiting line.

I couldn't watch them as they searched each donor for a good vein, poking and prodding with a needle, some taking as many as three or four tries before they found the right spot and got blood flowing. The flow of blood was even more nauseating than the stick of the needle, and I found myself studying the line of students waiting their turn rather than look at the repulsive procedure of stick and drain. I noticed that many of the other students were doing the same. When it came my turn to give, I nervously sat back in the chair and watched anxiously as the attendant swabbed my left arm with alcohol and applied a tourniquet. She asked me to make a fist. I turned my head and looked at the big clock on the wall while she inserted the needle. I studied that clock as though it was a Van Ruysdael oil on canvas, afraid of the needle, afraid of the blood, afraid to turn my eyes back toward my arm.

It was over before I knew it. I was so focused on the clock that I never felt her remove the needle and swab down my arm and bandage it up. I turned my face toward her with surprise when she said we were through. The orange juice and cookies made me wish I had waited until later in the day since I was still full from a breakfast of three bowls of hot oatmeal.

I rose from the recliner feeling good: good physically and great emotionally. Physically I felt fine. I'd expected to feel a bit sluggish and drained from the loss of blood, but there was no such reaction. I felt a little tired but just as strong as when I sat down in that recliner. I had no nausea or dizziness like some of the others. I suppose the orange juice helped in that respect, but this trifling reaction surprised me nevertheless. Emotionally I felt fulfilled. I knew my blood would go to help keep someone alive. It didn't matter that I didn't know who or when. It mattered only that it would happen. I looked at the patch on my arm and came to the realization that impressing the girls with the patch was no longer that important to me.

Chapter Eleven

DR. BLUMENTHAL BROUGHT me back to the present with his next question. "You never donated blood after your freshman year in college, right?"

"That's right."

"Why was that?"

"It was not a good experience."

"And yet you felt no ill effects when you gave blood as a sophomore in high school?"

"None at all," I replied. "I was a little tired at first, but by that afternoon in gym class, I was fully recovered and I felt great. In fact, I felt invigorated, like I was recharged."

"Hmmm," he said. He could be noncommittal at times. He merely gazed at me and fiddled with the clip on his pen. Since he didn't follow up on his own with another question, I decided to elaborate.

"I thought a big part of it was the recognition that my blood was going to do something good. As kids in school, we always talked about doing things for the greater good, but it was all talk. We never had the chance to do for the good of mankind. We were just kids in high school. But this really was something for the good of someone else."

He nodded and gave me an understanding smile that encouraged me to continue.

"I had always thought of the blood drive as something you did because you had to do it. Everyone did it. Peer pressure, and adult pressure, for that matter. My driving motivation was to do it first, before any of my peers in tenth grade. One-upmanship and all that stuff. But once I gave that blood, it was different. It was real. It was actually doing something for the common good. That may have contributed to my feelings of physical renewal."

Dr. Blumenthal and Corinne both said, "Hmmm."

"I know," I said, "it sounds like the idealistic babble of a high school sophomore. I can't help it. Remember, I was a high school sophomore at the time. Even so, I do remember feeling refreshed, recharged, whatever. I attributed it to emotional well-being. I still showed off my arm patch to all the girls."

"What about the next year?" he asked. "Did you donate at the blood drive again your junior year?"

"Of course! My junior year was even more prestigious. I was seventeen and didn't need a parental permission slip. I was up there with the seniors."

"Did you have any problem with that blood donation?"

"No. Everything went smoothly just like the first year."

Actually the second donation was just a little different from the first. I was a veteran at this, and there was no nervousness or needle anxiety to contend with this trip. I went first thing in the morning just as I had the year before. I wanted the whole day to show off my bandage. This time I only ate two bowls of oatmeal for breakfast, and I had two extra cookies with my orange juice.

I didn't get the euphoric pump from knowing I was giving to the greater good. That novelty had worn off. It was more of a routine. The thrill of being involved in a thing larger than myself just wasn't there.

Yet I did get the physical pump. Of course, I felt tired at first, but by midmorning I was not only fully recovered, I was rejuvenated. I felt stronger than I had ever felt, and I was energized as I had never been before. I wished it was soccer season so I could take advantage of all the energy and use it to help us win a soccer match. Instead, I applied it to stamina and weight conditioning. My speed in short runs like the one-hundred-meter dash was not affected, but my time in longer runs like the four-hundred-meter and eight-hundred-meter was faster. I had better endurance and more stamina. I also pressed twenty-five pounds more than I had ever pressed before. I was a dynamo.

This new level of energy did not disappear. It continued through December and on into January. This was particularly odd, since I was always low energy in January. The month did not agree with me, and if bad things were going to happen, they would happen in January. I don't know if the power eventually faded away or I just got used to it, but I continued to press weight at the higher level.

Chapter Twelve

CORINNE HAD SAID little to this point. She was an excellent listener. This enabled her to perceive what was going on much better than I did. When she did speak, her words were always backed up by that perception and her questions were always designed to enhance her understanding.

"Why are you focusing on the blood drives, Doctor?" she asked. "Do you think he picked up this disease there? That would be hard to believe."

"No, he definitely did not pick it up there. That's not how this disease is contracted. But the symptoms would manifest themselves whenever he gave blood, or lost blood, as we have seen. I'm trying to determine when the problem first appeared, and we may be able to do that through the timing of the blood drives."

"Oh, I can tell you when it first appeared," I said. "At the time it was not obvious, but looking back, it's easy. I gave blood again my senior year. It was way different that time. As I've said, the previous two blood donations resulted in increased strength and energy, but my senior year it was the opposite."

I recalled watching other students donate ahead of me. Most would rest briefly in the recliner after the needle was removed and the arm was swabbed and patched. Usually it was only as long as it took to eat a cookie and drink the orange juice. Then they would be on their way to class, no worse for the wear. But occasionally a student would not recover so quickly. He would take a few more minutes, then he would rise slowly and move cautiously toward the door. Or one might rise too quickly and fall back into the chair, dizzy and disoriented. Some merely remained in the recliner until an attendant came with a cold washcloth to wipe away the perspiration.

I sympathized with those who had reactions like that. It was through no fault of their own that they were squeamish, and it didn't lessen their contribution in any way, but I was thankful that I was not among them. High school kids can be merciless. Their teasing of classmates who responded less than perfectly was callous and ruthless. Drawing attention to another's flaw is an old ploy to distract attention from one's own. High school kids are experts at this and, some develop the skill even further in adulthood.

I was confident when I settled into the recliner. I had done this twice before, and each time had been a pleasurable and satisfying experience. I even watched as the worker searched for a vein, taking three tries to make an appropriate connection. I watched the blood flow through the clear tube into the plastic bag, changing it from translucent amber to ruby red. When the bag was full, I accepted my orange juice and cookie and lifted two more cookies from the tray.

I popped a cookie in my mouth, and it had a bitter taste to it. My head didn't feel the same, but I managed to chew and swallow the cookie. My eyes blurred, and the room spun. I looked for the clock on the wall but could only find a smear where I knew the clock was mounted. The room spun again, and I closed my eyes to shut out the vertigo. I took a small drink of the orange juice. It felt good going down. It felt bad coming back up. An appalling memory of cool grass, cold beer, and warm whiskey flashed through my mind. I could almost hear the splashing, bubbling of Pleasant Run as I turned on my side and threw up on the gym floor.

The oatmeal was the last to come up. By that time, they had hustled me off to the nurse's office where I could writhe and moan and whine without disturbing the rest of the school. Stomach cramps replaced the heaves as spasm after spasm shook through me. When they subsided, I lay curled in a fetal position, soaked with cold sweat, on a bed with crisp white sheets and fluffy pillows, wondering what I had done wrong.

The blood test results came back clean. I was healthy. I felt miserable. They said I must be coming down with the flu, so I took a few days off school. It was December, and classes were winding down toward Christmas break, so I didn't miss much. I also avoided the razzing I was sure to get from my classmates. So much for being first in the rite of passage. Last year was old news. How have you performed lately?

My illness did not develop into the flu. I never had a fever. I never had muscle aches or cramps other than the morning that I donated. I did not experience any other flu symptoms except for a dramatic drop in my energy level. This lethargy lasted through Christmas and well into January.

Mother coddled me. I had never been sick before, and the incident with the rain of shingles was the only time I had seen a doctor for other than a routine physical for soccer eligibility.

Just as I had gotten used to my increased energy the preceding two years, I was able to get used to my new, lower level this year. Back in school in January, my press weight dropped thirty pounds and my stamina fell below previous levels, but I was still able to function. I had developed into a pretty fair athlete, and that had not changed.

Chapter Thirteen

BEING AN ATHLETE had some advantages off the playing field. Kids that I had never met knew me by name because I played soccer. Often kids assumed athletes had abilities not related to their sport that they didn't have. As a result of this, my campaign for class treasurer went smoothly in spite of my distinct lack of experience, knowledge, or training in anything remotely resembling the handling of money. I'm sure I was aided significantly by my snappy slogan, "When it comes to the class treasury, Don't Pass the Hat!"

However, my political operation was hindered by my lack of campaign proficiency. I was just too inhibited to promote my candidacy effectively. I not only lost the election, but I finished a very distant third out of three. I have been told that if there had been four candidates, I would have taken fourth.

Even so, I like to think I affected the election in a positive way. I took a part of the popular athlete vote away from a boy who played strong forward on the basketball team. He finished a close second. I'm sure that as a basketball player, he knew nothing about handling money, so I did the class a big favor by preventing his election as class treasurer.

The best thing about that campaign was that I achieved my goal of spending quality time with Miss Rosen, my Spanish teacher and the love of my life. I recall her stunning smile flashing across her face every time I went to her with some inane question about campaign procedure.

"You don't need to get your slogan approved again, Hat," she said, her moist lips parting to reveal her perfect teeth. I loved to hear her call me Hat. It meant our relationship was closer than merely teacher-student. It was on a more personal level.

"I just want to make sure I follow the rules, Toby." I had seen her first name in paperwork but had never used it with her before. I had been looking for an opportunity to slip it in covertly in the hopes that it would eventually become the common form of address, outside of class, of course. She didn't notice my usage, at least she didn't remark on it. I decided not to push it and would not refer to her name directly for the rest of the conversation.

"Everything about your campaign has been according to the rules. You don't need to worry."

"I don't know how to do this," I said. "I saw the others making signs, so I made some signs, but I'm behind the curve. The others got all the good locations before I even got started. Lately they've been organizing rallies and giving speeches. I have no idea how to go about doing that."

"You don't have to do the same things they do. Just be yourself. Walk up to people, shake their hand, say, 'Hi, I'm Hat Maloney. I'm running for class treasurer, and I'd appreciate your vote.' It's surprising how far that will go."

"I'm too shy to do that. I can't just walk up to people and start talking."

"You know all the kids in school, Hat. You can talk to anyone. You're a popular boy."

Lift me up then shut me down. She called me Hat then called me boy. I was making no progress. She misinterpreted my look of distress.

"You're going to have to do that if you want to succeed in politics. Bashful never got votes."

"Thanks," I said, "I'll try." But I didn't try. I didn't care if I won; I just wanted to be close to her, and I managed that quite well.

I got her approval of each of my six signs, one at a time to maximize visits. She approved each of the sign locations one at a time. She approved my walk-up line and my exit line, two visits.

"I'd really appreciate your vote, Toby."

"I'll be happy to vote for you, Hat."

Practicing walk-up and exit lines with her allowed me to call her Toby without being conspicuous. I was feeling closer and closer to her as the campaign wore on. Then the election came and ended it all.

I no longer had convenient excuses to talk to her once the elections were history. My story about being too shy to walk up and talk to someone was not a campaign ploy; it was the truth. I couldn't just start talking to her out of the blue. That's why I wanted to visit with the Mexican roofer the day of my face and eye injuries. I needed fresh material to talk about with her. That idea didn't work out well, so I had little contact with her outside class from early November until January.

I didn't mention my fascination with her to anyone except Joe DeMarco. I think I brought it up that night when we got drunk. Amazingly, Joe kept the secret to himself. I don't know why he felt sufficient loyalty to me to respect my position on this, but he only spoke of it when the two of us were alone. Perhaps he felt some responsibility for the fiasco I caused that night. He really was not responsible even though he provided the whiskey, took the car without permission, and kept me out till well past 4:00 a.m. I made the decision to drink both whiskey and beer, and I made the choice to neglect my responsibility to my sister and my parents. He just wanted a piece of ass, and he did no harm to the car. I was already beyond recovery by the time he took the car.

One afternoon in January, when I was feeling particularly weary, I decided to spend a study hall period in the library. Joe and I were the only ones at the reading table.

"I can't figure out how to get close to Toby Rosen," I said.

"You going crazy over that woman?" Joe asked.

"I'm already crazy about her. I've been crazy about her for months. I need to get close to her."

"Ask her out for a date," he said nonchalantly.

"Are you crazy?"

"How's she supposed to know if you don't take her out? You never tell her how you feel. You just come up with lame excuses to talk to her for a minute here, a minute there. That's not going to get her to fall for you, Hat. You got to ask her out."

"I can't do that. Not yet."

"You better do something quick, Hat. Mr. Newman is going to ask her to go to the prom with him."

"What? Newman, the algebra teacher?"

"That's the one."

"Teachers don't go to the prom. What's that all about?"

"He's one of the faculty sponsors for the prom committee. He pretty much has to go. Besides, he's young and single, and she's young, single, and pretty. I'm telling you he's going to ask her to go with him. You have to head that off if you're serious about this thing you have for her."

"How do you know this?"

"I have my sources." His devil's grin hinted at the mischief playing out in his head. "I have the grapevine."

I took this potential threat seriously. The next day I hung back after Spanish class ended. I needed to talk to Toby. There was one girl in class that always had questions for the teacher after class was over. I think she was just trying to suck up to her. Today was no different, and her idiotic prattle was going to make me late for my next class. I waited anyway.

After the girl finally left, Toby turned to me.

"*Señor* Maloney," she said.

So it was back to that. No more "Hello, Hat." Just the formal greeting, "*Señor* Maloney."

"*¿Cómo puedo ayudarle?*" she asked.

"I need to ask you a question," I said. "It's not about the Spanish."

"Oh, okay."

"Um, I don't…" I stammered. "I um…I think…"

"I think you will be late for your next class if you don't come out with it, Hat."

She called me Hat. She still felt close to me. That was all the encouragement I needed.

"I would be honored if you would go to the prom with me."

It wasn't that hard after all. I just needed to know that the familiarity we had developed that fall still existed in the winter.

"Oh!" she said. Her lips formed a perfect oval for the brief moment before her hand found her mouth and blocked that beauty from my sight. Then she dropped her hand and her lips curled into a slim frown, and I saw in her eyes that she was going to say no.

I needed to stall. I couldn't let it happen. I needed a way to take the big question back, but it hung out there in the dry air between us, sucking the moisture from my lips and mouth and throat.

Before she could utter a word, I said, "You don't have to answer right away. You can think about it if you want. Think about it over the weekend."

"I don't need to think about it, Hat. You know I can't go to the prom with you. I appreciate the honor of your invitation, but it wouldn't be proper. I'm your teacher, you're my student. Thank you for asking me, but we can't do that. I'm sorry."

Bad things happen in January. That night Mother told us that she was going to the hospital for some tests.

Chapter Fourteen

THERE WAS A tension at the dinner table that night that was out of the ordinary for the Maloney family. We were a close-knit clan, and our dinners were our gathering together and sharing time. Since Dad worked the night shift, we were able to have dinner together as a family nearly every night. While Brian played football in high school, he missed the Friday night meals since the football players ate dinner together as a team on Fridays after the game. My soccer matches were either on Saturday afternoon or Tuesday right after school, so they didn't interfere with our dinner plans. After Brian went off to college, he then became only an occasional participant, although his frequency increased after football season ended in November. Muncie is only a little over an hour's drive, so he could make it home easily if it was important. Brian was at the dinner table that night.

Mother and Dad were reserved. They thanked Brian for making the trip from Muncie on a weeknight but otherwise left the three of us to our sibling babble. We knew something was up, for they had specifically asked Brian to come home, but we tried to act as though nothing was out of sorts.

"Do you believe Johnny Farrell asked me to go to the prom with him today?" Corinne said.

"What's wrong with that?" I asked, thinking about my prom proposal that afternoon.

"For one thing, it's a little early, don't you think? The prom isn't until May. That's four months away."

"He wanted to get to you before anyone else does," Brian said.

"Well, that's the other thing. Everyone knows I'm going to the prom with Bobby Mays. Why would Johnny think he could jump in ahead of Bobby like that?"

"He just figured it was worth a try," Brian said. "Did you tell him no?"

"Of course, I did."

"Did you tell him why?"

"Yes. I said I was planning on going with someone else."

"You didn't say who?"

"No."

"Did he give you the weekend to think it over?" I asked.

"Why would he do that?" Corinne dropped her eyebrow over her left eye and scrunched up her left cheek in a look of bewilderment.

"I don't know," I said. "Was he embarrassed when you said no?"

"No. I don't think so. I think he fully expected me to refuse. How could he expect otherwise? When a boy asks a girl to the prom, he already knows what the answer will be. Normally, he doesn't ask unless he knows she'll say yes. But then, Johnny Farrell is far from normal."

I wondered what Corinne would think of me if I told her that I had asked Toby Rosen to the prom that very day, that I had no idea what she would answer, and that I had offered her the weekend to think it over. It looked like there were at least two guys at Howe High School who were suffering the anguish of rejection that night. Not only did I need to deal with Toby's refusal, but now I knew my sister would consider me to be far from normal if she got wind of what I had done. I thought it couldn't get any worse than that.

Then Dad cleared his throat, and we all knew he was not going to give us good news.

"I think you all know that your mother has not been feeling well lately. She's had a persistent cough and difficulty breathing for some months now."

Dad paused, and Mother's cough added emphasis to his pronouncement. She rose and cleared some dishes from the table and carried them to the kitchen. Corinne and I gathered several more plates and tableware and took them to the sink as well. It appeared that Mother didn't want this discussion to take place, and Corinne and I didn't want to hear it either. Brian sat silently, waiting for the next assertion.

"She has also been experiencing a loss of energy. The doctor has been treating her for bronchitis and has given her some medicines for that. What medicine have you been taking for bronchitis, honey?"

Mother took the pill bottle from the windowsill over the sink and read the label. "Mucinex," she said. "He also gave me a strong version of Tylenol. Tylenol 3, I think it is."

Dad continued. "But there has been a buildup of fluid in her lungs. The doctor thinks she may have walking pneumonia. He wants her to go to the hospital. They'll run some tests and possibly drain the fluid from her lungs."

Corinne threw her arms around Mother and hugged her. Mother hugged her in return, patted her on the shoulder, and disengaged.

"It's no big deal. They do this sort of thing all the time. I'll be in the hospital"—cough—"tomorrow overnight and be back home the next day." Mother kissed Corinne on the forehead then turned toward the dishes in the sink. She leaned over the sink and coughed twice and then paused to catch her breath. "Paddy, I think it's your turn to wash tonight. Corinne, it's your turn to dry."

Dad was wrong about one thing. I had not noticed that Mother was not feeling well lately. I knew she coughed a lot and sometimes had trouble speaking long sentences without stopping for breath, but I hadn't thought much about it. Mother was always the one who took care of us; she was not the one who needed caretaking. For the past month, since the blood drive, I had been the one moping around, missing school, neglecting my chores, thinking I had the bird flu or some other dread disease. She had babied me and nursed me back to health and eventually got me up and back out to school; all the while she was the one truly sick. I wasn't even aware that she was not operating at full capacity.

I realized, as she leaned on the sink for support, that I was of little support for her.

“They can cure pneumonia,” Brian stated while carrying an armful of dishes into the kitchen. “It’s the common cold that has the doctors baffled.”

“That’s right,” Mother added, straightening her back and turning toward Brian. “Penicillin is still”—cough—“the miracle drug of our day.”

Chapter Fifteen

MOTHER WAS IN the hospital for two nights. They drained her lungs twice and put her on tetracycline. This antibiotic was more of a preventative than a cure. They wanted to be sure she did not develop an infection from the draining procedures. When she came home on the third day, she was given a thirty-day prescription for Augmentin. This medication was the latest version of Mother's miracle drug, penicillin. Actually, it was amoxicillin combined with clavulanate potassium.

"I'm a new person," she claimed as she got out of the car in front of the house. "I can breathe!" She coughed and leaned back against the car door. Proof of her statement was visible in the mist of her breath against the cold January air. She looked up at her three children waiting anxiously on the porch. We stood on the edge of the top step like kids that had been admonished not to leave the porch but who strained to be as close to leaving it as possible.

"Brian!" Mother called. "I'm so glad you could be here for my homecoming."

"I'm sorry I didn't visit you in the hospital, Mother. It's hard to get away during the week, and I had already come down on Wednesday night. It's easier to get away on Saturday."

I hadn't visited her either, but I didn't have a ready excuse, so I didn't say anything.

"There's no apology needed. I know you're working hard in college. I'm just happy you could be here today."

Dad came around the back of the car and, firmly holding Mother's arm, helped her climb the few steps to the yard level. They paused there and let her catch her breath. In spite of having visited Mother in the hospital last night, Corinne could wait no longer. She bounded down the porch steps and into Mother's arms. Brian and I followed.

"Are you really better?" Corinne asked.

"I'm as well as can be expected," Mother answered. "I can breathe again." She coughed. "I still have a little cough, but that will go away when this new medicine kicks in. I'm a little weary, but I just spent three days in the hospital. If that won't tire you out, you have better staying power than I have."

I doubted that anyone had better staying power than Mother did.

"Let's get into the house and out of the cold," Dad said, "or we'll all be coming down with pneumonia."

Corinne had hot chocolate ready. We filled our cups and gathered around Mother in the living room. Dad brought her a blanket from upstairs, and she wrapped up and sat back in her favorite reclining chair, enjoying her family and her escape from the hospital. She was finally at peace after a wearisome ordeal that left her agitated and restless. We talked of the events of the past few days while she gently fell asleep.

Mother was not cured, although she insisted she was. The Augmentin made her feel better for a short while, but her cough did not go away. She never returned to her former energy level. She laid blame for her lethargy on her hospital stay long after she should have recovered from that. I think she felt well again because her breathing was fuller and smoother due to the fluid drainage, but we feared that fluids were again building in her lungs. Even I noticed that she was fatigued and her cough was sounding raspier. But she fought through all that, and before long things were back to normal.

Chapter Sixteen

TWO MONTHS AFTER her return from the hospital, Mother was still suffering from fits of coughing and exhaustion, but she was adamant that she was well enough to go to the Saint Patrick's Day party at the church.

Although Our Lady of Lourdes Roman Catholic Church in Irvington was not officially an Irish church, it had plenty of Irish in the congregation, and the annual Saint Patrick's Day party was a longstanding tradition. This event was never missed by the Maloney family. In fact, Dad says he has been to every party since 1962. Since Dad was born February 17, 1962, that would have put him at exactly four weeks old when Saint Paddy's Day rolled around. I have often doubted this assertion, but he says that it was on a Saturday that year, which makes for a larger turnout, and since Grandma and Grandpa Maloney didn't want to miss such a grand party and they didn't want to leave their tiny baby with a sitter, the tradition of taking even the newborn babies to the party was started. Grandma says every word of it is true, but she would back Dad up even if he insisted the sky was green. In fact, I think one time he did say that the sky was green on the day he was born, and Grandma Maloney nodded and said, "Yep."

The church is located on South Downey Avenue and was only one block north of Grandma Maloney's house on Julian Avenue. She walked to church every morning and watched her three sons serve Mass as they grew into their teenage years. Later she walked to church each morning and watched Brian and me serve Mass as we did the same. Even when we lived way out east in Braeburn Village, we attended Our Lady of Lourdes Parish and we served Mass every morning before school.

When Mother announced on Wednesday, March 12, that she was going to the party on Monday, March 17, she left little time to prepare. Brian had to arrange transportation and cover for the classes he would miss on Tuesday; Corinne had to talk Bobby Mays into going with her even though he had basketball practice after school and a game on Tuesday night; and I had a sudden urge to ask Toby Rosen to go with me. Since it was not a school function, I saw no reason for her to refuse.

The next day I lingered after Spanish class, and that same girl was waiting to talk with Toby again. I let her go ahead of me because I didn't want her to hear me ask Toby to go to the party with me. She rattled on and on about some article she read in *Newsweek* magazine about trouble with drug cartels in Mexico. What did that have to do with learning to speak Spanish? I fidgeted while I waited, and she finally got the message and brought her commentary to a close.

Once the girl had left, Toby turned to me with a smile and a flip of her hair.

"*Señor* Maloney," she said. "*¿Cómo puedo ayudarle?*"

I conjured up all the courage I could muster, and before I could talk myself out of it, I said, "Would you like to go to the Saint Patrick's Day party with me on Monday?"

She looked stunned and stunning. Surprise registered in her eyes, and in the gleam, I could see that she was going to say yes. She blushed faintly from her cheeks to her ears, her pink skin contrasting with her jade-green earrings. The top two buttons on her blouse were open, and at this close vantage point, I could see the beginning of cleavage. I imagined her in my arms on the dance floor with her breasts pushing against my chest. I vowed to kiss her on Saint Patrick's night. What a glorious night it would be.

"We talked about this before, Hat. You know I can't go out with you."

Another broken vow. How many more vows would I break before it all caught up with me? That gleam in her eye was my imagination, not her anticipation.

"It's not like it's the prom," I said. "It's not even a school function. It's at the church."

"I'm still your teacher, Hat. It wouldn't be right."

"I don't suppose giving you the weekend to think it over would make a difference, would it?"

Her laugh settled my despondency. She was beautiful, and nothing could ever change that. Even in rejection, she made my heart soar.

"I'd love to be able to say yes, Hat, but I can't. I appreciate your asking me. I really do. But it just cannot happen."

I grinned at her as I turned and left the room, but my head sank into the collar of my shirt and my shoulders slumped forward as though a great burden had been placed upon them. I fought back a tear that I knew I had no right to shed, but the tear fought harder and it fell cleanly from my eye and landed on the Spanish book I carried in my hand.

Chapter Seventeen

THERE WAS A big turnout for the Saint Patrick's Day party even though it was held on Monday night. Brian managed to make his arrangements and arrived home in plenty of time to go to the party with the family. Corinne convinced Bobby Mays that this was a significant event for her family, and he agreed to give up some study time to go with her. His schedule was tight since he had basketball practice after school, but he picked her up with time to spare. He had turned sixteen since the Y-Teens dance and now had his driver's license. He was happy that he was not depending on me to chauffeur them. I can't say that I blame him.

Mother was doing great. She coughed a little every now and then but otherwise seemed fine. Dad had arranged for the night off from work and was ready for a good time. We planned on spending the night at Grandma Maloney's house so Dad didn't need to worry about having an extra beer or two.

We parked in the church lot and entered the side door into the Catholic Center. The party room was the gym with the bleacher seats folded back into the wall and the backboards, and baskets swung up on their hinges to the ceiling. Long folding tables with white paper table covers were set up across the floor with a large area near the stage cleared for dancing. Scattered instruments indicated that later there would be a live band performing on that stage. Green and white helium-filled balloons floated over the tables, their green and white ribbon tails anchored by ceramic shamrocks. Paper shamrocks and cardboard leprechauns were attached to the walls at various points about the room, and a long string of green cutout letters was draped from the ceiling, stretching from one wall to the other, that read "HAPPY ST. PATRICK'S DAY!"

About half the tables were occupied, and every indication was that they would all be filled soon. People were streaming into the room like shoppers into Walmart on Black Friday right after the doors were opened. Grandma Maloney saved a table near the dance floor, and we hurried over to it. It was a table for twelve, but she had pulled up two more chairs since we expected to have fourteen from our family. We were soon joined by Dad's older brothers, Uncle Joe and Uncle Bill and his wife, Terri, along with Cousin Billy, who was a junior at Warren Central High School. Aunt Mary and her husband were going to miss dinner, as would Cousin John, but all three would join the party later. Aunt Maggie lived in Boston, and her family would no doubt attend a similar function there. Although all the aunts, uncles, and cousins couldn't be there, Dad's family was still well represented.

Mother's family was there as well and, as usual, occupied two tables next to ours. Mother was the sixth child of seven children, and the only girl, so there were a few more Sullivans than Maloneys at the party.

The family surname was not originally Sullivan but was actually O'Sullivan. Thomas O'Sullivan came to America from County Tipperary in 1848 to avoid the potato famine and the British government discrimination against the people of Ireland. He changed his name in an effort to avoid the discrimination he encountered here in the United States.

Mother's brothers, Joe, Sean, Eddie, Liam, and Michael, showed up with their wives and most of the kids. Mark was Mother's only absent brother, and he was expected to arrive later. Grandma and Grandpa Sullivan were in their seventies but still could shake a leg on the dance floor along with the best of them.

The meal was a typical Irish dinner: beef stew, corned beef and cabbage and potatoes, and freshly baked bread. The beer from the taps was its normal pale color—these Irishmen didn't go for that commercialized green beer—and the bottled Guinness was a deep black.

After dinner, all the adults at the Maloney and Sullivan tables got a shot of Jameson Whiskey and toasted to Grandpa Maloney, who, before he died ten years ago, had promised to join the toast from heaven each year. They each in turn made some comment about Grandpa before taking their shot.

When it was Dad's turn, he said, "You were always there for me, Dad. I hope I can do the same for my kids." There was a glistening in his eye as he looked our way, and then he tilted back his head and shot the whiskey down straight.

When Grandma's turn finally came, she lifted her shot glass and smiled over her gathered family. Then she lifted her eyes to the heavens and said, "If you've had a shot with each of these toasts, Will, I would say you've about had enough." She downed her whiskey to the laughter and applause of all at the table. She slammed her glass hard on the tabletop just as the band began to play "My Wild Irish Rose."

I noticed that the shots they drank were considerably smaller than the half-cup servings I had the night I left Corinne stranded at the Y-Teens dance. Perhaps that was the problem that night.

Dad pulled Mother up from the table and dragged her laughing onto the dance floor. They glided smoothly together even without ever having seen the inside of an Arthur Murray Dance Studio. Every Saint Paddy's Day party was a reminder to me of how well they danced together as one, just as they danced together through life.

Brian saw a girl he knew and went to her table to talk with her, Corinne and Bobby moved onto the dance floor, and I was left alone at our end of the table. Just as I was considering going over to talk with Cousin Billy, I saw Mary Kelly strolling my way. Her green dress shimmered as she slinked across the floor, her red hair bouncing and her smile inviting. Since Joe DeMarco was not at the party, Mary was obviously available.

"Hello, Hat," she said as she slid into the chair next to me. Her long red hair flowed down around her face in waves, resting on her shoulders in perfect spirals, in beautiful contrast to the bright green of her dress. "Are you having fun?"

"Yes, I am. Are you?"

"Could be better. I saw your family taking shots of whiskey, but I didn't see you drink any. Have you sworn off?"

"I'm not old enough to drink whiskey. You know that."

"You drank it pretty well that night at Pleasant Run."

I chuckled. "Not that well. I got sicker than a dog."

"You were fine when Joe and I came back to get you."

"You have no idea, Mary."

"Well, you don't need to drink whiskey to dance with me. Would you like to dance with me?"

"Sure."

Mary's idea of dancing was not the same as my parents' dancing. Theirs was a floating, soaring movement; hers was a sexual ritual. I didn't need to pull her toward me; she snuggled right up to me. She ran her left arm all the way across my shoulders so that her hand rested on my left shoulder rather than my right. This stretched her body across mine, and I could feel the rise and fall of her breasts as she breathed. We moved across the floor, thigh pressing on thigh, and I began to feel a stirring in my groin. She moved a little to her left, and her right thigh slid between my legs and pressed against my growing erection.

"Mmm," she said. "You haven't sworn off girls, have you?"

"No. I haven't." I didn't know what to say. I just wanted her to keep doing what she was doing. I moved my hand down to the small of her back and pulled her body closer. I wanted to grab her hips and force her tighter against my thigh, but I was afraid someone would see me drop my hands. She must have read my mind. She moved her left thigh over and pressed herself hard against my thigh at the same time rubbing my cock with her other thigh. I was fully hard now.

"Let's go for a walk," she said and broke away from our embrace. She pulled me after her toward the door. I followed, looking to see if anyone would discern the bulge in my pants. No one was watching, and we slipped unnoticed out the side door.

The door opened into a hallway that led to the church proper. We followed it, running easily hand in hand, to its end where a door stood in the middle of the wall. That door opened into the front left area of the sanctuary. The great congregation room was dark except for several votive candles burning in the rack in front of and beneath the statue of the Blessed Virgin Mary. We crossed along the altar rail to the middle of the room. We both stopped to genuflect and make the sign of the cross in front of the tabernacle out of respect for the Holy Eucharist that was contained there. Then we continued on across to the door in the front right corner that led to the sacristy. I was very familiar with this room since it is where the priest and the altar boys get ready for Mass in the morning. Mary seemed familiar with it too even though I knew she was never an altar boy.

Once we were inside the sacristy with the door closed, I turned on the small light over the sink, knowing the light could not be seen from outside the room. Although the room was not large, there was plenty of space for three or four people to don cassocks and surplices and do all the other necessary tasks in preparation for the Mass. One wall was covered with hanging wall cabinets above floor cabinets with a Formica countertop and a single bowl sink and faucet centered along the wall. Those cabinets were chock-full of stuff. I could never figure out exactly what was in them or how things were arranged, but whenever Father Paul needed something, he knew right where to find it.

Mary turned to me and, wrapping her arms securely around my neck and pressing her body firmly against mine, kissed me long and hard on the lips. Our tongues intertwined, our bodies melted together, and I grabbed her butt as I had imagined on the dance floor, my hand swooping over the curve and the tips of my fingers nestling into the crease at the top of her leg.

"You seem to have lost something," she said as she rubbed her thigh against my formerly hard penis.

"We'll be finding that again very soon," I said.

"I can't wait!" She unbuckled my belt, opened the button, and pulled down my zipper before I could say "Irish eyes." My pants dropped unceremoniously to the floor, yet Mary had my underwear down before they landed. I was beginning to regain my erection when she dropped to her knees and took me in her hand.

"Yes, this is coming around," she said, stroking me back into full arousal. She ran her tongue lightly over the tip then sucked me into her mouth like a lollipop.

The air left my lungs, and all the blood in my body rushed to meet her lips. My eyes lost focus, and I became light-headed. I had never done this before, and the sensation surprised me. My thigh and buttock muscles began to quiver, and my balls tightened up close as I frenetically thrust ahead. She squeezed the base of my cock with her right hand and stroked slowly, my balls nestling into the palm of her hand as her lips tightened around the shaft. She bobbed her head in rhythm with her up and down strokes, and my thrusts, no longer frantic, fell into tempo with her movements.

She obviously had done this before. She established a cadence and stayed with it. I leaned back against the counter and let her work her magic, watching her red hair sway back and forth, back and forth.

Soon I began to feel an urgency, and I needed to pick up the pace. With fingers interlocked, I placed both hands behind her head and, while holding her in place, began pumping more rapidly. She responded with quicker strokes in time with my thrusts and ran her free left hand up the inside of my thigh and gently caressed my balls.

I felt like I was going to explode…and I did. She held me tight, her mouth never letting me slip out of its grasp. I thrust forward and ejaculated again. I saw that Mary's eyes were tightly closed. She was concentrating on my orgasm. One more thrust and I emptied my load.

The whole time Mary kept my cock in her mouth. Even as it shrank away to nothing, she continued to suck like she didn't want to miss one drop. She finally let it slide out clean and limp. She smiled up at me, her Irish eyes wide open now.

"Well, that was something," she said.

Chapter Eighteen

YES, IT WAS something. It was something that I had never experienced before. I was still light-headed, and I leaned back against the counter to recover. I began to feel silly standing in front of Mary with my pants and underwear wrapped around my ankles. Mary must have sensed my embarrassment. She freed my underpants and pulled them up, pausing to kiss my flaccid penis one more time before she covered me, allowing the elastic band to tighten around my waist. I was surprised that I started to stiffen again. She then raised my pants, and she too was surprised that there was a sizable bulge in my underwear when she tried to close the button.

"No more right now," she said as she tucked me into my pants and pulled up the zipper. "We need to get back to the party."

After Mary cleaned up at the sink, we returned the same way we had come. When we crossed the center aisle of the sanctuary, we again stopped to genuflect and make the sign of the cross. It occurred to me that we were being hypocritical by engendering this symbol of respect after what we had done in the sacristy. Isn't having sex in a sacred place the zenith of disrespect? I didn't know the answer to that, but I was sure of one thing: I wasn't going to bring it up in confession on Saturday.

We quietly retraced our steps across the sanctuary and exited into the hallway. An awkward silence engulfed us as we walked back to the gym. I was enthralled by my first sexual encounter but at the same time felt a weighty burden of guilt. I don't know which was heavier: the guilt over performing this act in the church sacristy or the guilt over being unfaithful to my true love, Toby.

"Is something wrong?" Mary asked as we approached the door to the gym and the party beyond.

"No, everything's fine."

"You're acting like there's a problem."

I squeezed her hand in an effort to assure her that any problem that existed was not of her doing.

"There's no problem. I'm just kind of mellow after…" I nodded my head back toward the church to reference what I didn't know how to put into words.

"Did you like the blow job?" she asked. Those were the words I was looking for.

"You bet I did," I said.

"Then will you walk me home after the party? My mom is probably totally drunk by now, and she'll fall asleep. She won't even know we're there. We can use my bedroom, and we can do anything we want. I like it doggy style. How about you?"

I felt myself getting hard again just hearing her talk that way, and physically, I certainly wanted to take her up on it, but I felt the guilt plunge down on me again, and I knew then that it was my lack of loyalty to Toby that was the heavier load.

I turned to Mary and took her in my arms while I tried to work out the best way to respond to her invitation. I didn't want her to feel rejected when I turned her attractive offer down. She mistook my action for yes and rubbed her body seductively against mine, causing my erection to rise once again. I held her close, quietly enjoying the embrace before starting to speak. She slid her warm hand down between my legs and stroked me through my pants. I waited another moment. Then I waited another moment. She removed her hand and snuggled against me, allowing my cock to settle between her legs. She closed her legs to tighten the space and give me more contact. It felt so good that I didn't want her to stop. But, finally, I decided that it needed to end.

"Mary. The blow job was really great, and I can't thank you enough for doing that for me, and it feels wonderful to hold you like this. I really mean it. You are a beautiful and sexy girl, and I sure would enjoy jumping in the sack with you, but I don't think it would be right."

"What do you mean?"

"I mean that I can't do this. I'm sorry. You look great and you feel great and you obviously turn me on, but I'm in love with someone and I feel guilty for what we did tonight."

She disengaged and stepped back like she had been slapped, a look of bewilderment on her face.

"You're in love?"

"Yes."

"With who?"

"I'd rather not say." This was not going well. I could tell she was going to try to pressure me into telling her about Toby, but I was determined to be strong.

"You think you're in love with Miss Rosen?"

It was my turn to step back. How did she guess that? Who else at school had guessed the same? Was I that obvious? I had to stall.

"Why do you say that?"

"Oh, Joe told me that, but I figured he was full of crap as usual. So, it's true. You think you're in love with the teacher."

"I am in love."

"How naive can you be, Hat? You don't know what love is. She's never going to go for you anyway. She's your teacher, for Christ's sake. She's old."

"She's twenty-one. I'm eighteen. Three years difference, that's nothing."

"She'll never give you a blow job like I just gave you."

"You're probably right. Thank you for that, Mary. It really was magnificent. If it wasn't for Toby, I'd surely go home with you tonight, and I'd willingly fight Joe for you tomorrow."

"I have an idea," she said, stepping forward, grasping my cock, and caressing it into stiffness again. "Why not go home with me, we don't tell Joe or anybody else, and you forget about fighting anyone? Tomorrow, you can go back to being in love with no one the wiser. How about it, Hat? Just for fun."

Once again, I was fully hard. Her hand was like a siren's song, and I didn't want to resist it. I hesitated, luxuriating in the pure pleasure of her touch. Then Toby's face came into clear focus in my mind, and I imagined it was her hand fondling me. What a joy that would be.

"It would be great fun, Mary, but I think not."

"Whatever," she said, removing her hand. She wasn't mad at me; she didn't appear to feel rejected. She was merely disappointed. She turned and went through the door into the gym, leaving me to cool down on my own.

I rejoined the family at our table a few minutes later. Brian had just finished dancing with the girl he knew, and Corinne and Bobby were returning from the dance floor as well. No one had noticed my absence. I thought it odd that Mother and Dad were sitting at an empty table on the other side of the dance floor, but they soon returned to our table.

"Your mother is feeling tired," Dad announced when they arrived at the table. "We are going to call it a night and head on over to Grandma's house. Please stay and enjoy the party."

"I think I'll head home too," Grandma said, and she rose to show she meant it.

Brian and his friend danced again, and so did Corinne and Bobby. I didn't feel like talking to Cousin Billy, so I went to the restroom. Standing before the urinal, I thought of what the night would have been like if I had gone with Mary. I regretted my decision to decline her invitation and decided to seek her out. When I returned, I saw Mary dancing close with Cousin Billy. It looked like her right leg was strategically positioned between his legs.

I left the party. I didn't know if I had done the right thing or if I was just a hopeless romantic with no chance of a future with Toby Rosen. Snow began to fall and quickly accumulated on the grassy church lawn and on the cold cement of the sidewalk. I walked up Downey Avenue one block to Washington Street and turned right. There was a place called Lazy Daze Coffee House that just opened on Johnson Avenue about four blocks up the street, and a hot cappuccino would make me feel a whole lot better.

Chapter Nineteen

I OPENED MY EYES and saw the most beautiful angel you could imagine. Her auburn hair fell loosely around her face as she leaned over me, and the concerned look in her eyes did not detract from her beauty, but enhanced it. A glow surrounded her head and filled me with awe and wonder and warmth.

As she reached over me, her white robes swelled like an egret taking wing, and the space around her shimmered like the heat rising off an asphalt parking lot in July. She was a mirage oasis just over the horizon on a clear Sahara afternoon.

"Have you finally come for me?" I said.

My head began to clear, and my eyes began to focus. The glow subsided and transformed into the ceiling fluorescent light, and my angel's face became my sister's, still an angel, but of this earth. Her eyes softened with my awakening, and she lifted the warm washcloth from my forehead. I felt the soft sheets around me and the firm mattress of the hospital bed below me and a curious disappointment in realizing I was still alive.

"I've always been here," she said.

She spoke the truth, and I knew she had.

Dr. Blumenthal peered at his watch as he held his fingers against my jugular vein. He then withdrew his hand, sighed softly, and slowly shook his head from side to side.

"Am I going to live, Doctor?" I joked.

"I really don't know, Patrick," he answered seriously, "for a moment I thought we may have lost you there."

"One minute you were fine," Corinne said, "then suddenly you were gone. You were talking about your bad reaction to the blood donation your senior year in high school, and then you just slipped away."

Tears were forming in her eyes, a reaction to the strain of responding to my episode, and she dabbed at her cheeks with the washcloth. She really thought I had died.

Dr. Blumenthal's face showed the strain as well. This was a man used to dealing with death, yet my incident stunned him. All his patients were on the edge and could slip over at any time, but I merely fell asleep and he reacted in the extreme. He too thought I had died.

"Am I that close to the end?" I asked.

He paused, giving his answer serious consideration. "I don't know," he said finally. "We have never dealt with a case like yours before. I've told you about the unique qualities of your illness. I use that term in its precise meaning. That is, you are one of a kind. So, I don't know how close you are to the end, as you so delicately put it. I do know that your shortage of blood, specifically hemoglobin, can cause you to be short of breath, lacking energy, and prone to passing out or just falling asleep. What else will manifest itself, I cannot say."

He paused again to let this sink in before he continued.

"Your pulse is slow but no slower than it has been since we brought you in yesterday. I think your condition is stable in a peculiar kind of way. Your body is not replacing the blood you have lost, yet your system is maintaining stability, but only at a lower level. I'm guessing that you will continue to have difficulty exerting yourself. You will tend to drift off to sleep as you just did. You may hallucinate due to insufficient oxygen supplied to your brain, but again, that is just a guess. Other than that, you are functioning normally."

"Normal? This is anything but normal. Did you know that I used be to a superstar athlete? I got an athletic scholarship to play in college, for Christ's sake. I had schools from all over the country knocking on our door, taking us out to dinner, begging me to play for them..."

"There's no need to be telling lies now, Paddy," Corinne broke in, "and you certainly don't need to be taking the Lord's name in vain like that. You should be asking for His help instead of cursing Him."

I wanted to scream, but I shut up instead. I didn't have the energy to fuss. I simmered in the warm sheets and wondered how I was going to replace that lost heat. Such a thing to be worried about at the fresh age of twenty-six.

"I'll be back to see you tomorrow, *Nessa*," Dr. Blumenthal said, moving toward the door. "I have something else we need to talk about, but I need to check on several things first."

I just nodded and turned on my side, facing away from the door so my back was toward the doctor.

"Good bye, Dr. Blumenthal," Corinne said. "Thank you for coming by."

She pulled a straight-backed chair up next to the bed and sat facing me. I had closed my eyes, but I could not keep them shut. I could not avoid her or the scolding that was coming.

"Why do you treat him that way? He saved your life. If he had not come seeking you, you would still be lying on that dirty basement floor in a pool of your own blood, surely dead and cold by now."

"I might have been better off."

"Don't say things like that. You know that's not true."

"What am I supposed to do, Corinne? I have no energy. I can't even get out of bed. Is this how I'm supposed to spend the rest of my life? This is not living—this is just existing. It's just being. To be or not to be? That is the question."

"I don't know God's plan, Paddy, but I have faith that He has one for you. You should talk with Him and ask for His help. Maybe He will let you see what He wants you to do."

"Corinne, when I drifted off a little while ago, you thought I had died."

"I feared that, yes. But you didn't die. You're still alive. You're still able to complete God's plan, whatever it is."

"I went back to that night when Dad told us that Mother was going into the hospital the next day for tests. He said she might have walking pneumonia. Do you remember that night?"

"Of course, I do."

"I remember you gave Mother a big hug like you thought she was going away for a long time. Did you know at that time that it was more than walking pneumonia?"

"How would I have known that? I'm not clairvoyant. I was only a sophomore in high school. I gave Mother a hug because she wasn't feeling well and she needed a hug. That's all."

"Mother kept getting worse all through the spring and the summer. With all those doctors' appointments, she had nothing to show for it. She was deteriorating, everyone knew it, and no one could do anything about it. And I had the cure running through my veins all along. The blood she had given me when I was born could have been her salvation."

"Paddy, you're not clairvoyant either. You didn't know that. You couldn't know that. None of us knew until yesterday. You can't blame yourself, and you certainly can't blame God."

I closed my eyes. She was wrong. I could blame God. He was the only one who knew at the time. He could have told me. He could have told one of the doctors. He could have made something happen so she needed a transfusion, and I would have given her my life-saving blood. But He didn't. He stood by while the cancer ate her alive from the inside out. He let her atrophy until she was a husk, and then He let her die.

"You weren't meant to save Mother," Corinne said. "You have some other purpose here. Mother lived her life to the fullest, and she accomplished what she was sent here to do. She had her children, and she raised all three of us in the Lord. She was successful, Paddy. We three are her successes. You and I and Brian are her legacy. She was happy, and she went to heaven when God called her."

I opened my eyes, and tears filled them. They overflowed, down over my cheeks and nose, across my lips, leaving a salty trail. I saw Corinne dab at her eyes with the washcloth.

"I miss Mother," I said.

"Yes, and so do I," she said.

Chapter Twenty

CORINNE WENT HOME for the night, and I was left with my demons. Logically, I knew that Mother's death was not my fault. But logic doesn't always override. I had the cure but couldn't use it. What good did it do to have the power but not know you have it? Why would I be given this ability if it was not to save Mother? I must have missed a cue somewhere, an entrance that I didn't make, a line that I didn't pick up.

I thought back to Mother's year of sickness. After several visits to the hospital and several rounds of tests, we knew this was more than bronchitis or pneumonia. With each passing month, Mother's energy faded away. The roses left her cheeks, and the gleam in her eyes began to dim. Finally they started her on chemical and radiation treatments. It was too late for surgery; the cancer had become too entwined with the normal tissues in both of her lungs.

Mother withstood the treatments with a strength that only she could possess. The chemo took away her hair but not her dignity. She wore a baseball cap with an IUPUI Soccer insignia on the front that I gave her, but she wore it sideways with the bill over her left ear. She said that was the way Rootie Kazootie always wore his cap, but he was before my time. The radiation sapped her strength and left burn marks on her chest. She told me a story about Polka Dottie, Rootie Kazootie's girlfriend, who loved polka dots more than anything else in the world. Mother said the burn marks weren't so bad because they reminded her of Polka Dottie.

One day, when only she and I were in the room, she told me that she never thought the treatments would be that hard to take.

She said she would never have agreed to them if she had known. When I asked her what she would have done instead, she didn't have an answer. We had no way of knowing that she was looking at the answer all along.

Her last five months were the fall of my freshman year at IUPUI. This was the worst of times, but it was the best of times. In spite of Mother's illness, it was the happiest time of my life. Perhaps that's why God chose not to reveal the power to me. Perhaps I was too happy at a time when I should have been grieving.

The fall semester didn't start off as well as I would have liked. I never recouped my full strength after the blood donation and my subsequent bout with the flu. I still had my speed, but my stamina was lacking. In spite of seven months of working endless hours in the Howe High School gym running the stairs, running laps, rotating through the workout machines, leg lifts with five-pound weights, jumping rope, and running the stairs again every day from February through August in an effort to regain my peak strength, my energy level did not improve. My hopes of immediately starting on the soccer team were dashed when my performance on the field was subpar. I had flashes of brilliance followed by periods of exhaustion. I could play for several minutes at high intensity but then needed to be relieved at regular intervals. The team needed someone with a higher level of endurance in the starting lineup, and I was relegated to a relief role. I played, but I played sparingly.

After a practice session in the early weeks of September, as the team was trotting off the field, heading for the showers, Coach Harrison yelled in my direction, "Better lay off the cancer sticks, Maloney."

I was so surprised that I stopped in midstride, causing two teammates behind me to crash into me and others to make quick adjustments to avoid a similar collision. Fortunately, we were not running full speed but merely jogging to the locker room, so there were no injuries other than to my pride. I trotted over to the coach to find out what was up.

"Did you call for me, Coach?" I asked, though I knew he hadn't. I just needed a walk-up line.

"No, I didn't call you," he growled. That winning smile that he flashed so readily at dinner last November was seldom seen on the soccer field this fall.

"I thought I heard you call my name."

"I didn't call you. I said you better lay off the cigarettes."

"Oh," I said, "I don't smoke."

"You play like you light up a pack a day."

"I would never smoke. I'm an athlete." I didn't know what to say. I had no idea where this was leading.

"What's with this getting winded all the time? You can't go ten minutes on the field without bending over, grabbing your side, and belly aching. 'Take me out. I'm tired. I need a rest.' What kind of athlete is that?"

"I'm sorry, Coach. I worked hard all last year. Believe me, I was in the gym every day running and conditioning. You can ask my coach. He worked with me. I wanted to start right away this year. I don't like sitting the bench. I don't understand why I don't have the stamina like I used to, but it's not from smoking and it's not from lack of conditioning."

"I better never catch you smoking," he said. "The last thing we need on this team is a nicotine nut. Do you understand me? We need people that want to play soccer. If you want to play soccer, cut the weeds. Now, get in there and get a shower."

Either he didn't hear me or he didn't believe me. It didn't matter which. I was more disturbed about my lack of staying power than he was. I wished it was as simple as quitting smoking. I could quit easily if that was the problem. I knew that wasn't the issue, and I knew that increasing the conditioning workouts wasn't the solution either. I didn't know what the answer was, and I didn't know where to begin looking for a resolution.

I was the last one out of the locker room. The practice had been particularly grueling, the brief conference with Coach had been disconcerting, and just taking a shower had sapped what remained of my energy. With a heavy load, I began the short walk to New York Street where I could pick up the Indy Metro and be delivered to within two blocks of home.

"Hello, Hat."

I recognized the voice immediately. I felt an old familiar pain in my stomach as I turned and saw the most beautiful woman in the world smiling at me.

Chapter Twenty-One

THERE SHE WAS, raven hair glistening in the evening sun, eyes like coral around deep black pools drawing me into them against my will but without a fight, her light pink dress waving gently in the late summer breeze like the flag of some tropical island country. She was a distant ideal. One I had pursued but had then resigned to the back cupboard of unachievable goals and inaccessible dreams yet dreamed of constantly. Now she stood before me, attentive to my simple word.

"Hello, Miss Rosen," I said.

"I'm not your teacher anymore, Hat. You can call me Toby if you want to."

A thrill shot through me like the shock of jumping dry into a cold swimming pool on a hot summer day. All last year I had worked in hopes of creating that familiarity, and here it was established with just two sentences uttered in an offhanded, even playful, manner. I needed to say something significant to cement the relationship.

"Does that mean we can go to the prom this year?"

With a laugh, she said, "I don't know about the prom…"

"I can give you the weekend to think it over."

She laughed again with a snort that made her human, that brought her out of that relegated cupboard, and I remembered that I still loved her. I had tried to put her out of my mind while training for my IUPUI soccer debut, but she was always there close in the background. Now she was close at hand.

"I've missed that wonderfully quick wit of yours, Hat. If you are interested, I'd like to join you for dinner. Where do you have dinner these days?"

"Usually at home with my family," I said.

"Oh, you still live at home?"

"Umm, I could call and let them know I'm not coming."

"That would be nice."

She was stunning. Her lips curled up slightly at each end, causing her cheeks to ball around her cheekbones and her eyes to slant almost imperceptibly yet sufficiently to give her an exotic look. She used no mascara, yet her lashes were long and thick and tantalizing. I fumbled with my cell phone and actually called the wrong number before I connected with Corinne and told her I would be late getting home.

"Where would you like to have dinner?" I asked.

"Let's go to the cafeteria in the University Hotel," she said. "I don't want to go anywhere fancy. I'd just like to spend some time catching up. Is that okay?"

"That sounds great to me."

It did sound great. There was nothing I wanted more right then than to sit with her and talk about anything...everything...nothing.

I had never been to the University Hotel before, and of course I had never eaten in the cafeteria. Toby was right. It wasn't fancy, but it was serviceable. There was a bulletin board near the entrance that was so crowded with flyers that you couldn't see any cork, and several notices had fallen to the floor. I picked one up and saw that someone was driving to Fort Wayne in October and needed riders to share the cost. There were little tear-off slips on the bottom with a phone number. I tried to find a spot to affix the notice back to the board, but it was saturated. I decided the notice would get more attention on the floor, so I left it there.

The cafeteria had a wide selection of cold sandwiches and a grill for burgers and hot dogs. Toby selected a tuna salad sandwich on rye with a root beer, while I chose two egg salads on wheat and Mountain Dew. We took our tray to a table for four in the corner near the window.

I mostly let her talk. I wished to bask in the ecstasy of her presence, enjoy the melodic sound of her voice, and admire the depth of her beauty. In high school I had invented reasons to go to talk with her, but now I just wanted to listen. And she wanted to talk.

She was unaware of the smudge of tuna salad on her chin. I thought to tell her about it, but I wondered how long it would take her to notice, so I let it slide.

"I didn't make much money as a teacher," she said, "but I had almost no expenses. As a graduation gift, Mom and Dad paid for all of my new furniture for my small apartment on Washington Street, and the utilities are included in the rent. All I had to pay was the monthly rent and food. I walked to school, so I managed to sock away more than $20,000 last year."

"And you're not teaching this year?" I asked.

She surprised me by wiping away the tuna salad with her napkin without any fuss. She was totally at ease with herself.

"No. I've decided to go back to school full-time. I never felt comfortable as a teacher. My bachelor's degree is in education, but I have a dual minor in Spanish and in biology. I can get a second bachelor's degree in clinical laboratory science in about one and a half years."

"The Indiana University School of Medicine is top notch."

"Yes, it is. And my mother says it's an excellent place to meet a young Jewish doctor."

I must have taken on an ill and distressed look because she immediately withdrew the remark and swore she was kidding. I didn't completely believe her, but I accepted the joke. What other choice did I have? It didn't matter anyway. I could not control those things, so I had to enjoy the moment while I had the moment.

"Don't you have a student loan or anything to pay back?"

"No, Daddy paid for school. When I told him that I wanted to go back, he said he paid for the first degree, but after that, it was up to me. If this twenty grand doesn't take me all the way, I can get a student loan at that point, but I think it'll make it, don't you?"

"I have no idea," I said. "My scholarship pays for all of this stuff. I haven't even thought about what it costs."

"By the way, I never did congratulate you on winning your scholarship, Hat. I remember the announcement when you got it, but we didn't connect around that time and I never had a chance to say anything after that. So, congratulations."

"Thanks. I just wish I was earning it."

"Don't you think you're earning it?"

"I scarcely play in the matches. I mostly relieve a starter when he needs a rest, usually right before half-time. In the second half, he's back in and I'm back on the bench."

"Don't you think that's an important role?"

"It's not the role that got me the scholarship."

"But doesn't someone need to be the relief guy? Without relief, won't the players get too tired to be effective?"

"Yes, I suppose so."

"You will earn the scholarship. You can't expect to be a superstar when you're still only a freshman. You need to be patient."

She reminded me of Corinne. She was lecturing me, yet she was encouraging me at the same time. It made the lecture easier to take.

We talked about our courses that semester. I was having trouble adjusting to the faster pace of college-level courses; she was having trouble getting back into the student mode. My courses were basic freshman engineering fare: psychology, chemistry, chemistry lab, calculus, and English. Playing on the soccer team also earned me credit in physical education. Her courses were junior- and senior-level diagnostic medical microbiology, immunology, physiology, and hematology. I was barely able to pronounce some of them.

After our light meal, we headed to the Indy Metro stop on New York Street. Her apartment was on East Washington Street, so we rode the same bus line from campus to the East Side. We were both quiet on the ride, digesting our dinner conversation. I was surprised when she got off at the same stop as I did, because she had not told me exactly where her apartment building was located. It turned out she lived only five blocks from my house.

Evening was settling in on the East Side, and the shadows were growing long. Although it wasn't necessarily a dangerous neighborhood, I suggested that it would be safer for her if I walked her home.

This would also give me a few more minutes in her company and give me time to build up my courage to ask her for a real date.

We walked down Wallace Avenue toward Washington Street. The street was narrow. With cars parked on both sides, there was room for only one lane in the middle. If two cars were on the street, one heading north and the other going south, one of the cars would have to pull into an empty parking space to let the other one pass. But the street was quiet this evening, and no one needed to pull over to the side.

The sidewalks were recently replaced with bright white concrete slabs, so the walk was even, unlike the old rough gray blocks in front of our house just three blocks north of here. The walkway stretched out in front of us like a white ribbon in the dark. The houses sat upon small grassy banks with cement steps up to the yard level, then wooden steps up to the porch. Most of the houses were large two-story duplexes of similar design, but a few were single-family homes. Each block had two or three houses with a For Rent sign in the yard. The signs were all the same, red and white with a phone number written in with black marker.

"Did you think about renting a house when you moved here, Toby?" I asked, relishing my new ability to call her by her first name.

"I looked at some houses," she said. "I may have even been on this very street, but they were too expensive. These houses are way too big for my needs. Even the duplexes have two or three bedrooms, and the rent usually doesn't include the utilities."

"So, do you like the apartment?"

"It's okay. Like I said, I don't need much, and it was close to the high school. I can see Howe from the balcony off my living room through the trees, and the walk to school was easy. The path through the little woods has a foot bridge over the creek."

"Run," I said.

"What?"

"It's called a run. Pleasant Run, to be precise."

"Oh, so that's why it's Pleasant Run Parkway."

"Yes. But it doesn't explain why we drive on a parkway but park on a driveway."

"That is hard to explain," she said with a straight face.

"And why is it that *fat chance* and *slim chance* mean the same thing?"

She jumped right into the game. "Why is it that *flammable* and *inflammable* mean the same thing?"

"Why is it," I said, "that time flies like an arrow but fruit flies like a banana?"

She laughed out loud. "I hadn't heard that one," she said. "That's really funny."

"There's more where that came from."

Her laughter was like the tinkling of ceramic wind chimes that Mother hung from a hook in the porch ceiling. It put me at ease and convinced me that I could ask her out and expect yes for an answer. Corinne would not be able to accuse me of being far from normal this time.

We then came upon East Washington Street, one of the busiest streets on the East Side. Fortunately, there was a traffic light at the intersection of Washington and Wallace, so crossing there was not a problem. We waited for the light to change while traffic streamed by at ten miles per hour over the forty-miles-per-hour speed limit. An 18-wheeler carried its own gale with it as it whooshed through the intersection.

Toby scooted close to me to block the gust, her pink dress flapping wildly in the wind as though a hurricane had invaded that tropical island country. I shielded her as best I could by wrapping her in my arms and blocking the blast with my body. She buried her face in my chest, and I held her there well after the wind died down and well after the light changed.

We almost missed the light. The duration of the green was not the same both directions, since Wallace was not as busy a street as Washington was, but with a last-second mad dash, we made it across the street without having to remain through another cycle. On the south side of the street, we paused for Toby to catch her breath. I controlled my breathing so she didn't notice that I was out of breath too. It wouldn't do for the soccer star to be out of breath after a mere fifty-foot run.

Her apartment building was one of those nondescript brick structures that you drive by a thousand times without noticing it. Constructed of brownish-orange and orangish-brown bricks, it appeared to be about six weeks early for Halloween. The front of the building faced west toward an asphalt parking lot that was nearly full of cars. It stood four stories high and didn't look like it had an elevator.

"Is this a walkup?" I asked.

"Yes. I'm on the fourth floor, so before I come down, I make sure I have everything. I wouldn't want to have to go all the way back up just for a book or a file."

"Why no elevator?"

"I don't know. None of these apartment buildings have elevators."

I looked up and down the street and realized that there were many apartment buildings similar to this one ranging from two to four stories. Some were constructed with red bricks, and some used the same brown and orange bricks that this one used. I had come through this area many times on my way to school and had never noticed these buildings.

"Thank you for having dinner with me, Hat. And thank you for walking me home."

The door to the building was an oversized solid oak slab of wood with no windows and a curved top that fit neatly into the gray stone archway. It reminded me of an entryway into some medieval castle. Toby slipped a key into the bolt lock and pushed the door open.

"Do you want me to walk you up?"

"No, thank you," she said. "That's okay. There's no sense in you climbing four flights of stairs."

She stood in the doorway with the open door behind her. The light from the entry hall reflected off her hair and cast her face in shadows. I couldn't read the expression on her face, and I didn't know if she was waiting for me to kiss her or waiting for me to go. I didn't want to spoil this perfect day by making the wrong move at the end, so I stepped back from the door.

"Okay then," I said cheerfully. "I'll see you."

"See you," she said.

I didn't catch any cheerfulness in her reply. I turned and started along the walk back to the street. I didn't hear the door close until I reached the main sidewalk. When I turned back, the doorway was empty and the door was shut.

I should have kissed her. She was waiting for me, and I walked away. How stupid! Corinne was right when she said I had never had a date. I didn't know how to act on a date. I never wanted to date anyone until I saw Toby, and now that she was available, I didn't know how to date her.

The walk home was a long five blocks. I chastised myself over and over for not kissing Toby. Two blocks from home, I realized that I hadn't asked her for another date. A minute later, I remembered that I had no way of contacting her—no phone number, no e-mail address. Now what?

Chapter Twenty-Two

I WAS TOO EMBARRASSED to tell Corinne about my encounter with Toby Rosen. She could only conclude that I was far from normal since I failed to ask her for a date when the opportunity was perfect and I failed to get her phone number. I could hear Corinne asking the inevitable rhetorical question, "How are you supposed to call her if you don't have her phone number?" The answer to that one is a puzzler.

"That is hard to explain," as Toby so flawlessly stated when we were walking down Wallace Avenue together.

The time we spent was so amazingly wonderful it was hard to believe all we did was eat some cold sandwiches, drink some cold drinks, and walk home and talk. We talked person to person, not student to teacher, not campaigner to election adviser, not starry-eyed lovestruck high school kid to beautifully dazzling young Spanish professor. It was more like starry-eyed lovestruck college kid to beautifully dazzling young college woman.

I would need to work on the issue of finding Toby again by myself. I was sure Corinne would be of no help. At least I knew where she lived. If all else failed, I could camp out on the lawn in front of her apartment building on Washington Street until she showed up. I might have to miss soccer practice, but love is worth the cost.

In chemistry lab the next day, I found myself daydreaming about standing in a field of green grass above rocky cliffs over the sea, like those that exist only in southern Ireland with the wind blowing strong from the sea, and Toby huddling beneath my coat with her arms wrapped around my waist and her head buried in my sweater and her hair blowing across my face and my arms secure around her shoulders. Nothing else happened in this daydream. Nothing else had to happen. It was perfect.

But it didn't get my lab work completed. Fortunately, it was an uncomplicated lab that involved merely measuring dry chemical ingredients and completing a short account of those measurements. My lab partner didn't mind doing the work, but there was an implicit agreement that there would be future labs that would be my responsibility.

I couldn't concentrate during my psychology lecture. I kept having that same daydream and didn't want to pull out of it. My notes were indecipherable scribbles, and my understanding of the lecture was lacking. A fellow student agreed to copy his notes for me in return for my notes from last week's lecture. This seemed like a fair deal to me.

I thought of Toby all day.

I didn't have lunch in the cafeteria as usual. Instead I went to the University Hotel and had a tuna salad sandwich with root beer. I sat at the same table that Toby and I had sat at the evening before and tried to remember what classes she said she would have today so that I might arrange a chance meeting outside the classroom, but I drew a blank. I looked for the flyer about the ride to Fort Wayne that I had left on the floor, but it was gone. I didn't really think that would help anyway, but I was getting desperate.

I skipped out of my chemistry lecture and walked around campus for a while then sat in the grass in the common area in front of the student bookstore, pretending to study and watched for her. I saw her in every dark-haired girl that walked by. After two hours of watching, I started seeing her in all the dark-haired guys too.

I had to give up on that method since we had a soccer match against Oral Roberts University that afternoon and I had to get over to the field. This problem was going to be more difficult to solve than I had first imagined.

IUPUI did not have a football team, so our soccer team got more exposure than soccer teams at a lot of schools. It was something for students to cheer about in September and October after baseball season was over. We would usually get several thousand fans at the matches in September and five to seven thousand in October if we were winning. If by November the team was not faring well, attention would shift to the start of basketball season.

Oral Roberts was the conference champion last year, and thus they generated a lot of interest this year. Three or four thousand fans had shown up for today's match.

I finally got Toby off my mind as we went through our pregame warm-up drills: sit-ups to stretch the thigh and back muscles and tighten the abs, toe touches for the back of the legs and calves, running in place to limber the joints, individual stretching to avoid muscle pulls and tendon tears. Last year in high school, stretching and calisthenics used to get my blood going and got me worked up and ready for a rough and tumble match. This fall they merely wore me out. I broke into a sweat doing the first set of stretches and was exhausted by the time we headed to the sideline for the pregame huddle. It was a good thing I wasn't starting.

After the huddle broke and I took my spot on the bench, I heard the voice that made my heart leap.

"Hello, Hat."

I turned and saw the most beautiful woman in the world smiling at me, again.

There she was, raven hair glistening in the afternoon sun, her IUPUI sweatshirt the same crimson and gold as all the other shirts and sweaters in the crowd but somehow brighter and crisper than those others. She stood on the other side of the waist-high cyclone fence that separated the fans from the field, a mere ten feet away from me. It was all I could do to refrain from jumping over that fence and taking her in my arms. I took a deep breath and exhaled slowly with relief. I wondered if she knew I had spent the entire day looking for her, yearning for her, fearing that I would never find her, dreading a repeat tomorrow of the horrible day without her today. She expectantly awaited my greeting.

"I never got your phone number," I said.

"I'll meet you after the game."

"Match."

"What?"

"It's called a match."

"Okay. I'll match you after the game."

"Meet."

"Okay. I'll match you after the meet."

"See you," I said.

She drifted back into the crowd, but she did not blend with it. The rest of the crowd was a blur of crimson and gold, but she stood out from it. Her bright smile shone like the beacon of a lighthouse on a star-filled night. Her eyes were wide and gazed back at me as though she had missed me too that day. How I wished it were true.

"Maloney!"

I jumped at the sound of Coach Harrison shouting my name. Surely, he didn't want me to go into the match so soon. I usually didn't enter until about two or three minutes before the end of the half. I sprang off the bench and ran over to the sideline next to Coach.

"Yes, sir," I said.

"Are you out here to play soccer or to flirt with the girls, Maloney?" he growled.

"To play soccer, sir." I wasn't sure that was true, but it was what he had to hear.

"You're supposed to be thinking about soccer, not some dumb co-ed. Now get back on that bench and pay attention to what's going on and get your head in the game."

I almost said "match," but for the second time within mere minutes, I refrained. I took a deep breath and exhaled slowly again and returned to my spot on the bench.

Oral Roberts was noted for its tight defense and last year had seldom given up more than one or two goals in a match. It promised to be a hard-fought battle, and I needed to have my mind focused on the game at hand if I was going to contribute in a positive way.

I feigned interest in the match, but all I could think about was Toby in the stands behind me. I couldn't turn to see her for fear Coach Harrison would see me and start another rant. I did manage to jump up and cheer when we moved the ball into scoring position.

When we lost the ball without a score, I turned to go back to my seat and stole a look into the stands. She wasn't there.

My heart fell in my chest like an anchor. Had she decided not to stay after all? Was it just a stroke of luck that she had shown up in the first place? I assumed she was there to see me, but maybe it was not a planned action. Maybe I was fooling myself into thinking she wanted to be with me.

I lost interest in the match. I sat moping at the end of the bench and didn't pay any attention to what was happening on the field. What did I care? I had no effect on the game anyway. I usually went into the match at the three-minute mark before half-time. College substitution rules required that the player I replaced could not reenter the game until the second half, so Coach wanted to make sure I could last through to the half-time break. There were times when I didn't think I would make it for three minutes.

This time was different. Matt Pipher, the player I normally replaced, twisted his ankle with a little more than four minutes left in the half. An injury timeout was called to tend to him, and Coach called me over to his side.

"You're goin' in earlier this time, Maloney," he snarled. "Do you think you can give me four good minutes?"

"Sure I can, Coach. Watch me," I said, but I wasn't certain it was in me.

I cast a speedy search for her in the stands, and my eyes immediately found her in spite of the sea of crimson and gold in which she swam. She jumped up and down and clapped and smiled at me. She thought I had it in me.

I don't think Coach was convinced. He said, "Okay then, get in there and do it." But there was a note of uncertainty in his voice.

I trotted onto the field, and the match began anew. We played a game of give and take, moving the ball back and forth at midfield with neither side gaining an advantage and neither side even attempting a shot. Several times I received a pass and made a quick move to my left, but the defender stayed with me and I had to pass the ball off. This defender was playing me very closely and very confidently. I don't know if he knew I was a freshman, but he certainly knew I was a substitute and he felt that he could dominate me.

We moved the ball well into scoring position but missed a score when the goalie made a nice save on an outside shot by our leading scorer. As the goalie put the ball back into play, I chanced a look at Toby in the stands. She was cheering me on with the energy of a two-year-old, jumping and waving and clapping and yelling. If I had that energy, I could not only be a starter, I could be a star.

Knowing she was watching made me acutely aware of every move I made. I was afraid I would run out of steam and embarrass myself and the team in front of her.

My teammate made a steal at midfield and moved toward the left. He was well covered and shot a pass over to me on the right side. I made a move to the left again, and my defender played it strong and tight with a stabbing attempt at a steal. I pivoted back to the right and pushed the ball past him. He was unprepared for that move and stumbled awkwardly as he tried to regain position. Free of him, I streaked toward the goal, the ball rolling rapidly before me. I saw a narrow opening to the net, and I left the ground as I swung my foot through the ball. The connection was solid, and the ball rocketed off my foot in the direction of the goalie. As I slid on my hip across the grass, I saw the ball curve to the right. The goalie dove through the air like an Olympic swimmer from the starting block and nearly reached the ball before it spun past his outstretched hand and into the net.

I decided against making the traditional celebratory run around the field after scoring a goal. I was exhausted. I lay on my back in the cool grass and celebrated as my teammates piled on top of me.

There was about half a minute left when I scored the goal. With the break that comes with a score, I was able to get my wind back and I finished the half with no problem. When time expired, I trotted to the bench. The fans were bouncing in the stands, and Toby was hopping right along with them. When she saw I was looking her way, she blew me a kiss. My first kiss was from a distance of fifty feet, but it thrilled me as though we were tightly embraced. I couldn't wait for the real thing.

We went into the locker room for the half-time break, my teammates still good-naturedly jostling me and slapping me on the back and congratulating me on my first goal.

Coach quickly put a stop to the horseplay.

"Okay, you guys!" he hollered. "We haven't won anything yet. We're up one to nothing, but that can turn around just as quickly as it happened. We've still got a half of soccer to play before we start to celebrate. You guys get your Gatorade and get back onto these benches. We've got a lot to go over before we go back out there. Now move."

He pulled me to the side as the others swarmed the Gatorade dispensers. I thought he was going to praise my play and thank me for my contribution, but he surprised me.

He dropped his voice to a low growl and said, "I guess that'll save your scholarship for ya…for a while, anyway."

Chapter Twenty-Three

MATT PIPHER'S FIRST half ankle injury was a minor strain, and he was able to start the second half. Even though I had scored the only goal in the first half, Coach did not treat me any differently. As always, I saw more action in the second half since substitution rules are different than in the first. Unlike first-half substitutions in which the relieved player cannot return to the match in that half, in the second half, the relieved player can return to the game. Coach's strategy was to put me in for Leslie, then Leslie in for Evan, then Evan in for Matt, then Matt in for me, each in two-minute intervals. That way Matt, Evan, and Leslie would each get a two-minute rest and I would be in the game for six minutes. This sequence usually occurred at about the midpoint of the second half in order to get maximum performance from the three starters and to be sure they were fresh for a strong finish.

When the time came for the routine substitution rotation, I was summoned to Coach's side.

"Okay, Maloney," Coach said. "We're going to do this the standard way. I don't care that you scored a goal your last time out and now you think you're a superstar. It's your job to see that we get through this rotation without giving up a score. We need to get the starters rested, and we need to protect our lead. Those are the objectives. I don't want any risky play that could jeopardize our position. Just control the ball until Matt comes back in for you. Do you understand?"

"Yes, sir."

During the next four minutes of play, Matt seemed to be a little late on the uptake. His passes were not crisp, and he was slow to respond when receiving a pass. His defender stole the ball from him and could have moved into position for a possible score except that Leslie made a nice cover play that allowed Matt to get back into defensive position. I thought I detected a grimace of pain on his face as he ran off the field when relieved by Evan. It was possible that his injury was more serious than the coaches thought when they slated him to start the second half. Conceivably, he would not relieve me after two minutes, and I would get to finish the match.

Evan intercepted a pass and quickly shot the ball ahead of me, giving me the chance at a great lead on my defender. Thoughts of a second goal boogied in my head as I raced after the ball. If I scored again, surely Coach would keep Matt on the bench for the rest of the game. But this defender was fast and, unencumbered by the ball, stayed with me.

Coach's words echoed through my ears. "Just control the ball until Matt comes back in for you." I pulled the ball back as the defender rushed past me. He deftly pulled up and covered me tightly. I knew then that I would probably not have scored if I had pursued the goal. This defender was in total control of his body, and his positioning was perfect. I passed over to Evan, and we reestablished control of the ball.

When Matt came in for me, it marked the end of my contribution to the event. I watched the final minutes from my reserved spot on the bench.

With the one-to-nothing victory secured, Coach permitted a bit of celebration in the locker room. He and the assistant coaches stood at the door as his players laughed and shouted and slapped each other on the back. It was a hard-fought win, and he knew we needed to release some pent-up tension. But he allowed it for a shorter run than my first half stint. After about two minutes, he called the team to order.

"Okay, guys!" he shouted. "Settle down now! Settle down! Listen up!"

When we finally quieted down, he addressed the team as a whole.

"This was a good win today."

We all cheered and shouted, "Yeah!"

"But it's only one win. We have a match next week with Oakland, and they're every bit as tough as this Oral Roberts team. Enjoy this victory, guys, because this is why we play the game, but don't celebrate too long or too hard. If we ever want to win a second game, we have to get back to work. No practice tomorrow. But we are back on the practice field as usual the day after tomorrow, Friday, three thirty sharp. Be ready to work harder than you've ever worked in your life. If you liked winning this match today, you will enjoy all the upcoming wins even more, but only if you work for them. See you all on Friday."

This was impressive. When practices started in August, we were all told that we would practice every day except game day—no exceptions, Sundays and holidays included. When we had full practice on Labor Day, we believed what we were told. Now we were given a day off. The announcement sobered us. The respite was cause for further celebration, but at the same time it impressed upon us the importance of the win. In a more serious mood, we prepared for the showers.

I stripped down and grabbed my towel, but as I headed for the shower room, I was stopped by Coach, his strong hand on my shoulder. I turned not knowing what to expect.

"That was a good play, Maloney," he said. "I thought you were going to try some crazy-assed shot on goal, but instead you pulled up and stayed in control and preserved our win. You may just become a soccer player before you're done here."

He gave me the smile he used so freely last November but so sparingly this summer, and I knew that I had saved my scholarship… for a while, anyway.

Chapter Twenty-Four

TOBY CAUGHT ME immediately as I exited the locker room. She materialized out of the crowd and seemed to jump into my arms. She gave me a kiss on the cheek and a grand hug that I wished could last forever. At that moment I didn't care about the scholarship except that it would allow me to play, which could generate more hugs like this one.

"What an exciting game," she said as she released me from the hug but remained close under my arm. "We need to celebrate."

"Some of the guys are going to the Student Union for pizza. Want to join them?"

"Sure."

We walked side by side on the asphalt trail. After a few steps, Toby slid her hand into mine. It felt comfortable there. It belonged there.

I couldn't believe things were going so well. I had scored a goal—the game winner; I had earned a begrudged compliment on my play from Coach Harrison; and I had Toby Rosen kissing me, hugging me, and walking hand in hand with me. How could the world get any better?

There was just one more thing I needed now. Pizza.

The Student Union Café was jam-packed with students and parents, and the sliced pizza line was forty customers long. Fortunately, the team had a reserved seating section and had advanced orders for several full pizzas and soft drinks, coffee, and tea. Five of my teammates were from Indiana, and two others were from adjoining states that were close enough for their parents to attend most of our home matches. Along with girlfriends, they filled the reserved section. Mother was not feeling up to it, so Mother and Dad decided not to come to the game today. I didn't encourage their attendance since I was not starting. In retrospect, I wish I had persuaded them to come given my performance. Toby and I found two seats next to Matt Pipher and his parents.

"How's your ankle?" I asked after introductions.

"It's fine," he said. "It was just a minor twist—nothing serious."

"It looked like it was bothering you in the second half."

"No, it's fine. It's going to take more than a little twist to get me out of the lineup. I know you'd like to step in there for me, but that's not going to happen."

Toby, bristling at Matt's tone, countered with, "If Hat continues to do all the scoring on this team, then Coach is going to have to find a way to start him."

She was astonishing. The flash of defiance in her green eyes was like the spark of a match on the striking pad just before it burst into flame. She faced him boldly, challenging him to dispute the truth in what she said.

Matt was caught by surprise by Toby's pointed rejoinder. His eyes grew wide with shock, and he reflexively jerked back, almost imperceptively, as though she had feigned a right jab at his nose. I saw his jaw tense and his lips purse while anger flushed his face as he formulated a retort.

Before he could respond, his mother spoke up. "That was a very fine shot you made. You must have practiced that move many times to get it down so well."

"Thank you, ma'am." She had effectively taken the heat out of the moment.

Small talk consumed the next fifteen minutes while we polished off the pizza. Toby and I parted with Matt and his family without further incident. She and I walked hand in hand once again across the grassy expanse between the Student Union and the library.

"So, you've decided to come to my rescue in time of need," I said.

She shrugged her shoulders. "I just thought he was being a jerk. All you did was ask after his injury, and he took it as an affront to his masculinity or a challenge for his starting position or something like that. I knew you wouldn't bring up scoring the only goal today because you're not a braggart, but the truth is, there was only one goal and you made it, not him."

This had all come out in a rush. She paused for a breath, and I gave her time to continue if she had more to say. The fire had rekindled, and she was all the more beautiful highlighted by the flame within her. She opened her mouth to speak further, but instead she paused again, took another breath, thought a third time about what she would say, released her breath in a slow and deliberate exhale, and then smiled sheepishly up at me. She was amazing. Her beauty shifted throughout all the changes she had just passed through without diminishing in any way.

"Was I wrong to jump in there?" she asked finally. "Did I mess up your relationship with your teammate?"

"I don't see how," I answered. "Matt and I don't have any kind of relationship. Usually I relieve him or I go through the six-minute substitution cycle. He and I are on the field together for, at most, four minutes. Besides, he's a senior. By the time I'm in a position to play more, he'll be gone."

"That may be sooner than you think, Hat. I was serious when I said Coach is going to have to find a way to start you. You were fantastic out there today. As little time as you played, you were the star of the game. That scoring kick was incredible, and everyone thought you were going to score again in the second half when you got free briefly."

"Yes," I said. "I thought I might score on that play too, but there's a funny thing about that."

"What funny thing?"

"After I made that goal in the first half, Coach almost acted like he was mad that I had scored. He even implied that he was about to pull my scholarship before that, but because I scored, he would have to wait. I can't figure out what I've done wrong, but I've gotten myself on his wrong side somehow."

We walked on in silence for a long moment. The sky was growing dark, and a single star appeared low in the east just over the City-County Building downtown.

"You said there was something funny about the second-half play, but then you talked about the first-half score. What was funny about the second-half play?"

"Well, when Coach sent me into the match in the second half, he told me not to try anything fancy. He told me to control the ball and keep them from scoring until Matt came back in. I had a good chance to score when Evan made that great lead pass, but instead of going for the goal, I pulled up."

"So, you were following Coach's instructions. But what was unusual about the play?"

"After the game was over, in the locker room, Coach paid me a compliment. He said I just might become a soccer player before I'm finished. He was talking about that pull-up play."

"That also sounds like he wasn't thinking about pulling your scholarship anymore."

"That's right."

We found a wooden bench along the walkway and sat arm in arm. Several more stars emerged overhead, and a warm evening breeze stirred the air. The sound of distant traffic provided a soft background for the chirping of crickets and the rustle of the gentle wind through the trees. September is one of the best months of the year in Indiana, and this was one of the best September nights ever.

We didn't say a word for a good five minutes. My thoughts meandered over the events of the last two days, examining them, analyzing them, turning them over and over in my mind. I tried to make sense of what Coach had said and done. I tried to figure out why Toby was attracted to me. I was puzzled by my inexplicable loss of stamina. Nothing was logical.

Toby sat silently with me. She must have been turning over her own thoughts and trying to solve her own puzzles. Her breathing was regular and uninterrupted and was the only sound she made…until she finally spoke.

"I wanted to be a teacher since I was in the fourth grade. I studied education for four years at DePauw University. I did my student teaching at Pike High School on the West Side. I thought I knew what I wanted to do for the rest of my life—that is, teach kids in high school. I thought I had found my purpose, but I had not."

She paused and looked up at the ever-increasing field of stars. The sound of the crickets grew louder as the breeze in the trees waned. With her left arm still wrapped around my right arm and her left hand still resting in my right, she placed her right hand under my right hand and cuddled close to me. She continued.

"For some reason that I don't understand, I took a minor field of study in biology. I never wanted to teach biology, but I just fell into it. I didn't think much about it. I just found that the courses fit my schedule and my inclination, so I completed the minor course work along the way."

She snuggled closer to me on the bench. I sensed that she was revealing something to me that was difficult for her to understand. I gave her the time she needed.

"This last year, after all those years, I discovered that I did not want to be a teacher. I now find that those courses I took in biology and other sciences, which were not required by my major field of secondary education, will prove very useful in my drive for a second degree in clinical laboratory science. It's a wonder that I took those science courses. Did I take them because I subconsciously knew I actually preferred that field? Or have I chosen this field because I already have so much course work completed in it? Or is there some other driving force? I don't know the answer."

I didn't have any answers either, so I let her continue at her own pace.

"What I do know is that you sometimes find your purpose where you least expect to find it. I suppose I was looking in the wrong place, asking the wrong questions of myself. I wasn't looking for a major move like this one, but it came along and grabbed me."

I suddenly realized that Toby was not talking about only herself; she was also talking about me.

"Are you sure this new direction is your true purpose?" I asked, not wanting to accept a new purpose of my own.

"As sure as I can be at this point," she answered honestly.

"Are you happy with this new purpose?"

"Yes," she said without hesitation.

I had plenty of hesitation in my mind. I didn't want to face the next question, the next role, the next purpose. I wanted things to be as they were last fall. I wanted to be the star, not the substitute. I looked at the night sky and saw a true star, and I knew I was not that. I asked the next question.

"Do you think I need to accept a relief role on the soccer team as my new purpose?"

"I think you need to ponder that and answer your own question for yourself. Just make sure you are asking the right question."

Chapter Twenty-Five

THERE MUST BE something about the Indy Metro that discourages conversation. Possibly it's the proximity of other people that might overhear or the jostling of the coach or the noise of the motor, but it is not conducive to dialogue. Toby and I rode home on the same line as the previous night, and we exchanged about eight words during the entire ride. That would be about twice as many as the prior trip.

We exited at the intersection of New York Street and Wallace Avenue and headed south toward Washington Street. The conversation started as soon as we were alone.

"I liked that Meg Ryan and Tom Hanks movie where they send each other e-mails and fall in love over the internet," Toby said. "What was the name?"

"I liked it too, but it was a little far-fetched," I said.

"Far-fetched? Why do you say that?"

"Just about everyone in the whole country has an—mail account, plus Canada for that matter, yet they happen to be right around the corner from each other, and they happen to be competitors in the book business. Too much coincidence there. Pretty far-fetched."

"True, but you have to accept some improbabilities when you watch a movie. The movies wouldn't be interesting without the little twists they put into them."

"Okay, I'll give you that. What about falling in love with someone just because you like how he writes an e-mail? That's a little far-fetched."

"Why do you think people fall in love?"

"I don't know about women, but men fall in love because the woman has the most enchanting eyes he has ever seen."

"Really? That's interesting." She flashed a look my way, and I was immediately enchanted. I stumbled and nearly fell over a rise in the sidewalk. When I looked back to see what tripped me, there was no rise, for the sidewalk was recently poured and was as smooth as a freshly raked beach. I had to cover my clumsiness with talk.

"Also, the skin of her cheek is smooth and begs to be touched, and her lips are moist and pleading to be kissed."

She stopped and faced me, flipping her hair back behind her ear with a sexy flick of her wrist. I should have taken her in my arms, touched those silky cheeks, and kissed those moist and pleading lips right then and there. But I was on a roll, and like an idiot, I had to go on.

"Also, she has a way of tossing her hair over her shoulder that draws him to her like a magnet, like an ant to sugar, or a butterfly to a flower."

She smiled wryly and started walking once again. "Or a moth to a flame?" she said over her shoulder.

"Ahh! The perils of love." I walked quickly and caught up to her. "Yes, like a moth to a flame. Like Jason's argonauts to the sirens of Titan."

Toby began to giggle though she tried to suppress it. She covered her mouth with her hand, but it was too late.

"What?" I said.

"Hat, you speak so eloquently, but you just made a major mix of references."

"What do you mean?"

"Well, first of all, Jason was the one who was tempted by the sirens, not his argonauts. Remember he had to be tied to the masthead while they sailed away so that he would not dive overboard or force them to turn back."

"Oh, you're right, Toby."

"Second, and this was what made me laugh, *The Sirens of Titan* was a Kurt Vonnegut Jr. novel and referred to the moon of Saturn called Titan. It was not in Greek mythology."

"Haha, that's right too. Sorry."

"I'm glad you can laugh at yourself. I didn't mean to break your run. You were doing quite well."

"Was I?"

"Yes. But I notice that all your explanations are physical attractions rather than emotional ones. Are you saying that love is merely a physical phenomenon?"

"Not at all. Emotional attractions translate into physical responses. That explains why when I look at you, I see the most beautiful woman in the world, while some other man may not agree with me. Your appearance has not changed at all, only the viewer and his perception of you are different."

"What a nice thing to say." She smiled at me, and her face glowed. Her hair caught the light of a streetlamp and sparkled like the surface of a quiet pond on a sunny afternoon. Her skin looked as soft and smooth as a rose petal, and her lips parted slightly, beckoning me to kiss them.

This time I seized the moment and the girl. I pulled her to me and, face to face, I looked into, fell into those enchanting eyes. She wrapped her arms around my shoulders and waited, eyes wide-open. I touched the tip of my nose to her right cheek and confirmed that it was indeed as soft as a rose petal. I closed my eyes and pressed my lips to hers.

It was every bit as wonderful as I had imagined it would be—this first kiss. We held our lips tightly together, not wanting the magic to escape. She slid her one hand from my shoulder to the back of my neck, then higher to the back of my head, holding me in place while she pressed her lips hard against mine. The bottom of her sweatshirt rose and exposed the soft skin of her waist to the night air and to my hands. I moved my hands around to her back until I could feel the vertebrae under my fingers. Then we slowly and gently began to massage each other's lips with our own. Her mouth opened slightly, and I slipped my tongue between her lips and found hers. Our tongues intertwined and caressed each other. She sucked my tongue to the roof of her mouth and ran her teeth gently over its rough surface. I had never felt such a sensation before, and the thrill of it settled in my loins, causing a great rush of blood to the area. My heart started pounding, and my breathing ran heavy. We held that position for a brief moment, then she released my tongue from her mouth and we lightened up. She relaxed her grip on the back of my head. I kissed her gently on her cheek and then her forehead, and she nuzzled her face into the curve of my neck under my chin.

I loosened my hold, removing my hands from under her sweatshirt, and in response, she dropped her arms so they no longer encircled my shoulders but now enclosed my waist. She softly kissed my throat then laid her head across my chest. I ran both hands up the middle of her back, stopping between her shoulder blades, and then pulled her tightly to me. Our pose was almost exactly as I had daydreamed in chemistry lab that morning. No grass, no cliffs, no sea, no overcoat, no blowing wind, and no hair flying in my face, but other than those minor differences, it was the same image. Perfection.

"What's going on down there?" a voice called from the porch of the duplex on the grassy bank to my right. "What are you kids doing?"

"We're moving on," I answered as we reluctantly released each other and walked down toward Washington Street hand in hand.

The light turned green our way just as we arrived at the corner, so I didn't get the pleasure of a repeat performance of an 18-wheeler-inspired hug, but we didn't have to sprint across the street either. After opening the big oaken door, she turned toward me, her silhouette backlit by the light in the entry hall, and silently waited. I could not see her face in the shadow, but I knew what I would see if there was light. I would see the deep sea-green of her eyes summoning me and her lips calling to me like the sirens of some Aegean island not called Titan, urging me to kiss her again. I was not going to make the same mistake I made last night. I took her in my arms and kissed her firmly on the lips. She responded by wrapping her arms around my shoulders and kissing me back. This kiss was briefer than the first but just as satisfying. We held our embrace long after the kiss and then gradually separated.

"Would you like me to walk you up to your apartment?" I asked, tentatively.

"No. You don't have to do that. I really need to do some studying tonight, and I have a feeling I wouldn't get any done if you came up. We'd probably talk about movies all night."

"I hope you don't think I didn't like that Tom Hanks and Meg Ryan movie just because I found it implausible. I really did like it. It's the old standard magic formula that everyone loves: boy meets girl, they fall in love, boy does something that makes girl mad, boy does something to make up for his error, boy apologizes to girl, and then they kiss and live happily ever after. How could anyone not like that movie? Especially starring Meg Ryan and Tom Hanks."

"I like happy endings," she said.

"So do I."

I set off for home. This time I had my happy ending. I had not only kissed her, I had kissed her twice. She had kissed me back. Man, had she kissed me back. I started singing "Your Kiss Is on My List" and floated across Washington Street. My feet barely touched the ground as I headed back up Wallace Avenue.

I was still flying when I crossed New York Street. It wasn't until I had to stop for traffic at Michigan Street that I came back down to earth. I waited while four cars went by, and before I stepped out to cross the street, I realized that I hadn't asked her for another date. Then I immediately remembered that I still didn't have her phone number. A quick replay of today's miserable morning and afternoon looking for Toby flashed through my head. There was no way I was doing that again tomorrow. But if I had to, I would search for her forever. If I parked myself in front of her apartment building, she would eventually have to show up. That would be a better option than losing a whole day wandering around campus hoping I would bump into her. What an idiot I was. I could not believe I did the same stupid thing a second time. A cloud of depression settled over my mind. If Corinne ever gets wind of this, I will never live it down.

While I stood still on the corner, afraid to venture out for fear that I would do another foolish thing and get myself into worse trouble, my cell phone rang. I flipped it open, and my caller ID displayed an unfamiliar number. It didn't pull any information from my address book either, so it wasn't someone that I talked to regularly. My depressed mood urged me to let it ring. I didn't know who it was, and I didn't feel like talking to anybody anyway.

The phone rang on for an eternity without switching over to my voice mail. I became irritated and punched the ignore button to shut off the ring. I must have missed the ignore button and pushed something else, because suddenly a voice came on the line.

"Hello, Hat."

My heart leaped. She had that power over me. Two words and I was a slobbering pile of protoplasm unable to think or act rationally. I stuttered some incoherent drivel into the phone and then stood panting, awaiting her response.

"I know the name of the movie," Toby said.

"Movie?"

"Yes. I remembered the name of the Meg Ryan movie. *You've Got Mail.* I figured you'd want to know so you could sleep tonight."

"Yes. That would have bothered me all night. How'd you get my cell phone number?"

"I called your home number. Your sister, Corinne, gave me your cell phone number. She didn't think it would be a problem. Is it?"

"No, no, of course not. I was just now wondering how I was going to get hold of you. I never got your number."

"You have it now."

"Yes, I do. Say, would you like to go out with me? Is it okay to ask you for a date over the phone? Or do I need to send you an e-mail?"

"Yes," she said.

"Yes what? Yes, you'll go out with me, or, yes, send you an e-mail?"

"Yes, I'll go out with you, and yes, you can send me an e-mail if you want."

"Great! Well, then I'll talk to you tomorrow, okay?"

"Sure."

"Bye."

It was all set. We were going to have an actual date. I did not ask her when or where or what. I would have to settle those questions with her tomorrow. I was too nervous to call her back right then. It was enough that she had said yes. I needed to send her an e-mail. Maybe she'd fall in love with me over an e-mail like Meg Ryan fell for Tom Hanks. I forgot to get her e-mail address. What will I forget next? I will have to face a million questions from Corinne tonight. Toby knew her name so they must have talked for a while before Corinne gave her my cell phone number. Corinne was going to want a ton of details about her, I was sure. Talking about Toby would be much more fun than trying to figure out how to get in touch with her. Now that I had her phone number, that would not be a problem. I was actually looking forward to the forthcoming cross-examination.

I opened my cell phone and carefully entered Toby's name next to her phone number from the caller ID. At least I had accomplished that much.

Chapter Twenty-Six

THAT NIGHT CORINNE became my official dating consultant. She advised me that dinner and a movie was a better bet for a first date than going to a dance where I might make a fool of myself or, worse yet, Toby might make a fool of herself. Corinne also cautioned me against museums and art shows since the potential boredom factor was higher when you weren't yet sure of the girl's tastes. Football games and other sporting events were to be reserved for later in the relationship after I knew her better and was more aware of her likes and dislikes. According to her, I had already made two potentially devastating mistakes by walking her home twice before I knew her well enough to be stocked with a sufficient supply of conversation material. There was the danger of a relationship-shattering period of silence occurring before we were comfortable enough with each other to appreciate these quiet moments.

I stated that we were already comfortable with quiet time and that we often experienced pauses in conversation while we walked or sat on a bench.

She said that boys always think that girls are comfortable with long moments of silence, but the reality is that the girl feels awkward. Corinne made me fully cognizant of the many pitfalls that could derail a blooming romance before it has even had a chance to bud. I didn't realize I had to be attentive to so many details. I thought I just needed to act naturally so she could get to know the real me, but Corinne said there's plenty of time for her to get to know the real me after she falls for me.

The next day I risked an awkward moment when I called and asked Toby to go out with me that upcoming Friday night. Meg Ryan and Tom Hanks were at it again in *Sleepless in Seattle*, which was showing at the on-campus movie theater that specialized in second-run movies. I figured that would be a safe first date, taking Corinne's advice fully into account and also considering my conversation with Toby the night before. She sounded enthusiastic on the phone, but Corinne had warned me about false enthusiasm. I wasn't sure how to read anything she said. According to Corinne, it might mean the opposite of what it sounded like. I decided to take it as it came.

Impatiently, I spent the next two days waiting out the time until our appointed meeting on Friday at six o'clock after soccer practice.

Thursday the passage of time was agonizingly slow. My morning English class was the most sluggish hour and a half of my life. We discussed Ernest Hemmingway's very short story "A Clean, Well-Lighted Place." The story is two pages long and is about nothing, literally. That didn't prevent a class discussion that lasted for the entire ninety-minute class period. A girl in the front row said that the main theme was man's inhumanity to man. I wanted to throw up. That was the sort of thing that a high school student who had not done the assigned reading would say to cover his lack of knowledge about the material. All I could think of was, "*Nada, y pues nada, y pues nada.*" I couldn't stand it.

Calculus class was also excruciatingly slow, but at least calculus makes sense. The sum of a sequence of numbers is a very specific number. It is never some other number depending on your viewpoint or depending on how you arrive there. The area under a curve is always a specific area regardless of whether you are young or old, male or female, Republican or Democrat. Give or take, that is. The ninety minutes of calculus class, however, felt more like nine hundred minutes.

After lunch at the cafeteria on Thursdays I usually go to the library for quiet study all afternoon until time for soccer practice. Today there would be no soccer practice because Coach Harrison had given us the day off. This day I decided that I needed to speed up the clock by taking a nap in the afternoon. I found a shady spot under a tree and parked my body on the grass, but closing your eyes does not guarantee sleep. Visions of Toby and me walking and talking and hugging and kissing and sailing and flying kites ate up all my fall-asleep inertia. I opened my eyes, and I found myself wide awake, lying on my back, in full awareness of everything around me including the tree branches swaying in the breeze directly above me, the cool air passing over me, the ant finding its way up my arm. After brushing the ant away, I checked my watch and found that I had been lying there for all of seven minutes. At this rate, it would be next year by the time Friday evening rolled around.

I was tempted to call her, but I didn't want to become a nuisance. I didn't want to be constantly in front of her, crowding her, or invading her time and space. Corinne had warned me against doing that. She didn't want me to smother her with my presence and thus extinguish any kindling flame that might be trying to fire up. Friday evening would come soon enough. I would just have to be patient and tough it out.

It was apparent that good old time was going to take his good old time, so I headed over to the library to get in some studying. It was possible that I would accidently run into her at the library, and I could see her and talk with her without being accused of smothering tactics, but this was not my lucky day. She was nowhere to be seen.

I hoped Toby would call me on my cell phone, but she didn't. Perhaps someone advised her against becoming a nuisance. Maybe she was told to avoid crowding me and to avoid invading my time and space. On Friday I must let her know that it was okay with me if she invaded my time and space. I wanted her to crowd me. "Please, go ahead, smother me, I don't mind." I'd tell her that the more I see of her, the better. Maybe she felt the same way.

Thursday afternoon and evening went by so slowly it was actually painful. It was like a gnawing at the back of my skull and a pounding at the front. This headache was too big even for Mother's Tylenol III, which Mother said would make you forget you ever had a headache. But everything was so slow, if I had entered a snail in the snail's pace race, my snail would have come in dead last. I couldn't concentrate on the studies and got very little accomplished. I prayed to God and asked Him to move it along a bit faster. I seldom asked God for anything, but this was an emergency, and given His great power, it didn't seem like I was asking a lot of Him. He may have answered, but I didn't hear Him; He may have granted my request, but I didn't notice. Perhaps it would have taken longer without His divine intervention, in which case it would have driven me totally insane, but I couldn't know for sure. Thursday night I could not sleep. Thoughts of Toby crowded out any weariness, there was no room for fatigue, the anticipation was so great, and the night dragged on and on and on.

Friday was even worse. Chemistry and psychology classes were a waste of my time because I could not focus on anything that was being said. Everything and everyone were performing in super slow motion. I must have looked at the wall clock more than three hundred times during the sixty-minute chemistry class. That did not speed up the movement of time. The psychology class was in a room with a broken wall clock, but I didn't realize the hands were not moving until well into the class. I had accepted the fact that time was at a standstill and the hands of the clock would not move ever again, and I was stuck in this time freeze, waiting for a Friday evening that was never to come.

Time did not speed up on the soccer field as it usually does. The two-and-a-half-hour practice session took six hours, or so it seemed. The enthusiasm level ran high after the win on Wednesday, and that translated into a spirited, fast-paced practice, but since I spent most of the session watching from the sideline, time still dragged on. The team was having fun. Even Coach Harrison was enjoying it. He didn't yell as much as usual, and he made no disparaging remarks to me. Still my mind was on Toby and not on soccer. Time crawled.

Chapter Twenty-Seven

I TOOK THE FASTEST post-practice shower of my life. I didn't break the record, which was posted and tied many times by Barry Webster, who never actually got wet when he showered, but I came very close. I had to balance my desire to hurriedly get out of the locker room and on with my date with Toby against my equally strong need to shower thoroughly to be sure that I didn't stink to high heaven and drive her away permanently.

When I exited the locker room, Toby was waiting there for me. The time had gradually passed, and we were together at last. After a century of waiting and hoping and praying for this moment to arrive, it was finally here.

"Hello, Hat," she said in that sweet, melodic voice that I had craved to hear for the past two days. Relief washed over me like the water from a locker room shower, cleansing me and rinsing me and ridding me of all the tension and anxiety that had built up in me over that time. I was alive and vibrant again just from hearing her voice. I pulled her into my arms and, cheek to cheek, squeezed her like I would never let her go.

"I missed you," I whispered into her ear.

We walked hand in hand to the Metro stop on New York Street and took the short ride into downtown.

At some point between exiting the locker room and arriving at the Palomino restaurant, the clocks started to move. I had checked my watch just before opening the door from the locker room. It was 6:10. After a five-minute walk to the Metro, a ten-minute ride to downtown, and a five-minute walk from the Metro to the restaurant, only twenty minutes should have passed, but my watch registered seven o'clock. Where did the extra half hour go? I thought about praying to God to ask Him to slow things down a bit, but I reconsidered and decided that I had better save my requests for something more important and more lasting, like love returned. I resolved that I would pray for that tonight.

"I've never been to this restaurant before," I said. "Do you know what's good here?"

"The mushroom soup is to die for," she answered.

"I can't think of much that I would die for, but I'm willing to give up some money. Do you think they'll take that instead?"

She giggled, and I heard Mother's ceramic wind chimes. I thought I might get Toby some wind chimes as a present. They would have to mimic her laughter to work as a viable gift.

"Do you have a porch or a balcony at your apartment?" I asked.

She was thrown off by my sudden shift of topic and had to pause before answering.

"Yes, I do. I have a small balcony off my living room that looks out over the woods along Pleasant Run. I can see the high school clearly from there. Why do you ask?"

"Oh, no reason." I didn't want to tell her that I was thinking about a gift for her that would necessitate access to a breeze for it to be useable. "I was just wondering if you could step outside to enjoy the fresh air without having to go down four flights and then back up again. Like if you wanted to take a short break from studying or something."

"Oh sure. I do take an occasional study break out there or if I just want to relax for a little while. There's a nice breeze that makes it very comfortable, especially this time of year."

The balcony has a nice breeze. That answered my next question without my having to ask it and without my having to explain why I asked it. Wind chimes would make an excellent present.

"So, mushroom soup it is. What else is good here?"

"If I tell you the linguini Bolognese is excellent, will you then ask if my apartment is air-conditioned?"

"Why would I ask that? What's the connection?"

"That's exactly what I was wondering," she said.

"Oh, the fresh air thing." I needed time to come up with an explanation for my question without giving away the idea of wind chimes as a gift.

"Yes. Why did you ask about my balcony out of the clear blue sky?"

"I can see why it would seem to be out of the clear blue sky to you." I spoke slowly in order to give myself a chance to concoct some reasonable story. This was quite a challenge. "But from my perspective, there was a simple progression of thought from mushrooms to balconies. You weren't in on those several steps, so the jump seemed unconnected."

"Okay, so tell me the steps."

"It started with the mushroom soup. That made me think about a mushroom farm in Pennsylvania that I read about in some magazine, probably *National Geographic*. The company that owns the farm is Moonlight Mushrooms, and it's the largest mushroom farm in the world. It's located in a former coal mine or limestone mine or something like that. The mushrooms grow well there because it's always dark, always the same humidity, and always the same temperature. It's a fascinating article. I could find it for you if you would like to read it. Of course, the workers on this farm have to work in this dark, humid mine all day long, so when they get their breaks, like a couple or three times a day, they like to go outside the mine to get fresh air and some relief from the dark. They scoot around in the mine on golf carts, and they use these carts to go out for their breaks. That made me think about you studying in your apartment last night without a break for fresh air unless you went down four flights of stairs and then back up again. Then I thought if you had a balcony, you could take a fresh air break without needing to go all the way down to the ground level. I'm glad that you have a balcony."

"Yes, it comes in handy."

"So, we will get the mushroom soup. I sure hope they use Moonlight Mushrooms. What else is good here?"

"The linguini Bolognese is excellent," she said.

"Does your apartment have air-conditioning?" I asked.

I heard the tinkling of ceramic wind chimes again. What a wonderful sound. I hope I can keep the breeze blowing so the sound of her laughter will never go away.

Chapter Twenty-Eight

NINE O'CLOCK CAME early that night. We had allowed two hours for dinner, which would give us thirty minutes to get back to campus for the nine-thirty movie. This should have been plenty of time, but we had barely finished our linguini Bolognese when the time to leave arrived. We decided to postpone dessert until after the show.

It was odd how the time had moved so slowly yesterday and today until after soccer practice, and now that I was with Toby, it was flying by like in that movie *The Time Machine*. If I had a time machine, I would jump over those times when I was away from Toby, and I would slow down time or even repeat it when I was with her. As it was, our date would be over before I knew it. If time kept accelerating like this, by next week we'd be sending our kids off to college, and the week after that we'd be reading bedtime stories to our grandchildren. Perhaps I should put in that request for a slowdown to God after all.

The theater on campus was not a real theater. It was a multiple-use exposition hall that could be set up for any number of different things. Last week it served as an art gallery containing a collection of charcoal sketches and water color and oil paintings by an undergraduate art student. At that time, they had used partitions to create smaller, more intimate spaces to display two or three paintings in a group. Earlier this week it housed a rock and mineral exhibition put on by the mineralogy department. The office partitions were removed, and the room was left open with several rows of folding tables covered with white cloth, elaborate displays of various rocks in cases set upon them. Tonight, the space was set up to show the movie *Sleepless in Seattle*. The tables were removed and replaced with folding chairs arranged in ten rows eight chairs long. Apparently, they were hoping for a big crowd. The chairs sat back from a white screen placed at one end of the room, and a projector was set up on a projector table at the other end.

For this show you needed to arrive on time because the movie started promptly at nine thirty. There were neither previews of coming attractions nor advertisements. Toby and I arrived at the last minute and took seats in the last row. The chairs were about one-quarter occupied, which meant about twenty viewers. I hoped the students that were putting on this program could make a profit with that small of a box office. Granted, they did not have to pay rent for the space, but they did have to pay for the movie rental and the equipment and the advertising and, probably, the chairs. I enjoyed watching movies in this environ because I knew it was put on by students trying to learn the ins and outs of commerce. Those students would in due course become business owners or corporate executives that would provide jobs for engineers like me.

Meg Ryan and Tom Hanks were magnificent as usual. Toby got the sniffles near the end, as did several other women in the room. The men held back, but I'm sure if they were alone, it would have happened to them as well. Not being a hopeless romantic myself, my eyes remained dry.

"I loved that movie," Toby said as we strolled across the common area toward the Student Union. It was after eleven o'clock, but we hadn't had dessert yet.

"They are quite the couple. If I was a movie producer, I would feature them in every romantic comedy I could lay my hands on. What a combination."

"But the movie didn't really resolve the problems of a long-distance romance," she said.

This comment took me by surprise. "Aren't you the one who said we have to accept certain improbabilities in movies?"

She smiled as she paused to consider her answer. "Yes, I did say that, and you were actually listening. I'm impressed. But an example of accepting an improbability is to not question the aspect that the young, intelligent, good-looking, and highly successful man that Tom Hanks portrays couldn't find love in Seattle. I accept that for purposes of allowing the movie to proceed with its premise, but I expect the movie to resolve the issues that the premise gives rise to."

"I think I understand that," I said. "So, you considered that he should have been able to match up with someone closer to home. What about true love, or finding the one person that's meant for you? What about fate?"

"I don't believe in fate. There's more than one person in the world who makes a good match. After all, he was married before, and that was apparently a good match. I don't believe there is a predetermined love for anyone. We have free will. That allows us to seek out what we want, and sometimes we make mistakes. Look at the divorce rate."

I wanted to disagree with her. My love for her was not a matter of my seeking her out. She was presented to me in some grand design. I had no interest in girls until I saw her, and then I became obsessed with her. I was fated to be with her. I loved her even after she rejected my first advances. I continued to love her when we had no contact other than Spanish class. I loved her through the summer when we had no contact at all. It was a predetermined course over which I had no control, my love dictating every move.

But I didn't want to disagree with her. Corinne had warned me not to discuss love except in the most abstract terms. She said that boys tend to start saying they love a girl before there has been enough time for love to take root. That can scare a girl away because she does not love him back. She told me to be careful with that word and just let the relationship grow in whatever direction it may.

"Good point," I said. "Some of those actors and actresses get married five or six times, and they still haven't found the one meant for them. By the same token, my parents met in grade school and have been a couple ever since. They never dated anyone else and got married shortly after finishing high school. They've been married over twenty years."

"That's wonderful. My parents have been married a long time too, and I think they're happy."

We arrived at the Student Union and paused at the door.

"Do you really want dessert?" I asked.

"No, I think it's getting too late for that."

We changed directions and changed the topic.

"How would you like to go for a frozen custard tomorrow? If I can get the car, we could drive up to Ritter's in the afternoon, have the dessert we missed tonight, and be back in time for me to go to soccer practice at three thirty."

"You have practice on Saturday?"

"And Sunday. Every day."

"Such commitment. I think I'd like to go to Ritter's with you tomorrow. Dinner is just not complete without dessert."

"Don't let me crowd you though. If I become a nuisance, you just let me know and I'll back off a little."

"Haha. You're not crowding me, Hat. I enjoy being with you. Why do you think you're a nuisance?"

"I just don't want to invade your time and space. I don't want to scare you off."

"I'll let you know before it gets to that, and you do the same for me. Okay?"

"Oh, you don't have to worry about that, Toby. You can go ahead and smother me. I won't mind."

We walked silently to the Metro stop and rode wordlessly out to Wallace Avenue as though a blanket had descended over us and we didn't want to disturb the security it provided. After departing the bus, the tranquility lifted and we could speak again. She broke the silence first.

"The movie didn't resolve any relationship issues. It only addressed the 'will you show up at the Empire State Building' issue, which really wasn't much of an issue."

"What did you need resolved besides the distance thing?"

"Nothing in particular, but there are always issues in any relationship."

The pause that followed was pregnant with overtones, the sounds of which were dissonant to my ears. I knew she was not concerned with issues in the movie but rather with potential problems with our budding romance. I did not want to address whatever concerns were on her mind right then. I wanted to follow Corinne's advice and face the tough questions after she had already fallen for me, when her approach would be from a more advantageous point of view. I remained quiet in the hope that whatever was bothering her would go away or disappear. That solution seldom works out, and sure enough it didn't work out this time.

"Look at us, for instance," she said, to my dismay. I knew it would come, but I was disappointed all the same when it did. "We have some very important issues that we are going to have to tackle eventually."

I didn't want to say it, but her statement was a lead that I was obligated to follow. It would have been cowardly not to respond in the prescribed manner.

"Like what?" I said reluctantly.

"You do know that I'm Jewish?"

"I surmised as much. Toby Rosen isn't your typical Irish name, you know, and I don't recall seeing you at Sunday Mass lately."

"And you are Irish Catholic."

"Patrick the Hat Trick Maloney, at your service, madam." I gave a little bow to try to bring some relief to the tension that had suddenly sprung up around us.

"Don't you think that's an issue?"

"Doesn't bother me. I haven't even thought about it."

"Maybe you should think about it. Tonight we had our first date, and I had a lovely time. I assume you are going to want to have a second date, and so do I. That means we need to do a little long-term thinking."

"That's funny."

"What's funny?"

"My sister, Corinne, told me to never bring up long-term issues until the relationship is firmly established as a long-term one. She says that is the surest way to scare a girl away before anything even gets started."

"Is Corinne your relationship counselor? That's awesome. She's probably right. I shouldn't have brought it up. I hope I haven't scared you away."

"Toby, you couldn't scare me away if you were a female werewolf."

"I'm glad to hear that, because it's going to be a full moon next week. You'll need to be prepared."

"I'll bring locks and cuffs, and I'll chain you to your bed before the moon comes out."

"That sounds a little kinky to me."

"Just a little?"

"Maybe a lot."

"Okay, then instead I'll bring lox and bagels."

"Maybe my mother will think you're Jewish."

That brought us full circle. After we both tried to get away from the subject, we couldn't help circling back to it.

"I know I'm going to have a problem when I tell my mother about you."

"Don't tell her. Not yet anyway."

"I'm going to have to tell her. Every day she asks me if I have met any Jewish doctors or Jewish med students. She says I'm in the ideal position right now, being a student in the Indiana University School of Medicine, and she doesn't want me to squander it."

"Well, I'm willing to convert to Judaism, but don't ask me to change my major."

"Don't even joke about that. You don't know my mother."

She admonished my lightheartedness, but she laughed out loud just the same. It was a welcome relief, but the respite was short-lived. Quickly her expression became serious.

"How are your parents going to react? Catholics aren't exactly known for being receptive to mixed religions either. My understanding is that Catholics don't even approve of other Christians."

"It's hard to say. I think they'll disapprove at first but come around later. Corinne was more taken aback that you are my former teacher than that you are Jewish. I am hopeful that she will tell my parents so that I won't have to. That will make it so much easier."

"You chicken! You have to face up to these things."

"Oh, I'll face the music, all right. It's just that I'll face only the wrath and not the shock of revelation."

Suddenly we were at her place. I didn't even remember crossing Washington Street. She fumbled with her key and at last opened the door. She turned to me just as she had the last two times we were here, light behind her, face in shadow. This time there was no confusion, no wondering what I should do, no hesitation. I pulled her to me and squeezed her tight. She squeezed me too, and we kissed, long and wet, our tongues fencing in the dark. We broke the kiss but did not break the embrace. I didn't want our time together to end. It had been such a long time coming and such a short time passing. I didn't want to face the coming night without her.

"I'll see you tomorrow," she whispered in my ear.

"I'll have to ask Dad for the car," I said. "I'll call you in the morning."

"Okay."

I wanted to add, "I love you," but I was sure that would only complicate things even further. Corinne had warned me, and she, after all, was my relationship counselor.

Chapter Twenty-Nine

AS I FEARED, time slowed to a snail's pace. Even though it was only eleven hours overnight, the night dragged on and on and on. I could not sleep for thinking of her. I could not find a comfortable position; the pillow was hot even when I flipped it over to the cool side. I tried my leg outside the sheet, then inside the sheet. Nothing worked. This was going to drive me crazy before long. When I finally called Toby at eleven o'clock the next morning, it seemed like a year since I had talked with her. Corinne advised me that it would be like this for about a week, and then the passage of time would revert to closer to normal. Time would always pass faster when I was with her and would slow down when we were apart, but I would adjust to it and it would become tolerable.

How did she know this stuff? I was Joe College; she was just a junior in high school. But she was dead on. She knew what she was talking about. Her advice made it easier to take, knowing that it was going to get better and that I would be able to handle it.

Over the next few weeks, as the nights took on a nippy edge and the leaves of the maple trees took on an orange and auburn tint, Toby and I spent a lot of time together. That made the speed of time issue easier to handle as well. I purchased a semester cafeteria pass for the evening meals. This was a disappointment for Mother and Dad since they enjoyed my time at dinner with them, talking of classes and campus and soccer. But it was much more convenient to have dinner on campus and spend time at the library or in the chem lab and so on. It was also more convenient to have dinner with Toby since she also had a cafeteria pass for lunch and dinner. I still had breakfast with the family.

Corinne didn't tell Mother or Dad about my new girlfriend. I guess she wanted me to face the shock of revelation as well as the wrath and the fury. I would eventually have to tell them myself, but not just yet.

For more than a month after Toby and I got together, I searched for wind chimes. I visited all the shops on campus and near the school but could not find the right ones. There were plenty of wind chimes available, but none had the right sound, the right tones. I checked out every store at Linwood Square Shopping Plaza, all along East Washington Street through Irvington and all the way out to Post Road. I spent an entire day at Circle Centre Mall downtown. I even spent time at Twin Airs Plaza and at Fountain Square but could not find a set of chimes that resonated properly.

Then Mother asked me to drive out to a craft store near Washington Square to pick up some yarn and some specialty items for her. While I was out there, I found the perfect chimes. These had eight ceramic hearts the size of my palm in eight different colors suspended from a ceramic disk by what looked like fishing line but which I'm sure had to be a more exotic material. The suspension lines were of eight different lengths, so the hearts climbed in a spiral up to the disk but were close enough to tap against one another when the air moved through them. In the tinkling of these chimes was her laughter. The clerk wrapped the wind chimes in bright-blue paper with yellow ribbon and a yellow and white bow, and I stowed the package away in my backpack. It would be the perfect gift.

Toby and I were set to have dinner at the school cafeteria that evening after soccer practice. It was Saturday night, but we just wanted to do dinner then study together at the library or one of the study lounges on campus. Many of our dates were like this. We didn't want to spend money on date activities when all we really wanted to do was spend time together.

Toby met me at the locker room door. We developed a routine that involved her saying, "Hello, Hat," which I loved because it reaffirmed our relationship in my mind every time I heard her say it. Then she would kiss me lightly on the lips before I returned the greeting, "Hello, Toby." Then we would share a hug and a cheek to cheek before we joined hands and walked off to wherever we were destined that day.

Usually it was to the cafeteria since practice was over at six o'clock and I would leave the locker room around six fifteen just in time for dinner. IUPUI students liked to complain about the cafeteria food, but I found the meals to be pretty good. They varied the menu enough that it never got boring, and the preparation and presentation, although not fancy and frilly, were appetizing. Tonight, the featured course was grilled rosemary chicken breast, parsley potatoes, spinach, and cooked carrots with German chocolate cake for dessert. The meal was fine, and the company was finer.

Toby sat across the table from me looking like a fashion model or a movie star or a goddess floating in the midst of white clouds high above some Greek mountain. Her outfit was plain, a solid gray silk blouse, two buttons open at the top, over a solid black cotton skirt, but her face glowed and her green eyes shined and her hair shimmered and her smile sparkled so that she might have been wearing diamonds and emeralds and mink. With her right hand she brushed her hair back behind her ear, revealing a dangling silver earring in the shape of a teardrop that matched the silver pendant on a thin chain around her neck, nestled between those two open buttons on her blouse. She was dazzling, and I couldn't look away. I felt like I too was floating among those high Greek clouds just by being there with her.

"So, how did practice go today?" she asked.

The question seemed so ordinary to be coming from such an extraordinary beauty. It served to bring me down from those high-flying clouds back down to earth.

"Same as always," I answered. I didn't like to talk about practice. Soccer was my great failure. After that exciting first goal against Oral Roberts, my contributions on the soccer field in the next eight matches amounted to relieving the real stars of the team so they would be fully rested and able to score the goals and win the games. We won five of those eight matches without me having to score a single point or even take a single shot. Toby's prediction that Coach would be forced to find a starting spot for me was falling flat.

"The problem," I continued, "is not my skill level. It's my energy level, or I should say, my lack of energy level. I can play this game. In practice, I can outmaneuver each and every one of these guys one on one, even two on one. I can outshoot all, but Evan and I defend better than anyone except maybe Leslie. I just can't keep it up for the whole match. I get tired so easily that I can't play even one half without collapsing of fatigue."

"Maybe you need to see a doctor," Toby said, not for the first time.

The problem with that suggestion was that if the doctor found something wrong with me that would prevent me from playing, I would lose my scholarship. Without the scholarship, there would be no school, no engineering degree, no time with Toby. That was not a satisfactory course of action.

"I think I'm just a little anemic. I'm trying to eat a lot more spinach these days." I gestured toward the two extra piles of spinach next to the cooked carrots on my plate as proof of my commitment to this solution.

"I don't think that's going to solve the problem, Popeye."

"It's worth a try. The extra iron in the spinach could give me just the boost I need."

"Maybe," she said. She didn't sound convinced.

After we finished eating, we sat in the halo glow cast by a sidewalk lamp on a wooden bench outside the cafeteria to enjoy the fresh air for a short while before going to the library to study. The leaves were not yet falling, but the chill in the air promised that they would be dropping sooner rather than later. Toby's eyes widened with surprise when I took the blue gift package out of my backpack.

"How pretty," she said, accepting the gift with a glint in her eyes. "Did you wrap this yourself?"

"Of course," I said, "with a little help from a friend."

She tore into the present like a child on her birthday. The pretty blue wrapping paper was in shreds by the time she got to the box underneath. When she opened the box and saw the ceramic hearts, a puzzled expression crossed her face. She struggled to take it out of the box, but the suspension lines kept tangling and the disk would not come free.

"I'm sorry," she said, "but I can't seem to get this out of the box. What is it?"

"Here, let me help."

I carefully untangled the lines and removed the chimes from the box. Holding the disk up over my head, I unwound the hearts so they hung separately below it. The pattern began to emerge, and the spiral formed below the disk. I blew softly on the dangling pieces, and they jangled together in a chorus of sound.

"Wind chimes," I announced, "for your balcony."

"Oh, how lovely," she said. "They have such a light and cheery tone."

"Like your laughter."

"Thank you. Will you hang them on my balcony for me?"

"Of course, I will."

Chapter Thirty

WE DECIDED TO skip the library and go straight to her apartment so I could hang up the wind chimes right away. This was a thrilling idea for me since I had never been past that big oaken door at the entrance to her apartment building. We usually ended the day at that door with a wonderful kiss and hug and sweet words of endearment. Sometimes I would offer to walk her up to her apartment, but she always declined. That door was a barrier; it was the gateway into the castle that held the fair princess who was safeguarded from all her potential suitors. I thought I would never be able to reach her heart unless I was able to get past that great door. If she was ever going to fall for me, I had to rise to the fourth floor. Tonight she had invited me up.

"Are there hooks in the ceiling of your balcony, or do we need to stop and get some?" I asked.

She gave me a strange glance before she answered. Her eyes narrowed and took on a faraway look as though she was seeing something just past my field of vision. Her cheeks lifted up slightly, causing thought lines to appear at the corners of her eyes. She shook her head and smiled as her eyes focused back on me.

"Yes, there are some hooks in the ceiling already. I have a couple of ferns and petunias hanging up there, but I didn't use all the hooks."

Her mind was on something else, somewhere else. She'd answered my question absentmindedly and then lapsed into her previous thoughtful state.

"Is something on your mind?" I asked.

"Yes, something was vaguely familiar, but I can't put my finger on it."

I gave her quiet time to try to recall the familiarity as we walked to the Indy Metro stop. She did not place it by the time we got on the bus, but as we crossed State Street, I noticed her eyes light up with recognition. She was virtually bubbling over with the need to tell me, but she observed the protocol of not discussing anything on the bus.

When we got off the Metro at Wallace Avenue, Toby grabbed my hand, gave it a healthy squeeze, and said, "That's why you asked about my balcony. It didn't have anything to do with mushrooms."

"What are you talking about?" I said.

"That night at Palomino's about a month ago, you asked if I had a balcony. It was because you wanted to give me these wind chimes, wasn't it?"

"Guilty, as charged."

"Why did you make up that crazy story about a mushroom farm? Why didn't you just tell me?"

"That mushroom farm is real. I didn't make it up."

"Okay. But why not tell me? Why the story?"

"I didn't want to tell you about the wind chimes because I wanted to give them to you, you know, as a surprise."

"But that was clear back in September. Why did you wait until now to give them to me?"

"I couldn't give them to you before today because I didn't have them. I've been searching all over town, but I couldn't find them anywhere. I just found them this morning."

"You've been looking for these wind chimes for more than a month? There must be fifty stores that carry wind chimes. What's with that?"

"You'll see when I put them up."

We walked on in silence, each of us in awe of the other. I was amazed that she could recall an immaterial conversation we had more than a month ago. She, I assume, was equally amazed that it could take me that long to buy a simple set of wind chimes.

When she opened the barrier door, I was tempted to take her in my arms and kiss her as I always did for tradition's sake and for good luck, but I was afraid that I would put a hex on this momentous occasion. I also didn't want her to think that I thought it was such a big deal.

Beyond the large oak door was an entry hall with a single evil light that cast shadows on young girls standing and waiting to be kissed that made it impossible for young boys to discern the intentions of the young girls. I gave that evil light an evil eye for causing me such anguish.

A staircase rose to the right, a pair of single bulb lights on each landing of the switchback illuminating the way to the fourth floor. I stepped on the first riser, but Toby moved on through the entry hall. I followed her into a room with a row of eight tall metal mailboxes built into one wall. Toby stopped at the last box and opened it with a key. She removed two pieces of mail, looked at them briefly, and then tossed them into the trash can in the corner without opening them. She closed and locked her mailbox and with a nod of her head beckoned me to follow her on through the room toward the back. I loved watching her perform her routine tasks as she made her way home. I felt at home myself that way.

We ascended a second set of stairs, similar to the first, in the back of the building. On the wall at the first landing was an old black-and-white photo of a building five stories tall with 1930 era, cars parked in front. The building was not familiar. We continued up the stairs to the second level where a hallway ran to the front of the building. There was an apartment on each side of the hallway, and at the other end was the first set of stairs. The next landing had another black-and-white photo of a different building from the same period as the other. This building looked familiar, but I could not place it. The third level looked like the second with two apartments alongside a central hallway. The photo on the next landing was a front shot of the old Irvington Theater back in its heyday. This was unmistakable since the Irvington Theater was an East Side landmark and was only a couple of blocks from Our Lady of Lourdes Roman Catholic Church. I thought now that the buildings in the other pictures might be ones that existed in Irvington years earlier, when the area was a more thriving center of commerce. On the fourth level was Toby's apartment.

We entered into the kitchen. The room was functional with refrigerator, stove, sink, cabinets, and counter space on the right. It was separated from the living room on the left by a three-foot-by-six-foot table built into the wall and surrounded by four wooden chairs. This served as her dining area. The living room was comfortably furnished with a couch, an easy chair, and an entertainment center that contained a television/DVD player and a radio/CD player. The far end of the living room had sliding glass doors that opened onto the balcony beyond. The open layout of the apartment gave a sense of size that the actual dimensions did not provide.

"Wow, Toby! What a nice apartment!" I said as she took my windbreaker and hung it with her jacket in the small closet just inside the door. I dropped my backpack on the table.

"Thanks. It's comfortable."

"Can I use the bathroom?"

She pointed to a hallway at the other end of the kitchen and said, "First door on the right."

As I entered the bathroom, I noted a door standing ajar at the end of the hall. The bedroom beyond the door was lit by a small blue ceramic lamp sitting on a bedside table. It seems that she left the light burning all day, perhaps to give the impression that someone was home and ward off potential burglars. A blue-and-white quilt comforter covered the bed, and a blue valance topped the window. In the bathroom was a pink shower curtain and pink bath towels. She apparently liked to match up the colors of the accoutrements.

"Would you like a Coke?" she asked when I returned.

"Coke is good, if it's caffeine-free."

I wandered into the living room, and on closer inspection, I saw that she had put some considerable effort into coordinating the look of her home. The carpet was the standard-issue dark brown typical of the apartments and rental houses in the area. I had seen many rolls of this same carpet on the maintenance trucks at Joe DeMarco's house whose father had several rental properties. The walls were painted bone white to accommodate any color scheme. Toby coordinated the colors of the furniture and the window treatments to complement and harmonize with these basic color requirements.

The easy chair was covered with cloth upholstery with thin vertical stripes of red and beige on a blue background. The couch was solid beige leather with two floral print pillows of beige, blue, and red. The two windows, one in the kitchen area opposite the entry door and one in the living room area, were covered by vinyl horizontal mini-blinds with valances across the tops with the same colors and design as the easy chair but with broader stripes. The sliding glass doors that led to the balcony were covered with vertical blinds that now stood open. These were topped by a valance of the same design and color scheme as the windows.

I walked up to the glass doors and looked out onto the balcony. Two dark metal chairs sat facing out toward the night, flanking a small metal table large enough for only a couple of glasses and perhaps a single cheese and cracker dish. From the ceiling of the balcony, four planters hung in a row above the wrought iron railing. Ferns dangled over the sides of the two outside planters, while pink and white and purple petunias climbed down from the two inside pots.

Toby brought two glasses filled with Coke and ice. She handed me one glass then opened the sliding glass door with her freed hand.

"Here's the famous balcony you've heard so much about," she said. "Not nearly as impressive in person as the tall tales I've spun, but serviceable nevertheless."

I stepped through the doors, the chill of the night air on my skin raising goose bumps on my arms. The balcony was small, the railing only four feet from the doors, but the view was large. Facing east, the lights of Washington Street stretched into the distance, past Emerson Avenue and into Irvington. I could almost make out the Irvington Theater, whose picture I saw on the stairwell landing. To the right, the trees of the Pleasant Run green space were still full of leaves and filled the horizon. Over the treetops rose the roof of Howe High School just on the other side of Pleasant Run.

There were six hooks screwed into the ceiling, and only four of them were in use. A gentle breeze stirred the ferns and the petunias. I thought this would be a great environment for the wind chimes.

"I could hang the wind chimes right here," I said, pointing to the empty hook next to a fern plant.

"Let me get it."

She opened the box and tried to extract the chimes but had the same difficulty as when she first opened the present. The lines were tangled and twisted. She handed me the box with a sigh of frustration.

"Just be sure to never take them down," I said. "Once they're up and hanging correctly, they won't get twisted up."

With two hands working, I was able to get them untangled and hanging properly, a colorful spiral of ceramic. The breeze flowed through the hearts, and they responded with a melodic song that made my heart leap.

"Thank you so much for the gift, Hat," she said. "They're awesome. What a lovely sound."

"Like your laughter."

She suddenly turned her face to me, her eyes knowingly appraising mine. She leaned into me, placing her hand on my cheek, caressing my chin.

"That's why it took you a month to find them. You had to have just the right sound, didn't you? In your mind, you had to have my laughter in the chimes."

"Of course, I did. What good would they be if they didn't reflect you? They would merely be ceramic and wouldn't be a proper gift at all."

She leaned against me again and turned her face up to me. Sliding her hand across my cheek over my ear and around to the back of my head, she pulled my face to her and kissed me with an enthusiasm I hadn't felt before. Her lips parted, and her tongue touched my lips then slipped between them to find my tongue. I wrapped my arms around her and squeezed her tightly to me.

The chimes laughed again as the cool breeze played a tune through them. Once more goose bumps rose on my arms, but I wasn't sure if it was the chill of the air or the heat of our embrace that caused them.

"It's chilly," she said. "Let's go inside."

She closed the vertical blinds over the sliding glass doors and turned to me again. She threw her arms around my neck and kissed me with a long and wet smooch. The goose bumps arose a third time, and this time there was no frosty draft.

Chapter Thirty-One

I DREW HER TO me, and we melted together, our tongues intertwined and our hearts beat as one. I brushed her hair away from her ear and kissed her there. I moved my lips down below her ear, and as I kissed her neck under her dangling, silver earring, I opened the third button on her blouse. She didn't stop me, so I opened the fourth button. I moved my face down and kissed under her chin, her perfume strong in the air, her skin glowing, and her breath warm on my ear. I opened the fifth button. I ran my tongue across her moist skin below the silver teardrop pendant and into the glistening valley between her breasts obstructed only by the narrow band that joined the cups of her bra. She raked her fingers through my hair, pulling my head closer to her, while sliding her other hand inside the back of my shirt. She caressed my shoulder, the muscles there tensing with excitement and anticipation, and massaged the nape of my neck, urging me on to the next and last buttons.

Her blouse fell open, and with an imperceptible wriggle, she let it drop soundlessly to the floor. I straightened and slid the straps of her bra over her shoulders, then slid the bra down to her waist. I took her breasts, so smooth and supple, in my hands, pinching the nipple of her left breast between my thumb and index finger, massaging her right breast, as my erection grew hard pressed against her stomach.

It was her turn to attack the buttons, and she did it swiftly and deftly and without pause. My shirt opened to her exploring hands, and my pectoral muscles took their turn at tensing. She laid her cheek against my chest, wrapping her arms around my back, drawing me firmly to her, kissing my breast, nipping my nipple with her teeth.

A shudder ran through me, collecting and settling in my groin. I pushed my cock harder against her, and she moved her hands to the small of my back, pulling me tightly to her again. I didn't want her to let go, but she eventually did, turning her face up to me with a smile, kissing me lightly on the lips.

"That feels good," she said.

I shrugged out of my shirt and tried to unfasten her loose bra behind her back but fumbled with it instead.

"It's easier to do it this way," she said as she spun the bra around her waist, bringing the clasp to the front. It was much easier that way. She slid the zipper of her skirt around to the front, and it was easier that way too. The bra and skirt joined the blouse and shirt on the floor in a disorderly pile.

She threw her arms around my neck and stretched her nearly naked body across mine, pressing her breasts against my chest, her lips against my lips, and her thighs against my thighs. I slid my hand under the waistband of her panties and caressed the smooth curve of her butt, my tongue finding her tongue, my rigid cock finding her crotch.

"Undo my pants," I said when we loosened our embrace.

She didn't respond immediately. A haze fell over her eyes, their sea-green luster fading to an olive drab, as she gazed at some faraway sight over my left shoulder. Then she lowered her arms to my waist and rested her face against my chest.

"What's wrong?" I asked, stroking her hair.

"It's my fault," she said. She started to sob softly. "I never should have let us go this far."

Tears streaked down her cheeks and mingled with the hair on my chest, but she did not release her grip around my waist.

"Why? What's the matter?"

"I can't do this with you." In contrast to her words, she held me tighter, conflicted, wanting me yet not wanting to want me.

"Why not?"

"You're not Jewish." She shuddered, and the tears flowed freely. She squeezed my torso as though she feared I would disappear if she let go. I squeezed her back, gripped with the same fear, caught in an evil curse that said Jews and Catholics could never be lovers. I held her silently, tightly to my body for several long seconds before I ventured to break the spell.

"We can work out the religious issues," I said. "Love will find a way."

I immediately regretted saying that. It sounded so childish. But she softened with my words, her grip around my waist loosening, her muscles relaxing, her stuttered breath evening, and her tears disappearing.

Without moving her face from my chest, she said, "Do you love me?"

"I do love you," I replied.

"Maybe love can find a way."

"Do you love me?" I asked.

"Yes, I do," she said, moving her hand across my belt, leading me slowly across the room toward the hall that led to the bedroom.

She sat back on the edge of the bed. I stood before her.

She had no problem with the buckle. As she pulled down the zipper, my cock trembled with the brief contact of her hand. My pants fell to the floor, revealing a bulge in my underwear. Using both hands, she slipped her fingers under the elastic waistband and pulled it forward and down. The waistband didn't clear my cock and pulled it down with it. Then it slipped over the tip, and my cock rebounded like a diving board after the diver's spring, bobbing in front of her face.

"Oh!" she said. "This won't be as hard as I thought."

"What do you mean?" I said.

"I thought only Jewish boys were circumcised, but I guess Catholic boys are too."

I recalled the lost luster in her eyes of moments ago, and I understood why she had been upset. It wasn't religious fear; it was physical. I hadn't thought much about it before, but at that moment, I was glad that I was circumcised.

She grasped the base and kissed the tip before engulfing the head in her mouth. She sucked gently as she slid her lips down the shaft as far as she could go, then back up again. I didn't think I could get any harder, but I did. She bobbed slowly down and up three more times, and then released me and smiled up at me, satisfied that I was ready.

I stepped out of my clothes, knelt before her, and kissed her bellybutton, running my tongue around its circumference. She giggled and I heard the chimes. I gently laid her back on the comforter and ran my tongue down to her panty line. I slid my hands under her butt and firmly grasped her cheeks. Then I kissed her left thigh and ran up to the panty line. I kissed her right thigh and ran up to the panty line. I kissed the inside of her left thigh, and as my tongue climbed higher and moved closer to her panties, I felt her tremble and her leg muscles tighten. I kissed the front of her panties and felt her pubic hair against my lips. I pulled her panties down over her legs, over her knees, over her feet, and deposited them on top of my underpants. I kissed her pubic hair again without any silk to block the way then ran my tongue down between her legs. She grasped the back of my head and pulled my face tighter to her, spreading her legs and arching her back to meet my exploring tongue. Her leg muscles shivered, and she gave out a delicate mewl. I moved my tongue in every direction I could, testing her while tasting her. She ran her fingers through my hair and then wrapped her legs around my neck, pulling me close with them, moaning softly.

I didn't want to stop. I loved hearing her moan; I loved feeling her quiver at my touch. I rejoiced that I could give her pleasure. Her sighs and whimpers excited me as much as her kiss or the feel of her body against mine. Her trembling caused me to tremble. In my euphoria, I almost didn't hear her call my name.

"Hat, come here."

I lifted my head to listen more carefully.

"Come here," she repeated, insistently.

I stood up. She threw the comforter aside, pulled the top sheet down, and fell back on the bed, her head resting on a billowing pillow. She reached her hand out to me, and I took it. I got into the bed at her side, not sure what to do, but I knew I wanted my body next to hers. I ran my hand over her breast and squeezed. She ran her hand up my inner thigh, gently and lightly tracing my balls with her fingertips. Then she slid her hand up the shaft of my cock and grasped it firmly, stroking, stroking. She pulled it toward her, and I rolled over on top of her. She made it easy for me, guiding me into her with her hand. I was able to figure out the rest. I plunged into her with a driving force, and she rose to meet me. With each thrust and withdrawal, she arched and retreated, matching my rhythm stroke for stroke. Soon we were both whimpering. I felt spasms in the backs of my legs and urgency in my balls. I grabbed her hips with both hands and tried to drive deeper into her. Her thigh muscles clenched, and she bucked back at me, her arms hugging my shoulders. She wrapped her legs around my legs as I exploded into her with a groan. I heard her suck in her breath as I emptied myself and began to fade away.

Chapter Thirty-Two

I AWOKE. I DIDN'T remember falling asleep or rolling over onto my back. Toby lay sleeping with her head on my chest, her left arm draped across my stomach, her breasts pressed against my abdomen, her stomach against my hip, and her left leg bent and wrapped around my left leg. It was an altogether quite comfortable arrangement. I glanced at the clock on the bedside table. Nine forty-five. We had slept for about an hour, but there was no need to hurry.

I placed my left arm over her shoulder and gently stroked her back. Without awakening, she tightened her hold with her left arm and squeezed my leg between hers. We held this position for the next ten minutes until she woke up.

"Hello, Hat," she said, kissing me lightly on the lips.

"Hello, Toby," I answered, hugging her close to me and sliding my cheek across hers. Our routine felt as natural while naked in bed as it had when fully clothed on campus.

"Did you have a nice nap?" I asked.

"Very nice. I feel reenergized."

She ran her hand across my stomach and then down over my abdomen, her fingers gliding through my pubic hair. There was a resurrection of my penis. I lay back enthralled with her touch and contented to let her find her way as she fondled my resurgence.

"You are reenergized as well, I see," she said, stroking me to full firmness.

Without letting go, she moved over me, straddling me, guiding me into her. I lifted my hips to meet her and to match her movements, but she placed her index finger across my lips to quiet me. I lay back, once again content to let her have her way with me.

She sat above me, her back straight, her arms extended so she could grasp the head board for balance and leverage. I placed my hands tenderly on her thighs. She moved her hips in a slow rhythm, alternating a gentle lift with a hard grind. She continued this at a steady pace, her eyes closed in concentration, while I watched her in wonder from below.

What an incredible sight to see, her naked body glistening in the lamplight, her breasts rising and falling with her breath and her tempo, the silver pendant swinging like a pendulum between them. Her hair fell around her face, swaying with the beat, her silver earrings flashing in and out of view. With her eyes still closed tight and her brow furrowed, she smiled then laughed—wind chimes. She stopped lifting her hips; instead she ground hard into my pelvis. I felt her thigh muscles tighten and tremble under my hands, and she moaned softly as she had done earlier. She shifted her legs down, straddling mine yet keeping my cock firmly implanted inside her. I moved my hands to her waist, helping to support her. She dropped forward, stomach to stomach, breasts to rib cage, her face buried in my chest, and wrapped her arms under my shoulders, squeezing me with her arms and upper body as well as with her legs. I moved my hands down to her butt, and although I could not possibly pull her any closer to me than she already was, I tried. She shook with spasm after spasm without making a sound louder than a whimper.

We held that tight embrace well after her body stopped shuddering. I didn't want to interfere with her full enjoyment of her release and the peaceful afterglow that followed. Gradually she eased her hold on me, and I let up, following her lead. She rose up and sat on top of me again, never having let me slip out of her.

"It's your turn," she said as she began to pump. I was already primed, and in short order, my well was overflowing. This time I closed my eyes, and in my peaceful afterglow, I drifted off to sleep.

She abruptly sat up in bed, waking me from a deep sleep.

"It's eleven o'clock," she announced, as though we had somewhere that we had to be.

She jumped out of the bed and wrapped herself in a housecoat that was hanging from a hook on the back of the closet door. As she tied the belt around her waist, she shook my leg although I was already awake.

"Come on, Hat, up and out."

"What's up?" I asked.

"It's time for you to go home."

"I thought I might stay the night."

"Nope. Not tonight. You've got to go to church with your family in the morning. I don't want your parents thinking that your Jewish girlfriend kept you up all night and made you miss Sunday Mass. This is going to be hard enough without getting that strike against us."

I reluctantly got out of bed and accepted the pants and underwear she handed me. I held the clothes in one hand and pulled her to me with the other hand. We kissed and embraced, and I started to get hard again.

"No, no," she said, pulling away. "We can't do that again tonight. Tomorrow is another day."

I didn't let her go, but I didn't press her either. I knew she was right. I had to get home. I was relieved by her promise of tomorrow, for I had feared that this might be a one-time fluke. Now, I could leave and go home and sleep peacefully in the knowledge that she would still be mine when I awoke in the morning. I embraced her one last time.

"This was my first time, you know," I whispered.

"Yes, I knew that." She smiled. "But it won't be your last."

I dressed, gathered my things, kissed her, said goodbye again, and left.

There was a distinctive chill in the air as I floated up Wallace Avenue that night. I loved the feel of it on my face. It reminded me by contrast of the soft warmth of Toby's skin and Toby's breath and Toby's touch.

I was happy to be moving into autumn after the long hot summer. Things might be easier to handle with a little nip in the air as opposed to the smothering heat that sucked the life out of you. This autumn, life was good, and that chill reminded me that I was indeed alive.

Chapter Thirty-Three

TOBY AND I didn't make love every night. Some nights we simply cuddled, some nights we merely studied together, other nights we didn't see each other at all. But most nights we jumped eagerly into bed and enthusiastically explored each other's body to our mutual satisfaction.

On those nights when Toby and I were not together, I had dinner at home with the family. Even I noticed that Mother was slowly disappearing. She was exhausted from the disease and from the treatments. I wasn't sure which was worse. Day by day she became thinner. Every morning she looked frailer than the night before. Sometimes she would come to the dinner table, but she never ate. Most times she would lie back in her favorite recliner chair and listen to our conversation from there. Our house was small, and the dining room was practically in the living room, so she was still a part of the dining experience even when she chose to remain in her chair.

Dad and Corinne became master chefs and alternated the tasks of preparing dinner each night. I could barely boil water, but on those nights when I ate with the family, I did the cleanup, both wash and dry.

On Thanksgiving Day, Brian came home from Ball State. Mother made the special effort to join us at the dining room table for the dinner that Corinne and Dad put together. There was turkey, of course, its skin baked to a crisp brown, and mashed potatoes with turkey gravy, cranberry sauce, and sweet corn. Mother had always spent Thanksgiving morning filling short cut pieces of celery with peanut butter and cream cheese for appetizers, but this year I assumed responsibility for that task. Corinne baked pumpkin pies, and they were nearly as good as Mother's. I didn't dare say that to either of them.

"Now that football season is over," Brian said, "I should be able to come home more often." The Cardinals won only four games this year and did not qualify to go to a bowl game.

"Sorry I didn't get up there to see any of your games, Brian," I said.

"That's okay, Paddy. I didn't get to see any of yours either. Believe me, I know how all-consuming college athletics can be. I barely had time for anything else."

"Yes," I said. "How did the season go for you?"

"Not so well. I got so used to winning in high school that all of this losing is taking a heavy toll on my psyche. We won only four out of twelve games this year, and that loss to Bowling Green last Saturday was tough. The college game is so much faster than high school. Before, when I found the hole, it was good for eight or nine yards or more. Now, more often than not, the hole closes up before I even hit it. I averaged just under three yards per rush attempt. A measly ground attack like that is not going to win very many games."

"At least you're playing. I'm the permanent sub."

"I didn't play all that much last year either. When I was a freshman, I mostly went in when the score was so lopsided that we didn't stand a chance of winning. Most of the third stringers got some playing time that way. When we were out of Coach's hearing range, we called ourselves the 'Spilled Soup Squad.'"

"How's that?"

"Well, at the end of the game, if the score was one sided, the winning team would send in their third stringers to mop up. We would send in our third stringers to be mopped up, so we must be the spilled soup."

Mother really got a kick out of that. She got to laughing so hard that tears came to her eyes. She lost her breath, and then she started coughing, then wheezing. Everyone jumped up and ran to her side. She motioned for us to sit back down, that she was all right. She took a moment to regain her, breath and then she smiled up at Brian.

"I can't laugh like I used to," she said.

We all sat back down at the dining room table; the humor of the moment had evaporated.

"Your team won some games this year," Brian stated.

"Yeah, we were twelve and seven. That's more wins in one year than we won in all my five years of high school. Not that I contributed to those wins. Even when Matt Pipher went out for the season with an injured ankle, I didn't move into the starting lineup. My backup, Lashawn Wilson, leap-frogged over me into the starting position."

"You'll have to work harder over the off-season," Brian said, "and earn that starting job next fall."

"Yeah," I said absently.

"Tell us about your new girlfriend, Paddy," Corinne said.

I was unprepared for that. I had been trying to come up with a smooth way to introduce to them, first, the concept of a girlfriend, then second, the existence of Toby Rosen, and third, the issue of religious diversity. I had decided that the best time to bring the subject up was tomorrow, and of course, today was always today. If I learned nothing else in Spanish class, I did learn the meaning of *mañana.* I thought that Corinne decided to let me take my time with the issue and choose the most proper occasion, but she apparently lost her patience with that approach. I guess she knew the meaning of *mañana* as well as I did.

All heads turned immediately toward me. The spotlight of attention was pouring on the heat, and my forehead became suddenly damp. The air became heavy and smelled of ozone as though a bolt of lightning had just struck a nearby tree. Then I realized that it wasn't ozone that I smelled but my own sweat. I turned crimson.

"So who's the girl, Paddy?" Mother asked. "Is it that Mary Kelly that you used to see in high school?"

I felt the blush drain out of my face as my cheeks went from crimson to deathly pale. How did Mother know about Mary Kelly? What did Mother know about Mary Kelly? How did she find out about our tryst in the church sacristy? How was I going to explain that sacrilege? Before I had a chance to open my mouth and confess the whole scene with Mary at the Saint Patrick's Day Party, Mother resolved the problem.

"She's such a nice Irish girl. I always hoped the two of you would find each other."

Color came back to my cheeks, and I slowly regained my composure as I recognized that Mother knew nothing about my time with Mary. Corinne gave me a look of suspicion, but I could deal with her later.

"I'm sorry, Mother," I said, "but I'm not seeing Mary Kelly. I am seeing another girl. In fact, we've been seeing each other for a couple of months now. Mostly we study together."

"So she's in one of your classes?"

"Well, no. She's in the School of Medicine. We don't have any common classes. We just spend our study time together in the library or in a study lounge."

"Tell us all about her, Paddy," Corinne said, encouraging me to continue. Corinne knew that Toby was older than I was and that she was my former teacher and that she was Jewish. All these things should have been major issues, but none of them bothered her. She knew that I was seeing Toby regularly and that things were getting pretty serious. She didn't know how serious.

"What can I tell you? She's five foot six, dark black hair, green eyes, and likes pizza. She likes Meg Ryan movies, not the war heroine ones, the romantic ones, especially with Tom Hanks."

"She's going to be a doctor?" Mother asked.

"No, Mother, actually she's majoring in clinical laboratory science. She'll be the one that runs the lab tests on blood and urine samples and does the analysis to see what's up. Stuff like that."

"What's her name, son?" Dad asked.

This was the giveaway point. I didn't know one Irish Catholic girl named Toby. As a matter of fact, I knew only one girl in the whole world named Toby. Maybe it could pass for an Irish name, after all.

"Her name is Toby," I said, "Toby Rosen."

"Now, that would explain why you haven't mentioned her before," Dad said.

There was no pause of surprise or sudden recognition. Dad had absorbed the information, processed it, analyzed it, and immediately understood the ramifications of the situation. There was no malice or concern in his voice. He was merely making a statement of fact.

Corinne was ahead of the game and sat with a shit-eating grin plastered across her face. She was actually enjoying my precarious condition. Brian was grinning too. I wasn't sure if he understood what was going on or not, but he seemed to be enjoying things as much as Corinne was.

Mother was a little slower on the uptake. She gazed at Dad with a puzzled look for several seconds before she turned to me. Then her look turned from confusion to understanding to apprehension.

"So, she's not Irish?" she said.

Dad, Corinne, and Brian burst out laughing. I couldn't help chuckling too. I didn't think I was going to be able to laugh my way through this, but at least this was a better start than yelling and crying and stomping and throwing things.

Brian stopped laughing long enough to interject, "Yes, she is Irish, Mother. Like so many Irish families, including your own family, they changed their name when they came to America. It used to be O'Rosen."

This time Mother laughed along with the rest of us, and her laughter did not degenerate into a coughing seizure; it slowly migrated from hearty to jovial to light, and then tenderly faded away. We all recovered eventually. Then Mother, dabbing her eyes with her napkin, asked a sobering question.

"Are you serious about this girl, Paddy?"

"Yes, I am quite serious, Mother. I'm in love with her."

Mother considered that revelation while a hush fell over the room. She gently shrugged her shoulders, smiled, and with a twinkle in her eye, gave me a wink.

"Well, why don't you bring her over here and introduce her to your mother? Maybe Corinne could learn to make some matzo balls or something."

"She'd probably prefer Irish stew," Dad said.

I felt a rush of relief as a great burden was lifted from my shoulders. This was easier than I thought it would be. I wished I had told everyone about Toby earlier, and maybe even brought her over to meet the family sooner, maybe even brought her home for Thanksgiving. I was delighted with their approval and elated that Toby would be readily accepted into the family. Dad brought me back down to earth.

"You realize this is not going to be all peaches and cream, don't you?" he said. "There are going to be some significant questions that the two of you will need to work out. Have you talked about that?"

"We've acknowledged that there are issues, yes. We haven't agreed to any solutions. I thought that telling you about her, and her telling her parents about me, would be the first steps, and then we could address the potential problems after that. She's not Irish. She's not even Catholic; she's Jewish. I know there are going to be things that we need to work out, but other people have faced the same concerns and managed to overcome them. I don't see why we can't do the same."

"Well, at least you know you need to talk about those things. You can't just ignore them and hope they will go away, because that's when they blow up in your face."

"That 'ignore them' approach was exactly the one I was hoping to take, but Toby thinks we need to talk things through. I guess we'll be following your advice, Dad."

"I hope you know that your mother and I are here to help you, son. You can talk about these things with us too—you and Toby both."

"Thanks, Dad."

"And maybe with one-on-one personal attention, she'll be able to drum some Spanish into your head. She didn't have a lot of success with that last year."

Dad never ceased to amaze me. He was tuned into the total picture better than I thought he was, and he didn't have a problem with what he saw. Sure, he was worried that we handle things properly, that we cover all the bases, and that we give ourselves the best possible chance for success. But he knew we could do exactly that, and because he knew that, I knew we could too.

Chapter Thirty-Four

TOBY AND I went the entire Thanksgiving weekend without seeing each other. It wasn't as bad without her as I thought it would be. I had plenty to do with chores around the house and football on TV. Detroit beat Green Bay 22–14, and Miami beat Dallas 40–21, both stunning upsets, on Thanksgiving Day; on Saturday Notre Dame bulldozed Stanford 57–7; and on Sunday the Indianapolis Colts lost to New England 38–34 in spite of a Peyton Manning led, nail-biting, heart-attack-generating fourth-quarter comeback that fell just short. By the time that game was over, I had couch sores on my butt from too much TV football.

I spent a good part of the day on Friday cleaning up the leaves in the yard that I should have handled in October and writing a long paper on a short story by James Baldwin that was due on Tuesday. The special assignment for that paper was to try to find the instructor's favorite pun within the story. The only thing close to a pun that I could find was a reference that the main character made a catholic gesture. Since *catholic* was not capitalized, I assumed he did not mean it in its proper-noun sense, that is, referring to the Catholic Church, but rather in its common meaning, which is universal. Not much of a pun in my estimation, but it was the closest thing I could find. Since I was a dumb jock and a civil engineering major, I couldn't be expected to pick up on puns the way the liberal arts students could.

We saw on the news that President George W. Bush went to Baghdad and served Thanksgiving dinner to the troops over there. The whole thing was hush-hush for security purposes until it was all over. The looks of delight on those soldiers' faces showed what respect they have for President Bush. That was a thoughtful thing for him to do. The news account reminded me to be thankful that our military was fighting hard to protect our country from terrorists.

Toby and I met for dinner as usual on Monday. It was odd to have the entire afternoon free without soccer practice. Since we completed the fall season last Saturday, practices were discontinued until we returned to school in January after the Christmas break. We didn't start the spring season until April, so the break in practice allowed us more time to prepare for the final exams that were coming the second week of December, and still have plenty of time to be ready for the spring schedule.

Toby met me at the front door to the library.

"Hello, Hat," she said.

It thrilled me every time I heard her call me that. It was a continuing reminder that we were lovers. It had been five days since we had seen each other, the longest stretch of absence since we got together in September, and it was particularly refreshing to hear her voice through the air rather than over the wire, or the wireless, as it were. She kissed me lightly on the lips, and I said, "Hello, Toby." We shared a hug and a cheek to cheek, as was our routine.

Routines have a settling effect on me. Following a routine means that everything is normal, in its place, and doing well. There is no need to be concerned about the state of affairs because the routine is working fine.

"How was your weekend?" she asked as we settled down at a table in the cafeteria.

Over tuna salad sandwiches, potato chips, and milk, I told her about her role in our Thanksgiving dinner conversation. She was pleasantly surprised by the warm reception, Dad's offer of consultation, and Mother's invitation to dinner.

"So which would you rather have, matzo balls or Irish beef stew?"

"I hate matzo!" she said.

"So it's settled."

"Your dad is so right."

"Yeah, he knew you'd want the stew."

"I mean about the other stuff."

"The Spanish? That's not your fault. I was never cut out to speak Spanish. Anyway, I'm in engineering. I'm not supposed to learn stuff like Spanish."

"You know what I'm talking about. We have a lot of issues we need to resolve. You may have laughed your way through the weekend, but we can't laugh our way through life. We have to face up to the problems if we're going to overcome them."

I decided that I needed something warmer to drink than milk. I went up to the coffee pots that were sitting on the warming pads and poured us each a steaming cup of decaf. Caffeinated coffee tended to keep me up at night, and I needed to get solid sleep in order to be in peak performance condition for soccer. Even though the season was over, I did not want to disturb that routine by drinking caffeinated coffee.

I hoped that the break in conversation would change the topic. I was not in the correct frame of mind for heavy problem solving. Of course, I was never in the mood for that kind of action. When I returned with our coffee, I tried to steer the conversation in another direction.

"Did you watch the Colts game yesterday? What a thriller. If Manning had thirty more seconds, he could have pulled that one out."

"No, I didn't watch the game. But I did tell my parents about us."

"You did?"

"Yes, I did. They took it much the same as your parents did. I can't believe them. My family is not strict Orthodox, but we have always observed the Jewish traditions. I thought for sure they would be outraged that you are Catholic. I guess that's better than Evangelist, but still. Instead, they were calm and composed and comforting, even. They, too, offered to help us talk things through with them. My dad said he can help us anticipate the adverse reactions from some of those in the family or friends that may not approve, and he can help prepare the way with others. My mother, of all people, said she will respect our decisions about how to proceed. She just wants to be able to offer counsel before we make those decisions. Can you believe that? My mother…"

"You sound like you're upset that they were receptive."

"No, no. I just expected great resistance and was kind of let down when that didn't happen. I thought they might even disown me or send me away to boarding school or something. I don't know. It was just so strange."

"I wasn't let down," I said. "I was thoroughly relieved. I was truly thankful that this would not cause a big fight over the Thanksgiving holiday."

"I'm actually surprised that you brought it up."

"That was Corinne's doing, not mine."

"I suspected as much. You know, Hat, we can't avoid the issues by not facing them. We have to address them in order to resolve them."

"I know that, but can't we do it tomorrow?"

Her look said no. This was a salient difference between Toby and me. Toby wanted to face the music, and I just wanted to dance.

"Okay," I said. "What would you like to address first?"

My blunt response took her by surprise. She was ready for a protracted argument about delaying discussion, but she was not prepared for an easy concession. She was beautiful when she was puzzled. She squinted her eyes and caused two creases to form above the bridge of her nose. Her cheeks took on a rosier tint, and her chin protruded ever so slightly as she clenched her jaw. Then her jaw slackened quickly, and her eyes relaxed, her forehead smoothed over, and her cheeks softened. She pondered my question and did not have a ready answer. I think she had many issues in mind but wasn't sure what was best to attack first.

"Well," she said, "the most obvious thing is our difference of religion. How do we handle that?"

"What's wrong with what we do now? I go to my church, and you go to your church. With Sunday Mass being available on Saturday, it doesn't seem all that different to me."

"That's just it, Hat. I don't go to a church. I go to a temple."

"What does it matter what I call it? Church, temple, you go there to worship God the same as I do."

"But you go there to worship Jesus. That's what matters."

"Why does that have to enter into it? Why do we have to let that get in the way?"

"What about when we have kids? How will we rear them? What will we teach them?"

"I've heard of couples that raise their kids in both religions. They follow the doctrines and celebrate the holidays and go through the rituals of both. Their kids learn both sides. Wouldn't that be a good thing for the kids?"

"What? You tell them that Jesus is God and I tell them Jesus is not God? How is that supposed to work?"

"What about Jews for Jesus? You could look into that."

"Jews for Jesus is an oxymoron. If you are Jewish, you do not believe that Jesus is God. If you believe that Jesus is God, you are not Jewish. I could never allow my kids to be taught that Jesus is God."

"I could convert. I could become Jewish. People do that. Sammy Davis Jr. converted."

"Oh, Hat! You don't know what you're saying. Converting to Judaism is more than going to temple instead of to a church. It's more than eating matzo and lox and bagels and saying 'Oy Vey.' It's far more than merely adopting customs, although it is that as well. It's a lifelong commitment to a new religion, a new way of looking at life."

"Marriage is also a lifelong commitment, Toby. We're not just talking here about going to a movie together. We're talking about raising kids, and that means marriage. Are you ready for that lifelong commitment?"

My little sister is wise beyond her years. She warned me not to bring up long-term issues like marriage, and I heeded her advice as best as I could. I had avoided that subject to this point, although I had thought of it, dreamed of it, yearned for it, time and again over the past several months. Now it was staring us in the face. I wasn't the one that brought it up. Toby was talking about our kids as if we were already married. How could we go to the kids place without going to the marriage place?

The look on Toby's face told me I should not have used that sacred word, *marriage*. Creases appeared at the ends of her eyes extending across her temples, and the skin of her face tightened. Her forehead crinkled, and her eyes glared at me as though I had been caught rummaging in her purse for secret, private things kept there. It was as though she didn't think that marriage was an integral part of the progression. Paradoxically, we could talk about kids that would somehow be ours, or going to temple together for the rest of our lives, or making lifelong religious commitments, but we must not mention the *M* word, unless, of course, it is part of a proposal of marriage. I don't understand that, but I recognize the fact.

"We are talking about religious issues here," she said, and the subject was averted.

"I'm just saying that I would do anything for you, Toby. I'm wholly and completely willing to convert to Judaism for you. I would die for you. I love you."

She was touched. The creases at the ends of her eyes disappeared. Her skin softened and then relaxed. Her eyes glistened, and she smiled that astonishing and soothing smile that could convince me to convert to Satanism if that was what she wanted from me.

"You can't convert for me, Hat. You have to convert for yourself. You have to believe it's right and true. You can't just do it for the convenience."

"I believe that you are right for me. You are my truth. I can convert for that truth. I said I would die for you, and that is the truth. I love you, and that is the truth."

Her next words were a comfort to me. I knew we could get these things ironed out because of those three words.

"I love you." She leaned toward me, and we lightly kissed.

"You need to give the idea of converting much more serious thought," she said. "I don't think you have considered all of the ramifications. It's more than following practices and rituals. It has to be a heartfelt and complete commitment."

I began to reflect on those things that she said. Yes, it was a big commitment, but I was already committed to her. My love was as heartfelt as any emotion could be. I would look forward to learning new rituals. Catholicism, after all, is full of rituals. Practices? Let me tell you about practices. All you need to do is attend one regular, normal, everyday Mass and you would be exposed to enough rituals and practices that your head would spin if they were all explained to you. Then try a High Mass. It's enough to drive you insane if you haven't been exposed to it slowly over the first fourteen years of your life.

Then she hit me with the big one.

"You know that it means denying Jesus."

I had not thought of it in exactly those terms. Of course, I knew that Jews did not believe that Jesus was the Son of God, but that was more a position of nonacceptance than one of outright denial. It's like a man on the street of Jerusalem, when asked if he was a disciple of Jesus, stating, "I do not know the man." A convert, however, is a different story. A convert must actively deny that Jesus is God after having been a Christian. It would be like Peter being asked if he was a disciple and him denying Jesus three times. That is a horse of a different color.

Chapter Thirty-Five

TOBY UNDERSTOOD THE magnitude of a decision to convert much better than I did. I had dropped that bomb without any serious thought. It was just my way of trying to close out the discussion in which I did not want to participate. But now that the suggestion had been made it had to be considered. She did not press me on it but allowed me plenty of time to mull it over. She acknowledged that there was no need to rush into any course of action since we weren't planning on marriage. Oops! I mean, we weren't planning any serious moves in the near future. Finishing the semester was the most immediate matter, and final exams were looming on the horizon.

School was a lot easier without having to contend with soccer practice. Besides the extra three hours available for study every day, including Saturdays and Sundays, there was also less pressure without the anxiety of winning or losing and of putting out my best performance. Fatigue was also a critical factor. During the season, I was always tired. It took forever to recover from the exertion necessary to practice. The games were actually easier than the practices, since I hardly played.

I found that I could absorb more in class once the season was over because I wasn't so weary. My attention span was broader and sharper, and studying became more productive. My grades showed improvement. Physical education was an automatic A for soccer play, and I already had As going in chemistry, chemistry lab, and calculus, but my English and psychology grades were coming in at the C level. The sea level is great when it's spring break and you want to be at the beach but not so great for college course grades. I got an A on the James Baldwin paper and was the only student to pick up on the instructor's favorite pun. That pushed me up to a B in English, so my only concern was psychology going into the final exams. I began to think that I was an actual student and that I had the potential to be a good one. I might even make a good civil engineer eventually. It was ironic that playing soccer made it possible to go to college in the first place but then interfered with my ability to achieve in accordance with my full talents.

The other factor that made school easier was that I was having the time of my life. I enjoyed every minute of the time that Toby and I were together even if it was just sitting next to each other in the library or on the Indy Metro. Without soccer practice, we had much more time to spend together. We went to the student movies on campus and even splurged and went to the Circle Center Mall downtown for a movie one afternoon. I don't remember the name of that movie, but it was full of explicit sex scenes. Toby and I took the rest of the day off, went back to her apartment, and made love about six times.

When we were finally too tired and too dispassionate to go at it again, we bundled up in our winter outfits and, with hot cocoa in hand, retired to the balcony. The ferns and petunias were long gone, the hooks that held them empty until the birds sang again in the spring, but the wind chimes still hung from their hook, awaiting the next breeze. The view from the balcony was enchanting. The day had been serene for early December. A gentle snowfall had laid a light frosting on the grass, on the branches of the evergreens, thick with needles and cones, and on the bare tree limbs along Pleasant Run. As the lights along Washington Street came up one by one, they cast a twinkling reflection off the new fallen snow. A gentle breeze stirred the wind chimes, and the evening air was filled with Toby's laughter, both imitated and real. It was a perfect ending to a perfect day.

Chapter Thirty-Six

A NOISE FROM THE corridor awoke me. I had been sleeping so soundly and so deeply that it took me several long moments to realize where I was. I was no longer on the balcony sipping hot cocoa with Toby. That was merely a happy memory. This hospital room was my world now, and I fully expected it to be my last locale. What other choice did I have? I could barely walk to the bathroom, and if I did, I could become so exhausted that I needed help to return. I usually chose to use the bed pan even though this was an embarrassing alternative. Sometimes even that effort fatigued me.

Dr. Blumenthal had explained all this to me in simple, layman's terms. The reasons for my malady were medically straightforward while significantly complex. Oxygen is critical to the proper functioning of all cells in the human body. This oxygen is delivered by the red blood cells. A shortage of red blood cells in my circulatory system meant that an insufficient supply of oxygen was being carried to the various cells. Due to the inadequate supply of oxygen, my muscles, for example, became fatigued easily. My other body functions were affected as well, but muscle fatigue was the symptom that was most outwardly apparent. Fortunately, my body protected my reason and my intellect by delivering proportionately more oxygen to my brain than to the rest of my body, which resulted in even less oxygen to the other cells.

When fatigue sets in, the body tries to provide more oxygen by forcing more rapid breathing. For most people, this natural remedy works well since more oxygen is pulled from the air, and after a short period of shortness of breath, energy is restored. That didn't work for me because it didn't matter how much air was forced into my lungs; with a shortage of red blood cells, the extra oxygen could not be delivered.

So I knew what the problem was, but I didn't know what to do about it and I didn't know why these things happened to me. The doctors were no help with the why, and what to do was a puzzle to them as well.

Although the lights were out in my room, it was not completely dark. A sufficient amount of light entered from the corridor to enable me to see even though the details were not distinguishable.

The winter roses that Corinne had placed on my side table stood tall in the vase of freshly treated water, each patiently awaiting the bee or butterfly that would find it and pollinate it. There would be no butterfly for these roses even though their fragrance was attractive and strong. They would share their splendor and their aroma for a short time, but there would be no future roses grown from this stock.

Will my time be any longer than that of these roses? If it is, what good would that do? I have no beauty to share with the world, no bouquet to enhance the day or the hour or even one minute of a person's life. I have only my blood to give, and to give that will surely kill me.

Yet, to live is to merely exist.

To be or not to be? That is the question. Hamlet hit the nail on the head with that one. What good is a life of mere existence? What purpose does it serve?

On the shelf on the opposite wall, the crucifix stood in the dim light, the silver Jesus suffering on the cross for all eternity. The crucifix had been my mother's favorite and had hung on the wall in the living room for as long as I could remember. On holy days, Mother would take it down from the wall and open it. The wooden cross had a hollow framework that was an inch and a half deep that contained four compartments, one in each branch of the cross. In the top compartment was a one-inch white candle; in the left branch was a small vial of holy water; in the right branch were matches for the candle; and in the bottom compartment was a rosary made from pressed rose petals that Mother's brother, Liam, had given to her after returning from his trip to Rome. At the intersection of the cross framework was a notch in which the crucifix itself could be inserted so that the framework could serve as a base and allow the crucifix to stand on a flat surface. Corinne had opened the cross and arranged it so the crucifix stood where I could clearly see it.

If Corinne had intended the crucifix to provide some level of enlightenment for me, it was not working. I could see no reason for all that was, no purpose for all that had happened, and no justification for the suffering and pain that I experienced when I could have been a star athlete, a top honor student, the savior of my mother, a good husband for Toby, a strong father and provider for my children, and who knows what else. All was cut short. For what?

I thought back to that evening of lovemaking and hot chocolate on the balcony at Toby's apartment. The future seemed bright for both of us. We had problems to face, for sure, but I was confident that we could face and solve any problem that came our way as long as we had each other. That might have been the last truly happy day of my life.

Chapter Thirty-Seven

I TOLD DR. BLUMENTHAL that I first noticed problems after the blood drive my senior year in high school, and this was certainly true, but the serious problems started after I gave blood during my freshman year at IUPUI. That was the turning point.

The annual Howe High School Blood Drive was held the first or second week in December. In 2003, it occurred on Wednesday, the tenth. I spoke before about what this blood drive meant to the students. It was also something of a tradition for alumnae and former teachers to return to give blood at the drive. It was like an informal high school reunion. I thought it would be a good thing for Toby and me to do together since we both had the connection with the school. She was not as keen on the idea. She said she was not well-liked last year by the other teachers at the school and did not feel welcome there. It was hard for me to believe that people would not like Toby, and I suspected that she didn't want the other teachers to see that she was dating me, her former student. At the same time I had to examine my own motives. I would certainly get a charge out of showing up with Toby on my arm. If Joe DeMarco or that algebra teacher, Mr. Newman, were there, I could gloat. Did I want to put Toby through an unpleasant return visit just so I could revel in some childish high school one-upmanship? The answer to that one was yes, but I had to be a man and refuse to do it.

We decided we would both give blood, but we would go at different times. Toby would be able to slip in and slip out while I could have my reunion for as long as I wished. We also decided that I didn't need to talk about our relationship with anyone at the school.

I arrived at Howe early in the morning. That was when I had given blood on the three prior occasions, and I wanted to follow the same practice. Toby said she would show up some time in the afternoon. We would meet at the IUPUI library at three o'clock, per our routine.

As always, the line was long, stretching from the girls' gym to the cafeteria. Previously, I had been aware only of the other high school students waiting to give, but this time I noticed teachers, guidance counselors, administrators, parents, and other nonstudents lined up along with the high school kids. One's perspective changes when one is no longer a student in high school. I stopped several times to say hello to guys and girls from my graduation class as I made my way to the back of the line.

When I reached the end of the line, I was pleasantly surprised to find Joe DeMarco and Mary Kelly there. I had not seen Mary since the Saint Patrick's Day Party in March and had last seen Joe DeMarco at graduation last June. My intense involvement in conditioning in order to physically prepare for college soccer had been at the expense of maintaining my friendships.

"Hey, Hat," Joe said. "What's up?"

"Nothing much."

"Hello, Hat," Mary said, her seductive tone and sexy smile reminded me of the church sacristy and brought a blush to my face. Her tenor wasn't lost on Joe either as he shot her an irritated look, though it didn't cause her to diminish her smile.

Mary was now a senior at Howe, and Joe was a freshman at DePauw University in Greencastle, Indiana. Going away to college did not weaken their friendship. In fact, Joe said he came home almost every weekend just to see her.

"So you guys are getting pretty serious about each other then?" I asked.

"Yes," Joe answered. "We've committed to seeing each other exclusively. It's kind of like going steady. I'll give her my fraternity pin as soon as I finish freshman pledging this April. Sigma Alpha Epsilon."

He beamed with pride as he said this. I wasn't certain if it was the commitment with Mary or pledging the fraternity that made him more proud.

"Congratulations," I said as I vigorously shook his hand. "I'm happy for both of you."

Mary shrugged when I glanced her way. I thought this may have been the first she had heard of this.

"So what have you been up to, Hat?" Joe asked.

I hesitated. I didn't have much to say. I didn't want to talk about Mother's cancer or my failures at soccer, and I couldn't talk about Toby. There wasn't much else in my life. I decided to keep it vague.

"Well, I'm seeing a girl at school pretty regularly. That's about the best thing right now."

"I'm glad to hear that," Joe said. "It's good that you've gotten over that Spanish teacher, Miss Rosen. I was worried about you. That was not a healthy situation."

"Really. Why do you say it was unhealthy?"

"You were all wrapped up in it—consumed by it. That's all you talked about, but there was never any future in it. I mean, she was your Spanish teacher, after all."

"I don't see what's wrong with that," I said. "The bigger problem is that she's Jewish. How to raise the kids will be the toughest issue."

"I'm just glad it's behind you," Joe said.

Joe did not catch my slip of the tongue, but Mary was not so slow on the uptake. She put her hand on my arm and looked me square in the eye.

"It's not behind you, is it, Hat? She's the girl you're talking about, isn't she? You're seeing the Spanish teacher."

The cat was out of the bag. There was no use in denying it. That would only make it more obvious.

"Yes, I am, but she's not my Spanish teacher now. In fact, she's not a teacher at all. She's a college student at IUPUI, and we became reacquainted on campus. Now we're like any other college couple."

"I wouldn't spread the word about that around here," Joe said. "Mr. Newman might get jealous."

"Mr. Newman never had any designs on her," I retorted. "He never asked her to the prom like you said he was going to. He never even asked her out on a date. He is a nonfactor."

"I don't know. That's not what my sources told me."

"Whatever. But you're right about not spreading the word around about us. It probably is better that you guys don't say anything to anyone. She and I have stuff we have to work out, and we don't need any other distractions."

"Mum's the word," Joe said. "Hold my spot in line while I go to the little boys' room."

After Joe sauntered away, Mary snuggled up close to me. She whispered so that those around us could not hear her.

"I think you're right to keep this under your hat, Hat." She giggled at her wordplay. "It would only cause trouble that I'm sure you don't need. But I can't help wondering..."

When she paused, I asked, "What?"

"Does she give as good a blow job as I do?"

I wasn't sure what she was fishing for, but I figured a compliment couldn't hurt. I whispered back to her.

"No one gives as good a blow job as you do, Mary. I will always remember Saint Patrick's night in the church, and I will always be grateful to you for that."

"Well, anytime you need a replay, just call me."

I gave her a gentle hug and told her I appreciated the offer and would be sure to keep it in mind. She stepped back, and we resumed our wait. By the time Joe returned from the restroom, we were ready to enter the gym.

When I saw the row of four recliner chairs along the far wall, the memory from last year's blood drive hit me. I had become sick after giving blood and had never fully recovered. I lost my energy, my drive, and I was never the same after that. I thought it was ridiculous to associate giving blood with my lethargy problem. Surely the problem was due more to the flu that I contracted around the same time than to anything else, but there it was, and I couldn't shake it. Nervous tension began to build in the back of my neck, and I started to feel anxious about donating blood. This was a different anxiety than what

I felt back in my sophomore year. Then, it was needles and blood and first-time jitters that made me uncomfortable. Now, the fear of possibly further sapping my energy and losing what little get-up-and-go I had left was filling me with dread. I knew this fear was unreasonable, for giving blood had nothing to do with my energy problem, but I couldn't let it go. I began to imagine black demons with yellow eyes standing by the doors to block my escape should I decide to run. Several of the blue-clad attendants morphed into dark bat-winged, hawk-clawed figures surreptitiously glancing my way to see that I was still progressing along the line to my eventual destruction.

"What's the matter, Hat?" Mary said. "You look as white as a ghost."

"What?" I said, snapping out of my nightmare. I knew that it was absurd to be frightened, but the fear was still there. My hands began to sweat, and I felt like I had to pee. I squirmed on my feet as I stood looking desperately around the gym for some sign of serenity, some object that would still the frantic beating of my heart and translate into a soothing balm for my ominous feelings of alarm.

Then I saw the clock. The big clock on the wall had been a fixture in the gym for as long as I knew. It stood the test of time while accurately measuring its passage. That clock had been a comforting sight when I gave blood my sophomore year. I had gazed on it to take my mind off the probing needle and the flowing blood back then. Now, that clock calmed my fear as I set my eyes on its sweeping second hand and relaxed in the knowledge that all things must pass. My hands became dry, my heart settled down, and I no longer needed to visit the little boys' room. My moment of panic was gone.

"I'm fine," I said to Mary. "I had a momentary queasiness about having a needle stuck in my arm, but I'm fine now. Thank you for asking."

Mary did not look satisfied by my answer, but what could I do? After all, it was the truth. I looked again at the clock, and I wondered how I could have been so afraid.

We finally arrived at the sign-in table. I didn't need to present a permission slip, but I did need to answer the short questionnaire. When I got to the question about Acutane, I had to ask what it was. When it was explained to me that Acutane is a medication for acute acne, I remembered that I had asked about that same drug before my first donation four years ago. I guess you never learn certain things no matter how obviously the knowledge is presented to you.

I was ready for the physical appraisal apparatus, which consisted merely of a blood pressure measuring cuff and an in-mouth thermometer. My heart rate and temperature were fine, but my blood pressure was depressed. I felt a little depressed myself. Was something or someone trying to tell me not to go through with this blood donation?

A nurse in pale-blue scrubs told me the blood pressure reading was barely within acceptable tolerances and was on the lower end of the range. She said the choice was mine. I was within acceptable standards, but if I decided to decline to donate, it was perfectly understandable.

I couldn't read Mary's expression, but Joe's face clearly expressed disdain at the idea of declining. I glanced up at the clock on the wall, and a feeling of calm settled over me. What kind of crazy thinking was I entertaining? There were no demons coaxing me toward the donor recliners, no enemies anxiously awaiting my fatal mistake, no competitors plotting the downfall and ruin of my career and my life. It was all in my mind, and running wild like a winter wind raging across the flat farms of Central Indiana, my imagination had adversely affected my blood pressure.

The nurse that stood before me was no demon. In fact, she was very pretty. Her smile was reassuring, and she applied no pressure in either direction. Go or stay, she was fine with either decision. I decided to stay and do my civic duty.

I was confident when I settled into the recliner. I had done this three times before, and only once had it been less than an agreeable experience. The other times had been pleasurable and satisfying. The worker searched for a vein, taking four tries before making a good connection. As I watched the blood flow through the clear tube into the plastic bag, changing it from translucent amber to ruby red, I had a feeling of déjà vu. Would this be a return to the good donations or a repeat of the bad? When the bag was full, I accepted my orange juice and cookie and relaxed back into the embrace of the recliner, awaiting the final verdict.

Chapter Thirty-Eight

MY HEAD BEGAN to throb. I took a bite of cookie. My mouth became dry. I took a drink of orange juice. The room began to spin. I closed my eyes but could still feel the spinning. My lips and tongue became warm, and my teeth began to ache. Saliva formed heavily in my mouth. I swallowed it back, knowing that was an early warning from my body that I was soon going to vomit. I tried to delay the inevitable by taking another bite of cookie. My mouth watered profusely around the cookie, and I could not bring myself to chew it. I tried to wash it down with more orange juice, which worked only partially. I pushed the remaining cookie to the left side of my mouth between my teeth and cheek and called to the attendant.

"I think I'm going to throw up," I said, though I did not think it. I knew it, and I knew it would be soon.

She promptly brought me an airsick bag and told me to sit back and relax. She told me not to fight it but to let it happen naturally. She said it was a normal and common reaction. This was not reassuring to me because I knew that normal was a temporary feeling of sluggishness followed by a resurgence of energy. This was clearly not normal for me.

But I followed her advice. What other choice did I have? I relaxed and waited for the heaves to begin and the cramps to follow close behind.

The heaves came sooner than I expected and more violently than I had ever before experienced. I filled the airsick bag and proceeded to fill a second bag. I didn't realize I had eaten that much that morning. I wished that I had eaten more when the dry heaves began, painfully tearing at my stomach when my stomach had no more to give. Cramps grabbed me, starting in my abdomen and moving up through my stomach and then concentrating their terrible forces in my chest. Then they spread out across my back with spasm after spasm. My biceps tightened up into knots that felt like rocks when I tried to unsuccessfully massage them. Then that effort caused the fleshy parts of my fingers and thumbs to tighten up and curl my fingers, not into fists but into claws so that my hands were in severe pain yet I could not move any of my digits.

"How are you feeling, Mr. Maloney?" the attendant asked.

I didn't know how to answer that simple question. I was not well. All my muscles were cramping at the same time and causing excruciating pain. That had to be apparent on my face. But I didn't want further medical attention for fear I would lose my scholarship. I just wanted to leave, to go home, to get into the medicine cabinet and take some of Dad's Vicodin that was left over from his kidney stone attack last summer.

"I'm doing much better, thank you," I said, though the pain surely was as evident to her as the vomit in my airsick bags.

"Are you certain?" she persisted. "We can move you to the nurse's office where you can be out of the spotlight, but we can still keep an eye on you until you actually start to feel better. It's no inconvenience to us, really."

I remembered last year's trip to the nurse's office. It spared me a ton of embarrassment and gave me a little time to recover before I had to face the world.

"Yes," I said, "I could use some extra recovery time and perhaps the nurse has some pain medication."

"What did you have in mind?"

"Vicodin," I answered. That was the only heavy-duty pain medicine I knew of besides morphine, which they gave Mother. I didn't think they would part with any morphine for a reaction to a simple blood donation.

"Vicodin is an addictive narcotic," she said. "We would need an okay from your personal doctor before dispensing any of that drug to you. Do you have a personal doctor?"

"No, I don't. Forget it." My muscles started to relax a bit, and the pain began to diminish. Maybe I just needed some time and not any drugs.

A male attendant brought a gurney, and they loaded me onto it. In the short ride to the nurse's office, I became dizzy as the ceiling rolled by overhead. I didn't realize the effect it was having on me until I became light-headed and my stomach began to turn. I closed my eyes and rolled onto my left side in a fetal position just as we reached the office. Inside I did not want to be moved and resisted every attempt to transfer me to a bed. I just wanted to be left alone.

"We might need the gurney if somebody else gets sick, Mr. Maloney," the female attendant informed me, and it was not an unreasonable request; however, I was in an unreasoning condition.

"I don't want to move right now!" I said. "I'm in great pain, and I need time to make the move!"

I guess my tone sounded sincere because they backed off and the female placed her hand over my forehead.

"You don't seem to have a fever, Mr. Maloney. Perhaps we'll let you rest here on the gurney, and I'll check on you in a few minutes. There's a nurse call button on the bed if you need anything."

Alone in the nurse's office, I began to relax. The quietude settled down around me, and I settled down with it. Dizziness and stomach queasiness drifted away while the cramps eased their hold on my muscles. I was sore from all the clenching and unclenching of muscles and dog tired from the whole ordeal. I didn't understand why a simple blood withdrawal would cause such distress and, I prayed to Jesus that it would not affect my soccer play. As an afterthought, I prayed to God the Father in order to cover my bases in case of a conversion to Judaism. Then I thought He would not be referred to as God the Father if Jesus was not His son. So I prayed to God, Jehovah, creator of all things.

"I'm merely a first semester freshman in college, so I hope You can understand and forgive my confusion on these things. But I hope

You will help me anyway and restore my energy so that I can keep my soccer scholarship, stay in school, and continue to love Toby in the way I'm sure You intend for me to love her. My love for her could only be Your doing, and I won't be able to fulfill Your plan unless I can stay in school. Thank You, Lord."

I found the energy to move from the gurney to the bed but was exhausted after the move. I managed to push the nurse's call button before I fell asleep.

Chapter Thirty-Nine

I DREAMED I was on the soccer field during a match and it was in the closing minutes of the half. I was as full of energy as when I was in high school. I was ready. I was at the top of my conditioning. I was champing at the bit to show what I could do. The ball was passed to me at midfield, and I moved swiftly with it to my right. My defender was slow and lagged behind by half a step. I abruptly changed my angle of progression sharply to the left and squibbed the ball between his legs, catching up with the ball as he stumbled past me. I was momentarily in the open, but Leslie's defender switched off and smothered me with a strong defensive position. Leslie was left unguarded. I made a side kick over to him. He didn't stop the ball to place his shot but merely changed its direction with a perfectly timed side swipe. The ball sailed past the diving goalie's outstretched hand into the net.

Leslie and I both took a celebration lap around the field before returning to the sideline where the team huddled. Toby was in the third row of the stands at midfield, and she flashed me her wonderfully sustaining smile. I returned her smile so briefly that Coach Harrison did not catch me flirting with her in the middle of a match.

"Nice shot, Leslie," he said. "Nice move, good setup, good pass, Patrick," he added.

I was not winded at all, even with the celebration lap. I was ready to get back into the game and ready to play at full speed. I wasn't sure which aspect of this dream excited me more: my rejuvenated ability to play soccer and the thrill of making a game winning play; the obvious approval of Coach Harrison and the college scholarship that came along with that; or the macho emotion of performing well in front of the one I loved. Before I could analyze this, I realized that recognizing it to be a dream meant that I was waking up. The painful reaction to giving blood was finished, but leaving this dream behind and returning to reality was depressing. I began to cry.

"Are you still in pain, Mr. Maloney?" The male attendant had returned.

"Yes…no, no, I'm okay now."

"It looked like you were crying, sir."

"It was the dream," I said. "It was sad."

I spent the rest of the day at home in bed as snow fell steadily across the silent city. The soccer dream did not return. In its place were scattered bits and pieces about demons, Joe DeMarco, Toby, Mother suffering in her favorite recliner, and other scenes all in a mish-mash with no logical timing or meaning to it. I awoke several times in a cold sweat but could not remember the details of what I had been dreaming.

At four o'clock I dragged myself out of bed and over to the window. A clean blanket of snow covered our front porch roof and the roofs of all the houses up and down the street. The bare branches of the trees were outlined in white. Cars parked in the street were lumps of white like marshmallows sitting here and there, waiting for a cup of hot chocolate. No cars traveled on Wallace Avenue, and there were no people in the street. The only activity I could see was Mr. Allen shoveling the snow from his sidewalk a few houses down the street. The snow continued to fall and to spread across the bushes and yards in gentle waves like the sprinkling of powdered sugar over a raisin cake.

I fell into the chair at my desk and checked my class schedule. I had missed two classes that day, chemistry and psychology, both lectures. I had found that most of the stuff discussed in the lectures was covered in the textbooks, and attendance was not taken, so I was not worried about missing those classes, but I was concerned about missing the study date with Toby at three o'clock.

I called her cell phone, but it rang over to her voice mail.

"Hello, Toby," I said. "I'm alive. I had a severe reaction to giving blood this morning and have been out of it all day. Sorry I missed our date at three. I love you. Call me."

I then sent the same message to her via text.

At the window I saw that Mr. Allen had either finished clearing his walk or had given up his battle against the snow. No other creature stirred. The world outside was as empty as a fresh sheet of composition paper. I knew there would be writing on it before long, but for now it was a mantle that covered everything, isolating me from Toby.

I turned back to the class schedule. This was the last week of classes with final exams set for next week. I usually had chemistry lab on Wednesday, but my lab partner was a chemistry major and was as good at chemistry as I was. We turned in our final lab work last week and had no final exam. That course was completed for an A.

I had two classes tomorrow, calculus and English. There was no final exam in English, and I merely had to get an A or B on my last paper to get a B in the course. That paper, which was turned in yesterday, was a discussion of a Kafka short story called "Metamorphosis." This story was about a man who turned into a giant bug overnight. I could see no redeeming value in this story, but I managed to write about two thousand words. It's amazing what you can do when you are not fatigued from soccer practice. Calculus was one of my strong courses. I had class on Thursday and final exam on Tuesday. I had a solid A in that course and was not concerned about the final. I knew the material and was sure I would get an A.

I had two classes on Friday, psychology and chemistry. I would complete those courses with final exams on Monday and Wednesday. The psychology final on Monday concerned me. I didn't understand the stuff, and if I was asked to write an essay on any aspect of it, I would fail miserably. I was carrying a C in the course, mostly because the tests were some multiple-choice questions, some fill-in-the-blank, and some single-word answers. I could follow it well enough to do okay on that kind of test, but if they had asked me to discuss Pavlov's dogs or Freudian slips or any such thing, I would be failing for sure. The final was 50 percent of the grade. The chemistry final was on Wednesday. Like calculus, I had an A going in, and I knew the material. They could even give me essay questions, and I would have no problem with them. I knew the theory, the mechanics, and the application. This course was an A waiting to be had.

Add in the automatic A in phys ed, and that works out to a fairly good semester:

Phys Ed	A	1 credit	4 grade points
Chemistry Lab	A	1 credit	4 grade points
Chemistry	A	3 credits	12 grade points
Calculus	A	4 credits	16 grade points
English	B	3 credits	9 grade points
Psychology	C?	3 credits	6 grade points

This translates into 15 credits, 51 grade points, and a 3.40 grade point average. The most important thing was to keep the psychology grade up to a C.

I worried that I hadn't heard from Toby. I knew I couldn't go out in this weather to meet with her, but I just wanted to hear her voice. I wanted to know that we were still together. I hoped she was not too upset about our missed date even though all we had planned was study in the library.

I went downstairs to see what there was to eat. Mother was asleep in her recliner, and Dad was asleep in his. The TV softly ran through a *Home Improvement* rerun. Corinne was not yet home from an after-school practice for the High School Holiday play.

I felt a twinge of anger that this play was no longer called the Christmas play. They pretended they were taking religion out of the schools, but really it was all focused on removing Christ. Holiday, after all, means Holy Day, as opposed to Christ in Christmas. Some of the things they taught us in science class could probably be called religion given the scant amount of evidence there was to support the notions. Maybe they should remove some of those lessons. The theory of evolution comes to mind. I guess it's called a theory because there is no proof and no lab tests. Unlike the law of gravity for which there are plenty of tests and tons of proof.

I acknowledge that belief in Jesus as God is a religion that requires an act of faith, but doesn't belief in multiple nonevident "missing links" require a leap of faith? Why is there no fossil evidence that tracks gradual changes in life forms? Why do new life-forms appear virtually overnight, particularly during the Cambrian period? To believe that the basic life-form, amoeba, mutated into a higher life-form in order to survive is absurd. If there were no higher life-forms at the time, what life-form were they threatened by that they needed to evolve? My experience and observation, limited as it may be by my youth, note that things tend to move toward their simplest state, as in chemical and physical reactions, not toward more complex states. Belief in the theory of evolution requires some giant leaps of faith.

Belief in Jesus as the Son of God, in fact, requires a much smaller leap of faith. According to the apostles, Jesus claimed to be the Son of God and claimed that He would rise from the dead. The apostles further claimed that they saw Him die and saw Him after having risen. Now this is certainly not enough to convince all people, since anyone can claim to have seen anything. But when you consider that Peter gave up a very prosperous fishing business to travel the world and preach of the Resurrection of Jesus, it has to make you wonder why. Why did he give up everything, and a considerable everything at that, for what promised him nothing in return? Why, when he was tortured by the Romans with some of the most extreme torture methods ever known to man, did he not change his story to save himself? Why, when he was crucified upside down until he died, did he not deny the Resurrection of Jesus? Peter had to have been firmly, thoroughly, and completely sure of his facts. He had to have seen Jesus die and return from His tomb three days later. How much of a leap of faith is it to believe Peter after what he gave up and what he went through to profess his belief in Jesus?

I wondered if this line of thinking was going to hinder my conversion to Judaism. Just as that thought entered my mind, I got a call from my favorite Jew.

"Hi, Toby," I said, sheepishly.

"Sorry I took so long to get back to you. I had my phone turned off in the library."

"I'm glad you did," I said.

"You're glad I turned off my phone?"

"No, I'm glad you got back to me. I was worried."

"You miss an entire day because you gave blood and you are worried about me? Did you see a doctor?"

The thought of seeing a doctor gave me the chills. The last thing I needed was to lose my scholarship because some doctor found some disease that would prevent me from playing soccer. But I didn't want to share this thought with Toby.

"No!" I said. "I rested for a while in the nurse's office, then I came home and slept pretty much all day. I just needed some time to recover, that's all."

"That's a lot just for giving a pint of blood, or did they take more than a pint?"

"I'm not sure they even got that much blood. I got sick right away."

"How do you feel now?"

"I'm okay, but I think I had better stay home tonight. I'll be fine by tomorrow. I have class until two thirty. Can I meet you at three tomorrow?"

"Okay! Library door at three."

"I love you, Toby."

"I love you too, Hat. Just take care of yourself, okay?"

"Okay. Bye."

I felt better having talked with Toby. It made sense for her to turn her phone off in the library. I didn't think of that. Why was I worried? No text message, that's why. I looked at my phone and saw the message indicator was lit. I accessed the message dated Wednesday, 3:58 p.m.

"Hat! Did you forget? Going into library. Turning off phone. Will check with you in about an hour. Love U. T"

I guess I should have checked my phone messages.

Chapter Forty

THURSDAY MORNING I still felt lethargic and listless, but I managed to get up and out to classes. Calculus class was devoted entirely to review for the final exam to be given next Tuesday. English class consisted of the return and discussion of our papers on "Metamorphosis." I received an A on this paper, which surprisingly pulled my final grade up to a B+ and raised that GPA expectation.

I didn't miss my three o'clock study date with Toby. Since I had only three finals and I felt comfortable with two of them, I brought only my psychology materials with me. I had to get at least a D on that final. The course material was a mystery to me, but if I could get enough facts into my head, I could pass the test and get a C– in the course. Now that I had a B+ in English, a C– in psychology would give me the 3.40 GPA. My soccer scholarship required that I maintain a 2.30 GPA. Any grade below a C– must be reviewed by the athletic director. I needed that psychology final to make it through without grade review.

"Hi, Hat!" she shouted, as I rounded the corner of the building and headed toward the library's front door. I stopped to gaze as she bounced and waved her mittened hand at me. I needed her. My unplanned absence yesterday left a hole in my chest bigger than any 105 Howitzer could make even if I stood five feet in front of it. We were apart at Thanksgiving, but that was by design. The abrupt and unexpected separation yesterday was a hard adjustment to make. I needed her near me. The look of excitement on her face and the way she leaped and jumped and beckoned me with her hand said that she needed me too. I had not thought about her feelings yesterday—only mine. What did she feel when we were apart? Was missing me a big disappointment to her? By the look on her face and the animation in her movements, I would say she missed me. But then, I was struggling to get a C– in psychology, so what do I know?

I walked the last fifteen yards to her side slowly. Although the thin coating of ice on the walkway suggested caution, that was not the reason for my prudence. Just as at my window yesterday I felt isolation, the two feet of snow on the ground and the chill in the air lent a feeling of remoteness, and my inability to pull oxygen from that chilly air gave a sense of altitude. I felt like I was at twelve thousand feet walking a forty-five-foot ridge in a wind that threatened to send me tumbling to my death with the slightest misstep.

"Are you sure you're okay?" Toby asked when I finally reached her.

"As long as you are by my side, I'm fine."

"Well, you should have worn gloves," she said, and then she kissed me lightly on the lips.

"Hello, Toby." I took her in my arms, squeezed her as best as I could with our heavy winter coats doing their best to separate us, and ran my cheek across hers.

"I got an A in the diagnostic medical microbiology course," she whispered as our cheek to cheek and embrace came to an end. "That means I only have two final exams next week."

"That's great," I said. "Let's go inside. It's cold out here."

In the library lobby we could hang our coats and get by with some quiet conversation without disturbing other students that were studying or doing research in the stacks or the study lounges.

"So, no final in diagnostic medical micro whatever? How did you arrange that?"

"Diagnostic medical microbiology. If you have an A or an A– after all the semester work, you can opt out of the final exam and take your grade as it is. The semester stuff is all lab work on the various machines. You run the lab tests, which get progressively more and more difficult, and use all the different machines and computers. Once you have successfully run all the tests, you get a preliminary grade and make a decision about the final exam. With a preliminary grade of A, it's a no-brainer."

"Just like my chemistry lab," I said.

"Except that this is a four-credit lab, not one credit."

"And it should be. That chemistry lab course was so easy I wonder that they give a full credit for it. You said you have only two exams next week. What other course did you manage to exempt the final?"

"Hematology doesn't have a final exam. It's all practical application. I'm pretty sure I have an A in the course, but I won't know for sure until class tomorrow."

"So what's that mean overall? How are your other two courses?"

"Solid B in both classes. I expect I'll get a B on both finals, so that's all the excitement there."

"So a 3.5 GPA. That's great, that's dean's team."

"What about you, Hat? How are your grades shaking out? Has psychology gotten any better?"

"Looks like an A in everything except psychology and English. English is in at a B+ and no final—"

"That's awesome, Hat," Toby interrupted. "So you got an A on the Kafka paper? You really pulled that one up."

"So I need to study psychology tonight. As long as I can pull out a D on the final, I'll make a C– grade. That's good enough to avoid grade review."

"Hat! You know you can do better than that. Shame on you for shooting for a D on the final. That's no way to go through college, settling for a D."

"I'm not shooting for a D. I'm just saying that I'm safe since a D will keep me off grade review. I'm sure I can do better than that and get a better grade than a C–, but the pressure is kind of off now."

"Well, you study up on your psychology, and I'll study up on my immunology and physiology. We can work here until dinnertime, then after dinner we can go to my place and I'll ask you psychology questions."

"Then can we look into your physiology?"

"Only if you pass psychology."

Dinner came and went. I got a lot of psychology crammed into my head in those few hours. I started to feel like I actually could pass the final exam. Walking from the Indy Metro stop down to Toby's apartment, we spoke little. For one thing the sidewalks were cleared only intermittently. We had gotten twelve inches of snowfall overnight, and the people in this neighborhood were not diligent about shoveling snow. Some walks were cleared, some walks were given a cursory pass, and other walks could not be seen. Mostly we had to guess where the walk was.

Another reason for our silence was my lack of enthusiasm for the evening before us. I wasn't fully recovered from the blood donation fiasco, and I didn't even have the energy to explain that to Toby. I just moped along through the snow.

Also, I felt embarrassment about missing our study date yesterday. I had never missed a rendezvous with Toby, and I didn't quite know how to apologize.

After about two blocks of silence, Toby broke the calm.

"Why are you so quiet tonight?" she asked.

"I don't know. I…um…*¡Yo estoy embarazado!*"

"Oh my god! You're pregnant! Am I the mother?"

"No, no."

"Who is she? I'll kill her!"

I laughed so hard I fell into a snowdrift. Toby dove in on top of me.

"Who is this wicked woman that would get you pregnant behind my back?"

Laughing, she stuck her nose in my face. I tried to pull her close. Once again our winter coats got between us.

"I'm sorry I messed up yesterday. I hope I didn't worry you too much, and I hope you aren't mad at me."

"Dogs get mad, people get angry, and I haven't had my rabies shots yet this month." She snarled in her high-pitched voice that reminded me more of a cat in heat than a dog with rabies, but I went along with it.

"Good girl," I said as I stroked her hair.

We found our way out of the snowdrift and down the street to her apartment. After a four-flight climb, she opened her door and we reached her kitchen. I collapsed into one of her wooden dining room chairs, dropped my head to the table, and struggled to catch my breath. I still wore my winter coat and backpack.

"Are you okay?" she asked.

"I'm exhausted," I answered between breaths. "I think I should rest up and then go home."

"No psychology questions?"

"I'm sorry, but I'm too tired."

"No physiology examination?"

"You know, that's the real shame. Too tired for that too."

"I think we may have a crisis on our hands."

"I'll go home and get a good night's sleep. We can meet at the library tomorrow and pick up where we left off."

"There's just one problem with that plan. A small problem, but a problem nevertheless."

"What's that?"

"Tomorrow, at sundown, begins Hanukah. I promised my mother I would go over to her house around three."

"What does that mean?"

"It's one of those things you will have to learn about if you decide to convert. It's just a minor holiday, but my mother loves it. It's fun for my nieces and nephews. For now let's just say I will be indisposed tomorrow night and every night for the next eight days. Next Saturday I will free up."

"What about your two finals?"

"I'm allowed out during the day. It kind of goes along with that female werewolf thing I told you about."

I had a brainstorm that would allow me time to get back up to speed and still allow for some physiology examinations.

"What time is your final on Monday?"

"I don't have a final until Tuesday."

"My psychology final is at nine o'clock. We were told the results would be posted by one o'clock. We could meet here at say two o'clock to celebrate, and I'll be gone anytime you want before sundown."

"That's interesting. We may actually have something to celebrate."

"How's that?"

"Think about it. If they can get the test results back that fast, the test must be a standardized test that uses computer readable answer sheets. That means multiple choice. Even you can pass a multiple-choice psychology test."

"You're right," I said. "I'll pick up the balloons and the confetti this weekend."

"Just make sure you get plenty of rest between now and then, Hat. I'll be primed for some celebrating."

"And so will I."

Having regained my breath and my spirit, I stood and faced Toby. She was truly sustaining. All I needed was her. All else was merely so that I could have her. She looked back at me, and I dared to imagine that she was thinking something along those same lines, but I dared not offer her a penny for her thoughts. She might be thinking something else entirely.

We kissed.

"Thank you for understanding, Toby. I'll be fully rested by Monday."

"You had better be, buster, or someone's going to pay."

Chapter Forty-One

I HAD NO PROBLEM sleeping Thursday night. From the time my head hit the pillow until I opened my eyes in the morning, I was out. No strange dreams, no midnight sweats, no chills. The problem was I didn't feel revitalized after the full night's sleep. I felt the lethargy pulling me down as I struggled to rise. I went through the motions of cleaning up and getting dressed, but I had no zest. I didn't want to face the day.

The Metro ride over to school was long and jarring. I developed an intense headache. I thought perhaps the bus was leaking carbon monoxide fumes into the coach, but no one else seemed to be bothered by it. The Michigan Street line went straight across town from the East Side to the West Side and right through downtown and the IUPUI campus. If I had needed to change buses, I might have just stayed at the bus stop. As it was, I made it to campus but that was all. I stopped in the School of Business to rest and warm up and didn't get moving again until well after my chemistry lecture was over. I didn't worry about missing that class, but I definitely needed to make it to the psychology class.

As I trudged across campus, I noticed that the snow no longer had the fresh white sheet-of-paper look. It was melting off the rooftops and forming icicles at the corners of buildings. Students had spoiled every open yard on campus by traipsing across the open fairways, leaving tracks and slush in their wake. Streets and parking lots were dark slush ponds, and cars parked there were covered with dirty snow and salt. The paper had been written on, and although I could not read the words, it reminded me of a Kafka story that had no message except to tell me that all was dark in the world.

I made it to psychology class and sat in the middle of the last row. My headache had intensified while walking across campus, and I couldn't focus on the lecture. It was a review for the test, which I needed badly, but I couldn't concentrate. I fantasized about recapturing my energy by eating spinach and other leafy vegetables. I ran through a garden grabbing heads of lettuce, and I climbed a plum tree to gather fruit. I heard Toby's voice softly whispering in my ear, saying, "I don't think that's going to solve the problem, Popeye." I stared at the lecture hall ceiling as these images danced across my mind's eye and played with my emotions. I returned from my reverie when students began to rise and shuffle out of the lecture hall. I waited for all the other students to file out before I got up to leave. I didn't want anyone to notice my sluggish steps.

It was only two thirty, and I had not done anything but walk to class, yet I was worn out. Since I wasn't meeting Toby that afternoon, I decided to go home. I would use the weekend to rest and study and come out fresh on Monday, ready for my psychology final. After that, it would be an easy downhill coast to wrap up the semester.

My walk to the New York Street Metro stop was just as bleak as my walk from Michigan Street. The snow no longer outlined the tree branches, and they stood dead and bare in the afternoon gloom. The sky was gray and featureless, and a cold wind started up from the west. I pulled the collar of my coat tight around my neck and my stocking cap down over my ears. I was glad I had worn gloves today.

When I reached the Indy Metro stop, I was alone. I felt the cold closing in around me. The Metro stop was just a green sign at the side of the road. There was no shelter, there was no wind block, and that frigid December wind blew from across the White River unimpeded down West New York Street, bringing an arctic freeze and a melancholy I had never experienced before.

"It's the twelfth of December," I said aloud, though no one was close by to hear. I began to sing to try to cheer myself up.

"On the twelfth day of Christmas my true love gave to me, twelve…?"

I couldn't remember what twelve things my true love gave to me. Trying to remember was too much work. I gave up and sank into a mild depression.

Chapter Forty-Two

I DIDN'T STUDY MUCH over the weekend, but I spent time with Mother. I hadn't been doing that very often lately. Dad was exhausted from the burden of working nights and caring for Mother days. Corinne had given up her weekends so that Dad could get some rest. Because I was home this weekend, she was able to go out with her friends on Saturday while Dad was able to sleep through the afternoon.

Mother spent a lot of the time sleeping while I relaxed in Dad's recliner next to her with my psychology book open on my lap. But when she awoke, her concerns were for my welfare, not hers. You would have thought she wasn't sick but merely resting.

"How are your grades, Paddy?" she asked during one of her waking moments. "I haven't seen any reports."

"My grades are good, Mother. The grade report will be out sometime after final exams. The finals are this week. I expect to get around a 3.4 GPA."

"What does that mean exactly?"

"It's about a B+ average. I expect four As, a B+, and a C."

"That sounds fine, except for the C."

"I'm working hard on that course, but that's probably the best I'll be able to do."

"What about your girlfriend? You haven't brought her around to meet me yet, Paddy. You said you would bring her for dinner."

"Yes, I will. We've both been very busy preparing for finals. Besides, she's not quite ready for that yet. She's still trying to get used to me."

"Perhaps after finals are finished, then? Maybe she could come for Christmas dinner?"

I laughed softly at the thought. "We'll see, Mother. She may have some trouble with that. I'll talk to her."

"Yes. I can see where she may have a problem with that. She will probably want to spend Christmas with her family."

Mother drifted off to sleep as I wondered what Christmas was like at Toby's house. Did they go about their day as though it was no different than any other day? I thought this would be next to impossible with Christmas so blatantly evident around them. We Christians could blissfully carry out our business as important Jewish holidays such as Rosh Hashanah and Yom Kippur passed by unpublicized and unnoticed. But even the nonreligious aspects of the Christmas season, like shopping for Christmas gifts and Frosty the Snowman cartoons on TV, were in your face from Thanksgiving until Christmas Day. Their religious culture must be deeply ingrained to withstand the constant soft pressure of the massive Christian culture around them. Then I recalled that they have withstood more insidious pressure from many quarters over the course of history, and they continue to do so today. There are factions, and even entire countries, whose sole purpose for existence is to exterminate the Jews. But the devotion of the Jews is strong, and those maltreatments and persecutions have only served to make them stronger.

Mother awoke and asked for ice. She was eating very little these past few weeks, and she was rapidly losing her girth. She was literally shrinking before our eyes. When supper was prepared, she always said she was not hungry right now and implied that she would eat something later, but when later came along, she was still not hungry.

She hardly drank anything either. A small sip of water was all she could manage at any given time. Her drinking glass sat mostly unused on the table next to her recliner.

But she always wanted ice. She liked to have the ice cubes chipped into small slivers that she could run across her lips and thus relieve the dryness caused by her dehydration. This was a temporary measure at best since the source of her dry lips was on the inside, not on the surface and could not be remedied by any cure we knew.

Mother kept getting worse as each day passed. Her breathing became a staccato series of short gasps, her cheeks hollowed out, and even her voice began to change. Her melodic laughter was gone—replaced by a hoarse, hacking cough. She spoke in a sandpaper tone that crackled like a burning log. Her parched throat and larynx would allow no smoother sounds.

And she slept.

The morphine was necessary to ease her pain, but it also induced sleep. Mother drifted into and out of sleep several times over the course of an hour, so it was difficult to sustain an extended conversation. Mostly, we watched television.

I didn't tell anyone in the family about my lethargy or about my reaction to giving blood. I didn't want to worry Mother in her condition, while Dad and Corinne had enough to be anxious about with Mother's care. When I came home early on Wednesday after the blood drive, I merely said that I didn't feel well and went to bed. No one gave it another thought. As the weekend passed, I began to feel a little stronger, and I decided not to dispel their breaktime with my petty problems. Mother's illness was the issue in our family, and she deserved as much attention as we could give her.

Chapter Forty-Three

WHEN MONDAY ARRIVED, I was ready to go. The snow still covered much of the open space, but the streets were clear and the sun was bright in the cloudless eastern sky. I felt a vigor that had been missing for the past five days, and I knew I would pass the psychology exam. I made it to the lecture hall with more than fifteen minutes to spare and waited anxiously for the test papers to be distributed.

Good news! The entire exam consisted of true-or-false questions. This was a godsend. Not only had I crammed single items of information into my head over the past week, but I always did well on binary tests anyway. I knew I would pass that test even without the smartest girl in the class sitting within peeking distance.

We were given fifty minutes to take the test, but I was confidently finished in thirty-five minutes. I didn't bother to check my answers. I would only be second-guessing myself, and if I changed any answers, I would probably change more from right to wrong than wrong to right.

After turning in my answer sheet, I called Toby.

"The test was pretty easy," I said. "All true-false questions. I'm certain that I passed."

"That's great. Are you coming over here now?"

"I'd better wait to be sure. They say they'll have the scores and the final grades posted by one o'clock. I'll call you when they're up."

"Sounds good."

"How's Hanukah going?"

"It's fine."

"That's it? It's fine, nothing more?"

"Hanukah is not that big of a deal. My mother likes to make it fun for the kids, and she needs my help to do that. That's all."

"Okay. I understand," I said, though not understanding at all. "I'll call you when I know my grade for sure."

I spent the next couple of hours in the library, trying to study for the calculus final, but I made little progress. I could only think about the psychology test. At twelve fifteen I closed my calculus book and headed back to the psychology lecture hall, hoping the results might be ready early. The graduate assistant was just closing the posting cabinet door when I arrived, and I was able to see the grades without fighting a crowd.

I couldn't believe what I saw. My test score was 96 percent, and my final grade for the course was a B. This was way beyond my wildest expectation. I knew I always did well on binary exams, but I never imagined that I would ace the final and pull out a B in the course. As long as I got an A on each of my last two finals, I would have a 3.66 GPA for the semester. I was going to make the dean's list.

Toby was ecstatic when I called her, and she told me to get over to her place right away to celebrate. I hurried over to the Indy Metro stop and waited for the bus. What a difference a weekend can make. This was the same stop that I found so cold and depressing on Friday. On Monday it became a warm and welcoming point of access to Toby. The bright, sunny day helped, the A on the exam certainly helped, the prospect of a celebratory afternoon with Toby unquestionably helped, but there was something else at work here. Adrenaline can help you accomplish great things even when you have a shortage of red blood cells.

The bus ride to the east side was smooth and settling. I too began to settle. The adrenaline high that I had been riding since breakfast rapidly dissipated as the streets rolled by. The crisis of passing the psychology test was over and my natural body chemistry reestablished control. I felt the pull of weariness on my legs, my arms, my lungs, my entire body, once again. Although the thought of Toby anxiously awaiting my arrival energized my excitement, it did not excite my energies.

The walk down Wallace Avenue to Washington Street was long and lonely. Even with the sun shining on this bright December afternoon, the air was cold and the people huddled within their warm homes rather than venture outside if it wasn't necessary. The sidewalks varied from clear to icy to snow covered and made the walking treacherous. I could not have moved faster even if they had all been clear and dry.

I called Toby from the sidewalk in front of her building and told her I was on my way up. It had taken longer than planned to get to that point, and I still needed a brief rest stop before commencing the four-story climb. When I finally knocked on her door, she was energized; I was exhausted.

I managed to go through our greeting routine without collapsing, but my embrace was not enthusiastic, my kiss was lackluster, and my profession of love eternal was less than the passionate expression Toby had come to expect.

My bag contained only my calculus book, but it was like unloading an albatross when I dropped it on the table. I shrugged out of my winter coat and hung it on the back of one of the wooden chairs.

"Congratulations!" Toby said as I settled into another of the wooden chairs. "Ninety-six percent is awesome. I knew you had it in you, Hat."

"I can't believe they gave a true-or-false final exam," I said as I struggled to catch my breath.

"They know that most of the students in the class take it only because it's required. Every student, regardless of their major field of study, must take Psychology 101. Same for English 101, Chemistry 101, Speech 101, and so on. They don't make it easy, but they don't want to ruin your GPA on a freshman general requirement course either."

"I don't have to take Chemistry 101."

"Sure, but you're taking a higher-level chemistry. What is it, Chemistry 105 or something?"

"106."

"See! You skipped 101, 2, 3, 4, and 105."

With a chuckle, I said, "103 and 105 are labs, but you're right. A couple of guys on the team took 101, and they both said it was easier than their high school chemistry class. They were thankful for that since they are both business majors and don't really care about the chemistry."

It was now Toby's turn to chuckle as she placed two tall, thin, stemmed glasses on the table in front of me. She opened the refrigerator and withdrew a dark-green bottle with gold foil wrapping around the neck.

"The important thing is to be exposed to the ideas so that they're not totally foreign to you," she said as she removed the foil and began working on the plastic stopper. "No one expects you to be able to psychoanalyze anyone, and no one expects a business student to be able to do a chemical analysis. But if you are a chemical engineering graduate, you had better be able to do a chemical analysis and be able to explain your findings to a nontechnical businessman, who, in turn, should be able to understand your findings after some reasonable explanation."

"Which succinctly explains why we all go to college."

"You mean besides the drinking."

As she said this, the bottle popped and shot the cork to the ceiling, leaving a small indentation in the drywall. The cork fell harmlessly to the floor, while a spray of champagne misted the air and bubbled over the mouth of the bottle onto the table.

"Wow! You are dangerous with that thing," I yelped.

She got her mouth over the lip of the bottle and sucked up the overflow before much champagne spilled over. This image caused a stirring in my loins that I had not felt since before the blood donation. Toby got the picture, and her cheeks glowed with a rosy blush as she smiled seductively over the still-fizzing champagne.

"So," she said, drawing out the "oh" and maintaining the sexual image by slowly running her hand up and down the side of the sweating bottle. "What is the appropriate reward for acing a psychology final exam?"

I rose and took her in my arms.

"I think a glass of champagne is an excellent idea," I said, "but only after a lingering kiss and a loving embrace. Then we'll see where to go from there."

We kissed and embraced. I kissed her neck and noticed that she was wearing the silver teardrop earrings that she had worn the first night we made love. The memory of that night enhanced my excitement.

"I missed you this weekend," she whispered as I kissed her gently behind the dangling earring and pulled her not so gently to me.

"I missed you too."

"Let's do the champagne later," she said, opening the top button on my flannel shirt.

I answered by pulling her Indiana University sweatshirt up to her shoulders. She raised her arms and let me pull it over her head. I was about to toss the sweatshirt on the floor when she stopped me.

"There's champagne on the floor. I'll clean it up later, but let's go into the bedroom for now."

I trailed her to the bedroom. An element of concern crept into my mind as I watched her stride down the hallway, her breasts bouncing under the restraint of her bra, her backside swaying provocatively in her tight blue jeans. I felt plenty of excitement and an irresistible yearning to be with her, but I did not have an erection. She liked to coax me to full strength using her mouth, but it was never actually necessary. I normally would have been hard and ready just by watching her suck the top of the champagne bottle. But today there was only a simple stirring where there should have been a rush of heat.

When we entered the bedroom, I put aside my concern and moved against her from behind. I encircled her waist with my arms and kissed the nape of her neck while pushing my groin against her butt. Without relinquishing contact, I undid the clasp of her bra, letting it fall forward while I reached around and cupped her breasts in my hands.

She responded by tossing the sweatshirt and bra onto the chair and leaning back into me. She arched her back, giving full fill to her breasts while at the same time pushing her rear firmly against my crotch. She laid the back of her head against my right shoulder, letting her hair fall over my back, nearly reaching my shoulder blade and stretching the front of her neck before my lips. I kissed the side of her neck and her shoulder while massaging her breasts, the nipples hardening between my index and middle fingers. The feel of her against me and in my hands was thrilling and should have had me in a state of full rigidness, but her nipples were the only things hardening.

I moved my hands down to the front of her jeans, opened the button, and pulled down the zipper. I slid my right hand inside, working my fingers down the front of her panties and caressing the mound of her pubic hair through the silk. She spread her legs slightly as I moved my hand lower and caressed more firmly. She emitted a soft moan. I loved that sound. I dropped her blue jeans with my left hand then spread my fingers across her abdomen and held her tight against me as I continued to stroke her with my right hand.

She dropped her hands and, reaching back, grabbed a belt loop with each hand on each side of my hips and pulled me tighter to her. I still did not have an erection.

I released her as she stepped out of her jeans and spun to face me. We kissed, and her mouth opened immediately to receive my tongue. I tasted the urgency of her need and felt an equal need myself. She went through the buttons on my shirt so fast that I thought they were popping off rather than opening. She sat back on the bed and went to work on my belt while I finished slipping out of my shirt and undershirt. I tossed the two shirts on the chair where they mingled with her sweatshirt and bra. She got my jeans open and let them drop to my ankles. I stood before her in my underwear, as eager as a puppy, more excited than an eight-year-old on Christmas morning, breathlessly awaiting what was to follow. But there was no revealing bulge.

Toby glanced up at me with a questioning look, and all I could do in answer was shrug. With both hands she slipped her fingers under the elastic waistband and pulled it forward and down. My underwear fell easily with no obstruction to block the fall. There was no springing diving board bouncing in her face, no bobbing appendage begging to be kissed and caressed, not even a semihard member that perhaps promised, with a little persuasion, better things to come.

I was as completely turned on as I had ever been, but this did not manifest itself in an erection. My penis hung as limp as a wet washcloth and did not give any sign of stiffening.

"What's up with this?" Toby asked. "I thought you were glad to see me."

"I don't know what's wrong," I said. "You've turned me on but…" I shrugged, not knowing what to say.

"You don't look like you're turned on."

"Believe me, Toby, I want you more than ever, but it's not working. I don't know why. Everything worked fine last week."

"Yes, it did," she said as she grasped my penis and gently squeezed. "Everything worked fine." She laid it across her palm. It fit perfectly in her hand, nothing extending beyond the edge of her palm. She bent forward and placed it in her mouth, the entire length fitting easily within, and massaged it with her tongue. She gently caressed my balls and created a warm tingling there but received little response from my still flaccid penis.

Her mouth felt wonderful and astonishingly stimulating yet did not produce an erection. The warmth in my balls expanded and extended into my penis, but that was the totality of my response. I wanted to hold her and make love to her, but I knew that was not going to happen today. I let her suck me until she gave up and lay back on the bed.

I stepped out of my pants and knelt before her. I kissed the inside of her thigh and then ran my tongue slowly across her hot, moist skin, inching my way up to her panties. I felt her thigh muscles tense as my tongue approached her heat. I nuzzled my nose against the wet spot on her panties and sniffed in the aroma of her arousal. She lifted her hips as I pulled her panties down. I tossed them on the chair with the other clothes.

When I turned back to her, the sight I enjoyed was the most magnificent vision imaginable. I could see her entire body, from her feet and lower legs dangling over the edge of the bed to her head propped up on a pillow, her sea-green eyes gazing back at me over her breasts, which were rising and falling with her bated breath. Her skin glistened with a film of perspiration that gave her a heavenly glow. The triangle of her black pubic hair thinly covered her pelvic mound and pointed the way to the object of my desire. Yet my desire created no working response.

I bent and kissed her other thigh, intending to move up slowly. She grabbed my hair and lifted my face so she could look me in the eye.

"So, Hat," she said, "what do you intend to do when you get there? Do you think you are going to have any response or not?"

"I don't know whether I will or not. As you know, this has never happened before. It doesn't look like I'm going to get up. But maybe this will work for you. Do you want to try?"

"I don't think it will work," she said, but she still pushed my face back down between her legs.

I obliged. I kissed her gently before inserting my tongue. I moved it up and down, left and right, and round in circles. She responded by grabbing the back of my head and pulling my face tighter to her. I thrust my tongue as deeply into her as I could reach and wriggled it around as she arched her back and raised her hips to meet me. I placed my hands under her hips and held her up as she began to buck. I repeated the entire cycle many times over the next fifteen minutes or so, and my tongue and jaw muscles began to tire and ache from the strain, but I continued to manipulate her in the hope that I could satisfy her need even though I could not raise an erection.

After a while, she stopped moving with the rhythm and did not respond to the touch of my tongue. She ran her fingers through my hair, but she did not pull my face toward her. Her abdomen, thigh, and buttocks muscles relaxed, and her legs fell lazily apart. She did not chase me away, but neither did she invite me in. She had tried her best and so had I, but I knew she was no longer interested in pursuing the allusive release that just did not want to happen.

My tongue was about to fall off anyway. The muscles at its base were revolting over the workout they had undergone and were threatening to cramp severely. I never had a cramp in my tongue, and

I didn't relish the thought of having one now. The muscles in the rest of my tongue were in good shape, and I could have continued indefinitely with them, but the muscles at its base were through for the day.

I laid my cheek against her thigh, and we both relaxed without a word.

Chapter Forty-Four

TOBY WAS NOT in the best of moods. She was obviously not satisfied by our oral lovemaking, and she was not shy about letting me know that. She did not want to cuddle afterward, and she did not want to take a nap as was our usual custom. Instead, she gathered up and sorted our clothes, handing me mine and slipping back into her own. When we emerged from the bedroom and entered the kitchen, she was visibly irritated by the champagne mess we had left earlier, yet she did not want me to clean it up or even help. She wanted me to go.

It was not yet three o'clock and nowhere near sundown, yet she insisted that she had to get to her mother's to further the Hanukah fun. I took the hint and gathered up my coat and backpack and was on my way home within minutes.

The full impact of the oral sex began to hit me as I walked up Wallace Avenue toward home. I stopped several times to rest along the way and found that it was becoming harder and harder to get moving again after each subsequent break. I made a final rest stop just a few houses down from our house. A giant oak tree grew in the narrow strip of ground between the sidewalk and the curb, pushing the cement of the walkway up and spreading the concrete, crumbling, across its bark. I dropped my backpack on the walk and leaned my shoulder against the tree.

My tongue and jaw muscles were fully recovered from their aerobics, but the memory of the strain was still fresh in my mind. As hard as I had worked, I could not bring Toby to a climax in this manner. What if I could never raise an erection again? How would

Toby react to that? She enjoyed our sex as much or maybe more than I did. She was clearly upset with this episode of impotence. What if I could never perform again?

"One instance of failure doesn't mean that it will always be that way," I said aloud. It probably was due to the rush, and then deprivation, of adrenaline. I remembered reading that when the adrenaline is pumping, a man could lift a car, but once it stopped, that same man might collapse into a ball of jelly, unable to lift even his own arms. But my lingering and persistent lethargy argued against such rationalizations and amplified my anxiety that this might be the first of many instances.

Perhaps I needed to improve my oral technique. Toby had given me no guidance in this area and I went purely on instinct, yet she seemed to enjoy the method I employed. Apparently, it worked well as a prelude but not so well as the main feature.

I thought of Mary Kelly and our session in the church sacristy. She was very good at what she did and had no trouble bringing me off. I didn't know if it was easier with boys, but she sure liked doing it and was successful at it. She had proceeded with ease and kept at it without pause, seemingly without exertion, for quite a long time. I thought of my aching tongue and jaw muscles and gained a new appreciation for Mary Kelly.

"What are you doing out there, boy?"

Mr. Allen had come out onto his porch and apparently was concerned that I might be stealing his oak tree.

"Just resting, Mr. Allen. I'll move on in a minute."

"Is that you, Brian? You go ahead and rest as long as you like, son. You deserve it after all the yards you racked up on the football field."

"It's Patrick, sir."

"Oh...well, you can rest there too, then."

"Thank you. I'll move on shortly."

Mr. Allen went back into his house, and after a few more minutes, I moved on to mine, no problems solved, no solutions contrived.

Chapter Forty-Five

I SLEPT WELL MONDAY night. My anxiety over my potential impotence notwithstanding, I was too exhausted to do anything other than sleep. I awoke and prepared for the day in my now usual state of lifelessness. I was not excited about the calculus final exam scheduled for nine o'clock that morning. This was a routine test on material that I knew inside and out. I merely had to show up and go through the process. Showing up turned out to be more difficult than I anticipated, and going through the process was next to impossible.

I struggled to get dressed, collapsing onto my bed several times before I managed, through sheer determination, to don a heavy flannel shirt, blue jeans, and thick wool socks. I didn't want to face the daunting tasks of putting on my boots and confronting the winter day. I caught the bus on time, but I had to rest at the School of Business and did not get moving soon enough to start the exam on time.

I had lost fifteen valuable minutes of exam time by arriving late, but even if I had two extra hours to work on the test, I would not have passed it. Most of the test covered fairly simple concepts of summation theory and application in which the most difficult aspects were knowing what each variable meant and its proper placement on the sigma symbol. The rest of it was logic and simple mathematics. I should have breezed through this test, but my mind drew a complete blank. After making a few notations on my test paper, I realized that I was marking time, not answers. I took my nearly blank blue book up to the graduate assistant after only forty-five minutes.

"Finished already, Patrick?" she asked.

"No, not really," I answered. "I must be getting sick or something. I can't remember a thing. I haven't finished the test, but I can't take it today. There's something wrong. I think I'm getting sick."

She glanced through my blue book and, seeing that it was virtually empty, turned to me and said, "Are you sure about this? I've worked with you all semester, and I know that you understand this stuff better than anyone else in the class."

"I just can't do it today," I said. "I don't know why, but I can't do it."

"Okay," she said. "I don't know anything about makeup exams, but I'll turn this into Professor Lutz and tell her what you said. I don't know what she will do with this."

"Thanks," I mumbled, as I stumbled out the door and into the cold winter morning, not knowing where I was headed but wanting to be anywhere but where I was. I hurried into the Liberal Arts building, which was the next building over, and sat on one of the plush couches in the lobby.

I didn't know what to do. I thought about calling Toby, but what would I say? "Hi, sorry I couldn't perform yesterday. By the way, I couldn't perform on my calculus test either, and now I'm going to flunk out of school." That would be a wonderful conversation. Instead I spent the next hour brooding.

I finally decided to go home. I still had my chemistry final at ten o'clock on Wednesday, and as long as I made it through that with the A that I expected, I figured I could argue my way into a makeup exam in calculus. All was not lost.

It had not snowed since last Wednesday, six days ago, but it had remained cold the entire week. The icicles that had formed on the buildings in the slight warming on Thursday still hung from the corners, from the gutters, and from the tree branches; but they did not drip. They were frozen solid. The snow still covered the yards, and the streets and walks were glazed by a thin coating of rime but were generally clear. My breath steamed in front of me and then frosted my eyebrows as I made my way to the Indy Metro stop.

Chapter Forty-Six

MOTHER AND DAD were asleep in their recliners when I got home. This was the way they now spent most of their days: Mother tranquillized by the morphine and Dad tranquillized by the burden of his responsibilities. After a full night of work, Dad came home to face continuing duty at Mother's side. He didn't complain, but he was physically drained by the double shift day after day.

I slipped by without waking them and climbed the stairs to my room. At my desk I immediately opened my chemistry book and laid my chemistry notebook next to it. I was determined to get the A in chemistry that I deserved. Nothing would stop me. There would be no excuses. There would be no brain skip tomorrow. Tomorrow I would ace the chemistry final.

When I awoke, I was sprawled across my bed, still fully clothed, and completely unaware of how I had gotten from the desk to the bed. I was glad that I had removed my boots before I sat down at the desk. The window was dark, so I knew I had slept the entire day away. A beep told me that I had a text message. I removed my cell phone from my shirt pocket and saw that the time display said it was 3:23. The problem was with the date: Wednesday, December 17. I had slept from early afternoon until 3:23 in the morning, and I didn't remember studying a lick.

The text was from Toby. "What up, Hat? How'd the exam go? I think I did well on the Health Sciences, but I won't know until later this week. We didn't make arrangements yesterday, but how about we meet at the library at 1:30? T"

The text was sent at 1:15, just about the time I sat down at my desk to study. I could not have met her at one thirty, but I could have let her know that. Now it was too late to answer her.

I got up and went to the window. The full moon shone so brightly that the bare trees cast spooky shadows on the street and gave the impression of daytime to the neighborhood. I could clearly see the roofs of the houses still covered with week-old snow. All except for the Van Landingham bungalow. They must not have gotten insulation when they replaced their roof last year because the snow was completely melted from their rooftop. They didn't realize that they were heating the whole neighborhood.

My chemistry text and notebook were closed and stacked neatly on the corner of the desk with my favorite pen lying diagonally across. It appeared that I had made the conscious decision to quit studying. I had no idea how long I actually studied, if I studied at all, but I now made the conscious decision to return to bed. I had to have a good rest before the exam, and I also knew that further study would not improve my grasp of the material anyway. This time I removed my heavy clothes and climbed under the covers.

When I awoke, the sunlight streamed in through the open curtains. I blinked in confusion and then sat straight up in bed. This was a bad sign, since my bedroom faced the west and the sun did not touch those curtains until the afternoon. I grabbed my cell phone and saw the time was one forty-five. My chemistry exam was given at ten o'clock.

My cell phone beeped and showed five text messages, all from Toby. I didn't want to read them. I didn't want to answer them. How could I explain the total screw-ups of the last several days?

All was lost.

Chapter Forty-Seven

I SULKED. IT WAS the best I could come up with in the spur of the moment. In just one week I had turned my life completely around. I was now flunking both of my two strongest courses, my grade point average would plummet to 1.79, I would lose my scholarship, I would surely be tossed out of school, and I was afraid to answer text messages from my girlfriend. I wasn't sure which of these was the worst state of affairs.

I hung my head. Why was this happening to me? I had always been a conscientious student, a hard worker, and a skilled athlete. Now, not only was I unable to play ten minutes of soccer without collapsing, I was also unable to take a test on material that I knew thoroughly, unable to wake up and get out of bed for an important final examination, and unable to make love to that girlfriend that texted me so often. What did I do to deserve this?

I allowed myself to sulk for a full fifteen minutes, but I could spare no more than that. This was a critical time. If the situation was to be saved, I had to act quickly. I called Toby first.

"Hat! Where are you? What's going on? Why haven't you called me or answered my texts?"

"I'm sorry, Toby. I've been sick."

"Too sick to pick up the phone and call? Too sick to send a text? I've been worried. Don't you think you owe me at least a phone call when you disappear into thin air like that? Don't I count for anything?"

"I'm sorry, Toby. You're right. I should have called after the calculus test yesterday when I was feeling sick. Instead, I came home. All I could think about was getting home and going to bed."

"You need to think about people other than yourself once in a while. I was worried sick."

"I'm sorry. I should have called. I slept right through the day. I didn't get your text until I woke up at three in the morning, and it was too late to text you back. I didn't want the beep to wake you up."

"What about this morning? Why didn't you call me when you got up?"

"I did. I mean, I am."

"What's that mean?"

"I just now woke up, and I called."

"You slept through two days?"

"I slept from when I got home at one o'clock yesterday afternoon until about three o'clock this morning. Then I slept from three until just a few minutes ago."

"Oh. So you really were sick then." Her voice assumed a softer, more tolerant tone. "What's the problem, Hat? Are you feeling better now? Did you call a doctor?"

The thought of calling a doctor scared the hell out of me. I knew that if I told a doctor about my energy problems, he would find something seriously wrong with me that would cost me my scholarship. I could not let that happen. I would have to work this out without the help of a doctor. I decided to ignore that part of Toby's question.

"I don't know what the problem is. I haven't felt good since I gave blood last Wednesday. That blood donation sure drained me, but any ill effects shouldn't be hanging around this long. That was a week ago. Maybe the blood donation weakened me so that my natural defenses were down and I caught a bug. I don't know, but I sure have been dragging since then."

"Hat! You said you slept until just now. What about your chemistry final?"

"I missed it."

"Oh, Hat! What are you going to do?"

"I don't know. I might flunk out. I don't know what to do."

"You've got to call your chemistry teacher and explain the problem. Maybe he'll let you take a makeup exam."

"I think I'll do better than that. I'm going over to campus. I make a better argument in person than over the phone."

"That's a good idea if you feel up to it. And call the doctor. You need to get to the root of this problem."

"Yeah, I will."

Chapter Forty-Eight

PROFESSOR CHARLENE LUTZ sat serenely in her high-backed stuffed leather chair, calmly studying my calculus grade records while I sat nervously in an uncomfortable low-backed rough wooden chair across the desk from her. The wall behind her was covered by several dark stained wooden bookshelves supported by two lateral files. The shelves were laden with thick, hulking textbooks on solid and plane geometry, analytic geometry, trigonometry, and integral calculus, as would be expected of a mathematics professor, as well as texts on other subjects such as physics, pricing theory, macroeconomics, and econometrics. The shelf on the lower right contained several books of fiction, including *Stranger in a Strange Land* and *The Moon Is a Harsh Mistress*, both science fiction novels by Robert A. Heinlein; *The Invisible Hand* and *Run and Gun*, two suspense thrillers by John W. Fosnaught; and *Watchers*, a supernatural thriller by Dean Koontz. Her office was small, accommodating only her bookshelves with files, desk chair, desk, computer work station, and two wooden visitor chairs. But she was the only occupant and could organize her space as she saw fit. It appeared that she organized it quite well, judging by the clean, clear glass desktop that contained only a pen holder, a calendar, a handwritten note, and my blue book from yesterday's calculus exam.

She peered at me over her eyeglasses with a look that prompted more questions than provided answers. She glanced back at the grade report, adjusting her glasses to reading position, and then suddenly dropped the report onto her desk. She picked up my blue book and opened to the first page. Frowning, she turned in her chair to fully face me.

"Mr. Maloney," she said. "Tell me. Do you know what *n* stands for?"

"Yes, ma'am," I answered. "The *n* represents the number of periods in a summation series. It tells you how far to carry the summation. For example, in a discounted cash flow such as a mortgage calculation over a period of fifteen years, *n* would equal one hundred and eighty."

"That's correct. That was the first question on yesterday's exam. You know the answer today, but yesterday you scribbled n=…and then nothing but scratch marks."

She turned the first page toward me, and I saw that what she had said was true.

"What was the problem yesterday?"

"I don't know, ma'am. I think I was getting sick. I couldn't get my brain in gear. After the test, I went home and slept right through until two this afternoon. It must have been some kind of twenty-four-hour virus or something. I can assure you that I know the calculus pretty well. I just need another chance to show you that I do."

"Your grades in the class to this point sustain that notion, and Ms. Kramer, your graduate assistant, has come to your support as well," she said, fingering the handwritten note. "I'm inclined to allow you to take a makeup exam."

I breathed a sigh of relief as I considered that I might be able to salvage the semester after all.

"Of course, I will have to devise an entirely new test since you saw the test we gave. And I will be sure to make this test significantly more difficult than the original to justify allowing you this special dispensation. I hope you are in agreement with these provisions?"

"Of course, I agree," I said "Thank you for letting me do this. I won't let you down. I promise."

"It will take me some time to prepare an appropriate exam, so I will assign you a temporary grade of I, which stands for Incomplete. This will be changed to the earned grade after you complete the exam. Do we have a current phone number on file for you?"

"Yes."

"Okay. We will be in contact with you after the first of the year to schedule a makeup test. Thank you for coming in, Mr. Maloney, and I wish you well."

"Thank you, Professor Lutz. Thank you very much."

* * *

Dr. Linda Leedy's office was very different from Professor Lutz's. The office itself was larger, but it was occupied by two teachers rather than one, giving each less space. They tried to compensate for this by combining the visitor seating area for two teachers into one space between the two desks. This might have worked out okay except that there were piles of books, magazines, reports, papers, and various sundry other items taking up most of the floor, desk, and shelf space. The clutter even extended to the window ledge.

When I introduced myself, Dr. Leedy recognized my name immediately although we'd never met. The chemistry class she taught contained four hundred students and consisted of a textbook, lectures given to the class as a whole, quizzes administered by graduate assistants in groups of fifteen to twenty students, four major exams, including the final, and the chemistry lab that was officially a separate course but had to be taken in conjunction with her lecture class. She knew few of the students personally but saw their quiz and test results and reviewed their lab work after it was graded by the graduate assistants.

"Mr. Maloney," she said, shaking my hand vigorously. "I'm so glad you came in today. I was worried about you. Hold on a second. I have your file right over here."

She went to a stack of manila folders on the floor under the window, and after sifting down through the top three or four, she found the one she wanted. My file was not a thick one, and I assumed my lab reports were kept in a separate place. She cleared some space on her desktop and placed the open file there as she relaxed into her desk chair. She motioned toward one of two chairs facing the opposite desk and invited me to sit. The visitor chairs were exactly like the ones in Professor Lutz's office, but the desk chair that Dr. Leedy occupied was standard issue, not high backed and not stuffed leather.

I started to feel more comfortable about my position. Yes, I had slept through the final exam, but I still had a lot going for me. My grade was a solid A, and I had never missed a quiz or an exam before. In fact, I had never missed a class until last week. She had said she was worried about me. Did that mean she would cut me some slack and let me take a makeup test as Professor Lutz had agreed?

Dr. Leedy was a very young doctor, not more than thirty, with a freshly scrubbed look to her face. I wondered if she washed her face and hands every time she left the lab.

"Mr. Maloney. You missed the final exam this morning."

It was not a question; it was a statement of fact. I let it stand on its own merit. She obviously had more to say, and I didn't see the value in interrupting her, but I nodded my head in agreement and encouraged her to continue.

"Do you realize that could result in a failing grade for the entire course?"

Her tone suggested that I was not going to be as cordially received here in the chemistry department as I was by the mathematics department. My face must have registered the panic and alarm that I felt because she immediately changed her tone from harsh and accusatory to warm and tender.

"We have not yet made a decision in this matter, but you must know the seriousness of this omission. Why did you miss the exam this morning?"

"I'm very sorry that I missed the exam, Dr. Leedy. I must have caught a twenty-four-hour bug or something. I started to get sick during my calculus test yesterday. I wasn't able to take that test, and I went home and slept for more than a full day. I woke up at around two o'clock this afternoon."

"So you missed my exam because you overslept?"

"It wasn't as simple as that. You make it sound like I was too lazy to get out of bed, but that was not the case. I was sick with something."

"You were sick this morning, and now you're well?"

"I feel a bit better now. I don't think I'm completely over it, but I think I'm well enough to take the test if you'll let me."

"Well, I don't think I can do that, Mr. Maloney. It wouldn't be fair to the students who got up this morning and made it in to take the test at its scheduled time."

"What if I take a more difficult test? Professor Lutz has agreed to give me a harder test as a makeup for the calculus test that I missed. Could we do something along that line?"

"My final exams are as difficult as they get. No, that would not be possible."

"Then take 10 percent off my test score. That might drop me to a B in the course, but I would have to accept that. I can't fail chemistry. Please, help me, Dr. Leedy. I didn't do this on purpose."

"I'm sure you didn't, Mr. Maloney."

As I was pleading, she was looking at my folder. I think she was impressed by the high scores on all the quizzes and the three big exams. She raised her eyebrows as she read some aspect of my file, and then she closed it and laid it back on her desk.

"You completed your lab work early."

"Yes, ma'am."

"Why did you do that?"

"Ma'am?" I wasn't sure what she was getting at, but I needed to be careful with my answer. It could make or break my chances for a makeup test.

"Why did you finish your lab work early?"

"Well," I stalled as I thought my answer through. Finally I decided that the truth was the best answer. I didn't have a reasonable alternative, and the truth would probably flow more freely and more sincerely than any fabrication.

"I had a very good lab partner. We both enjoyed the lab work, and we enjoyed working with each other. We learned a lot from the lab assignments, and we helped with each other's learning experience. This made the labs a lot of fun, so we just kept working at them. The next thing we knew, we had finished them all. If I am going to work with him on my next lab course, I have to pass this chemistry course.

Otherwise, I'll have to take this one again and I'll be a class behind him."

Something in my answer registered with her. She smiled and opened my folder again.

"You have all As on your exams, your quizzes, and your labs. There must be a way that we can get you through this final exam debacle. I am going to report a temporary grade of I for your transcript. I will take your situation under advisement and consult with my department staff. I will let you know what we decide and how we will proceed. In the meantime, sit tight and wait for my call."

"Thank you, Dr. Leedy," I gushed. "Thank you so much."

Chapter Forty-Nine

"That's wonderful, Hat." Toby sounded as relieved as I felt. "Make sure you call your coach or the athletic department and let them know what's going on. Then come on over. I've still got some champagne left from our aborted party on Monday."

The champagne glasses were full when I arrived. I felt a little awkward. The last time I was in her apartment, I couldn't get it up and the champagne was a not-so-subtle reminder of that episode. Toby didn't notice or didn't care. As soon as I was out of my coat and we had run through our greeting routine, she handed me a glass and proposed a toast.

"I took my last final, and you made your final arrangements today," she said, lifting her glass to eye level. "No more school worries until next year. Here's to a successfully completed first semester."

"And to many more," I said as we gently touched glasses.

I had drunk champagne before but not so often that I knew good from not so good. This champagne, however, left no doubt. It tingled in my mouth before I swallowed, and the swallowing was as smooth as milk. The almond flavor lingered on my taste buds even after I put my glass back on the table, and I could still taste it on Toby's lips when we kissed.

I held her close. After Monday's fiasco, I wasn't sure if she would want to hold me again. I thanked God that she was back in my arms. She was why I did what I did. She was why I sang in the morning and why I smiled on the bus to school. She was the reason I counted the minutes until three o'clock knowing I'd see her shining green eyes at that time.

She was the cause of my joyously skipping up Wallace Avenue in the late evening with her scent still strong in my nose, knowing I was leaving her behind but also knowing I would see her again the next day. She was why I did all those things and many things more. She was why I lived.

I kissed her behind the ear and nuzzled my nose there, sniffing the scent of a new perfume. She dropped her arms from around my neck and adroitly unbuttoned my shirt. She slipped the shirt over my shoulders, down my arms, and onto the floor. She then slid her fingers beneath my undershirt, sending a shiver up my back along with her hands.

"Do you like it?" she asked.

"Boy, do I."

"I know you like my hands on you, silly. I mean do you like the perfume?"

"Yes, I do. What is it?"

"Mist of Vallarta. It's my new favorite. One whiff of it and any man turns into a raging sex maniac."

"Too late for me, I'm already there."

"Then I guess it will drive you over the edge."

"Let me smell that again," I said, snuggling my nose behind her ear.

It didn't take long for us to get naked. It was fantastic just holding her, her arms wrapped around my shoulders and back, her breasts pressed against my chest, stomach to stomach, thigh to thigh, her soft skin hot against mine. Kissing her neck, I didn't want the moment to end. I just wanted to hold her in that lover's embrace forever.

But she wanted more. And I was not going to be able to give it to her. As beautiful and sexy as she was, with her dark hair hanging seductively over her left eye and concealing half of her face, and as intimately as we touched, her whole body melting into mine from head to foot, I did not have an erection.

She broke away.

"Toby, I'm sorry."

"You've been saying that an awful lot lately."

"What am I supposed to say?"

"I wish you didn't have to say that. I wish you would quit doing things you're sorry for. I wish we could go back to how it was a week ago, two weeks ago."

She started picking up our intermingled clothes just as she did on Monday right before she threw me out.

"I don't know what's wrong."

"You've been saying that a lot lately too. But you don't seem to want to find out what's wrong."

"What do you mean?"

She stopped picking up clothes, stood straight up, and looked me dead in the eye.

"Have you talked to a doctor? Have you called a doctor for an appointment?"

"I didn't know this would happen again. I thought Monday was a freak occurrence."

"Oh, Hat. I'm not just talking about sex. You've lost your drive, your energy. That's why you sat the bench on the soccer team. You have the speed and the agility and the skill to be not only a starter but a star, except that you don't have the same energy you had a year ago when you won your scholarship. And it's getting worse, not better. This sex issue is just the latest manifestation."

She returned to the clothes, sorting hers from mine, and I knew this was my last chance to save the evening.

"I can try to satisfy you with my tongue. I have plenty of stamina there."

"Hat! You're not listening to me. It's not just the sex. You've got to see a doctor. You've got to find out what's wrong with you."

She thrust my clothes at me like an exclamation point to close her statement. What else was there to say? "Here's your underwear, what's your hurry?" I guess it was time for me to leave.

After dressing, I hesitated before I gave her a goodbye kiss. I wasn't sure if she wanted that or not. She kissed me back.

"I love you, Toby," I said.

"I love you too, Hat," she answered.

That made my day. She was mad at me, but she still loved me. That I could handle.

"Call a doctor!" she said as I slipped out the door.

I wasn't so sure I could handle that.

Chapter Fifty

CHRISTMAS WAS ALWAYS the happiest time of the year. Yes, it is the celebration of Christ's birth and the ensuing promise of redemption from sin, which should be enough in and of itself, but it also meant the expectation of gifts, two whole weeks of vacation from school, decorating the house and the tree, singing Christmas carols, great Christmas movies on TV, and the promise of a succulent turkey with all the trimmings for Christmas dinner. But there was even more to it. Everyone we knew seemed genuinely happy and caring and loving. In our family, the best in everyone came out during the Christmas season.

This Christmas was different. We had a tree, but it wasn't as fully decorated as usual. Dad and I both were too tired for the task, and our lack of enthusiasm rubbed off on Corinne and Brian. Mother didn't pay much attention to it. In previous years Dad and Brian and I outlined the entire house with colored lights, but this year we managed only to encircle the front door. We decided to dispense with singing carols for the time being. No one was in the mood.

Corinne's report card was the only bright spot—straight As as always.

Dad and I went to see the Holiday (Christmas) Play and cheered proudly for our Corinne, but there were two people missing from the party. Brian had stayed home with Mother so we could go. We didn't feel much like celebrating after the play. We wished everyone Merry Christmas and laughed and smiled, but we made an early exit. To the casual observer, it might have seemed like Christmas as usual, but there was an underlying melancholy in the Maloney household.

The arrival of my grade report didn't brighten the mood any.

Brian's grade report came in the mail on the same day as mine, Monday, December 22. That was the extent of the similarity between the two. His grade report contained two Bs, two Cs, and his normal one credit A for football, giving him a 2.62 GPA. His report was received by Dad with admiration and by Mother with praise.

My report contained two one-credit As, one B+, one B, and two Is. There was a temporary GPA calculation of 1.79 because they assigned zero grade points for the Incompletes, and there was a letter of explanation accompanying the report. The letter stated that I had one year to complete the course work and convert the incomplete grades to permanent grades. If I did not complete the course work within that time frame, they would be automatically revised to Fs. The letter also explained that until the course work was completed, I would be placed on academic probation.

This report was not well received by Mother and Dad. I knew I should have intercepted the mail before they saw it, but the grades came sooner than I expected and I was not set up to do that. Anyway, I had already explained to Mother and Dad about the Incomplete grades, and although intellectually they understood that those grades would convert to As once I took the finals, emotionally they were not prepared to see Is on my report and a GPA of 1.79. The accompanying letter did nothing to soothe the sting. Dad was angry; Mother was worried.

"What the hell were you doing that you couldn't finish your schoolwork?" Dad's face turned red as Santa's coat. I feared that he might burst a blood vessel in his forehead. "You have the opportunity of a lifetime, and you squander it. You don't have any idea what the value of this schooling is, do you?"

I thought I knew the value of college. I saw Dad working all night, every night for very little pay. His work was honorable and he provided for his family, but I knew he wished he could do more. I wanted to do more.

"Yes, sir," I said. "I do know the value. I explained to you before that these grades will become As after I take the makeup exams. I will have a 3.66 GPA."

Mother could only believe what she saw on the report: a lousy 1.79 GPA and academic probation. Her watery eyes told the whole story. She looked like a lost puppy with her eyebrows pinched and drooping and her gaze fixed on some faraway spot somewhere outside the room, outside the house. With all that she had to be concerned about with her illness, she was worried about me.

"Mother," I said, though I don't think she was listening to me, "there's nothing to worry about. My grades are going to be fine. I will actually make the dean's list when these grades are finalized."

"Dean's list? With a 1.79?" Dad was making himself angrier and angrier as he spoke. "You must mean his list of flunkies."

"Why would you say that? Why don't you understand what these grades mean? I've explained this to you. These Is will change to As, and I will make the dean's list."

"Academic probation is the only list that I can see you have made. After all we've done—"

I interrupted. I couldn't help it. I was becoming angry too.

"What have you done?" I shouted. "I got the scholarship. You haven't had to pay a penny for my school. I went to all the classes. I did all the studying. I did all the lab work. I went to all the soccer practices, and I worked my ass off. You didn't do any of that. I wrote all the papers. I took all the tests—all but two—and I've arranged to handle that deficiency. If that's not good enough for you, then that's just too bad."

"Don't you talk to me that way, Patrick! This is my house, and I won't stand for it."

"Then I guess I'll just have to leave."

I didn't want to leave. I just wanted to be somewhere else. I didn't want to be fighting over something that was going away in a couple of weeks. I couldn't understand why they were making such a big deal about two temporary grades that would disappear once I took the makeups.

I had my coat on and was out the door before I had given it two thoughts. The cold air cooled me down quickly, and before I reached the front walk, I regretted rushing out. But it was too late; the deed was done.

I walked down Wallace Avenue with no objective in mind. I just wanted to be away for a while. After they'd recovered from the shock of the GPA and the academic probation, I told myself, they'd realize that what I'd said was true. Dad's reaction was partly due to the stress of caring for Mother and the fear of where her disease was taking her, and Mother worried about everything and everyone. Perhaps it took her mind off her own circumstances.

I had problems of my own. Of course, Toby was right. I needed to see a doctor. The big problem with that was possibly losing my scholarship. If the scholarship went away, the rest would be academic. Maybe I could get a prescription for Viagra and thus solve my problems one at a time. Will Viagra work for a nineteen-year-old, or does it work only for old men?

As I was contemplating this question, I turned the corner at Walnut Street and walked toward Dequincy Street. Traffic was light this Monday before Christmas, but there was one car on the street. It pulled to a stop at the curb at the intersection of Dequincy and Walnut, and after a short pause, someone got out of the passenger side and stood by the car on the sidewalk. As I drew near, the car pulled quickly away, and I saw that the passenger was Mary Kelly. She turned to walk down Dequincy Street without noticing my approach.

"Mary!" I said in a voice that carried through the crisp winter air, louder than I had intended.

She turned toward me, grabbing the collar of her coat with both hands and squeezing it tight against her throat. She was startled to hear my voice so close when she didn't expect anyone to be near.

"Who's there?" she asked, tentatively.

"It's Hat," I said more softly. "Hat Trick Maloney."

"Oh, Hat," she sighed with relief. "You scared the hell out of me. How dare you sneak up on me like that?"

The words were chastising, but the tone was playful. She moved closer to me and flashed me her sexy smile. I couldn't help but recall when that smile was wrapped around my shaft in the church sacristy. I felt a tingling in my groin.

"What are you doing out on this cold, cold afternoon?"

"I was just going for a walk. You know, fresh air."

"Well then, will you walk me home? It's only half a block to my house."

"Sure."

We walked together in silence for a short distance, and then I spoke.

"Why don't you have your ride drop you at your house instead of up the street?"

"I don't want my mother to know who I'm hanging out with so I always get dropped off there at Walnut Street. I get picked up there too. Remember when you picked me up there that one night?"

"Yeah, I remember. It wasn't just me though. You actually were with your boyfriend, Joe."

"Yeah, my boyfriend." She sounded uninspired. I recalled that she was unenthused at the blood drive two weeks ago when Joe announced to me that they were going to be pinned. It was as though she had heard that for the first time and was not all that impressed by it.

"He is your boyfriend, right?"

"He likes to think so. He's been hanging around so long that he's become like a habit. Other guys don't approach me because they think we're a couple, so I end up doing everything with him. I guess I'm stuck with him."

"You better decide pretty soon whether you want to be stuck with him or not. He's planning on giving you his fraternity pin when he gets it. Once that happens, it's a short trip to the altar. If you don't say no, that will be it. I know it's none of my business, Mary, but that's no way to choose a life partner."

"I know that, Hat, but how do I stop it? He's always there. There's never a chance for anyone else."

"You need to tell him you don't want his fraternity pin, for one thing. You need to do that as soon as possible. You can't just let him go on thinking you want to be with him. You have to tell him no, and the sooner the better. It will never be easier than right now. It only gets harder and harder the longer you put it off."

We came to her front steps and stopped. I never knew exactly where she lived, only that her house was on Dequincy Street. I looked up at the white aluminum-sided duplex she called home and acquired a newfound appreciation for our three-bedroom single-family home on Wallace Avenue. It was difficult for me to comprehend that this house, which was much narrower than our house, contained two homes. But it was easy to see that it did since it had two sets of front steps and two front doors separated by two narrow single windows. The front porch stretched across the width of the house and was shared by both sides, and the porch roof was common to both. The north, or left, side had Christmas lights strung around the door, the single window, and under the gutter along the porch roof to the midpoint. There was an electric candle in that single window and another in the lone second-floor window on the north side of the house. The south, or right, side had no decorations at all. I wasn't sure which side was Mary's side, so I withheld comment on the decorations.

"Now your mother is going to know you hang out with me."

"My mother's not home. She's at work."

"But you had your ride drop you off up the street?"

"Oh yeah. I always have Joe drop me off up there whether Mother is home or not. I don't really want him to know when my mother's not home."

"I see."

"Would you like to come in? It's cold out here, and I could make us some hot tea or hot cocoa."

Thoughts of Toby briefly passed through my mind. She might wonder about my going inside with Mary, but it was awfully cold out here this afternoon, and a cup of hot cocoa sure sounded appealing.

Chapter Fifty-One

MARY LED THE way to the decorated door on the north side. Somehow I knew she lived in the decorated side; she was Irish after all.

"They don't decorate next door?" I asked.

"I don't even know if they're Christian. They just moved in three months ago, and the only thing I know about them is they fight a lot. I don't see them much, but I hear them through the walls, screaming at each other and at the children, calling each other names, their children constantly crying. It's nothing but noise all the time except when they're not here."

We entered her home. Inside the house was even smaller than it looked from the outside. The front door entered directly into the living room, which had the one window that looked onto the porch. A couch and chair faced a flat-screen television, and the room was filled. The front room passed quickly into a dining area. The Kellys did not have a dining room table, and this area served as additional sitting space with two stuffed chairs on the right. The Christmas tree stood on the left, shining with tinsel and garland before three side-by-side windows looking north toward the house next door. A plastic angel was perched atop the tree, looking out over the home, standing guard. A stairway, with a strand of silver and gold garland woven through the banister and spindles, led to the second floor from the back left of the dining area. Another doorway stood to the back right beyond the stairwell.

Mary led me through this doorway to the kitchen, which, it turned out, was the biggest room in the house. A large metal-frame table with a Formica top occupied the center of the floor space, and four kitchen chairs surrounded it. In its center sat a bright-red poinsettia, perfect for the season. I sat at this table as I watched Mary make hot cocoa.

"So, you think I should tell Joe to get lost?" Mary asked.

"I wouldn't put it that way, Mary. You would need to be a little gentler than that. But I think you need to decide on the answer to that question for yourself. Do you want to stay with him, or do you not? What I'm saying is, don't take the default answer, the answer that comes automatically. Think about it. Think about what you want. Then the answer will come."

"I think I know the answer already. I just don't want to face up to it. I want to be broken up, but I don't want to break up. Does that sound silly?"

"Not at all. I know exactly what you mean. You want the hard part, the 'telling Joe you're through' part, to be over and the 'getting on with life' part to begin."

"That's exactly what I meant, Hat. It's amazing that you understand me so well."

She placed two cups of hot cocoa on the table, along with spoons and napkins and sat next to me. We sipped our cocoa in silence for a short while.

"How's your girlfriend, Hat? Is everything going well?"

I didn't know whether to tell her the truth or not. We seemed to have established a good rapport, and the only way to get some answers was to talk to somebody. She might be able to give me some good ideas about what to do. At the same time, it was all very embarrassing. How could I expose myself to possible ridicule by telling her about my problem? I vacillated.

"I guess all is not rosy in Loveland," she teased. "Your hesitation tells it all." She laughed easily. I thought she might laugh at me, at my impotence.

"Tell me," she continued. "What's the trouble?"

I continued to waver. I was finding out that it's a hard thing to talk about even when you want to talk about it.

"I think I know what it is," she said. "It's the same trouble men have with women all the time. She doesn't want to suck your cock."

My expression must have made her think she had guessed correctly, because she focused in on that issue.

"Is that it? Boy, she doesn't know what she's missing. She should try you out and see how you fit. I know, I've been there. Your cock is great."

"Thank you," I said, "but you're the one that made that session go so well. You knew what to do. I didn't."

"Look. There's an easy solution," she said. "You continue to do all the things you do with her. The stuff she doesn't want to do, you come to me. That way, she doesn't have to do anything she doesn't want to do and you still get what you want. Everybody's happy."

"What about you?" I asked.

"I'll be happy if all I get to do is suck your cock. But maybe we could work out a deal for some extra benefits and we won't have to tell her about them."

"Man, that solution sounds great," I said. "Too bad it won't solve the problem."

"What do you mean? Why not?"

"Because that's not the problem. Toby is perfectly willing to do that."

"Bless her heart. So what's the trouble then?"

I faltered again. I had thought that talking about blow jobs would make it easier, but it only made it harder.

"You're the one?" She was guessing again, and I hoped she had guessed right. "I can't believe it, Hat. You can't refuse to go down on her, especially after she does it for you. Turnabout is fair play, you know? She deserves your attention as much as you need hers."

"No, no, no," I said several times before she heard me and let me break in. "That's not the problem either, at least not directly. The problem is…I can't get an erection."

The silence was deafening. If there ever was a time when you wanted the people next door to start arguing, this would be that time. Mary just looked at me with no sign of which direction she was going to go. Her expression was blank. Was she going to laugh?

I didn't think so, or she would have done that by now. Was she going to shrink away from me like I was a leper? That was hard to tell. Was she going to cry because she would not be able to enjoy what she liked so much? Then I recognized her expression. It was not blank at all. It was puzzlement. Her eyes narrowed, and her brow creased. Her lips pursed and lifted slightly on the left side. She was trying to figure it out. She finally broke the quiet.

"You didn't have any trouble at the church on Saint Patrick's Day. If I remember correctly, you were up and down several times that night."

"That's true," I said.

"So you just have trouble when you're with her, not with me."

"No. I had no trouble with her at all. In fact, it was always fantastic. It's just the last couple of weeks that I haven't been able to do it."

"Are you sure it's not just her? Have you tried with anyone else in the past weeks?" She moved her chair closer so that our knees touched to make sure I understood that she was willing to give it a try.

I understood that perfectly well, and the tingling in my balls made me think she might be right. Maybe I couldn't do it with Toby but I could with Mary.

"No, I haven't tried with anyone else."

This was clearly an invitation, and Mary did not miss the meaning. She slid her hand up the inside of my thigh, causing the tingling to spread across my groin, but she teasingly did not touch any private parts.

"Stand up," she said, taking my hand in hers.

She remained seated as I rose and stood in front of her. She unbuckled my belt and opened my jeans as I took a quick survey of the windows. The windows to the rear of the kitchen were uncovered, but they were high and small and faced the backyard. The one to the left was covered with curtains and sheer lace. I didn't think anyone would be able to see what we were doing unless they came right up to the window. That was unlikely.

She pulled my jeans down over my knees and left them there hugging my calves. There was no bulge in my underwear yet. She massaged me gently through my underpants. The sensation was thrilling, and the tingling spread to wherever she touched, but that was as far as it went. No erection.

I began to regret my doubting Toby. I should have known it wasn't her fault but mine. I was grasping at straws when I thought Mary might be able to do what Toby could not.

Mary dropped my underwear to reveal my flaccid penis. She took it in her hand and stroked to no avail. She covered it with her mouth and massaged it with her tongue, trying to suck the stiffness into it. It would not come alive. She sat back in the chair, disillusioned.

"I'm sorry, Hat," she said. "I've never had a problem like this before. I can't get it going. I don't know what I'm doing wrong. I'm so sorry."

"Mary," I said. "I told you it's me. It's not you. I had this unreasonable hope that it wasn't me, that the problem was with Toby, but I was wrong. I shouldn't have let you do this. Thank you for trying, but it's my fault and nothing can be done."

"I wish I was able to help you," she said, laying her cheek against my tense thigh. She kissed my limp member in one last ineffective attempt at arousal. "I was hoping to have some fun with this too."

"You still may be able to help me, and have some fun while you're at it. I have an idea if you're up for it."

"Oh, yeah? What's that?"

"You could teach me how to use my tongue. I haven't been able to satisfy Toby, but if I learn the proper techniques, I might be able to make her happy that way. Are you willing to do that for me?"

"Do you just want verbal instruction, or are you willing to practice on me?"

"I think specific direction and practice are necessary for me to learn. I want you to tell me where to place my tongue and my lips, how to move them, how fast or how slow, and then I want you to show me. I want to do what you say to do, and then you tell me if I'm doing it right or not."

"You might need a lot of practice."

"I'll practice until you say I've got it right. I really need to learn how to do it. It's my only hope of keeping Toby."

"You're doing this for her? You want to go down on me so you can make her happy?"

"It's the only way I can see to hold on to her."

"You really love her, don't you?"

"Yes. I'd do anything for her."

"Is this why you came looking for me today?"

"I didn't plan this. You just happened to appear as I was out for a walk. I think God intended for us to run into each other when we needed each other."

"So you think God sent you to me. I'm not so sure about that, but I do think this is my lucky day."

Chapter Fifty-Two

AS I SUSPECTED, Mary was an exceptional teacher. She taught me when to kiss, when to suck, when to lick, and when to thrust my tongue as deeply as possible. She taught me how and when to curl my tongue and how and when to flatten it. She taught me to run my tongue in circles, saying this was a critical skill. She was dedicated to the task of turning me into the best oral lover ever.

I was dedicated to learning everything she could teach me. We practiced all afternoon, and I'm certain that she had several orgasms, but she said that I still needed work on some of the techniques if I really wanted to satisfy Toby. I agreed to come over to her house again the next afternoon for more lessons and more practice.

Toby and I had dinner at her apartment that night. I didn't try any of the new stuff Mary had taught me. I decided to wait until Mary said I was ready. Besides, my tongue was really tired. Toby and I just cuddled in front of the television and watched *It's a Wonderful Life*.

It truly is a wonderful life if you're with the one you love. I was lucky to have my love with me, and I needed to make sure she stayed with me. I knew we would have dinner again the next night because we had made that a date. But beyond that, who knew?

There were four areas that I needed to address in order to feel secure with Toby, and three of them seemed to be under control. The four areas to address were sexual performance, academic performance, athletic performance, and conciliation of religious differences. Mary was teaching me to handle the first, and the makeup tests would resolve the second. I felt confident that Toby and I would overcome the religious difficulties, but athletic performance was the one area that troubled me. I barely made it through the first soccer season, and I knew that my physical condition was worsening. I didn't need Toby to tell me that; I could feel it.

But I didn't know what to do. I didn't know who to ask. If I brought it up to anyone, I ran the risk of exposing the problem to someone that would cause me to lose the scholarship. If that happened, all would be lost. For now, all I could do was bide my time and see what happens.

I went to Mary's house the next afternoon as promised. She didn't show me any new techniques, but she made me practice the old ones over and over again. She had at least two orgasms, and I began to think I had this mastered. I laid my cheek on her abdomen, inhaling her scent, and listened to her breathing as she gradually settled from hyperventilation to a slow rhythmic pace.

"I think I'm ready to try this stuff on Toby," I said once I knew she was fully relaxed. "You got off on it, right?"

"Oh, yes I did. Thank you."

"So am I ready?"

"Yes, you're definitely ready, Hat. And thanks to you, I'm ready too."

"What do you mean? You're ready for what?"

"I'm ready to break it off with Joe. I think the right time will be shortly after the New Year. I don't want to mess up his Christmas and all the parties coming up, but I don't want to drag it out either."

"What did I have to do with that decision?"

"What you said yesterday made me think more seriously about our relationship. I realized that I don't love him. Not the way you love Toby. He's more of a convenience than anything else. I don't want to spend my life with a convenience. And then today..."

"What about today?"

"Today you showed me that even the sex with him isn't that great. You gave me better sex today than I've ever had before, and you can't even get a hard-on. Oh, I'm sorry. I didn't mean to offend..."

"No offense taken. True is true. But, Mary, you can't just drop him because we had a good session here. You could teach him just like you taught me."

"No. That's not possible. You truly wanted to learn. It was easy and fun. Joe's not that way."

"I don't want to be the cause of your breakup."

"You're not the cause; you're the catalyst. You didn't write the letter; you just delivered it. The truth was always there for me to see; you just removed the blinders."

"You know that I can't continue to come over here every afternoon, don't you?"

"Of course, I know that. Once a week will be sufficient."

"Mary!"

"Just kidding. But seriously, you're welcome anytime. If things don't work out with Toby, or if you just want to get off the plantation once in a while, call me."

"Thank you, Mary."

I kissed her navel and then moved up to lie even with her. She rolled me over onto my back and placed her cheek on my breast, draping an arm and a leg over me. She moved her hand down over my stomach, over my abdomen, between my legs, and fondled my penis. There was no activity.

"Why do you think this happened?" she asked.

"I don't know why. I don't know a lot of things. But I'm sure of one thing: God has a plan for me."

"God made you lose your hard-on?"

"I don't know exactly. I do know He sent me Toby. I fell in love with her the moment I saw her, and now she loves me. That could only be God's doing. When this problem fell on me, He sent me to you for a solution. This will help save Toby for me. That, too, has to be God's doing. He has some plan for me and Toby that will be revealed when the time is right."

Chapter Fifty-Three

WHAT A FOOL I was back then! God's plan indeed! How could I have ever believed that God would put together a plan that involved afternoon sessions of oral sex with Mary Kelly that were supposed to save my love life with Toby? How convoluted was my thinking that I would even come up with that approach? How naive could I have been to think that such a process was reasonable? But I was only nineteen, I was in love, and I was in trouble. I was also desperate.

Now I'm twenty-six, and I'm not any better off. I lie in this hospital bed just as desperate and in greater trouble. God has not shown any master plan to me. All that has come of my life is one mess after another. There is no guiding principle that has developed, no philosophical answers have been revealed, and no singular accomplishment has been achieved that justifies my existence. I'm nearly at the end, and there is no time for triumph now. There is nothing. Ernest Hemmingway was right when he wrote, "*Nada, y pues nada, y pues nada*" in his very short story, "A Clean, Well-Lighted Place." I made fun of that story when I read it as a freshman in college, but now I find it describes my life. Maybe that girl in the front row was right when she said that the main theme was man's inhumanity to man. I made fun of her too, but what do I know?

As I think back on that time, I realize that the plan actually experienced some limited success for a short while. About two weeks to be precise. From a couple of days before Christmas until just after the New Year, Toby and I enjoyed oral sex often, and frequently it ended with orgasm for Toby. I don't think she was fully satisfied with that method, though, and she persisted in pushing me to see a doctor. Her faith in doctors and modern medicine was unshakable. If she could see me in this hospital bed today, with doctors galore around me and none of them knowing what's going on with me, and none of them having the slightest idea of what to do with me or how to treat me, I wonder how steadfast she would be in that faith.

But what other choice did she have? She wanted to have children, and that was not going to be possible with me if my condition continued. And she was concerned for me. She was as afraid of me losing my scholarship as I was. She was more fearful for my general health than I was. I would have gladly given up my ability to play soccer if it would guarantee a life with Toby. I would have given up sex forever if it would assure that I would have Toby by my side for just as long.

But those are not the kind of choices we are given in real life. My choices now are life or death. To be or not to be? It's as simple as that. It was so much more complicated back then, or so it seemed.

And then the New Year came, and as always January came with it. Bad things happen in January.

Chapter Fifty-Four

JANUARY 2, 2004, started out great. The sun was bright in a clear blue sky, and all the snow had long ago melted away. The air was unseasonably warm, the streets were dry, and the grass was Kelly Green on the lawns. If you didn't have a calendar, you might have thought it was April.

I was in the backyard resetting a fence post that had been pushed up by the ice in the last freeze when Dad called me in to the phone. It was my cell phone, not the landline.

"Good morning, Mr. Maloney," said a voice that was vaguely familiar. "This is Dr. Linda Leedy with the chemistry department. How are you today?"

"Oh, yes, I'm fine. How are you?"

"I'm very well, thank you. I'm calling to let you know that we have decided to allow you to take a makeup exam for the final that you missed in December. We made this decision based on your previous work in the course, and we believe that you were not trying to get out of an exam for which you were not properly prepared. We can administer this test on Monday or Tuesday. Which day would work best for you?"

"Monday is good."

"Fine. Can you come to my office at ten o'clock?"

"Yes, that's great. Thank you, Dr. Leedy."

I had barely clicked off when the phone rang again.

"Hello, Mr. Maloney. This is Professor Lutz. I wanted to see if you could take your makeup exam this Tuesday at nine o'clock."

It was a lucky thing that I had chosen Monday for the chemistry test.

"That's perfect, Professor Lutz. Thank you so much."

I returned to my task in the backyard. The resetting was easier than expected since the weather was good and the ground was soft. I patted the last of the loose soil around the fence post and took a minute to admire my work. The fence was tight, the post was straight, and in a day or two, the ground would settle and all would be secure. The day, the month, the year was going extremely well. It promised to get even better because I had a date with Toby that evening. We were going to one of her favorite restaurants, the Italian Garden, on East Washington Street on the far east side near Post Road.

Things seemed to be falling into place. By Tuesday the Is on my grade report would be converted to As, the GPA would be recalculated to 3.66, I would come off academic probation, and I would go onto the dean's list. There would still be problems to face, but I could face them one at a time and handle them. I didn't realize it was all a pipe dream and that January 2, 2004, was about to become the blackest day of my life.

When I went back into the house and Dad saw that I was finished with the fence post, he called all of us together in the living room. When he made announcements in this way, it was never good news. Good news would be shouted up the stairs or yelled into the backyard. "We're going on a picnic," he might bellow, and then the gathering would begin. This was different; this was going to be bad news.

"Your mother and I have had some long discussions," he began, "and we've consulted at length with her doctors. You all know that her condition is getting worse. The fact is that the cancer has spread beyond both of her lungs and is now in her brain and her ribs. It may have invaded other parts of her body as well. She is suffering intense pain, and the only thing that can be done is to treat that pain. There will be no cure."

Corinne burst into tears, and Dad hugged her close to him. We already knew these things to be true, but we never spoke of them. The telling was like a final confirmation and an admission of the hopelessness of the situation. None of us wanted to admit that, and none of us wanted to face it. Now that Dad had said it, it could never be taken back.

"We can no longer give her the care she needs here at home. The attention and the medicine required to quell the pain and to make her as comfortable as possible can only be given at a hospice that is designed for these conditions. Mother is going to move into the hospice this afternoon."

"Oh, Daddy," Corinne cried. "Why can't she stay here with us? We can care for her better than anyone else could."

"No, honey." Dad's eyes were tearing up also. "They have special monitoring, and they have access to all the drugs that will keep Mother out of pain. It will be easier for Grandma and Grandpa Sullivan to visit her there, and for her brothers too. I want her to stay with us just as you do, but this is best for her, for her comfort."

Mother didn't say a word through all this, but she shook her head in affirmation of all that Dad had said. Her eyes contained no tears but only a wistful misting, and her face contained no sign of fear but only a melancholy set of her cheeks and mouth.

An ambulance took Mother away. The siren did not shriek, the lights did not flash, and the tires did not squeal. It pulled slowly away from the curb as though it had all the time in the world. After all, there was no hurry. Mother was leaving her home for the last time, and there was no need to rush that.

Once Mother was settled in and adjusted to her new surroundings, we decided that she did not need the four of us hovering over her. We thought that rotating visits would be better for her and for us. Dad and Corinne decided to stay, while Brian and I went home. Grandma and Grandpa Sullivan were going to visit later that afternoon and would give Dad and Corinne a break. It was agreed that I should go on my date with Toby and Brian would come over later on tonight. I would come to see Mother tomorrow.

How quickly the irregular becomes routine. I always found that routines help you handle day-to-day difficulties by keeping things in their place and therefore making life more comfortable and predictable. This establishment of a routine was not so comforting.

The mail had already arrived when Brian and I got home. It was mostly junk, but there was one interesting piece. It was a letter addressed to me from the IUPUI Athletic Department. I tore open the letter, and my eyes immediately focused on a single sentence in the middle of the page. The sentence was in bold print. It read,

> *Due to your failure to maintain a cumulative GPA of 2.30 or better and due to your status on academic probation, which is in violation of your scholarship agreement, your athletic scholarship has been canceled effective immediately.*

My chin fell onto my chest; I dropped into the nearest chair. I closed my eyes and began to whimper. Brian came over to see what was wrong. I didn't answer his queries. I merely dropped the letter on the floor and continued to cry. He picked up the letter.

"You need to call your coach, Patrick" he said. When I didn't respond, he shouted, "Right now!"

I opened my eyes. "I tried to call him several times since I got my grade report. He's been out of the office on Christmas vacation. I've got the Incompletes taken care of with makeup exams. I thought the athletic department would know that or would check with those classes or at least would call me to see what's up before canceling my scholarship."

"Then you need to call the name at the bottom of that letter and explain that to him."

I called and talked to Mr. Ross, assistant athletic director, who could not help me. I needed to speak either to Mr. Wilson, the athletic director, or to Coach Harrison, both of whom were on vacation and would not be in until Monday. I decided to pay the athletic director a personal visit after the chemistry exam.

The day that had started out like a dream had turned into a nightmare, and it wasn't over yet.

Chapter Fifty-Five

I MET TOBY IN front of her apartment building, and we took the East Washington Street line out to the far east side. In spite of the mild temperature, we took our winter coats and gloves because the forecast predicted that cold, winter weather would return.

Toby and I seldom talked while riding the bus, and with the disagreeable happenings of the day, I was not in a talkative mood anyway, but I sensed a different edge to Toby's silence. I hoped her day had not been as bad as mine.

We didn't pick up conversation during the half block walk from the Indy Metro stop to the Italian Garden and had said fewer than twenty-five words to each other by the time we settled down in our booth.

The Italian Garden was a little mom and pop restaurant that was downscale in the furniture department but definitely upscale in the aroma and taste departments. The air was filled with the scent of tomato sauce and spices, the tang of Italian sausage, and the warm fragrance of freshly baked bread. The walls were decorated with prints of coastal scenes of Amalfi, Sorrento, and Capri, and Dean Martin sang of pizza pie moons, wine-enhanced stars, and Italian soup on the sound system.

The waiter was a big guy with broad shoulders and arms as big as my legs, reminding me of Rocky Balboa, but he handled the place settings with the finesse of an illusionist and magically set placemats, silverware, napkins, water, and bread before us in the time it took to remove our coats.

There were no cloth table covers and the napkins were paper, but the bread was magnificent covered with garlic butter. We knew from experience that the meatballs and the eggplant and the lasagna and everything else was good enough to write home about.

Dean Martin finished his serenade of *amore*, and Frank Sinatra began to croon of two ships passing in the night. Toby and I had not yet begun to talk. I thought someone needed to break the ice.

"So, how was your day?" I said.

"Fine." There was no expounding. There was no "how was yours" in return. Only silence. There had to be a problem. I like to take the direct route.

"Toby, is there a problem?"

"Yes, there is a problem, Hat. We need to talk."

"Okay, let's talk about it."

"I don't know where to begin."

"There's that much, huh?"

She gave me a distressed look. She didn't want to joke around, and she thought I was about to dismiss the problem with a laugh. I had to assure her that I would listen seriously to what she was about to say.

"Okay, Toby," I said. "Tell me what's up. We'll work it out whatever it is."

"You don't seem to be concerned about our future. You don't listen to me. And I can't trust you. How's that for a start?"

"Pretty intense. Can we do it one at a time? How am I not concerned about our future?"

"You have these important physical issues that impact all aspects of our future, but you won't address them. Your fatigue is scary. It's unnatural. It affects not only your soccer but also your school work and everything else. Last year in high school, you were the most vibrant athlete on the soccer field. This past fall you couldn't play more than five minutes without requiring a long recovery. And you're getting worse. Why won't you see a doctor? Why won't you try to find out what's wrong and get it fixed?"

"You're right. I do need to see a doctor. I've been afraid to go for fear that they would find something that would cancel my scholarship, but that doesn't matter now. I promise you I will go to a doctor next week."

"You've said that before."

"No, I mean it. I'll go to a doctor as soon as I can. I have my makeup tests scheduled for Monday and Tuesday, but I promise, right after that."

"Don't forget about the sexual thing too. That has to be related to the fatigue. How are we supposed to have children? You need to get that fixed."

"Okay."

"What do you mean, 'it doesn't matter now'? You said you were concerned about losing your scholarship, but it doesn't matter now. Why doesn't it matter anymore?"

"It still matters, but if I can't do what I need to do physically, I'll lose the scholarship anyway. I wanted to make sure I got at least two semesters paid before I risked seeing a doctor. I may have a problem with that anyway."

"Why? They'll pay your tuition next week, and you'll have two semesters paid for."

"I got a letter today saying they canceled my scholarship because of my incomplete grades."

"Oh, Hat. You didn't talk to them about your grades? You didn't call them like I told you to do? You see? You don't listen to me. You don't pay attention to anything I say."

"I tried to call Coach Harrison, but he's been on Christmas vacation."

"He went on vacation during finals week? I don't think so."

"I couldn't get hold of him. I thought they would check with the teachers or with me before they did something like this. But it may be all right. I'm going to see the athletic director on Monday after my chemistry test."

Toby studied the print of Capri. I knew she wasn't satisfied with my answer.

"Toby," I said. "I promise you. Monday afternoon I will talk to the athletic director. I'll explain about the grades. I'll show him my chemistry test results and my new grade. I'll explain to him that I'm taking the calculus makeup on Tuesday. He'll reinstate my scholarship. I'm certain of that."

She didn't appear to be impressed.

"I'll call a doctor and make an appointment before I go to take the exam on Monday. I don't know what to tell you about that, but I'll see what he says. I'll tell him the whole story, and I'll do whatever he tells me to do."

Things worked out great for Old Blue Eyes. He and his stranger lady friend became lovers, and all was "Scooby Dooby Do" forever after. Events were not going so well for me.

Toby opened her menu and took a shot at perusing it, but I could see that her heart wasn't in it. Over the sound system, Tony Bennett lamented leaving his heart in San Francisco. My heart was on my sleeve.

I had never seen Toby this way before. She didn't believe my repeated promises. She didn't want to hear my excuses. I understood her frustration, but I didn't know how to convince her that I was serious.

The waiter came by to ask if we wanted drinks. When we said we were happy with the water, he left us alone to decide about dinner, but he had succeeded in breaking her away from the menu.

"I love you, Toby," I said. "I'll do anything for you. I'll call a doctor first thing on Monday. I promise."

"Do you mean like you promised not to tell people about us at the blood drive?"

I'm not certain if a fly flew into my mouth or not, but it dropped open so wide and for so long it could very well have happened without me noticing.

"You look surprised. I guess you didn't think it would get back to me, but it did. I guess you didn't think it mattered to me, but it does. You told me you wouldn't say anything, but you did, and you didn't bother to tell me that you did."

I was stunned. I was totally unprepared. I had completely forgotten that I had told Joe and Mary about Toby and me. It seemed like a hundred years ago. It seemed like the world had turned inside out since I gave that blood donation that morning and all that transpired before it had become irrelevant. But it wasn't irrelevant. It was here to haunt me now.

I sat back in the booth, closed my mouth, and swallowed hard. I wiped my lips with the paper napkin and tried to regain some composure.

"It's true," I said at last. "It slipped out when I was talking with Joe DeMarco. I didn't mean to tell him. I was just talking, and I accidently gave it away. I'm so sorry, Toby. I didn't intend to do it."

"And you didn't intend to tell me about it either."

"I'm sorry I didn't tell you. So much happened after that...I just forgot about it."

"You broke our agreement, and then you forgot about it."

"I gave blood and got sick. I was so sick I missed classes, I missed two final exams, I couldn't—"

"Yes. I know all about your problems, and they're so much more important than any little promise you may have made to me. You think you're the only one that has problems. Well, you are wrong."

"I'm sorry, Toby. I am truly sorry. I didn't realize it was that important to you. You know I would never hurt you intentionally. It was a slip of the tongue. I forgot about it because I was sick and I didn't see you right away to tell you about it. I didn't know it was so important, or I would have paid better attention and I would have never said anything in the first place. I love you. Please forgive me."

She didn't forgive me right then, but she was softening. She didn't throw it back at me; she just let it hang out there in the air with the smells of spaghetti sauce and Italian sausage and the sounds of Italian singers.

"Please trust me," I said. "I will never hurt you again. I will keep my promises. I love you. Please forgive me and let me make it up to you."

She took a sip of her water. She was definitely coming around. She didn't commit, but I knew she was considering it. That was half the battle, and I was sure I had won that half. In a minute she would go the rest of the way, forgive me, and I would be home free. This time I would follow through. I would call a doctor first thing on Monday, take my exams on Monday and Tuesday and get my GPA back up, see the AD on Monday afternoon and get my scholarship back, and love Toby for the rest of my life.

"Can I trust you, Hat?"

"Absolutely."

She looked questioningly into my eyes. I hoped she saw sincerity there. She needed to see it, not hear it. She needed to feel it, to believe it.

Like a man drowning in the sea, I fell into her eyes as I had so many times before. I couldn't speak. I was mesmerized, but that was okay. There was nothing more to say. It was up to her now.

"Oh, Hat," she said, softly. "I…"

Her eyes suddenly swung upward and to the right, and her expression changed to surprise and confusion. I snapped out of her spell, regained my senses, and turned to see what had caused the abrupt shift in mood.

Striding menacingly toward us was Joe DeMarco, anger flushing his cheeks, tension pulling at his clenched jaw and tightened lips, and hatred filling his piercing eyes. Toby and I instinctively drew back as he approached. He came swiftly upon our booth and pounded his fist hard on the table edge. It was fortunate that we had not yet ordered dinner, for the spaghetti would have been on the floor. Toby's glass of water was safely in her hand, but mine found its way into my lap.

"You son of a bitch!" Joe shouted. "You've been screwing around with my girl. I'm going to drag you outside and beat the shit out of you."

"Joe! Calm down!" I said as I lifted the now empty water glass from my soaked blue jeans.

Joe threw a punch, and his fist caught me squarely on the outside corner of my left eye. A searing pain shot through my eyes and forehead as my head snapped back and my legs kicked out. If we had been at an open table rather than in a booth, I would have toppled over, chair and all. As it was, my head was cushioned by the booth back, and the only thing to reach the floor was the water glass that fell from my hand.

Landing the punch took a lot of the steam out of Joe. Rather than pursuing his distinct advantage, he stepped back and simmered. I covered my eyes with my hand and shook my head as the pain subsided.

"How could you do that?" Joe shouted, not quite so loudly. "You're supposed to be my friend."

Toby had been frozen with surprise by Joe's unexpected appearance, but now she spoke up.

"What's this all about?"

"Your boyfriend has been sleeping with my girl." Joe was beginning to control his anger. He did not shout his response, but his voice cracked with emotion. "Now she wants to break up with me."

Toby turned to me, waves of fury undulating across her face, her sea-green eyes bright with rage. "So I can trust you? Absolutely?"

"Toby, it's not like that."

"Oh, yeah?" Joe said. "She told me all about your problem getting it up. It's like that, all right."

Toby threw her water in my face.

Before I could recover from the shock, she was on her way to the door. I rose to chase after her but was confronted by the waiter. He must have thought I was going after Joe to continue the fight because he stepped in front of me, blocked my movement, and forced me back into the booth.

"Settle down, boy," he said. "This fight's over, right now."

"My girl…" I said, pointing to the door.

"All of you are out of here," the waiter said, "but only one at a time. She's gone, so you go next." He pointed to Joe. "And I don't want you guys meeting up in the parking lot to finish things off. If you do, the police will be here to settle up."

I sat frustrated as Joe left. I wanted to rush out to Toby to explain, to set things right, to win her back. But Rocky Balboa could crush me with only one of his mighty arms, and he didn't want me following too closely behind Joe. I had to sit and wait my turn.

I don't think it mattered. I don't know that I could have set things right with Toby anyway. What was I going to say to her? I did it for you? Even though that was the truth, it sounded so hollow now.

How could she possibly believe that I spent two full afternoons in bed with Mary Kelly and the only reason was to try to learn how to become a better lover for her? It was a likely story. It was something you made up on the spot when you didn't have time to concoct a better excuse. It was like telling her I could read the expression in her voice and know whether the answer was *Sí,* or *No.* I wish I had seen the absurdity of it earlier. I wouldn't have done it.

Or maybe I would have done it anyway. Mary Kelly was a seductive girl, and the time I spent with her was erotic and fun. I might have been fooling myself, telling myself I did it for Toby, when all I really wanted was to have Mary. I remember that there was the thought in the back of my mind that I might be able to get up for Mary when I couldn't for Toby. It was a blind shot, but I took it anyway, and then I rationalized it away.

Rocky Balboa let me leave. He cautioned me again about not mixing it up with Joe in the parking lot or any place near the restaurant. He even invited us back when we were on friendlier terms.

I rushed out to the street to see if Toby was still waiting at the Metro stop. I saw the doors close behind her as the bus pulled away from the post. I had missed her by seconds. She found her way to a seat without looking my way. I couldn't tell if she was crying or steaming. I didn't know how I could alleviate either response.

I considered chasing the bus and flagging it down, but the next stop was probably two blocks away and I didn't think I could run that far. The bus would not stop unless someone was waiting at the sign. I watched as it lumbered through the green traffic light a block away. Like the ambulance took Mother away from her home, that bus steadily and surely took Toby out of my life.

Chapter Fifty-Six

WASHINGTON STREET IS long and straight. I was able to watch the running lights of the bus for about five blocks before it became impossible to distinguish them from the many other traffic and Christmas lights. At that point, I hung my head low, knowing that the last cord between us had been severed. I felt my chest tightening and my lungs constricting as my eyes blurred and my world spun. I staggered sideways and leaned against a parked car, gasping for air. I bent over at the hips and placed my hands on my knees, metronomically inhaling and exhaling in purposeful breaths as though my body had lost the ability to perform these involuntary functions on its own. I didn't know that breaking up had actual physical responses, but here I was, having a heartache attack.

"Are you okay?"

Joe DeMarco was standing a few feet away, unsure of whether to help me or leave me in my misery. I waved a hand in signal that I would be all right in a minute. I knew the physical reaction would pass, but would I really be all right?

"I think I just lost my girl," I said, straightening my back but not yet standing erect.

"I guess that makes us even then," he said.

I leaned against the parked car and tried to straighten up. I managed to unbend a little more and was able to look Joe in the eye.

"I'm not the reason that Mary broke up with you, Joe. Yes, I talked to her about it. She said she wasn't sure what she wanted to do. She didn't know that you intended to give her your pin until that morning over at the high school when you told me. I just advised her to ask herself what she wanted for herself before she made a commitment to you. I said it wasn't fair to you for her to let you think you were on your way to a permanent relationship if she was going to back out later. Was that wrong?"

"Yeah, right," he sneered, "you were just thinking about me, concerned for my welfare, when you jumped into the sack with my girl. I'll tell you what, though, I'm glad you can't get a hard-on, because Mary will never be satisfied with half a man. I know she'll come back to me because I can give her what she wants and you can't."

"Joe, you're wrong about that. There's nothing between Mary and me. I'm not in love with Mary. I'm in love with Toby Rosen."

"Yeah, and I'm glad your brother knew where you and Miss Rosen were going tonight. This was something that had to be done in person with both of you there. I loved the look on your face when she threw that water on you. Priceless!"

There was no use in arguing any further with Joe. What good would it achieve? I needed to save my best arguments for Toby. I had to get her back. Maybe after she has slept on it, she would be more receptive to explanation. Maybe she'd think about how much she loved me and needed me and would find it in her heart to forgive me. The stuff I did was stupid and unfeeling, but we couldn't let it get in the way of our happiness. I'd make it up to her somehow.

Joe decided he had won the battle and left in his car. I had not put on my coat in my hurry to catch Toby before the bus came, and the night air was turning cold. I shivered as I slipped into my coat and pulled on my gloves. I continued to shiver as I walked to the corner bus stop. Snow began to fall. I was not warming up in spite of wrapping my scarf around my face and neck and pulling my stocking cap down over my ears. I remembered the bus stop on New York Street on December 12 when I got so depressed in the cold. That was nothing compared to this. Back then I still had Toby on my side. How could I have gotten depressed knowing she was still with me? I never considered that I might not have her. Now I had to consider it. It was reality.

The snow fell in earnest. It stuck to the parked cars and on the sidewalks and on the awnings in front of the stores. The wind picked up and blew the snow sideways, beautiful white streaks across darkened windows. Traffic thinned as though all those drivers knew exactly when the weather would change and planned their trips so they'd be home when the first flake fell. No one moved on the sidewalks. Everyone was where they wanted to be on this cold night. Everyone but me, that is.

I was not where I wanted to be. I wanted to be with Toby. In the Italian Garden, at her apartment, on the bus—it didn't matter. I wanted to be with her. I wondered if I would ever be with her again. I shivered as the winter stormed around me.

Chapter Fifty-Seven

DAD AND I went to the hospice together on Saturday, but he stayed for only a short while. He'd been working six nights a week for extra money and had worked Friday night. This was after getting no sleep during the day on Friday when we took Mother to the hospice. He didn't want to leave her on Saturday afternoon, but he would have collapsed if he didn't go home and get some rest.

The hospice was a quiet place. The patients and their visitors alike were waiting out the final days of their disease. There was no hope of recovery. There would be no joyful reunions; there would be no returning home. A hushed mood of calm acceptance permeated not only the people but also the walls, the furniture, the very air we breathed.

I sat at Mother's side as she drifted in and out of sleep. Each time that she awoke, she asked for ice chips. We kept a cooler with ice and soft drinks near the bed to accommodate her. I picked out a small chip of ice and ran it across her dry lips. The melting ice gave her temporary relief and made me feel like I was doing something useful.

"How was your date with Toby last night, Paddy?"

"It was fine, Mother," I lied.

"Where did you go?"

"The Italian Garden."

"What did you have to eat?"

"Um…we had, um, spaghetti and meatballs."

"Both of you?"

"Yes, why not?"

"You both had the same thing?"

"Yes, Mother," I answered, a little too snappy. There was no sense in worrying her about the fight. How could I explain that to her anyway?

"I'm sorry that we never had her over for dinner. I would have loved to meet her."

"She would have loved to meet you too."

"It's okay with me if she wants to come over here. It's not like having her at home, but…"

"I'll tell her."

Mother closed her eyes. I wasn't sure if she had gone to sleep, but I welcomed the opportunity to drop the subject. My future with Toby was uncertain, and I didn't want to have to go into details about it with Mother. Then she surprised me by changing the subject herself.

"Your grades will be fine, Paddy," she said without opening her eyes. It was as though she was reassuring me. "I know you have taken care of that. I'm not worried."

"Yes, Mother. There's no need to be concerned."

"I wish you would have your supper at home, though." She opened her eyes and turned her head toward me. "You don't have the same vigor you've always had. I do worry that you're letting yourself get run down with that cafeteria food all the time. Corinne makes a fine meal, you know, and your father has come a long way in the kitchen himself."

"I think I'll eat at home more this semester," I said.

She was satisfied with that answer and turned her head back to gaze at the ceiling. Eventually she closed her eyes and drifted off to sleep.

When Mother slept, the silence was suffocating. There were no sounds of conversations or laughter or music or radios or televisions. No one or no thing would dare break the somber mood that cloaked the building like a fog of gloom. Even the brightness of the sun reflecting off the snow outside the narrow windows could not penetrate the thick curtains and dispel the darkness and shadows within.

I took a can of root beer from the cooler. The spritz of opening the can resounded throughout the room and echoed down the hallway, disturbing the quietude with its impertinent release. Mother opened her eyes and turned my way to see what had caused the sound.

"I'm sorry," I said. "I didn't mean to wake you."

"No problem," she said. "I wasn't really asleep."

Minutes passed without a word until finally I asked the question that had been on my mind for more than a year.

"Mother, were you always in love with Dad?"

"From the moment I first saw him in church at Our Lady's. He was quite a big boy, you know, and I couldn't help notice him among all the other little fellas. I knew right away he was the one because God told me so. It took some time to convince your father of it, though."

"So God wanted you and Dad to be together?"

"Of course, He did. He wanted you and Brian and Corinne to come into this world. That could only happen if your father and I married."

"God told you this?"

"Paddy, God doesn't speak like you and I speak. God puts the knowledge that you need in your head and in your heart. You know what God needs you to know to follow His plan. I saw your father, and I knew what God's plan for us was. I didn't need to hear a voice to hear God."

"Is it like that with everyone?"

"I believe it can be. If you open your heart to God, He will reveal His plan to you. You only have to ask Him."

"How do you know that it's God speaking? Maybe it's just wishful thinking. Maybe it's the devil."

"You will know in your heart that you are doing God's will. The devil cannot fool you unless you want to be fooled."

"What about this, Mother?" I gestured about the room. "Is this God's will?"

"Yes, it is. I have fulfilled my purpose on earth, and now God is calling me to be with Him."

"Why doesn't He want you to be with us?"

"Only He knows the answer to that."

I wasn't content with her reply, but I couldn't think of any more questions that might lead me to satisfaction. She went back to sleep, and I brooded.

Chapter Fifty-Eight

I CALLED TOBY THAT evening. I wanted to give her time to think things over, but I didn't want to give her too much time. If we were going to get through this bump in the road, we needed to do it pretty soon.

Mother's remarks about knowing God's plan gave me the courage to act quickly. I knew this was God's plan. I fell in love with Toby the minute I saw her in high school, and I think she fell in love with me then too. She resisted because of the teacher-student issue, but then she sought me out at IUPUI when that was no longer a problem. Maybe she enrolled at IUPUI just to be with me. It had to be God's will that we be together.

She didn't answer the phone, so I left a voice mail. "I love you. Call me." Maybe she was in the shower. I sent her a text. "I love you. Please call me." She didn't call. I gave her forty-five minutes before I sent another text. "I have a doctor's appt on Wednesday. I love you. Please call me." She didn't call. Maybe she left her phone somewhere. Maybe she left it at the Italian Garden when she rushed out last night. Maybe she didn't want to talk to me.

I gave her another forty-five minutes, and when she didn't call, I decided to call her using Brian's phone so she wouldn't recognize the phone number on her caller ID. She answered on the second ring.

"I'm sorry, Toby," I said to the deathly silence on the other end of the connection. "I know it sounds bad, but I can explain everything. You just need to know that I love you."

Silence.

"Will you give me another chance? I love you, but I can't explain it over the phone. I need to see you, to talk with you. Will you meet me tonight?"

Silence.

"I made a doctor's appointment. Wednesday afternoon. I'll get everything taken care of. I'll do anything you want. Please, just give me a chance."

Silence.

"Toby?"

"I don't think we should meet tonight," she said.

"Tomorrow? You name it. Any time is okay with me."

"I don't think we should meet tomorrow." Her voice was as cold as the winter blow that I felt on East Washington Street last night. I had never heard that chill in her voice before.

"What do you want to do?" I ventured.

"I think we should break it off, Hat."

"Break it off?"

"I think that would be best all around. I think we have too many differences and too many problems to make it work."

"We can work out all the problems. Love can find a way, remember?"

"Yes, I remember. But you don't want to work out the problems, Hat. You just want to keep kicking the can down the street. That's not how I handle things."

"I will. I promise. I'll do anything you want."

"I think it's too late for us. I'm going to find that Jewish doctor and make my mother happy."

"You can't live someone else's dream," I said. I felt like I was talking to Mary Kelly.

"It's my dream too, Hat. It's what I really want. I want to find a nice Jewish boy, doctor or not, where there aren't all the complications. I want to raise my kids in a nice Jewish family and not be concerned about whether my husband is going to die any minute of exhaustion or skip his appointment because he was afraid to see the doctor or convert back to Catholicism for whatever reason. I don't need the complications."

"I pledge to you I won't go back. I'll start the conversion right away. I'll be Jewish before you finish your degree."

"No, Hat. You won't. I won't let you. We need to stop now. We need to break it off now."

"What about God's plan for us? God meant for us to be together. We need to follow His plan."

"That's enough! We are finished. I'm sorry, Hat, but I don't want you to call me anymore."

"But, Toby…"

"Goodbye, Hat."

That was the last I spoke with her. Not a fun and friendly conversation like we used to have. It was tense and curt and cold as the January night.

When I looked out my window into that night, I saw the bleak future ahead of me. A future without Toby was no future at all. Where did this fit in God's plan?

There was no plan.

Chapter Fifty-Nine

I TOOK THE CHEMISTRY test on Monday morning and scored 97 percent. I didn't even have to think. It was all automatic. While I waited, Dr. Leedy graded the test, submitted the results, and changed my grade from Incomplete to an A. She gave me a copy of the signed change report to show to Mr. Wilson, the athletic director.

My meeting with Mr. Wilson was a waste of my time. He was impressed with my grade but said the decision was not his to make. I needed to talk with Coach Harrison. If he agreed to reinstate my scholarship, then it would be done. I scheduled a meeting with Coach Harrison for the next afternoon.

Tuesday morning I took the calculus test and scored 100 percent. Professor Lutz was not available, but the graduate assistant had the authority to change my grade. She also gave me a signed copy of the change report. My GPA jumped from 1.79 to 3.66 in two days. The graduate assistant also gave me a printout showing my new GPA.

I was nervous as I approached Coach Harrison's office. I hadn't talked to the coach since the last soccer match, and I wasn't sure what his reaction would be. I should have felt confident that he would be pleased with the new grades, but he was an unpredictable sort.

"Maloney," he bellowed, as I entered his office. He rose from his desk chair and extended his hand. I shook his hand with as firm a grip as I could muster. I knew he loved a firm handshake. "Sit over here." He pointed toward two leather chairs at the side of his desk and moved into one of them. I sat across from him.

"What can I do for you?"

"I'd like you to reinstate my scholarship, sir."

"Well, I can't just do that. You are on academic probation and have a GPA below scholarship standards, you see. You have violated the terms of your scholarship."

"My grades were Incompletes, not F'. The 1.79 GPA was incorrectly assigned and has been corrected. The Incomplete grades have been changed to As, my GPA has been changed to 3.66, and I am now on the dean's list."

I handed him the grade change reports and the new GPA printout. He studied them as though he would be given a test on the content. He handed them back to me with a smirk.

"Those are fine results," he said. "I'm really happy that you have turned that around and gotten your head together. A good education is something you will never regret. I was afraid when I saw your report that you would be flunking out of school, but I see now that you are going to do fine."

"So you will reinstate my scholarship?" I asked.

"No, I'm afraid not. You did go on academic probation, even though it was only temporary, and your cumulative GPA was below the 2.30 minimum allowed. It's above that minimum now, but the terms of our agreement required that it never go below that level. As I said, I'm glad that you have recovered from that mess, but I can't give you back the scholarship. I'm really sorry about that."

"This is not about my grades. You've wanted to take my scholarship ever since I showed up for practice. You've just been waiting for an excuse that you think you can get away with. You could snap your fingers right now and I'd have that scholarship back, but you don't want to do it. Why is that? What did I ever do to you?"

"That's not it at all, Maloney. If I could bend the rules, I would, but I can't. I'm just the coach. I do have to tell you that I was disappointed in your on-field performance this fall. The way you played in high school, I thought you had the makings of a superstar. But you picked up that cigarette habit, and it just destroyed your ability to perform athletically. I don't understand why you did it, but you just ruined yourself."

"I have never smoked a cigarette in my life."

"Well, you could have fooled me."

"Coach, there's something physically wrong with me. I don't know what it is, but it's sapping my strength. I'm telling you the truth. I have never smoked cigarettes or anything else for that matter. I have a doctor's appointment this week, and I'm going to find out what the problem is. When this problem is eliminated, I will become that superstar that you saw in me. Please give me a chance. I need the scholarship, or I won't be able to stay in school. I won't let you down, Coach."

"I'm afraid you've already let me down, boy. No, I'm not giving you the scholarship. There are other kids out there that are dying to go to school. That scholarship is going to one of them."

"But, Coach, just give me this semester. I'll prove to you that I can play. You won't be able to get a replacement student that quickly anyway. You won't be able to get anyone until next fall. By then I will have shown you what I can do."

"I already have your replacement, Maloney. He's going to enroll next week for the spring semester."

"But, Coach…"

"This meeting is over. Goodbye, Mr. Maloney."

"But—"

"Get out of my office."

Chapter Sixty

I DIDN'T TELL ANYONE about my meeting with Coach Harrison and the loss of my scholarship. Brian was the only one who knew about my letter, and he went back to Ball State on Sunday night. My semester didn't start until the twelfth of January, but his started on Monday the fifth.

I don't know why I hid it from Dad and Corinne. I guess I was too embarrassed to talk about it. Over spaghetti and meat sauce, Corinne asked about my test results, and of course, I had good news to share on that front. I showed Dad my new grade reports and the printout of my new GPA.

"So you made the dean's list after all," Dad said. "I guess I shouldn't have doubted you, son. I'm sorry that I did."

"Dad, there's nothing to be sorry for." I felt guilty letting him apologize when he was actually right. I had blown my chance for a college education. I would have to drop out of school. I didn't understand the value of school, or I would have never let this happen. Dad was right about me all along, yet now he was apologizing. I wanted to tell him, but I couldn't bring myself to do it. I was ashamed.

"I'm glad you got that cleared up, Paddy," Corinne said. "I was worried that you were going to flunk out."

I looked her way, and her expression suddenly changed from cheerfulness to puzzlement. She could always read me, and this time she read me perfectly. She knew there was more to the story than I was telling.

Corinne and I cleared the table while Dad went upstairs to sleep awhile before going to work for the night. She and Dad had alternated visits with Mother that day, and he was worn out. I ran hot soapy water into the sink to prepare to wash dishes while she put the leftover spaghetti and sauce in containers in the refrigerator. When the first washed and rinsed dish reached the drying rack, she snatched it out with a dish towel and began to wipe it dry.

"So, you now have a GPA that's worthy of the dean's list. Tell me, what is the problem with that?"

"No problem."

"Paddy, I know when there's a problem, and there's a problem now. So why don't you just tell me what it is?"

"There's no problem. My grades are what you see."

"Hmmm. So, how are things going with Toby?"

"Fine."

"Oh, so there's a problem with Toby too?"

"No, there are no problems. My grades are good, Toby's good."

"I can't help you, brother, if you don't confide in me."

I briefly considered telling Corinne the whole sordid tale but quickly decided that I could not. I was too embarrassed, too ashamed. It would be humiliating to admit to my kid sister some of the things I had done. She knew things were not right, but she didn't know just how wrong they were.

"I told you, there are no problems. I'm just tired. I took two draining exams in the last two days, and I'm tired. Okay?"

"Okay. But you better not be too tired to go visit Mother tonight. Daddy and I spent most of the day with her, but she needs your company tonight."

I spent Tuesday evening at the hospice with Mother. I told her about the changes in my grades and my GPA, but I didn't tell her about the meeting with Coach Harrison and the loss of my scholarship. Why worry her? I would eventually have to tell everyone and own up to it, but not tonight. It's all just too complicated.

"Paddy," Mother said, "Your father and I are so proud of you. We knew you'd get those grades up to where they belong. You will be a fine engineer one day. You'll build great bridges and safe roads."

"I hope so, Mother."

How could I become a fine engineer when I no longer had my scholarship? So what if I had the brains? So what if I had the drive to take the tough courses? So what if I had the will to do the heavy lifting. Lack of money was going to prevent that from ever happening.

"I know you will," Mother said. "It's in God's plan for you."

"What do you mean? Did God tell you that?"

"Not in so many words, Paddy. God doesn't usually work that way. But it's obvious that He has given you the talent and the intelligence to make that happen. You've chosen that field because He has led you in that direction. Your purpose in life has to be to complete His purpose."

"So everything has a place in His plan then," I said. "How can that be when so many things don't fit? So many people live lives that have little meaning. Some die before they have a chance to accomplish anything. Kids drop out of school before they learn enough to be productive in society. How does all that fit in God's plan?"

"We don't see God's entire design, Paddy. We only see a small part of it. I've been lucky enough to understand my role. Many people don't get to see even that small bit."

"Your role is to leave us now when we're all so young?"

"My role was to bring you into this world, to raise you to be a good, God-fearing person, and then join Him in heaven so I can learn the totality of it all and watch you fulfill His promise."

I couldn't hold back my tears as I realized how much I had let her down. She didn't know it yet. She was intent on Brian and me and Corinne making as much of our lives as God gave us the ability to accomplish. I had thrown it all away. I dabbed at my eyes and wiped the tears from my cheeks.

"You don't need to cry for me, Paddy. I'm going to where I want to be, where I'm supposed to be."

She had misunderstood my tears, but I let that go. She didn't need to know why I cried. I leaned forward and kissed her on the cheek.

"I love you, Mother," I said.

"I love you too."

We didn't say any more, and she closed her eyes. I thought she was asleep for the next twenty minutes, but she suddenly spoke as though there had been no lull in our conversation whatsoever.

"Why does it take so long?" she asked.

"What?"

"Why does it take so long to go to heaven?"

Chapter Sixty-One

THE PHONE RANG at just after ten o'clock. Dad was getting ready to go to work, and I was lying awake fully clothed on my bed. I knew what the call was about as soon as the phone rang. We all knew. I heard Corinne rush from her bedroom into the upstairs hallway. I continued to lie on the bed until I heard Dad open the door to his bedroom.

"Oh, Daddy," Corinne cried.

I stepped into the hall and saw Corinne clinging to Dad, her face buried in his shirt. Dad gazed over her head at me, a tear forming in his eye. He motioned me to join them, and we stood together there at the top of the stairs.

"I've got to call off work," Dad finally said. "Then I'll call Grandpa Sullivan. Patrick, will you call Brian?"

I had never made a call like that before, nor had I ever received one. I had no idea what to say when Brian answered the call. I could only sniffle into the phone.

"Patrick," Brian said, "has Mother passed away?"

"Yes." I was relieved that he had taken up the burden that I could not carry.

"I'll come home tomorrow."

My only previous experience with death in the family was when Grandpa Maloney died in 1993. I was only eight years old and didn't understand what was going on. I stood on the sidelines back in 1993, and I did the same in 2004. Dad made all the arrangements with the church and the Oakley Hammond Funeral Home. He wrote the obituary for the *Indianapolis Star* and the *East Side Gazette*. He called many of our family members and asked them to pass the word. The funeral would be on Friday.

Corinne was only five when Grandpa Maloney died, but she must have been paying closer attention than I was. She dove right into the preparations for Mother's wake. She started baking cookies and cupcakes and pies on Wednesday morning, and she called Dad's sister, Aunt Mary, to get the women in the family organized. They would work out the provision of meals during the mourning period.

People began showing up at the house.

Aunt Mary came over at noon with two large chicken casseroles for our dinner that night and a brown bag full of bologna, lettuce, and tomato sandwiches for our lunch. She had spoken that morning with Aunt Maggie in Boston, who would be flying in with her husband on Thursday afternoon and would need to be picked up at the airport.

I volunteered to do this and was grateful to have a task. I was the only one, it seemed, that didn't know what to do.

Soon after that, Dad's brother, Uncle Joe, arrived carrying a case of Miller High Life. He asked me to get the bag from his back seat. When I retrieved it, I noted that it contained two fifths of Jameson Irish Whiskey. The case of beer was stored in the refrigerator, and the two bottles of whiskey were stowed in the cupboard next to it.

Others stopped by, bringing food, drink, and other supplies, including more beer and more whiskey and offering sympathy to the family. All stayed only briefly as they knew we were busy making arrangements. I wasn't busy, but Dad and Corinne surely were.

Dad met Brian at the door when he showed up at around two o'clock. He had been standing by the window watching out for him. The two of them hugged long in the cold with the front door standing open.

Corinne came bounding out from the kitchen and joined the embrace, while I stood awkwardly off to the side. Corinne noticed, as always, and opened her arm to me. I stepped into the circle, and we four were as one.

The wind blew cold, and we broke our hug to close the door. We sat in the living room while Dad filled us in on the plans. There would be open showings at the Oakley Hammond Funeral Home tonight from seven to nine, Thursday afternoon from one to four, and Thursday evening from seven to nine. Father Ben would lead a prayer at the funeral parlor at about eight o'clock Thursday night, and the funeral Mass would be at Our Lady of Lourdes Church at eleven o'clock Friday morning. The funeral home was just across the street from the church at 5342 East Washington Street, so everything was conveniently close.

Dad and Brian and I wore coats and ties to the funeral home. Corinne produced a black dress that I didn't know she owned. She was lovely, as she always is. All of the visitors were family that night since word would not get out as quickly to friends. Even so, the showing was crowded. Both Dad and Mother came from fairly large families, and they were there in force. Mr. Oakley led the family in prayer shortly before closing, and we took the cue and headed home.

Most of the family followed us home. I don't know how we fit everyone into those small rooms in our small house, but somehow we managed. There were Dad's two brothers and Mother's six brothers and their wives and Dad's older sister and her husband and a number of their children. Grandma and Grandpa Sullivan and Grandma Maloney were there as well. I think there were upwards of thirty-five people or more in our little house.

I remember that Grandpa Maloney's wake was an unruly affair with rowdy family stories and loud laughter and much singing and more drinking. But Grandpa Maloney was sixty-eight when he died, and his death was not unexpected. Although Mother's passing was certainly anticipated, she was only forty years old and her youth put a damper on the celebration.

Things started slowly. There was quiet talk of everyday events and quiet tears shed sparingly. Cookies and cupcakes were consumed calmly, and drinks were nursed. I opened a Miller High Life even though I seldom drank beer and sat in the kitchen with Dad and Brian and others.

Uncle Joe moved about the house with a bottle of Jameson and gave everyone a shot, even those too young to drink whiskey legally. Once everyone had their shot in hand, he stood in the center of the dining room where all could see and hear him unimpeded. He cleared his throat with a soft cough, which brought everyone in the house to silence and raised his glass to the heavens.

"She was a fine woman," he said. "Too fine for the likes of you, Michael Maloney, but for some reason she chose you and she surely made you a better man for it. She gave you these three fantastic kids, and although she was with you for only a short time, she gave you a lifetime of wonderful memories. Here's to Kathleen."

I gulped down my shot along with the rest of the family and felt the burn all the way down. I coughed in reaction, and my eyes began to water while memories of Pleasant Run Park flooded back. I decided I would toast with beer for the rest of the night.

Somber tributes to Mother by Uncle Bill and Aunt Mary followed, but Grandma Maloney got everyone to laugh when she asked Mother to say hello to Grandpa Maloney, assuming he was actually up there in heaven.

Then the stories began to flow. Mostly they were family stories of youthful exuberance and friskiness, weddings gone awry, Saint Patrick's Day parties gone to beer and whiskey, and newspaper route tales of families that hid behind the curtains when the carrier boy came to collect payment. All the men in both the Maloney and the Sullivan families had been altar boys at Our Lady of Lourdes Church. Altar boy stories dominated the night.

The funniest story, I thought, was about Dad and Uncle Bill serving as altar boys for Aunt Mary's wedding. In those days they had Sanctus bells on the steps of the altar for the server to ring three times during the Mass. They were first rung during the consecration of the bread and wine into the body and blood of Christ. The server is kneeling on the bottom step of the altar at this point in the Mass. The bells are to be rung again when the priest presents the Host, which is the body of Christ, to the congregation, and again when the priest presents the chalice filled with wine, the blood of Christ. If the servers are to participate in Communion, they are to kneel on the top step of the altar to be given the host, so after the server rings the Sanctus bells for the consecration, he places them on the top step so they will be at hand and can be rung during the presentation of host and chalice. This is a simple matter of routine during the Mass. Part of the routine is to place the bells back on the bottom step after the third ringing. This piece of the procedure was forgotten by Dad, and the bells remained on the top step after Communion was over. Later in the Mass, the altar boy must move the enormous Bible and the book holder from one side of the altar to the other. The Bible and book holder are carried in such a manner that the altar boy cannot see any obstruction in his way. Of course, there is not normally any obstruction in the way of moving the Bible, unless one forgets to place the bells back on the bottom step of the altar. After Dad lifted the Bible and book holder, he proceeded across the altar, tripped on the bells, and sent them tumbling down the altar steps, loudly ringing out the music of the error Dad had made as they rolled all the way to the altar rail. Dad and the Bible also went tumbling down the steps, chasing after the bells. The Bible flew across the floor, skidding to a halt at the foot of the pulpit while Dad did a belly flop at the foot of the altar. Steam was streaming from Aunt Mary's ears as she watched this spectacle from her place at a kneeler just inside the altar rail. Uncle John, the groom, her husband-to-be, was laughing out loud.

The same thing was true tonight. Aunt Mary didn't see the humor in that story and endured it with a scowl while Uncle John enjoyed it with a howl.

Grandpa Sullivan had been a fine Irish tenor in his youth. He had even tried to make the big-time as a singer in New York City, and at age seventy-eight, he could still croon with the best of them. Tonight, he brought tears to the eyes of all around by singing "I Will Take You Home Again, Kathleen." Then Mother's brother, Uncle Liam, broke out with "Sure, It's the Same Ol' Shillelagh" and got everyone to singing. "When Irish Eyes Are Smiling" and "If I Knock the L from Killarney" soon followed. After a rousing rendition of "McNamara's Band," we sang our own made-up verse that went like this to the same tune:

Oh, Ireland was Ireland when England was a pup,
And Ireland will be Ireland when England's time is up.

Well, I'm an Irish Catholic and I go to Sunday Mass,
And every Limey son of a bitch can kiss my Irish ass.

Mother always said that she didn't like our singing of that verse. She thought it was crude. We always sang it anyway, and she always laughed when we were done.

The wake went on well into the night with song after song, story after story, and toast after toast. I restricted my drinking to beer alone after the first commemoration, and by the last, I was certainly glad that I did. Several of the men were drunk and the wives drove home. Aunt Mary appeared to be sober, but she asked her husband, John, to drive this night.

Finally, only the four of us were left: Dad, Brian, Corinne, and I. We all wanted to go to bed, but at the same time, we wanted to linger. The closeness and harmony of the family was a sustaining feature of the gathering. Dad and Brian had not restrained themselves as I had. If we were out somewhere, they would have asked me or Corinne to drive them home.

"Now what am I supposed to do?" Dad asked.

"Mother is where she is supposed to be, Daddy" Corinne answered. "It's what she wanted."

"Yes, I know," Dad said. "But why couldn't she have been with us for just a little while longer?"

"She didn't want to remain in this world with her disease. She wanted to join God in heaven where she would be cured."

"But how will I live without her?" Dad began to cry.

"We will all have to learn how to do that," Brian said.

We sat silently at the kitchen table for four or five minutes, and then Dad announced that we all needed to get to bed. Tomorrow was going to be another busy day.

Chapter Sixty-Two

FUNERALS AND WAKES are for the living. Mother didn't need the toasts and tributes; she was far better off than we were. Dad needed the support of his brothers and sisters. The joking and drinking and singing were their way of standing by him in his time of need. Grandma and Grandpa Sullivan needed the support of their other children in the same way. We all needed to have family around to help us get through the first few days. I wondered how we were going to handle it once everyone left and we had to restart our lives without her. That's when it would get really hard.

Thursday's activities were similar to Wednesday's. Food and drink arrived in the morning, visitation was conducted at the funeral home in the afternoon, I drove out to the airport to pick up Aunt Maggie and her husband between showings, and we went back to the funeral home in the evening.

There were many more visitors that evening as word of Mother's death got out and friends and neighbors joined the family in mourning. The wide parlors of the Oakley Hammond Funeral Home were overflowing, and extra chairs had to be brought out. Some of the visitors congregated on the sidewalks outside but crowded into the funeral home when Father Ben gave the prayer at eight o'clock. After that the crowd slowly dispersed.

The party at the house Thursday night was as rowdy as Wednesday's. It was mostly the family once again, but a few others joined us. Mr. Allen, from down the street, stopped in and spent most of the time quietly observing from a vantage point near the front of the living room. During a lull in the singing and the storytelling, he pulled me to the side and gave me an offer of condolences.

"I'm sorry about your mother, Brian," he said. "I had a lot of respect for her, and she is certainly going to be missed in the neighborhood."

"Thank you, Mr. Allen." I didn't bother telling him that I was not Brian. "I really appreciate you saying that, and I will pass it on to my dad."

"This is kind of an unusual party, isn't it?" he continued. "I mean, with your mother passing away and all."

"No, sir," I said. "We celebrate the passing of a loved one as a joyous occasion. We tell family stories and sing favorite songs to honor our mother and our family. She's gone to where she was meant to be from the beginning, so we are happy for her. We celebrate."

He nodded his head and said, "I see."

I also saw. I had not thought of it in those terms until I spoke the words. The speaking helped clarify it in my mind and helped soothe the pain in my heart. Yes, it was going to be a tough adjustment living without Mother. We were all so used to having her near and seeing and feeling and touching her and being touched by her love. Yes, there were many more tears to be shed. I didn't kid myself in that regard. Yes, there would be an emptiness that no person could fill, a need that could never be satisfied, a vacuum that would forever be left void, but she had finally moved on to where she wanted to be. Her extended wait was over. It took a long time for her to go to heaven by her own reckoning, but I'm sure it was worth the wait. With this realization, I knew we would move past our grief and survive this loss.

Mr. Allen shook my hand and shook me out of my reverie. "Thank you, Brian," he said. "I've got to go home now. Thank you for having me over."

"Thank you for coming, Mr. Allen."

I meant that sincerely.

Chapter Sixty-Three

I CONSIDERED GOING OFF to school each day and pretending I was still enrolled just so I would not have to tell Dad that I had lost my scholarship. I could probably get away with that for the entire semester. I would have to face the music when it came time for grades, but later would be better than sooner. Right? I could spend my time studying on my own. I could buy the books for the classes I had scheduled. You didn't have to be enrolled to use the bookstore. Maybe I could become a self-educated civil engineer. I could take the certification exam and prove that I knew the stuff without having to produce a degree. I could fulfill God's promise, as Mother saw it, and follow His plan even though I had totally screwed up the process thus far. Perhaps I could redeem myself that way.

Who was I kidding? I had no intention of completing the course work. This whole idea was just a ruse so that I would not have to fess up. I didn't want to tell Dad—or Corinne, for that matter—that I had failed him and Mother and the family. I didn't want to have to admit that I was a screw-up and a failure. I was a coward.

Dad, Brian, Corinne, and I spent Saturday and Sunday unwinding together at home. The many family and friends that had spent the previous several days with us had moved on and returned home. They left behind much food, so we only had to warm up lasagna or reheat the beef stew or microwave the chicken casserole and we had our meal. School started again for Corinne on Monday, and Brian also needed to be back at Ball State for class on Monday. Dad did not have to return to work until Monday night. We had the weekend to relax and reflect on what had occurred the previous week.

On Sunday afternoon, as we four sat quietly in the living room, Corinne brought things to a head.

"So, what classes are you taking this semester, Paddy?" she asked innocently.

I had not yet decided on whether I was going to confess or deceive, so I stalled for time.

"I, umm, I'm taking the next level class in the series in both chemistry and calculus." I had not thought my deception out far enough to have come up with a class schedule. I could not remember what the natural progression was for a freshman civil engineering student.

"That's not a full schedule. What else are you taking?"

"I haven't decided."

"I thought you had to register for your classes last week," she said, suspicion creeping into her tone.

"Yes," I said, not sure of how to proceed. I looked at Brian and then at Dad. Both of them wore expressions of doubt and misgiving.

"I'm going to audit two classes for a week to see if I want to take them," I continued. "Eastern religions and European geography."

I was a terrible liar. That was one skill that I had never mastered. I didn't fool anyone. Dad, not being familiar with how college courses worked, was unsure but unbelieving. Brian and Corinne knew right off that I was lying.

"And if you decide not to take those courses, what then? Audit some other courses? Come on, Paddy."

Corinne was on to me. I couldn't carry the lie. I might as well confess.

"I'm not registered for any courses." I paused, and then continued. "I lost my scholarship. I had to drop out of school."

It was easier than I thought it would be. Once the central truth was out, the rest was effortless. I merely had to tell the story—edited, of course.

Dad was clearly disappointed but still supportive. He said he would go with me to see the doctor once I rescheduled my missed appointment. He also said he knew of a place that was accepting applications for employment. Perhaps I could work and save some money and return to school in the fall with the help of a student loan.

Brian said he would check with the student affairs office at Ball State to see what other sources of financial aid there might be. Corinne said she would do the same with the high school guidance counselor. My family came to my support so swiftly I was startled. I had expected Dad to fly off the handle, but he didn't. I had expected Brian to chastise me and Corinne to give me a good talking to, but they didn't. All three accepted my predicament and rallied around me, giving me ideas on how to proceed and encouragement to do so. I wished I had talked with them when my troubles first started. I saw now that hiding my problems was a big mistake. I vowed not to make that error ever again.

On Monday I scheduled another doctor's appointment for Thursday afternoon, and I put in three applications for jobs at Precision Propeller, Robert's Welding, and Sparkling Image Car Wash. It took me all day to make those three applications. I had never applied for a job before and didn't realize how frustrating it could be. There was never enough space on the form to answer the question, even if the inquiry was merely for your address. One would think that application forms for a business located in Indianapolis would allow room to write "Indianapolis" in the city space.

None of these businesses was very interested in my level of education. There was one line that asked for the last grade of school attended. Graduated? Check yes or no. There were many lines allocated to previous jobs, with starting and ending dates, job descriptions and duties and responsibilities, reason for leaving, supervisor's name, and other related data. There were a lot of blank spaces in these areas on my applications. This was not a good sign.

I figured that I needed to get a lot of applications out in order to improve my chances of landing a job. I set a goal to make at least six more applications the next day. I managed to get seven applications filed.

I needn't have bothered because Precision Propeller called Tuesday evening with a job offer. They must have been impressed by my high school diploma. I could start work the next Monday.

Chapter Sixty-Four

THE DOCTOR'S APPOINTMENT on Thursday was set for three o'clock, but I went over to his office in the morning to visit the lab. They wanted lab results to be available for the doctor when I showed up at three. I was concerned about this visit because they needed to draw blood, and I feared a reaction like the one in December at the blood drive. I need not have feared. They drew barely enough to fill a small vial, and my sole reaction was a brief dizzy spell. I was glad that I had given the urine sample first so I needed only to sit a few minutes in the waiting room until I was recovered.

Dad went with me to the afternoon appointment to provide moral support. It wasn't necessary that he do that. I wasn't afraid of the doctor any longer—I was actually looking forward to a treatment—but I appreciated his effort all the same. The problem with his presence, though, was that I was too inhibited to discuss my erection issue with the doctor. I provided details about my poor soccer performance and my severe reaction to giving blood and my problems taking my final exams, but I never mentioned an erectile dysfunction issue.

The doctor found that I was mildly anemic and suggested that I take iron supplements. I told him that I had taken iron last month and it didn't help. He suggested I give it more time. He had no answers and no further suggestions. He did not think a referral to any type of specialist would be appropriate. It was a waste of our time and money. We had plenty of the former but damn little of the latter.

After the disappointing doctor visit, there was little more that I could do. I had to hope he was right and that eventually the iron supplements would solve my problem. I should have known that was a fool's choice. My devastating reaction to the blood donation and the impact that had on my final exam performance should have warned me that this was no simple case of mild anemia. How could mild anemia have destroyed the wonderful relationship that Toby and I enjoyed? But I was only nineteen years old and didn't know any better. Dad was older and certainly wiser, but he didn't have all the facts.

The one good thing I had going was the job with Precision Propeller starting on Monday.

Chapter Sixty-Five

PRECISION PROPELLER MADE boat propellers, both aluminum and steel. I was assigned to the steel plant. I knew nothing about propellers, steel, or hard work. That's not to say I didn't earn my keep. As an adolescent I earned money with a paper route, cutting grass, shoveling snow, and other odd jobs around the neighborhood. I contributed half my earnings to the household fund and was allowed to keep the other half. I could spend or save as I desired. I mostly saved. After all, what did a kid have to buy? But I had never encountered work that was as exhausting as what I did at Precision Propeller.

I was hired in as a general laborer. That meant I had no specific skills and had to be placed into a job that I could learn quickly and where I would become productive right away. That meant I became a sand mold hookup. I would also be available to fill in when the regular guy called off work.

My first day on the job, after I was issued my hard hat and safety glasses, I was placed with another laborer named Bruce Glover, who showed me the ropes. I learned the location of the shower and locker room, where we would also eat lunch. I learned that I needed to get a padlock so I could claim a locker to store a change of clothes. Bruce let me put my brand-new plastic lunch bucket next to his dented metal lunch pail in his locker for today, but tomorrow I was on my own. I learned that I needed to bring a towel but not soap or shampoo, which was provided. I was advised that shaving in the shower or at the sinks was frowned upon, but brushing teeth after lunch was accepted and expected. I was also cautioned to never forget deodorant because there were always girls looking for sweet-smelling guys at the Sunset Bar and Grill down at the corner of Twenty-First Street and Ritter Avenue. I learned many other important things like these from Bruce before I ever set foot in the actual work zone. Eventually, however, we had to go out on the floor and get some work done.

When we left the locker room, we entered directly into the foundry. This was a huge open room about half as long as a soccer field and a good forty to fifty feet wide. On each side of that width, vertical steel support beams stood like soldiers in a column, spaced about twenty feet apart, extending to the far end of the room, creating a large work bay. These I-beams held up a slanted metal roof about sixty feet over our heads. At about half that height, they supported a double track for an electric overhead traveling crane that ran the length of the building.

A few steps into the work bay area, I realized it had a sand floor. The sand was intended to absorb and restrain any molten steel overflows, help the steel cool and harden, and contain the splash area so that once the steel cooled, it could be lifted into the scrap barrels.

To my left was a long pit running in front of three massive furnaces that stood shimmering in the hot dusty air that swirled around them. I remembered the giant boiler back at Howe High School, which had the same magnitude but not nearly as much attitude. From their position at the head of the work bay, these three ruled the foundry. When the first furnace arrived at its appropriate level of temperature and liquidity, it sounded a warning horn like a fire drill alarm that echoed throughout the work bay and brought all other work to a standstill. The electric overhead traveling crane rumbled down the elevated tracks carrying an enormous steel bucket with a pour spout protruding from the front and what looked like a steering wheel on the side. The crane operator expertly maneuvered the bucket into the pit in front of the first furnace.

I was momentarily blinded by a searing brilliance when a gate in the furnace face was opened and a dazzling sun-like radiance burst through the dusty foundry air. When my eyes adjusted to the glare, I saw that there was a pour spout on the furnace as well. A hinged base allowed the furnace to be tilted forward, and a river of red and yellow molten steel flowed, like lava down a volcanic mountainside, smoothly into the bucket. When the bucket was full and the oven was empty, the furnace returned to its original upright pose and the crane moved the bucket up the bay and positioned it over sand molds that had been prepared and placed on the sandy floor.

Bruce handed me a shovel and motioned for me to follow him as he followed the crane. The bucket operator used what I had thought was a steering wheel but was actually a gear mechanism to tilt the bucket forward. The spout on the bucket was much smaller than the one on the furnace, and the stream could be very accurately controlled. The steel ran easily into a guide hole at the top of each sand mold then spread out and covered the top of the mold when it was full. As the crane and bucket moved from mold to mold, Bruce and I swathed each completed mold with sand to help it cool. This was the first productive task I performed for Precision Propeller, and it felt good to be doing something useful rather than talking about lunch and soap and shampoo and showers.

When all the sand molds were filled, the crane carried the bucket off to some unknown destination up at the far end of the bay. The bucket operator followed the crane, but Bruce and I did not.

"Good job," he said as we stowed the shovels in a tool closet. "Well done."

I smiled at him. This was not differential calculus, and the task of shoveling a coating of sand over steel-filled molds was not a job I would ever expect to screw up, but this was his life and he was proud to do the job well. "Thank you," I said.

"Now we've got to stock that furnace for the next heat," he said. "We've got about two hours before ol' furnace number two comes up. During that time we need to restock number one for tomorrow's work. Those molds we just poured will cool off while we do that, and they'll be ready for us to deliver them up to the shakeout when we're done stocking. Then we'll have to put out those new molds across the floor to be ready for the second heat. Two hours is plenty of time to do all that, but we can't dally. You follow me?"

"I follow you. Lead on, Macduff."

"What's that?"

"Yes, I follow you." I needed to be careful with my literary references. Bruce was not a literary man. He was a man of the girls at the Sunset Bar and Grill down on the corner of Twenty-First and Ritter.

The crane reappeared carrying a barrel that was even bigger than the bucket it had just taken away. The barrel was about half full of scrap steel. The crane operator placed the barrel alongside the first furnace and waited while Bruce disconnected the hook.

When Bruce opened a door in the side of the furnace, I expected a wave of bright light and heat to wash over us, but the oven had cooled in the time it took to pour the molds, and although there was still plenty of heat inside, it was not enough to overwhelm us standing next to it. Bruce stooped over and peered inside.

"You see those electrodes up there?" he asked, gesturing at three large conical features pointing down from the top of the oven like stalactites in a cave—a very bright cave.

I stooped over and saw them and nodded my head.

"Always be sure they are retracted clear to the top when you stock one of these ovens. If you break one of them, they cost about a million dollars, and they will break if you throw a piece of scrap steel in there and hit one."

I nodded, knowing he spoke from experience.

"The furnace operators always retract them after the heat, but just to be sure they're completely out of the way, I push the Up button right here before I throw anything in there."

I was surprised to learn that the furnaces were electric. I'd assumed that it was necessary to burn coal or coke in order to generate enough heat to melt steel, but Bruce informed me that was the case for making steel from iron, not for melting it. He told me about a steel mill up in Gary where he used to work that had gas furnaces. In that plant they didn't make the steel or melt it. They just wanted it hot enough to do mind-boggling things with it, like punch a hole lengthwise through a thirty-foot-long, two-foot-diameter solid steel cylindrical ingot to make a seamless tube. Unbelievable!

We spent the next half hour tossing bits and pieces of scrap steel into the oven. Bruce would select a piece, lift it from the barrel, turn, and toss it into the oven. While he turned and tossed, I selected and lifted; and while I turned and tossed, he selected and lifted. This slow process was not the main source of stock for the furnaces but was a way to recycle scrap. There was another primary loading mechanism that was automated that fed small blocks of steel into the ovens. We fed mostly arms and stems from the propeller molds, and once in a while, we found a malformed propeller blade.

Manually loading the furnace was draining work. I had to stop to catch my breath several times during the thirty-minute exercise, but Bruce kept right on selecting, lifting, turning, and tossing each time I paused. I felt like I wasn't carrying my share of the load, but I simply could not keep up, even though I was twenty years younger than Bruce.

Once the scrap barrel was empty, we returned to the sand molds on the floor. They were now cool enough to handle, and we had to deliver them to the next operation to make room for the next set of molds for the second heat. Bruce showed me how to hook up the chains so the crane could carry the molds. Each mold was a steel-encased cylinder about two feet high and two and a half feet in diameter with four-inch-long steel posts protruding horizontally at the four compass points. The trick was to drop a chain below two of the posts and another chain below the other two posts. This provided stability to the connection when the crane lifted the chains so the cylindrical mold would not tip over and spill out its sandy contents. One mold could be set on top of another, and the chains easily dropped to the lower mold. Four molds could be taken each trip in this manner.

Bruce told me to follow the crane up to the shakeout and release the chains from the molds whenever the crane operator placed them on the floor. I was to wait there while the crane returned with empty chains back to Bruce to pick up the next load of molds. This was significantly less physically demanding work, and I was easily able to keep up the pace. In fact, there was quite a lot of dead time while I waited for Bruce to stack up each load.

I used the dead time to watch the shakeout operator. She had her own smaller hand-operated crane and a set of chains that she used to lift the molds one at a time from the floor and place them on top of the shakeout table. The shakeout table consisted of a set of steel roller bars that vibrated, bounced, and jiggled with a noisy clamor. There was sufficient space between the bars for the loose sand that resulted from all the vibration to fall under the table, away from the mold casing, and away from the newly formed propeller blades. When most of the sand was removed, the remaining casing and propeller blades were rolled off the table by hand. The blades were to move on down the line to the next step in the production process, while the casings were to be returned to the mold building section.

I had read about the assembly line process in school but had never witnessed it firsthand. I always imagined that it was like that old *I Love Lucy* episode where Lucy falls behind in the timing and screws up the whole process. This was nothing like that. There were staging areas between steps, so there were not production backups. The molds the shakeout operator was working on were from yesterday's heats, not today's. The individual jobs were more involved than merely screwing the same part in place over and over again. Each job contained various tasks and had a distinct beginning and a distinct end. There was an element of accomplishment even in the simple task of getting the molds from the pouring floor to the shakeout. I could see what we had achieved that morning in the piles of molds standing at the shakeout and the cleared space on the sandy pouring floor.

Once the floor space was cleared, Bruce and I helped the crane operator move new molds into the pouring arena. The whole process was repeated as the second furnace produced a second heat then repeated again with the third heat from the third furnace. The workday ended once we placed the last mold on the pouring floor in preparation for tomorrow.

Chapter Sixty-Six

WORKING AT PRECISION Propeller was rewarding in many ways. The pay, a couple of dollars over minimum wage, was good for an inexperienced nineteen-year-old. Of course, this was important, but I also realized a good deal of satisfaction by being a productive member of the team. I learned the value of getting up and showing up for work every day. I saw that others depended on me to do my job so they could do theirs. It was not unlike the soccer team where each player had his role to play. The passer needed a receiver, the driver needed a blocker, and we all needed the goalie or all would be lost. We even needed the relief guy so the starters could get a break. Once again, as a general laborer in this propeller plant, I was the relief guy. It was a valuable position, and these were invaluable lessons.

But the work took a lot out of me too. My fatigue problem did not go away just because I was no longer in school. When the work was slow and steady, as when we moved the molds, I could handle it okay. But when we stocked the furnace from the scrap barrel, I could not keep up the pace with Bruce. If the bucket operator misjudged and poured a little excess steel into a mold, it would overflow onto the sandy floor, and Bruce and I would have to scramble to cover the overflow with sand. This small bit of extra exertion would deplete my reserves. Then, after the overflow cooled, I had to dig it out of the sand and throw it into the scrap barrel. As a result, I was physically drained each day after work.

On top of that, the plant was not on the Indy Metro line, so I needed to walk six blocks to Twenty-First Street to catch the Metro.

The first leg went only about five blocks from Ritter Avenue to Emerson Avenue, where I had to switch lines to the southbound route. This leg took me the thirteen blocks from Twenty-First Street to Walnut Avenue, where I could walk the five blocks west to Wallace Avenue. This may not sound like much of an effort to get home, but in my deteriorated condition and after a full day of lifting and tossing scrap steel, I just wanted to collapse into Mother's recliner and not move for two or three hours.

After a couple of weeks of this routine, I thought it might be better if I rented a place close to the plant so I could walk to work. There was a place for rent on Bolton Avenue that was only a few blocks from Precision Propeller, and it was available immediately. I got two week's pay on February 6, and the bulk of that paycheck went toward the four hundred dollars rent for February. Dad paid the one-month deposit, and I moved in on February 7. The landlord didn't care that I was only nineteen or that I had been working only three weeks. He only seemed concerned that he got the full eight hundred dollars in cash up front.

The house was a small yellow brick duplex with a living room, kitchen, two bedrooms, and a bathroom on each side, all on one floor. A sliding window about four feet by eight feet consumed the entire wall next to the front door. There was no front porch but only a cement stoop at the top of three cement steps. The front yard sloped gently to the street.

Across the street was a playground consisting of swings, a teeter-totter, and a merry-go-round adjoined by an asphalt basketball court with two backboards and hoops, one at each end. Beyond the basketball court was an open grassy area large enough for a good game of football. The rest of that square city block was thinly covered with oak and maple trees and scattered picnic benches. The park made the street look inviting and friendly, although no one peopled it on this cold February day.

The back of the house also had a cement stoop at the kitchen door and a yard that opened onto an alley. The people in the other half of the double had three beat-up cars parked in the yard. Rust was the dominant color among these vehicles. One of them looked as though it had not run in years. Weeds grew high around the four flat tires, one headlight was busted, and the windshield had a crack running its length. The other two looked serviceable although decrepit.

I didn't own any furniture, so it only took a couple of hours to move. Dad let me take my bed, desk, and bookcase from my room, and Aunt Mary gave me her old couch that was stored in her basement. Cousin Kathy had a futon that she never used, and Uncle Bill provided a floor lamp. The furnishings were sparse, but it was plenty for me. Since I didn't know how to cook, I didn't need pots and pans. I bought some paper plates and plastic spoons, forks, and knives and was ready to face the world.

The next several months passed quickly. I spent my time either working, eating, or sleeping. Most of the time dinner was Domino's delivered pizza or double whoppers with cheese from the Burger King at Twenty-First and Arlington. I managed to buy lunch meat, lettuce, tomatoes, mayonnaise, and bread so I could pack a lunch for work and cereal, milk, and a single bowl so I could have breakfast in the morning. I spent the weekends at home with Dad and Corinne, sleeping in Brian's bed most Friday and Saturday nights. The Saint Patrick's Day Party at the church was my only entertainment, and Mother's absence put a damper on that event.

I had never experienced paying bills and was surprised that most of my paycheck was eaten up by rent, gas, electric, and water bills. The gas bill alone through February and March was astronomical. I thought that a small brick unit would be easy enough to heat, but apparently the key features for energy conservation are the windows. These windows leaked like sieves, especially the big sliding window in the front. I also noticed that the snow on the roof melted faster on my side than on the other side. It reminded me of the Van Landingham bungalow across from our house on Wallace Avenue. This meant poor or no insulation, but only on my side of the house. In late April, I had the heat turned off and still spent half the summer paying off the balance on the gas bill. Fortunately, the water heater was electric, and I could live without gas until next winter.

Looking back, I realize that the main reason I had trouble paying the bills was because I missed work on a regular basis. I was worn out. I often called off sick on Wednesday to give myself a break in the middle of the week. I was paid by the hour, so when I didn't work, I didn't get paid. The midweek breaks were necessary, however, or I would not have made it to Friday.

I knew that the people who lived next door had children because I could hear their screeching voices over the blasting TV through the walls, but I never saw anyone all winter. When I left for work each morning, all was quiet on their side. In the evenings there were lights and the television on in their home, but I never saw any people.

In February I had bought a plastic folding lawn chair so I could sit at my desk in the second bedroom. As the weather warmed in the spring, I spent more time in the evenings sitting in that chair in the front yard. One Wednesday, when I had called off sick from work, I sat in the bright three o'clock sun, enjoying the warmth and watching the budding trees in the park across the street lightly swaying in the gentle breeze. That's when I met Michael Jones.

My first impression of Michael was that he was built like a wall. After I got a closer look, I realized he was bigger and more solid than most walls that I knew. When he emerged from his home, I wondered that he was able to fit through the front door. He wore a T-shirt that was as big as a tent and that hung down to his knees, covering his shorts. The bright orange of the shirt set off his deep ebony skin, and the picture of Jimi Hendrix on the front was bigger than life. He had to go at least four hundred pounds.

"Hello, neighbor," I said.

A smile spread across his wide face, and his teeth beamed like polished porcelain. It was like curtains opening to the midafternoon sun in a dark room. This day was bright, but his smile was brighter.

"Hello," he replied.

Michael was a friendly sort, but he had an extremely bad case of body odor. The smell intensified as he approached me, and the waft of wind was not sufficient to disperse the stench. He was sweating profusely, and I guessed that he had not bathed in many days. That was no wonder, since I couldn't see him fitting into a bathtub or a shower.

He worked as a cook at the Bob Evans restaurant on Shadeland Avenue, mostly making omelets or fried eggs and bacon. The first thing he told me about his job was that they never gave him enough hours. He averaged around fifteen hours per week at minimum wage.

"How do you manage on fifteen hours a week?" I asked. I didn't tell him I made more than minimum wage. "I get between thirty-two and forty hours every week, and I can't pay all the bills. And you have a wife and a couple of kids."

"Three," he said. "I have three kids."

"I don't know how you do it."

That's when I met Latisha Pitts. She was tiny next to Michael. Anyone would look small next to Michael, but Latisha had a head start. She was all of five feet two inches tall and did not break a hundred pounds. She appeared from the side of the house, and when she walked into the mild breeze, I thought it might blow her away. She sashayed up next to Michael, and her pink T-shirt and light-brown coloring contrasted sharply with his orange shirt and black skin.

"Hi, I'm Patrick. My friends call me Hat."

"I'm Latisha," she said. "You're the new guy next door?"

"Yes. You must be Michael's wife."

"We're not married. He's my fiancé. If we got married, I'd lose the money for the kids. We like to keep it this way."

Michael Jones and Latisha Pitts had been living together for six years. They had three children ages seven, five, and two, which provided a healthy check from the government each month. Latisha also got a government check to pay for classes, which she attended every Monday, Wednesday, and Friday. She couldn't explain to me what the classes were training her to become. She only knew that she had to go to the classes or she would lose her kids' checks. Since she went to class, the government also paid for child care while she was in school, but this check went to her grandmother.

"That money can't go to the same address as where you live," Latisha explained. "My gran'ma gets it even though she don't never watch the kids. She's rippin' me off. I'm thinkin' 'bout changing child care services."

I didn't understand how they could get the government to pay for them to have kids. It didn't make sense to me, but they knew how to work the system. They told me they were on Section 8, which meant the government paid their rent. It also meant there were periodic government inspections, and three years ago the Section 8 people made the landlord put new tightly sealed energy-saving windows in their unit. They didn't make him change the windows in mine, so the old drafty, energy-wasting windows stayed.

Latisha brought Michael a straight-backed chair from her kitchen and then took the kids over to the playground across the street. Michael and I sat together in the yard. Fortunately, I sat upwind from him.

"So, if you get all these checks from the government, why do you work at Bob Evans?"

"A man's got to have something that he accomplishes in his life," Michael said without hesitation. "I make breakfast for dozens of people. I can see their smiling faces through the order window, and I know they're smiling because the eggs are good, done the way they want them done, and I made 'em."

I was just beginning to develop an element of respect for this man, when he started laughing. When Michael laughed, it sounded like we were in an echo chamber. His stentorian voice bellowed out each staccato syllable, which reverberated off the houses and the trees and drowned out the whisper of the wind. His whole body shook, causing his orange T-shirt to ripple with waves and causing Jimi Hendrix to dance as though he was into a rendition of "Purple Haze."

When he stopped laughing, he explained.

"All those checks she told you about? They're all made out to her. I don't see a penny of that money."

That was all he said, but I got the picture.

Chapter Sixty-Seven

MY ENERGY LEVEL started to pick up with the renewal of life in the spring. As the flowers bloomed and the trees budded and the birds returned from their winter migration, I felt rejuvenation in my whole being. The mild May temperatures were neither so cold, as in February, that they made you want to wrap up and stay in bed, nor so hot, as in August, that you didn't want to do anything but lie in front of a fan. I was able to work five days a week on a steady basis from May through late July, although I was bushed each evening after work. I spent more evenings sitting in the front yard, and my new friend and neighbor often joined me.

I began to think that my case of mild anemia, or whatever it was, had gone away on its own, my body had cured itself, or the iron supplements had worked a miracle. Sure I was tired every day after work, but who wasn't? The work at Precision Propeller was arduous, and it was not abnormal to be drained by the time the shift whistle sounded. But I was recovered by morning and able to make it back to work, and that was more than could be said for a lot of men.

But when a hot spell hit the Midwest the last week of July, I knew I was not cured of my ailment. The sun heated the air outside, while the foundry furnaces heated the air inside. Even the dark of night could not cool down the heat from the day. Temperatures ran from ninety-five at night to one hundred or more in the afternoon. It was even hotter in the foundry. I moved from one oven to another to another. I couldn't function in the oppressive heat. I called off sick twice that week in July and four more times in August, yet in spite of much shorter work weeks, I was still beat.

Michael found me sitting in my lawn chair in the backyard in the shadow of the house one Wednesday afternoon in late August. I had to escape the heat of the sun and of the house, but I was afraid to go into the park across the street for fear that someone from work would see me there.

"No work today, Hat?"

"I called off sick."

Michael had never mentioned the use of illegal drugs in the many times we had talked. He didn't mention it that day either. Without a word, he pulled a self-rolled cigarette from his pocket, lit it, and drew the smoke deep into his lungs. He held his breath in as he held the joint out to me. The sweet smell of marijuana drifted to my nose mingled with the sour stench of Michael's body odor. I ignored the body odor and took the joint from his hand.

I had never smoked anything before, not even cigarettes, the testimony of Coach Frank Harrison notwithstanding, but I had no trouble smoking that joint. I drew a full toke into my mouth and then inhaled a full breath deep into my lungs, just as Michael had done. I expected it to burn, not the heat of a shot of whiskey, but the burn of smoke from a bonfire, yet it did not burn. It went down as smooth as fresh air from the woods. I expected to cough it back out immediately, but I did not. I held it in as long as I could, which was not nearly as long as Michael did. He was the expert, and he had bigger lungs.

When I exhaled, he flashed his wide smile and held his breath in a while longer just to show me he could. When he finally did exhale, the stream of smoke was barely discernible. He had absorbed most of it.

"This is good stuff," Michael said as he moved over to the stoop at my kitchen door and sat. It's good that the stoop was made of cement, because I don't know of a wooden step that could have handled his weight. Once his butt settled, it covered the entire stoop with some hanging over the side. It was good that there was a gentle breeze blowing from the south so that the biggest part of his body odor drifted away from me toward the neighbor to the north.

"Let me have another hit."

I had no idea if this was good stuff or not, but I needed a diversion. The second hit was as smooth as the first one, and I started to relax. After several hits, I began to feel a little dizzy. Not so much from the grass, but from holding my breath. I felt little effect from the smoke.

When the joint burned down to a butt that was too short to grasp between his fingers, Michael placed a metal clip on the end and held the smoldering stub up to his nose so he could continue to inhale the smoke. He faced toward me, into the draft, so the smoke was brought up to his face.

"Now that's a roach you don't want to exterminate," he said in a squeaky hold-your-breath voice, while handing the bit over to me.

Following his lead, I turned away from him and faced into the breeze. I held the stub up to my nose and inhaled the smoke while closing my eyes to the stream that flowed around and across my face. This time it did burn some as the heat passed through my nostrils and my sinus cavity, but still I did not cough.

We burned through three joints. I don't know that I was high, but I was certainly relaxed. My legs felt heavy, and I knew that I would not be able to lift them when I tried to get up. It was good that I didn't want to get up. With closed eyes, I explored the feel of the afternoon heat burning into my cheeks even though at the same time I could distinguish the cool breeze on my face. I felt the hairs on my forearms stand up as the air moved over them, and a shiver ran up my arm over my shoulder and down the middle of my back. My body became as heavy as my legs, and I felt my torso melt into the plastic straps of the lawn chair and become one with it.

"Michael," I said without opening my eyes.

"Yo!"

"What did the Buddhist monk say to the hot dog vendor?"

"I don't know. What did he say?"

"Make me one with everything."

Michael didn't laugh, but I did. It started as a hiss and a snigger and a snort and evolved into a low chortle. Soon it developed into a full-fledged laugh, and my eyes even began to tear. I knew the joke wasn't that funny, but it took hold of me and wouldn't let go.

Michael's expression merely added to my delight. He didn't get the pun. His face was blank at first but changed to merriment as my laughter progressed. He too eventually began laughing without knowing what he was laughing about.

After a short while, our laughter subsided, and we sat quietly for a few minutes.

"So," Michael said, finally breaking the spell of silence, "he wanted everything on his hot dog?"

We started into another round of uncontrolled laughter and tears. I never explained that joke to him, and he never got it on his own.

Michael just wasn't all that familiar with Buddhist monks, but he did know a lot about other things. He knew a lot about some very important things.

I noticed a pair of tennis shoes dangling from the power line that ran across the alley. To get the shoes in that position, you had to tie the laces together, then, standing directly below the power line, toss both shoes up in parallel, one shoe to one side and the other shoe to the other side of the wire. When the shoes passed the line, the laces would catch on the wire and wrap around the line. Once they were in place, they could never be retrieved because everyone knew that power lines were dangerous and you don't mess with them.

That was the message. Michael informed me that the shoes were the mark of the local gang that haunted these alleys. It was like a dog pissing on a tree to stake his territory. If you wanted to operate in this neighborhood, you needed to deal with them.

I had never run into any gang members in the time I had lived there. Of course, most of that time was winter, and I was usually inside the house or I was at work. Even so, I did walk to and from work and down to the Burger King sometimes. I also walked over to the grocery store at Twenty-First and Ritter and returned with brown paper bags in my arms. I imagine I would have looked like an easy target for some gang to hit on. But I never felt intimidated or threatened by anyone. I guess gang members don't operate so well in the cold weather.

"Why waste a good pair of shoes?" I asked.

"They don't use their own shoes to mark," Michael said. "They take them from some kid to set an example."

"Have you seen them do it?"

"I didn't see this one, but I saw something worse when I lived over on LaSalle. There was a gang over there—a bunch of kids, fifteen or sixteen years old—that ruled the street. They had shoes up on the wire and graffiti on the garage doors and all that crap. They mostly were involved in some break-ins and stealing and other petty stuff, but they also sold drugs. Not just weed. Cocaine, meth, smack, you name it.

"One day this kid that lived a couple of houses down the street—he wasn't in with the gang—but he decided he was going to throw his old beat-up sneakers up on the line. I don't know why he did it but he did.

"Those hoodlums got pissed off big-time. They dragged that kid out into the middle of LaSalle Street in broad daylight and beat the shit out of him. Then they brought out a step ladder and a pair of hedge trimmers and made him climb up the ladder and snip the laces on those shoes. That kid was scared of the wire, but he was more scared of the gang. He went up and clipped those laces even though he knew he could get killed doing that."

"Didn't you try to stop it?" I asked.

"Those gangsters had guns. I would have been shot dead if I so much as moved off my porch. Latisha called 911, but the police didn't get there until after the action was over. They found the kid sitting on the curb, bruised and bleeding and crying, while the gang scattered."

"Did they catch the gang members?"

"No, man, no one said who they were. Not even that kid that got beat up. He knew better."

"How do you put a stop to that kind of stuff if no one will talk against them?"

"We moved over here about that time."

"And now there's a gang over here," I said, but the irony was lost on him.

I wondered what I would have done if I had been there and I had seen that beating. I'd like to think that I would have intervened, but then, we all think we would have intervened, yet so few of us actually do. We call 911 and the police arrive too late to do anything, and we think we've done our part. But then again, what good would it have done if Michael was shot and the police found him bleeding in the gutter next to that poor kid? The gang would have taken the kid out a few days later and done the same thing. Then they'd have taken Michael out and done him some more.

"Yeah, man," Michael said. "Now there's a gang over here, and you need to watch your step."

Chapter Sixty-Eight

THE HEAT WAVE broke one week later on Wednesday, the first of September. Around two in the morning, a thunderstorm shook me awake, rushing through the trees, splashing on the streets, and banging at the windows. I ran around the house closing the windows and securing the doors. My last stop was the front door, and by then I was completely out of breath. I leaned against the sliding window in the front of the living room and watched the rain beat down on the world outside. The rain was falling away from the house, so this window was not getting wet. I decided to open the front door and watch the storm from the front stoop.

I remembered many evenings in junior high and in high school sitting on the front porch with Mother, Dad, Brian, and Corinne, watching the rain. We often sat without a word for long periods, merely enjoying the wonder of God's world. I missed those quiet nights with my family. It seemed like years since I had moved from the family home, but it was only seven months. I was going to turn twenty years old in just a few weeks, and there I was thinking like an old man reminiscing about the good old days.

There's something about running water that is revitalizing. Whether it's a small stream or a great river or a placid lake rippling in the breeze or the ocean surf pounding on the shore or merely a light drizzle, flowing water has a soothing effect on me. A girl I once knew in high school told me that running water, especially water bouncing off rocks like a churning river or a waterfall, gives off negative ions that your body absorbs. She said these negative ions are good for your system and that's why people like to be near the water. I don't know if all that's true, but this thunderstorm invigorated me.

Or perhaps it was the break in the heat. The temperature dropped into the midseventies that morning, and I went to work even though I had planned on calling off sick again. Bruce was actually surprised to see me since Wednesday was my typical unscheduled day off.

"You need to be careful about calling off sick, Hat," he warned. "They're watching you. I get the feeling that if you had called off again today, they were going to fire you."

The possibility of getting fired had never occurred to me. I thought they just didn't pay you and that was it. I guess they actually want you to show up and do your job. With the weather getting back to normal, I was able to work five days a week again, and the threat of dismissal faded away.

But I still enjoyed partaking of a joint or two with Michael in the evenings and on weekends. He started making me pay for my consumption, but with the two of us smoking, we were able to buy in slightly larger quantities than he had before. This made it cheaper, so Michael welcomed my participation. The gangbanger that sold the weed to Michael also welcomed the increase in business.

I got the gas turned on again when the nights started to turn crisp in mid-October. There was no problem with Citizens Gas Company because I had paid off my account the previous summer, but there was a problem for me since I had grown used to not having a gas bill. Suddenly, I was paying for heat and for smoke. It was a good thing I was able to work the full forty hours a week.

Actually, it was good for only a short while. In December the weather turned bitter cold. We got little snow, but the wind must have been shipped in directly from the Arctic. The walk to work exhausted me even though it was only a few blocks, and I had to leave half an hour earlier to allow some recovery time once I got there. The cold took what little life energy I had and sealed it up in an ice box.

I called off sick twice in December. I would have called off more if they hadn't closed the plant on Christmas Eve day and New Year's

Eve day. But in spite of those two breaks, I called off sick again on Wednesday, January 5. The next day, on Thursday, January 6, they fired me. Bad things happen in January.

That morning, I went back to my half a double and went back to my bed and went back to my lethargy. I didn't know what else to do. I slept all day, but when I awoke, I did not feel refreshed. I took a shower, but I did not feel cleansed. I called Domino's Pizza for delivery, but when the pizza arrived, I did not feel hungry. I sat in my living room, nibbling half-heartedly at a slice of pizza, when my cell phone rang.

"Hello, Paddy," Corinne said.

She didn't have to tell me she was crying. I could hear the sniffling and the sadness in her voice. My first thought was that she and Bobby Mays had broken up. They had dated each other for several years, and Brian and I had assumed that they would eventually get married. Corinne had seemed as happy as ever when we were all together at Christmas and at New Year's, but these things could happen quickly. Look at how fast Toby and I fell apart.

"What's the matter?" I asked.

"Today's the day, Paddy," she said as she broke into a full-blown bawl, her breath catching in her lungs.

I could envision her pretty face streaked with tears, her eyes red and swollen. In my imagination, she wiped at her eyes with a handkerchief as she struggled to get her breathing under control.

"What day is it?" I asked.

"Today's the day that Mother passed away."

I had forgotten. One year ago today, my mother had died and I had forgotten. I was so wrapped up in my own problems that I didn't even think of her. I didn't think of Corinne or Dad or Brian either. It didn't occur to me that they might be struggling with the loss. It didn't occur to me that we might need each other's support on this black anniversary. As was becoming more and more typical for me, I didn't know what to say; I didn't know what to do. I sat for several moments with my mouth wide-open but with no words emerging from it. In that time, Corinne regained her breath and recovered her composure.

"Are you there, Paddy?"

"Yes, yes, I'm here."

"I miss her so much," Corinne said. "Sometimes I see her in my dreams, making breakfast or walking with me to Linwood Square. Sometimes I wake up and think it was all a nightmare and I'll run downstairs to see if she's in the kitchen stirring the oatmeal. She's not in the kitchen anymore."

"No, she's not."

It was a lame response, but I could do no better. I couldn't muster any wise words of support for my baby sister. I couldn't bring a spark of encouragement to my voice or a declaration of faith in God's plan and assurances that all would work out for the best. I didn't have it in me.

I didn't believe that anymore. I had lost my mother I had lost Toby, I had lost my scholarship, and that day, I had lost my job. All was not right with the world.

Corinne and I talked for a while about other matters. Her relationship with Bobby Mays was in excellent shape. School was going well, and her grades were good. I said my job at Precision Propeller was going fine even though I was very tired at the end of the day. She thought that was a normal thing, and she was glad that the job was working out so well.

I felt bad about lying to her, but I didn't want to burden her with my job loss. She had just recovered from her depression over Mother, and she didn't need to hear that I was fired. One fit of tears was enough for one day.

Or was I ashamed to admit to her that I couldn't handle working for a living? How was I going to explain this to her and to Dad and to Brian? "Oh, I didn't like going to work every day, so I took a little time off. You know, time for me." Right! That would go over big.

I couldn't answer those questions, so I didn't tell anyone.

I began to fret about my finances. I had already paid my rent for January before I was fired, so I was good for a month on that account. On Friday, January 7, I got paid for the last two weeks of December. They were both short weeks due to the holidays, and the check was proportionately short. I got another paycheck on Friday, January 21, but it was for only two days. I would soon be broke.

Chapter Sixty-Nine

MY NEW FRIEND and neighbor and smoking partner, Michael Jones, it turns out, knew a lot about how to survive when things turn bad. He had an overabundance of ideas that would help me get through the next few months. Not all of them were legal and none of them were morally upstanding, but the more time we spent discussing them, usually over a joint, the more appealing they became.

I decided not to pay my utility bills. Michael advised me that the government would not allow the utility companies to disconnect my utilities in the winter because that would not be humane. I wondered about the truth to that, but sure enough, I went all winter without paying for gas, electricity, or water, and they didn't turn them off. The gas finally went off in early April, but the electricity and water were still on when the landlord kicked me out.

Michael advised me on the landlord front as well. When February came, I didn't send in the rent as I usually did. I waited for the landlord to call me. He called around the sixth and told me he hadn't received the rent payment. I acted surprised and insisted that I had mailed him a money order just as I had each month for the past year. Fortunately, I had never missed a rent payment before that, and the landlord believed my story. I told him I would contact the PL$ Money Order people and put a trace on the payment. He said he would wait to hear from me. I didn't call him back.

I continued to delay payment of the rent with excuses provided by Michael. "They made an error in my paycheck and shorted me." "I was expecting them to send me an overtime check, but I hadn't received it yet." "We had a death in the family, and I had to pay for the funeral expenses since there was no life insurance." That one hit close to home.

Because of my first twelve months with a perfect payment record, and with Michael's guidance, I was able to stall off the landlord through February, March, and April. Finally, he gave me a notice to vacate the house by April 17. I would have moved out then, but Michael told me we weren't through yet. He said I didn't have to move until the landlord got a court eviction order. I knew this was true when the landlord angrily backed down and told me he would get that order. He said I had until May 3. Michael said that was the court date, but the court would give me until May 7, and even then, I would not have to move out.

"This is starting to feel like it's a game," I said as I took a hit on our shared joint.

"You bet it's a game," he answered. "If you play the game right, you could get over on that landlord for as much as six or seven months. Don't bogart that joint now."

"How about I go into court and complain that the landlord never fixed anything?" I said. I wanted to contribute some of my own ideas to the contest. "I could say the bathroom sink leaked since the day I moved in, and the electricity kept going on and off and on and off."

"Not a good idea. For one thing, that never works. The judge will just ask you why you want to stay in a house where the landlord doesn't fix anything. Then you're stuck. Besides, you're not going to court at all."

"Not going? The judge will find against me for sure if I don't show up."

"The judge is going to find against you anyway, man. You haven't paid your rent since January. You are guilty as sin, and the judge is going to order you to move out."

"So that's it then?"

"No, that's not quite it. If you don't move out on your own, which you will not, the landlord can't move you out by himself. He has to get the constable and a moving company scheduled to do a forced move-out. That's going to take about two weeks. He may not realize right away that you didn't move out, and that's some extra time right there. That puts us out to around May 24 or May 25 or maybe even as late as May 30. The constable will deliver a notice telling you the move-out date so you can move out before that and he won't have to come out to the house."

"Wow! So I've got about another month and a half then."

"No, you're not leaving so soon. We've got too much dope to smoke to have you leaving us yet. The day before they come with the moving truck, you go over to the court and file a paper called a 'Motion to Set Possession Aside and Stay Writ.' That will stop everything in its tracks. It is just amazing what that little piece of paper can do."

"What does that mean?"

"It means you tell them you never got any notice and you weren't aware that anything was going on until the constable gave you the move-out date. The judge will sit on that for a couple of weeks and then set another court date one day near the end of June. Then he'll give you until July 2 to move out. Again you don't move out on your own, and the landlord schedules the constable and the moving company. When the constable gives you the forced move-out date, probably around July 18, you plan to move out the day before."

"So that gives me three more months without paying any rent? Are you sure this is how it works?"

"Sure I'm sure. I've done it myself. This way you get from February to mid-July for free. That's five and a half months. You could have gotten more, but you are a terrible liar. You could have strung out the landlord a lot longer than you did, especially since you paid your rent so faithfully for the whole year. Once he files with the court, the time period is kind of fixed at about three months, but only when you use the 'Set Aside Motion' technique."

The whole plan sounded like a pack of bullshit until he came up with the actual name of the paper I would file with the court. Then I believed him. I followed his advice to the letter, and the plan went exactly as prescribed. I moved out of the house on Bolton Avenue on July 17.

Chapter Seventy

CORINNE HAD HER high school graduation party on Sunday, July 3. Friends and relatives gathered in our backyard for hot dogs and hamburgers cooked on the open grill and baked beans stewed in a Crock-Pot. Corinne made potato salad, and I brought potato chips fresh from the Marsh store. Beer and soft drinks chilled in several coolers as people milled around, talking about the promising future ahead for Corinne and her fellow classmates.

I had not told anyone in the family about losing my job or about the rent and utility delinquencies. Even at the Saint Patrick's Day Party I managed to avoid the subject. This time I could not get around telling Dad about the eviction since I would have to move in about two weeks. I tried to broach the subject gently, but things came to a head quickly.

"I'm going to have to look for another place to stay," I said as Dad meticulously turned the burgers on the grill. I'd learned from Michael Jones that people no longer "lived" someplace; they merely "stayed" there.

"What do you mean? Why are you moving?"

"I've got to move. I can't pay the rent."

"Why can't you pay the rent? I don't get it. You make good money at that plant."

"I've been laid off."

Dad paused his grilling and looked at me. There was no suspicion in his eyes. The lie was accepted since he had been laid off many times himself, especially when he was new to the workforce.

"Oh my," he said. "Well, you can get another job. Ask the landlord to ride with you until you find work. He seemed like a reasonable guy, and it won't take that long to find another job now that you have some serious work experience."

"I can't do that. I've already fallen behind in the rent. He won't ride with me any longer."

"What about all the money you've made? You've been working at that plant for more than a year. You've got some money saved up, don't you?"

"No, I don't have anything saved. The utilities were more expensive than I thought they'd be. I've already spent what little I put away."

"Patrick, it costs money to move. If you can get him to work with you until you can find something else, it will save you money in the long run."

"I can't get him to work with me, Dad. I'm being evicted."

"Evicted? You mean you're being thrown out?"

His voice rose so that everyone at the party heard his proclamation. I think even the neighbors may have heard it. I sheepishly looked around and realized that I should not have brought this up during the party. The first eyes that I caught were Corinne's, and I knew that I had just ruined her time. This event was supposed to be about her, and I had just made it about me.

"Yes. I'm being thrown out," I whispered in the hope that Dad would whisper too.

"That's a fine thing." He did not whisper. "And what has happened to the security deposit?"

"That's gone," I whispered again.

"So now you want me to come up with another deposit so you can move to a new place and then get evicted from there. Is that your plan, Patrick?"

"No. That's not my plan."

I dropped my soft-spoken tactic since it wasn't working and raised my voice level to match his. I didn't care at this point who overheard our argument. Anyway, it was too late to save Corinne's party. Once again I had let her down and left her stranded, but I couldn't help that now.

"I just thought you might want to know that I'll have a new address, but I guess you don't care about that. You don't care about my school or about my job or about my life. I'm nothing to you. I may as well leave. Not that you'd notice."

Dad was visibly shocked by my words. He stepped back as though I had landed a punch squarely in the middle of his chest. I regretted my crazy outburst, but it was too late. Once the words are out there, you can't take them back. You have to own them, good or bad.

I then did what I do best. I fled the scene. I pushed my way through the backyard to the alley, down the alley to Walnut Street, and across Walnut toward Dequincy Street. I stopped at the corner of Walnut and Dequincy to catch my breath and regain my senses. This had all happened without forethought. Now that it was too late, I tried to think.

I came up empty. I knew that I had hurt Dad badly with my ill-chosen flare-up, but I had no idea how to repair the damage. I knew I had spoiled Corinne's graduation party, but I could not come up with a way to put the fix to that either. I still had two weeks before I would have to move, but I had no plan.

I thought back to a cold December day when I stood on this very corner talking to pretty Mary Kelly. That conversation launched the idea that she could help me save my relationship with Toby. I made a bad decision that day. I think I made a bad decision this day too. I couldn't remember the last time I had made a good decision. I decided to try Mary Kelly again.

I walked the half block to her house and climbed the steps to her porch. I hesitated there, unsure of myself. What would I say? Why was I there? What if she rejected me? I hadn't spoken to her since our two-day romp in the sack that culminated in my breakup with Toby and her breakup with Joe. More than a year and a half had passed since then. She would have every right and every reason to reject me.

What if she didn't reject me? I couldn't perform in bed any more than I could a year and a half ago. What else was I expecting from this visit? What else would she expect?

I decided that this was not a good idea, and I turned to leave without having knocked. As I turned, I heard the door open. I turned back.

"Can I help you?"

Mary Kelly stood in the doorway. No, this woman was an older version of Mary. Her hair was auburn like Mary's and hung long around her face and shoulders. But unlike Mary's well-brushed and curled tresses, this woman's hair hung straight and limp and looked as though it had not been washed recently. Her face was prematurely crossed with wrinkles and had the ruddy tone of someone that drank too much, too often. She squinted in the afternoon sunlight, her eyes bloodshot and her eyelids drooping as though the effort to hold them open was too much for her.

"Is Mary home?" I asked.

"No, she's not. Who should I say asked for her?"

"Oh. It's not important. I was just in the area and thought I'd give it a try. Thank you anyway."

"I'll tell her you came by."

I left the porch as the door closed behind me. I walked back up to Walnut Street and turned right. I could catch the Metro on Emerson Avenue about five blocks over. I still had some time left in my place on Bolton Avenue. I would have to use that time wisely if I was going to find a cheap place that included utilities in the rent.

Chapter Seventy-One

CORINNE, AS ALWAYS, was quick to forgive. As I lie in this hospital bed—unable to fend for myself, unable to walk to the bathroom, not even able to get up and put that crucifix back in its cross holder so that I don't have to look at it—I marvel at her resilience. How many times had I let her down? How many times had I stolen her thunder? How many angels can fit on the head of a pin? Too many to count. That crucifix truly represented her approach to life. She is Christlike in her ability to forgive.

A couple of days after her party, she showed up at my place on Bolton Avenue with a gift for me. She told me that I missed her big announcement by leaving the party early. She was awarded a full academic scholarship to attend the Indiana University School of Nursing. She wouldn't be needing all the money she had saved over the years, and she wanted me to have eight hundred dollars to help me get back on my feet. Of course, I would pay it back once I was reestablished and in good standing.

I never repaid the eight hundred dollars. I never had eight hundred dollars in my hands again. Even when Dad paid for me to move into the house on Temple Avenue, he paid that money directly to the landlord. I never touched it.

I owe her so much more than eight hundred dollars. That money bought me a place to "stay" when I would have been out in the street. It bought me time to find a job, which took longer than Dad expected since my work experience was not as serious as he thought. I couldn't use Precision Propeller as a reference because my departure was less than reputable. I would not have survived the summer without her generosity. I owe her my life, such as it is.

The apartment I rented on Washington Street was similar to Toby's in that it included the utilities in the rent. That's where the similarity ended. It was an efficiency apartment, which meant it had a bathroom in addition to the main room. It was kind of like a hotel room except it had no maid service, no room service, no air-conditioning, and often no heat. It had hot running water in the summer and cold running water in the winter. But they didn't need references, only cash up front. This worked for me.

I drifted from job to job over the next several years, working mostly in fast food for Wendy's, Arby's, Burger King, Taco Bell, and McDonald's. I thought the work at Precision Propeller was hard, but it doesn't compare to grilling burgers at McDonald's. That is some grueling work. The job at the Bob Evans restaurant on East Washington Street was the best of that bunch. I was the host and cashier, which meant I seated people, poured coffee, and took their money. I also helped bus tables, but I tried to avoid that aspect of the job.

The most stimulating job was with Jackson Hewitt Tax Service. They offered a free course on income tax preparation in the fall and hired anyone that could pass their course. It paid minimum wage, as did all the other jobs, but there was an additional commission for each tax return that I prepared. The job lasted only from January to April, but I took that job each winter from 2006 to 2009. I worked as many hours as they would give me since their offices had heat and my apartment did not. That commission, which was paid at the end of the tax season, helped pay my transition costs when I was looking for work, come April 16. This was the only company that hired me that didn't end up firing me. I think it was because the work was more cranial and less physical than the others. I could handle cranial. A big downside to the job was that I had to miss the Saint Patrick's Day Party every March because we were open until ten at night, but at least I was working.

Time dragged during those years. I had no *raison d'être* but to stay alive, and that's all I managed to do. Brian and Corinne moved forward with their lives.

Brian was graduated from Ball State in June 2006. Even though his grades were lackluster, he was still admitted to the graduate program in education at Ball State University. He got the job as assistant football coach at Muncie Central High School and taught tenth-grade English while attending part-time at Ball State. As a teacher, he applied his skills and his education toward changing lives.

Corinne's grades at Indiana University were spectacular. She justified her academic scholarship every semester with As straight down the line and finished with a 4.0 GPA. While some nursing students take five years to finish, she was graduated in May 2009, after four years of study, and took a position at the Indiana Heart Institute. As a nurse, she applied her skills and her education toward saving lives.

I applied for unemployment compensation—again.

Was that the best I could do? With all my intelligence and all my athletic ability, all I could accomplish was the completion of an unemployment benefits application. I should have been ashamed of myself, but I wasn't. This mess, after all, wasn't my fault. My fatigue on every physical job I held was a medical condition that I could not control. I did my best on every job I held, but my best was not good enough. I was constantly tired, and my low energy inevitably led to my dismissal, except from Jackson Hewitt Tax Service.

When Corinne finished nursing school, a general feeling of celebration enveloped the family. I was again on good terms with Dad because for all appearances, I had righted my errant ways. Even though I changed jobs often, they were menial jobs in the fast-food industry, and moving from job to job in fast food was not unexpected. From Dad's perspective, my real job was in tax preparation, and this was necessarily seasonal.

About a week after Corinne's graduation, Dad arranged a job interview for me as an assistant custodian at School #15, the Thomas D. Gregg Elementary School on Michigan Avenue. My boss at Jackson Hewitt gave me a good recommendation, and with Dad's referral, landing the job was a cinch. And as with almost all my jobs, landing it was the highpoint.

Chapter Seventy-Two

DAD WAS EXCITED about my having a real job again. One that was not seasonal. He was so enthusiastic that he paid my deposit and first month's rent on a one-bedroom half double on Temple Avenue that was only two blocks from the school.

The house was wood frame painted green with gold trim. I felt like I needed to buy one of those cheese-head hats and become a Green Bay Packers fan. It had a living room, dining room, kitchen, bathroom, and one bedroom all on one floor. There was a full-size porch in front and a big yard in back. I worried about cutting the grass, but that porch was going to be used to the utmost. It also had a full basement, which would be a useful place to hide my stash. The basement steps were steep and narrow, but as long as I was careful, that would not be a problem.

The unit next door was vacant and had a For Rent sign in the yard. I wondered if a new version of Michael Jones would move in and become my smoking buddy.

Unlike my apartment on Washington Street, this house had heat, but I had to pay for the gas. Since I had left Bolton Avenue with a large unpaid bill, there was no way the gas company would turn on the gas for me. Because there was one water meter for both sides of the double, the water and sewer were included in the rent and I had no issue with the water company. The electricity was still on in the previous tenant's name, so I got a free ride for a while on that one. But I had to do without gas for the summer.

By the time September rolled around, I decided I needed to have the gas service turned on before the nights started to chill out. About the same time, the previous tenant's electricity credit ran out and the power was turned off. I needed to do something about the utilities.

Back when I lived on Bolton Avenue, and I wasn't paying my utility bills, my old neighbor and smoking partner, Michael Jones, had told me about how he had once put the utility bills in his sister's name. I decided I needed to try the same technique, only in my brother's name. This wouldn't cause a problem with Brian because he lived in Muncie and the utilities didn't cross-check all their accounts with utilities that were out of town. And since I planned on paying the utility bills, it wouldn't affect his credit rating.

I talked the landlord into giving me a lease in my brother's name. I told him my brother was not going to live there but that he was going to pay my utilities for me. The landlord was only interested in getting his rent each month, and he didn't care what I told the utility companies.

Both the gas company and the electric company required a photo ID along with the lease before they would provide service. Getting the fake lease had been easy. Getting Brian's driver's license was harder.

Brian didn't come home much in the summer and fall because of football, but he did come home for a two-night visit in late September when Muncie Central played Howe. Both teams were expected to be strong contenders for the state title, and it was widely thought that the winner of this game could go undefeated on the year. Muncie beat Howe that night, and Brian was very much in the mood to celebrate the win. Dad, Brian, and I drank beer until three in the morning, then we collapsed into our beds. In spite of Brian being a light sleeper, I managed to slip his license out of his wallet without waking him that night. I had no plan of how to replace it. I just let him think he'd lost it.

In no time at all, I had gas and electricity at the house. All was well.

Chapter Seventy-Three

ALL WOULD HAVE been well if it hadn't been for my fatigue issues—and, of course, the grass.

As the assistant custodian, my job involved emptying the waste baskets every day after school and taking the trash to the collection point. I cleaned the restrooms and vacuumed and mopped all the floors every evening. Once a week I waxed and buffed those floors. But this work was not overly physical. I had an electric-powered cart for collecting the trash and a service elevator at my disposal. The vacuum was a very light ride on my back. Automated waxing and buffing machines did all the work themselves; I needed only point them in the right direction. Only the mopping was done the old-fashioned way, and all these tasks were made easier by the fact that the school building was practically brand-new. All the floors were newly laid tile, and the machines flowed over these new floors with an ease that made a custodian's job nearly effortless. My fatigue problems never got in the way.

For the first few days, the head custodian worked with me until I knew the routine. After that I was on my own. He worked the day shift from seven to three thirty, and I came in at that time to relieve him. Once he saw that I showed up, he could go home. I was a diligent and faithful worker and could be trusted to complete all my assigned tasks on my own without his supervision.

The work was easier through the summer. There were fewer students in the summer program, and not all the rooms were used. I adjusted the job so that if the trash can didn't have anything in it, I didn't vacuum and mop the floor in that room. This gave me plenty of time to do the rooms that were used, along with the great hallways, and still have time for a lengthy smoke break in the middle of my shift.

The grass helped me cope. It was my sole source of relief from the realization that I had not amounted to much. Dad was happy that I was working. He repeatedly assured me that the work of a janitor was honorable and important. I had a hard time swallowing that. He said I was a valuable and productive member of society. I felt like I was not utilizing my natural gifts in math and the sciences. I was glad that he was satisfied, but I needed a diversion. Grass helped me deal with my frustration, and it didn't interfere with the work.

The method of skipping the unused rooms worked fine through the summer, but when the full complement of students showed up in late August, it was no longer feasible. There were no unused rooms. The restrooms took longer to clean, and the trash cart filled up more quickly, requiring several trips rather than just one. My smoke break had to be eliminated.

In mid-October the school went on fall break, which was actually just a long weekend. For fall break, I reinstated the smoke break. When the students came back the next week, I rearranged my workload so that I could retain my smoke break. Each night I designated one room (on a rotating basis) that would be vacuumed but not mopped. One unmopped room would never be noticed, and this gave me some extra time to light up and enjoy a joint. After a week of this, I designated two rooms to skip each night. Then I could enjoy two or three joints.

The last two weeks of December were a breeze. There were no students and no teachers. My smoke breaks lasted most of the shift. It was hard to readjust when they returned in January, but I managed to cut my consumption back to two joints per evening.

One evening I decided to have a third joint. I was a little ahead of schedule and figured I could squeeze in one more smoke. If necessary I could stay a few minutes over my shift to finish the work.

The head custodian woke me up about five minutes after I lit that one up. That was the end of that job. Bad things sure do happen in January.

Chapter Seventy-Four

DÉJÀ VU! I was right back to where I had left off five years ago. Fired from my job, unable to pay the rent, unpaid utility bills piling up, no money put back for a rainy day, and storm clouds forming on the horizon. If I'd spent less money on weed, I might have had some banked to help weather the coming storm. Of course, if I had spent less money on weed, there would be no storm brewing.

The really sad part was the timing. Only two weeks earlier I told Jackson Hewitt Tax Service that I would not be returning this season. Another opportunity lost. Even fast-food places were not willing to take a chance on me anymore.

I started showing up mornings on State Street where jobless guys hung out waiting to get picked up for day work. At first I was picked every morning because I was bigger than most of the Mexican guys and looked like I could do the job. But I was usually unable to do the work satisfactorily, and more and more often I found myself walking away with the scrawny guys that were never picked.

I managed to get through the winter on the money from the day jobs and from odd jobs like shoveling snow only because I did not pay my utility bills and I gave the landlord only enough money to keep him riding. The fact that the other side of the double was empty since I moved in indicated that he had a hard time renting this place. He kept threatening to throw me out, but if I gave him a sad story, a hundred dollars, and a promise to catch up eventually, he would give me another month even though the rent was four hundred and I was four months behind.

In May they cut off the gas. I had lived without gas before, so I was not overly bothered by that. In June they sent me a letter saying the electricity was cut off, but it never actually went off. They just quit reading the meter. I worried every day that I would wake up without power, but that never happened.

Money came easier in spring and summer. Contrary to popular notion, it does rain in Indianapolis in the summertime, and as a result, grass-cutting jobs were plentiful and more reliable than shoveling snow in winter.

Life was not great, but it wasn't all that bad either. I had enough money to keep myself in grass and food. What else did I need? For sure, I was going to have to face up to the issue of heat come winter; eventually the power was going to actually be shut off; and I probably would be evicted sooner rather than later; but those troubles were to be faced in the future. I was living in the now. Unfortunately, now is very short-lived.

In June, Brian was offered the head coaching position at Warren Central High School on the Indianapolis Far East Side. He spent the summer preparing for the fall season but did not move to Indianapolis until August since he had one final course to finish at Ball State in order to complete his master's of education degree. He then rented an apartment at our old stomping ground, Braeburn Village. Fortunately, the gas was included in the rent at Braeburn Village. Unfortunately, the electricity was not. Brian was not able to get the power turned on because I had ruined his rating with the power company. He then checked on the gas and water and found that his rating with the gas company was also ruined.

I found that my rating with Brian and Dad was ruined. There would be no more funding of rent or deposits. There would be no more late-night celebrations of football victories. I would no longer be welcome at the Saint Patrick's Day Party. Even though I had missed the last six parties, this was a tough blow to take.

Only Corinne remained. Her capacity for forgiveness is endless. In September, my birthday passed. Dad and Brian did not acknowledge it. Only Corinne brought me a small gift of cigarette papers.

"I noticed you've been rolling cigarettes, Paddy," she said. "I wish you wouldn't smoke, but this is the only gift I could think of for you."

She is observant. How I managed to keep the grass out of her sight is a miracle. I wanted to roll a joint right then, right in front of her, and offer her a hit, but my stash was secreted away in the basement and hard to get to, so I didn't.

I was not invited home for Thanksgiving. Corinne brought me a plate of turkey and the fixings on Friday. I had nothing to offer her. I had spent all the money I had on an electric space heater that I hoped would keep me from freezing to death as the winter closed in around me.

Christmas was a cold and lonely time. Snow thinly drifted down from the sky and blew across the lawns, but none stuck to the ground or to the street or to the broken sidewalk, leaving a vacated feel to the neighborhood. The trees were empty of their leaves, and several of the houses were empty of people. The street was dark and empty, and so was I.

Once again, I was not invited home. I spent Christmas Eve hunched under a blanket on the floor next to the space heater. I was out of food, out of grass, and out of options. I could hear the Bad Boyz arguing in the house two doors up the street. I'm sure Santa Claus had finished his rounds when the shots rang out. There was no question as to what they were.

Michael Jones used to say, "When they start poppin' tops, don't even go near the window. You never know when one of those toppers will come through and get you."

That was sage advice, which proved perceptive that night because one of those toppers did come through my front room window and would surely have gotten me if I'd been curiously watching the action. I ignored it, and I ignored the two guys that ran past my bedroom window immediately after.

But I couldn't ignore the cops that showed up half an hour later. I spent the bulk of the early morning hours of Christmas painstakingly explaining to the police that I had heard and seen nothing other than my window glass breaking, which I thought was a dream. "Yes, I live here. Yes, I have a lease. No, I was not involved in the ruckus up the street. No, I don't know who lives there. Yes, you may remove the bullet from my front room wall." I wanted to make a recording and play it each time a new cop came on the scene. The cops were done by noon, and the street resumed its quietude.

Corinne showed up around four.

"What happened to your window?" she asked as she laid her packages on the floor and walked over to the place where the police had pried the bullet from the drywall.

She turned and looked at me when I didn't immediately answer. I didn't want to go into a long explanation, but I couldn't come up with a reasonable lie. Then I figured, what the Hell? It didn't really matter anyway. It wasn't my fault, and there was nothing that either of us could do about it. The truth was the easiest way.

"There was a small shootout last night," I said.

"A small shootout? What is a small shootout?"

"There were some shots fired out in the street. One came through my window. I wasn't hurt. I was in the bedroom."

"Paddy, you need to come home," she cried. "You can't continue to live here without any heat, with shots being fired through your window."

"Dad won't let me come home."

"Daddy will let you come home. He loves you, and he misses you."

"He hasn't talked to me since August. Not on my birthday, not even on Christmas."

"All you need to do is reach out to him. Call him. Tell him you're sorry about the gas bill. I know he'll forgive you if you reach out."

"Okay, I will." I wanted this line of conversation to end.

She handed me her cell phone. I took it before I realized what it was. I just stared at it.

"Call him."

"I don't know what to say."

"Say 'Merry Christmas.' I think that always works."

She smiled, and I saw in her smile that she believed that's all it would take. But life is not that simple, and this problem was more complex than an unpaid gas bill. There was the gas bill, no small matter in and of itself, but there was also the electric bill and the lost custodial job, the lost Precision Propeller job, and all the other lost jobs. There were also the lost rent and deposit payments and all the back rent I had not paid both here and on Bolton Avenue and those utility bills on Bolton. More importantly, there was the lost trust. How could I look Brian in the eyes after stealing his driver's license? How could I face Dad after lying to him so many times I can't begin to count and after playing on his faith in me time after time? How could he ever believe me again? No, I didn't think "Merry Christmas" was going to resolve this one. I fumbled with the phone for a minute then handed it back to her.

She dropped the phone into her overcoat pocket as she rushed toward the door. Before closing the door behind her, she turned back to me, tears filling her eyes, and said, "The gifts are from Daddy and Brian. We will all be praying for you, Paddy, and I hope you will pray for some guidance yourself."

Then she was gone, my sister, the only one left that gave a care for me. She had left behind her packages and implied that they were gifts for me from Dad and Brian, but I knew better. I opened them one at a time. None of them had a note saying who they were from. Corinne could tell me they were from Dad and Brian, but she could not bring herself to forge their names on a note.

There were three packages. The first contained a fluffy green-and-white comforter with a shamrock pattern design. This would serve me well on the coming frosty nights. The second contained soft leather hand gloves with warm wool lining. I tried one on, and it fit like a glove. The third revealed a pair of heavy winter boots also with wool lining. When I reached inside the boot to feel the lining, I felt something else instead. It was a plain white envelope, unsealed, and with no name on it. Inside the envelope were twenty-five new crisp twenty-dollar bills. I tried on the boots, and they fit like boots. They must be a gift for me, and that included the money.

I wore the new boots and gloves along with my old overcoat and blue jeans out into the cold that afternoon. I took some of those twenty-dollar bills and bought a stock of food, but not before I bought a restock of Colombian Red smoking weed. I had my priorities straight.

Chapter Seventy-Five

ON CHRISTMAS NIGHT ten inches of snow fell across central Indiana. Normally that would have paralyzed the city, but this year the day after Christmas was a Sunday, and no one was going anywhere anyway. I was glad that I had not waited to stock up on smoke and food, and I spent the next week huddled under that new comforter next to the space heater, staying warm and getting high. I didn't spend all the money that Corinne had given me, so I didn't worry about going out in the weather to earn anymore. I had what I needed as long as I didn't run out of matches.

New Year's Eve came and went without my notice. There might have been some firecrackers shot off in the neighborhood, but who could tell them from the other shots that happened all too frequently? My landlord didn't fix my broken window, so I had unobstructed listening pleasure to everything that was going down, none of it interesting. I didn't mind that the landlord didn't fix things; after all, I wasn't paying him much, but I was afraid that one of the homeless guys would think the house was abandoned. Often one or more of them would break into a vacant house and set up homestead. The next thing you know, the house was burning down because they started a fire to keep warm. I didn't need the hassle of chasing away vagrants.

On New Year's Day, the weather warmed and not a day too soon. I had plenty of weed, but I ran out of food. It wasn't five degrees above zero anymore, but I still needed to bundle up in my old overcoat and wear my new winter boots and gloves to go to the store. I didn't want to carry the balance of my grass with me. I hid it in the basement, and I found the new boots cumbersome when I was negotiating the narrow flight of steps. I nearly tripped and fell down the stairs, but I managed to catch myself. I stashed my grass in its hiding place behind a couple of nearly empty paint cans, green and gold, and had no trouble going back up the stairs.

When I stepped onto the front porch, I became invigorated. The temperature was probably around twenty-eight degrees, but the sun was shining and the air was still. When the chilled air flowed into my lungs, they expanded in welcome reception of the fresh burst of oxygen. I had definitely been stuck inside the house for too long. The snow was deep on the porch and in front of the house, but mine was not the only walk not shoveled. The boots would serve me well on this supply trip. I made sure the door was securely closed and locked before setting out.

It didn't take me long to get the supplies I needed. There was a Hispanic Mercado at the corner of Michigan Avenue and Forest Avenue only two blocks away that carried any type of groceries you may want. Most of the whites and blacks in the neighborhood didn't shop there merely because they assumed they only carried Mexican stuff like hot peppers, tortillas, picante, and guacamole. It didn't occur to them that Mexicans might also like to eat potatoes, corn-on-the-cob, and Rice Krispies. I toted a full bag in each arm and headed back to the house. I wasn't gone more than twenty minutes, but that was probably fifteen minutes more than they needed.

I knew there was a problem before I reached the house. The two extra sets of footprints in the snow to and from the front porch were my first clue. The front door standing wide-open was my second. One of them had entered through the broken window and then opened the door for the other from inside. It was obviously two of the neighbors since they were in and out in the short time that I was gone. They had to have seen me leave, and then they pounced.

I sat the groceries on the front steps and approached the house cautiously, calling out as I entered. No one returned my call. I stood motionless for a minute in the front room, listening. Not a sound. I slowly exhaled. They were indeed gone. All the money I had in the world was in my pocket. There was nothing to steal. I hoped they would spread the word.

I retrieved the two bags of groceries from the porch steps and deposited them in the kitchen. I was hanging my overcoat in the hall coat closet when it occurred to me that I did have something that was worth stealing. I went into the bedroom and discovered that I was right. My electric space heater was gone. So was my new Irish comforter.

I hated these people that I lived among. They weren't my neighbors. *Neighbor* was too good a word for the likes of them. That's probably the reason why they called it the hood. There was no neighborhood here, only hoodlums. They would never make a move to help me or anyone else. They would just as soon see me freeze to death. They knew that space heater was the only barrier I had against the winter, the only thing keeping me alive. They had to know, or they could have guessed that the comforter was more than a blanket to me. Those things had no meaning to them. It was all about the money. It was merely my life in exchange for their few dollars.

Anytime an investor tries to improve the area by fixing up an abandoned house, they move in and steal the newly laid carpet or remove the new aluminum siding to sell for scrap, getting pennies on the dollar. Or they remove the water lines—particularly if they're copper—to sell the pipes for scrap. They'll tear through newly hung drywall to get at those pipes. Is it any wonder there are so many vacant houses and so few people willing to invest? Is it any wonder that my landlord doesn't want to fix a broken window? I would never invest a penny here.

I suddenly remembered the only other thing I had that was worth stealing. What about my Colombian Red?

I rushed to the kitchen and threw open the basement door. No longer wearing my overcoat but still wearing my heavy boots, I moved swiftly down the narrow staircase, but I only made it halfway down before my feet got tangled up with each other and I tripped, tumbling headfirst to the cement floor below.

I don't remember the pain, only the sight of my blood spreading out slowly on the soiled floor before my eyes as I lay prostrate—my left cheek, eyebrow, and forehead driven hard across the rough surface. I was conscious long enough to see the bloody river reach the sewer drain, uncovered and filthy in the middle of the floor.

Chapter Seventy-Six

"Is he alive, Doctor?"

"He's alive, but we've got to get him to the hospital soon."

"The 911 operator dispatched an ambulance. It should be here any minute."

Disembodied voices echoed close above my head. As much as I tried, I couldn't open my eyes. It was as though they were stapled shut. I couldn't remember where I was until the cold, damp feel of the basement floor crept slowly into my hands and arms, which were pinned under my chest and stomach. Hands reached under me and gently turned me over onto my back. I felt a blanket under me, and my head fell back into a pillow. Another blanket was thrown over me and tucked in around me. My whole body was cold in spite of the blankets, but I didn't shiver; I couldn't move.

I was dimly aware of being maneuvered up the stairs on a stretcher and then transferred to a gurney. I blacked out in the ambulance and awoke in the hospital. I had no idea how long I lay on that basement floor or in that hospital bed.

I opened my eyes to one of the most beautiful sights in the world. Even with her eyes reddened with tears, Corinne was a vision to behold, her auburn hair flowing around her perfect cheeks and chin, her face aglow, and her smile dazzling.

"Hello, Corinne," I said.

"Oh, Paddy," she cried as she threw herself onto the bed and hugged me. "You really are alive."

"Yes, I think I am."

I realized then that my face was heavily bandaged. I raised my hands to my face and found that my hands were also bandaged.

Corinne got off the bed and straightened herself and the bedcovers.

"What day is it?" I asked.

"It's Sunday, January 2."

"I was out for a whole day," I said.

"You are so lucky that Dr. Blumenthal came looking for you, or we might not have found you for several days. I can't bear to think of what would have happened to you."

"I'm fine."

"No, I don't think you are fine, but you are alive."

"Who is Dr. Blumenthal, and why was he looking for me?"

"Actually, I knew him from a class he taught at the IU School of Nursing. But that's not why he tracked you down."

"Okay, I give up. Why did Dr. Blumenthal track me down?"

"Did I hear my name?"

A tall, lanky guy in green hospital scrubs entered the room and approached the bed. He extended his hand to me. I could barely lift mine to reach his in return. The bandages prevented a solid handshake, but the gesture was acknowledged.

"Hello, Mr. Maloney. My name is Dr. Blumenthal, and I will be happy to answer your question, but first a little on your current status."

The doctor carried an air of authority and credibility. I liked him immediately and trusted him with no reservations. It may have been the graying at his temples or the honest smile. Whatever the reason, he had my attention.

"You are stable and doing quite well considering your fall. You must have broken that fall with your hands and saved more serious injury to your head. You do have abrasions on your hands, so it seems to follow. You also have some serious abrasions on your face and forehead, but fortunately you did not break anything. You were very lucky."

He leaned over me and examined the several bandages on my face, lifting one after the other to check the progress beneath. He made some notations on my chart.

"Head injuries tend to bleed heavily and don't stop readily, so there was much loss of blood. It will take a little time for your body to recover from that. The injuries have been cleaned and dressed and will heal in no time. There is no sign of infection, but your IV has an antibiotic included just in case."

"So I'm going to live?"

"It appears that you are."

"So why were you looking for me?"

"You are a unique individual, Mr. Maloney."

"My name is Patrick, but you can call me Paddy or Hat if you like."

"Okay, Patrick it is. Well, Patrick, I am an oncologist. That means I treat cancer patients. I also study cancers in the hope of finding cures. You, Patrick, are a cure for cancer."

"What do you mean?"

"Let me explain. Seven years ago, I had a patient named Joan Gray, who was deep into the third stage of lung cancer. Even though she was a relatively young woman, only fifty-five at the time, her cancer was in both lungs and had spread to her liver and her kidneys. Her prognosis was not good, and we did not expect her to live for much more than a year."

Dr. Blumenthal paused his story and moved a straight-backed chair up to the side of the bed. He sat for a moment, silently studying my chart in his left hand as I contemplated Joan Gray's situation. It was similar to Mother's condition, and it occurred at the same time. He continued in a slow and solemn voice.

"In December of 2003, Joan Gray was in an automobile accident on Arlington Avenue at about Tenth Street. She was in critical condition and had lost a significant amount of blood. I was called in because I was her treating physician for the cancer, but I was not involved in her treatment for this accident. She was given a blood transfusion that included the blood you donated at Howe High

School on December 10. Mrs. Gray recovered fully from her injuries in the car crash partly due to your donation of blood."

"I'm glad that my blood was used to help her. But what does this have to do with her cancer?"

"Everything."

Dr. Blumenthal moved my chart from his left hand to his right. He paused to gather his thoughts, then he continued.

"You see, after she recovered from the crash, she began to recover from the cancer. The cancer began to slowly withdraw, little by little. It took about four years for it to completely disappear. It took us another three years to analyze this miracle before we finally figured out what had happened and what had caused it. It was your blood, Patrick. Your blood saved her from her crash injuries, and your blood saved her from her cancer. You are a miracle. You are *Nessa.* Your blood is a natural cure for cancer."

"I don't understand. How can that be?"

"Let me try to explain. All cancer cells give off what we call volatile compounds. Your blood cells have the ability to identify this volatile compound emission, trace it to its origin, and tag the emitting cell so that it can be recognized by the white blood cells of the host body. Once the white blood cells recognize the cell as a tagged cell, they will remove it from the body. This is a natural process called phagocytosis. It's quite simple, actually. We now understand what your blood cells do. We just don't understand how they do it."

Understanding bloomed within me, and anger blossomed along with it as the full implications of this revelation dawned on me.

"My blood is a natural cure for lung cancer?"

"And other cancers, at least liver and kidney cancer. We have not been able to test it, but we suspect it will work on many other cancers as well."

Anger and anguish rose in equal measure, and my body quaked with building tension. If I had only known, I could have done something.

"And it has always been this way?"

"Yes, as far as we can tell. At least it was this way seven years ago when Joan Gray received the transfusion of your blood."

I burst from pent-up pressure and screamed with all the ferocity my lungs and vocal cords could muster.

"Seven years ago my mother died of lung cancer! Now you are telling me that a transfusion of my blood would have saved her?"

I tried to throw my blankets off so I could jump out of bed and throw a waste basket across the room, but I couldn't get my arms to work. There was no energy. I threw a fit instead.

"Get the fuck out of my room! I don't want to see you. I don't want to hear you, you bastard! Get out of my sight!"

Both the doctor and Corinne left the room in a hurry. I fell back into my pillows and fumed. My anger turned to despair, and I rolled over and cried into the sheets.

Chapter Seventy-Seven

THE SHIFT NURSE woke me to take my temperature, my pulse, and my blood pressure. All three were extremely low, but she didn't comment on them. I asked her to check my IV since it didn't appear that anything was flowing through the tubes. She fiddled with the bags and the tubes and then assured me that all was working properly. I was being given fluids, nutrition, and antibiotics intravenously, and I was also allowed to have regular meals and drinks.

I'd had lunch at 12:45, which according to the wall clock was only half an hour ago, but I was still hungry. I asked her if I could order more food, and she said she'd find out about that. She checked my water pitcher and, noting that it needed to be refilled, took it with her out the door. She returned in a few minutes with a full pitcher, which she placed on my side table.

"You'll have to wait until dinnertime to order more food," she said, "but I brought you some crackers that will help tide you over."

She put the crackers on the side table next to my water glass and a box of Kleenex.

It's a good thing I didn't look out the window this morning, because if I had, I would have nothing to do this afternoon. There was a television set mounted on the wall, but I never got into TV. In school, I was too busy with soccer and study; after that I didn't have the money or the inclination to buy one even though my neighbors Michael Jones and Latisha Pitts had their TV on high and always.

Through the window I could see the top of a great white oak tree and the sky. Getting out of bed would sap my energy, so I had to be satisfied with that view. Even with so little to see, the contrast was startling. The white oak was lacking leaves as you would expect on January 2, but the sky behind it was deep blue and freckled with billowing clouds reminiscent of a summer day. The disparity was like my condition: alive in that I breathed and ate and talked, yet not quite alive in that I merely existed and had no purpose.

Corinne appeared at the door, toting a plastic Walmart bag. She sat the bag on the shelf along the wall and came around the bed to give me a kiss.

"Good afternoon, Paddy. I hope you're feeling better."

"I feel great," I said. "I feel like I could play a good round of soccer. Then I think I might go out dancing."

"You never went out dancing in your life!"

"But I did play a good round of soccer back in the day."

"Yes, you did that. And maybe you will again, with the help of Dr. Blumenthal."

The mention of his name brought back the memory of my flare-up this morning. I briefly flashed anger, then remorse as I realized that neither he nor Corinne was responsible for the news; they merely delivered it.

"I'm sorry about my outburst this morning, Corinne. I was angry and frustrated, but I shouldn't have taken it out on you."

"It's okay, Paddy. I understand your frustration. But there's nothing that can be done about Mother now. Now we need to focus on you. We need to help you get better. That's going to take effort from me and Dr. Blumenthal and from you, Paddy. We all need to work at this."

"Yes," I said, but work was the farthest thing from my mind just then. "So, what did you find at Walmart that I could possibly need?"

Corinne looked puzzled for a moment and then realized I was asking about the bag she had brought. She went to the bag on the shelf and removed Mother's wooden cross with the silver crucifix. She disassembled the cross and affixed the crucifix so that it stood on the shelf where I could clearly see it. She returned to my bedside without comment; Mother's crucifix spoke for itself.

"Thank you, Corinne." The crucifix meant more to her than it did to me, so I truly appreciated her bringing it to me, but I didn't think it was going to help my recovery.

"Daddy is working double shifts this week in order to accommodate vacations so he may not come to visit for a couple of days."

"If ever..." I said.

"Paddy! Don't be like that. It's not his fault that you've treated him the way you have. It's completely your fault. But he will forgive you if you just reach out to him. All you need to do is call him."

"Yes, Corinne, I know."

"I have to go to work now, but I'll be back in the morning. I sure hope Dr. Blumenthal has some good news by then." She leaned over to kiss me goodbye then reached into her purse and extracted a small package. "I almost forgot. Here are some breath mints for you to use until they get you a toothbrush and some toothpaste. See you tomorrow."

"Very funny," I said.

"I'm not kidding. You need them, sure 'n begoraugh."

She giggled on her way out the door. Her giggle always made me feel like singing. But even though I felt like singing, I just didn't have the energy and there was no one to hear me anyway.

I sighed and closed my eyes. I recalled when we three—Brian, Corinne, and I—would sit on our front steps and sing into the night. We'd sing the popular songs of the day for sure, but we also sprinkled in some of the Irish songs that Mother and Dad loved so much. When we did that, Mother and Dad would often join us. So many times, I remember, Corinne did not know the words and she would start to giggle. Her giggle would spur both Brian and me on, and we would finish the song with strong voices, hand flourishes, and much fanfare. I longed for those days when my greatest worry was whether or not I knew the words and could keep up with my brother.

I heard Corinne's giggle, and I saw her smiling face fresh in my memory. I started to sing with a feeble but honest effort:

> When Irish Eyes are smiling,
> Sure 'tis like a morn' in spring.

In the lilt of Irish laughter,
You can hear the angels sing.

The shift nurse came in to check my vital signs, and I stopped singing.

Chapter Seventy-Eight

HOSPITALS ARE IN their own time zone. I don't mean that the clocks are an hour behind or an hour ahead. I mean that time moves at a different speed than everywhere else. A friend that had several surgeries told me that time speeds up when they knock him out. He said that before he would go under, they would ask him to count backward from ten. He would count ten, nine, eight, seven…and then he would wake up and the surgery would be over. Now that is fast.

But time in the hospital can also go very slowly. That was the case Sunday afternoon and Sunday night. I once had a class in a room where the wall clock was broken, yet its hands still moved faster than those on the clock in my hospital room. The shift nurse checked my vital signs every hour or so all through the afternoon and night. A lab technician poked my finger and took a few drops of blood every couple of hours. I was rapidly running out of unpoked fingers. Every time I drifted off to sleep, they woke me up for one reason or another. I spent the entire time in bed, but by morning I was exhausted.

Corinne arrived around eight o'clock, and I was so relieved to see her that I let out a whoop like a bronco busting cowboy. I immediately grabbed the breath mints she had given me and popped one into my mouth.

"I'm not taking any chances," I said.

She giggled then gave me a good morning kiss.

"So you must have had a good night to be in such a good mood," she said.

"Just the opposite," I said. "It was the worst night of my life. They kept poking and prodding me all night long. I barely got a minute's sleep. I don't know what they were looking for, but I don't think they found it. No, I'm in a good mood now because you are here."

"What a nice thing to say, Paddy." She gave me another kiss. "See! You can be a gentleman if you set your mind to it."

Dr. Blumenthal entered the room. The look on his face did not indicate whether he had good news, bad news, or no news at all. His smile was friendly but not revealing.

"I thought I heard signs of life in here," he said, nodding to Corinne. "How do you feel this morning, *Nessa*?"

"I sure don't feel like a miracle, Doctor. I feel more like a pin cushion. What was all the poking about?"

"We needed to test your blood to see how well you are recovering from your blood loss. We have been working on your tests all night."

"So how am I doing?"

"I have a rather long answer to that question."

"I have all day, Doctor."

"Everyone is different," he said, "but you, Patrick, are truly unique."

He paused to let this sink in, glancing at Corinne to see that he had her attention as well, and then he continued.

"Let me briefly describe, in layman's terms if I can, how the circulatory system works. A primary ingredient that all cells need to function is oxygen. The air we breathe contains oxygen, among other things, and when we fill our lungs with air, the red blood cells extract the oxygen and carry it to all parts of our body through the blood system. When you run, or otherwise exert yourself, your muscles use that oxygen to expand and contract and make your body move. The more you run, the more oxygen your muscles burn up until they start to become depleted. When that happens, they demand more oxygen from the blood, and you breathe faster and heavier to get more air into your lungs. Your heart beats faster in order to pump your blood faster so you can grab more oxygen from your lungs and deliver more to your muscles. Does this all make sense?"

"Sure," I said. "I remember most of that from tenth-grade biology class."

"Good. So do you remember that a red blood cell typically remains functional for around one hundred fifty to one hundred seventy-five days?"

"I don't remember all the details, but yeah, I know they need to be replaced regularly."

"Every day, all day long, and especially at night, the typical body is replacing worn-out blood cells. It's a constant process, like painting the Golden Gate Bridge. As soon as you get to the other end, you need to start over at the beginning again."

"I understand that," I said. This discussion was starting to get interesting. I wondered what it had to do with me.

"The bones not only form a framework to support your body and allow for mobility. They also contain marrow, which is where your blood cells are manufactured. I'm sure you have noticed when eating a chicken that the bones are softer at the ends. Your bones are similar in that they also are more porous on the ends. This is where the new blood cells are distributed into the bloodstream to replace those worn-out cells that are removed from the stream."

He shifted his clipboard from his left hand to his right, and I recognized that he did this because he was about to shift his explanation from the general to the specific.

"Your red blood cells are different in a number of ways. I explained the cancer-detecting property to you yesterday. I pointed out then that this characteristic is not known to exist in anyone else anywhere in the world. Last night we learned that your red blood cells do not wear out the way normal blood cells do. They don't need to be replenished every five or six months. In fact, we think they may last for as long as twenty years, maybe even longer. Their carrying capability diminishes very, very slowly. Like the cancer tag, this quality is unique to you. It is not known to exist in anyone else, anywhere in the world, and is the primary reason you are still alive today."

This revelation was a shock to me. Not the revelation that my blood cells were different than other people's blood cells, I knew that already; or that they were the only ones of their kind in the world, I was told that yesterday morning; or that they were virtually immortal. These things did not register as all that important. But the idea that my life was somehow in danger was a stunner.

"What? Otherwise, I would be dead? Why do you say that? What do you mean by that?"

I looked at Corinne, who was as shaken as I was. Her face drained of color, and fear registered there just as it had when we first learned of Mother's lung cancer. We both turned back to Dr. Blumenthal.

"You have a condition known as aplastic anemia, which means that your bone marrow is not manufacturing red blood cells for replacement of worn-out cells. This is an idiosyncratic condition. Excuse me, by that I mean, it is a condition that is rare and unpredictable. It is usually fatal, as you can imagine."

"Fatal?"

"Yes. When your red blood cells die and are not replaced, your body has no way of providing oxygen to the cells. Death is the imminent result, usually within a few months. However, in your case, since your blood cells have a much longer productive cycle, it may take twenty years or more."

I could take twenty years to die? That's kind of like living, I thought. Since no one knows when they are going to die anyway, what difference could this knowledge make? I could get hit by a truck tomorrow if I could only get out of this bed and out to the street.

"Is there a cure?" Corinne asked.

"No. There is no cure. The condition is rare and often isn't diagnosed until well into the critical time frame, so there has been little research toward a cure."

"So you're saying that my bones don't make red blood cells, but because the ones I have don't die, I can live with this for twenty years or more?"

"That is our speculation. Of course, you are the first case of this kind, so we don't really know."

"But I'm twenty-six years old now. Why aren't my blood cells already dead? How could I still be alive today without replacement blood cells?"

Dr. Blumenthal didn't have time to respond to my question when Corinne threw out a question of her own.

"How could he have matured physically if his body doesn't manufacture red blood cells? He needed to be able to generate additional blood as he grew from a baby to an adult."

"I can address both of those questions with one answer," he said. "You have not had this trouble your whole life. At some point after you matured, you acquired the condition."

"Are you saying I caught it from someone else?"

"No. It's not an infectious disease and is not contagious. It can be caused by overexposure to radiation or to toxins like benzene, but more than likely, it's an adverse reaction to a drug. Have you ever been treated for attention-deficit hyperactive disorder, ADHD?"

"No, I haven't."

"So you've never been given carbamazepine. What about epilepsy or seizures? Have you taken felbamate or phenytoin?"

"Never heard of them."

"You probably have not had malaria, but have you taken quinine for any reason?"

"Nope."

"I'm sure you have not had typhoid, cholera, or meningitis. That pretty much rules out chloramphenicol, except for the eyedrops, and it's not generally used for that anymore."

"Eyedrops? I went to an eye doctor once," I said, recalling my misadventure with the Mexican roofers. "It was that place on the corner over there."

I pointed out the window toward the intersection of Ritter Avenue and Sixteenth Street where the medical office building stood. Both Corinne and Dr. Blumenthal looked out the window, then looked at each other, and then looked back at me.

"She gave me a prescription for eyedrops."

"Do you remember what prescription it was?"

"It was prod something acetate. It cleared up my eyes in a couple of days."

"That could be prednisolone acetate. Did it say Pred Forte on the bottle?"

"Yeah, something like that. She said it was a steroid, so I asked her if it would disqualify me from competing in sports. I was an athlete in school, you know, and I didn't want any Barry Bonds issues haunting me down the road. She said I would be fine."

"Yes. Prednisolone acetate is a steroid, and it does not contain chloramphenicol, so that was not the source of your problem. Besides, chloramphenicol is more commonly found in underdeveloped countries, and the risk of contracting aplastic anemia from chloramphenicol eyedrops is somewhere around one in ten million. It's extremely rare."

"But didn't you just tell me that I am one in nine billion?"

"Yes, I did. As a matter of fact, I did."

Chapter Seventy-Nine

WAS THERE EVER going to be a stop to all this good news? First, my blood cures cancer, but it's too late to save Mother; second, my blood does not die; and that's convenient because, third, aplastic anemia prevents my body from producing any more blood. What could possibly top that trio?

"I'm having trouble swallowing all of this," I said, "let alone digesting it. What are the ramifications? Are there treatments? What do I do now?"

Dr. Blumenthal looked perplexed, and he shook his head slowly. "As I've said, we have never encountered this before. I have a team of nine professionals working on your case, and it is our top priority. We are literally moving through unknown territory here. We have very limited options and can only guess as to what may happen next. We are working on an action plan for you, but we do not have anything concrete right now. I will have more information for you later today, and I will certainly keep you informed as things progress. I can only ask you to be patient with us while we work this out."

"Oh, I'm a great patient, Doctor, and I'm getting plenty of practice."

Dr. Blumenthal chuckled. "I'm glad you can maintain a sense of humor, *Nessa*. It's an important survival tool, and we need all the tools we can get."

He turned and headed for the door, then stopped and turned back.

"Oh, one more thing. Do you mind if I tell Mrs. Gray that you are here? She's the woman who received your blood and recovered from her cancer. I'm sure she would want to visit with you to thank you. Would that be okay with you?"

"Sure thing. Tell whoever you want. The more the merrier. I don't exactly have a crowd of visitors, as you can see."

"That's fine. I'll call her this morning."

Corinne stood by the window, the sun highlighting her hair and surrounding her head in a halo. I thought it was going to take an act of God to turn this quandary around, and He sent me an angel. How could anything go wrong as long as Corinne was watching over me?

"I'm sorry I wasted your money, Corinne," I said.

"What money was that, Paddy?"

"The eight hundred dollars you gave me from your college savings."

"What did you do with that money?"

"I used it to get the apartment on Washington Street."

"I gave it to you for that purpose, so you didn't waste it."

"But I never paid you back."

"You paid me back when you said you were happy to see me this morning."

Corinne is my sister and I've known her all of her life, but I still can't figure her out.

"So what do you think about your situation?"

I didn't want to think about my situation. What was to think about? I could die now, or I could die later. What is so different about that? Isn't that what everyone faces every day? I know my cause of death ahead of time. So what? I still don't know when, and I surely don't know why.

"I don't think much of it," I finally said. "It sucks."

"Dr. Blumenthal seems like a good man and a smart man. He and his team are working on the problem. Maybe they will come up with something. But in the meantime, Paddy, you should be prepared for the worst. You need to pray to God for guidance. He will let you know what is best, and He will help you with any decisions you have to make."

"Yes, Corinne, I will do that."

She knew I would not, but she didn't press it. She knew I would break if she pressed too hard. The occasional reminder and the subtle comment were her style. She prayed that I would come around eventually.

After the nurse checked my vital signs one more time, I dozed off. Those lab boys had apparently taken enough blood through the night, so they left me alone this morning. I managed to get a solid couple of hours of badly needed sleep.

When I awoke, Corinne was chatting with an older woman that I had never seen. Corinne immediately noticed that I was awake and cut off the conversation.

"Welcome back, Paddy," she said. "You have a visitor."

Corinne and the woman stood, and I saw that she was probably average height for her age, about five foot five, but next to Corinne she looked like a midget. She was in her early sixties, and she carried her age well. Although she had some laugh lines at the corners of her eyes, her face was generally wrinkle-free. Her hair had just a hint of gray which was probably due to the skill of her hairdresser.

"Patrick Maloney," Corinne said, formally, "I would like you to meet Mrs. Joan Gray. Mrs. Gray, this is Patrick Maloney."

"I am so happy to meet you, and please call me Joan."

"Okay, Joan," I said, "and you can call me Mr. Maloney."

Joan flinched at my unexpected response and said "Oh."

Corinne did not flinch. "He's joking, Joan. You can call him Patrick or Paddy or Hat. He answers to all three." Her eyes flamed at me and demanded that I be on my best behavior.

"Oh, okay, Patrick, I'm glad to meet you, and I hope you're feeling better. I understand you had an accident at home. Most accidents happen at home, you know."

"Yes," I said, "that's why I'm thinking of moving."

"Ha ha, that's good. And quick. You have a good sense of humor, Patrick. It's important to laugh at life, or it will get you down eventually. That's probably the most important lesson I learned in my fight against the cancer."

"How long did you have cancer, Mrs. Gray?" Corinne asked before I could interject another wise remark. I decided to let them have their conversation without interruption. It took too much effort to keep coming up with witty comments.

"Apparently I had it long before it was detected. It had already spread across both lungs by the time I was diagnosed. I was on chemo and radiation treatment for more than a year when they discovered it in my liver. Six months later, it showed up in my right kidney. I was given six to ten months to live, and we discontinued the treatments. They weren't working."

"So you had resigned yourself to die within a year?"

"Yes. I had initially taken a leave of absence from school for the treatments, but eventually I had to quit. All of my energy was sapped. Both the cancer and the treatments take it all out of you. The one thing the cancer gives you is time to set things right in your life. Not a whole lot of time, but more time than an automobile accident does."

"Then you actually had an automobile accident."

"Yes, and I have you, Patrick, to thank for saving my life with your blood donation. Thank you for doing that. Your blood not only saved me from my car injuries but, Dr. Blumenthal tells me, it actually destroyed my cancer. I don't fully understand that, but I certainly appreciate it."

I looked at the wall clock and did not reply.

"Are you fully recovered now?"

"Yes. They tell me my cancer is not in remission but is completely gone. There are some scars on my lungs, but that's about the only evidence that I was ever plagued by the cursed thing. I'm back teaching the third grade again, and I hope to continue teaching those kids until they drag me out kicking and screaming. Patrick, I owe you a great debt that I can never repay. You gave me a new lease on life, and I'm trying my best to make the most of the time you provided me. I don't make much money as an elementary school teacher in the IPS system, but my husband has done well in his construction business and he is willing to pay your hospital costs for as long as you need to stay. We hope that will help you recover from your infirmity."

It was time that I got into the act here.

"I don't need your money, Mrs. Gray," I hissed. "I don't want it. I don't want to hear about how grateful you are that you got my blood. That blood should have gone to my mother, not to you. My mother needed that blood. She deserved it, not you. If I had known, you would have never seen a single drop of that blood. You can leave now. Go back to your snot-nosed school kids and leave me alone."

Joan Gray sat straight in her seat. This time she did not flinch at my outburst.

"You did an unselfish thing when you gave that blood so long ago, Patrick. I see that you have now grown into a very selfish man. That's too bad. I feel sorry for you. But we are going to pay your hospital bills anyway. We will do it for that generous school kid that donated blood without asking for anything in return and inadvertently saved my life in more ways than one. We will hope and pray for his survival of this hospital stay, and we hope you don't suppress him for much longer."

She rose and kissed Corinne lightly on the cheek. She touched my foot through the blanket and then turned and left.

Chapter Eighty

"That certainly went well." Corinne stood next to my bed with her hands on her hips, peering intently at me. "One might have thought she had stolen your piggy bank with the way you tore into her."

"I couldn't stand to hear her talk about how well everything was going for her. She got my lifesaving blood, while Mother was on her deathbed. It should have gone to Mother, not her."

"No one knew what your blood could do, Patrick. You didn't know it, and she didn't know it. Treating her rudely cannot change that. It just makes you look bad. She came to thank you, and you threw her out. She offered to help you, and you turned her away. How many offers of help do you think you can refuse before you run out of offers?"

"I could get tons of offers. Do you have any idea how valuable my blood is? Cancer patients would pay a fortune to have just a pint of my blood. One transfusion would cure their cancer forever."

"And how would you spend that fortune, Paddy? Would you buy a fancy casket? How about a nice plot with a good view of the city at Crown Hill Cemetery? We could buy a good bit of Jameson Whiskey for toasts at your wake."

"What are you talking about?"

"I'm talking about your blood, brother. You lost quite a bit of blood when you fell down the steps and cracked your head. It was all over the basement floor. Why do you think you can't get out of bed without assistance? You're not making new blood, and you lost a bunch when you fell. Do you think you have blood to spare to sell to anyone?"

I had not thought it through. She was right. My problem all along was insufficient blood. My poor soccer performances, my inability to take my exams, my inability to work long hours, and my depleted sexual performance were all due to lack of blood. My body was not replacing the blood I lost. How much had I lost? A vision of blood streaming into the sewer drain in my basement suddenly filled my mind's eye. I shook my head to chase that image, but the thought lingered.

"I'm not going to get better, am I?"

"We don't know the answer to that question, Paddy."

"I'm never going to be able to sell my blood or give my blood or do anything with my blood. I'm barely alive now. If I lose another pint, I will surely die. This cancer-curing capability is a total waste. It's never going to cure anyone besides Joan Gray."

"I would guess that you are very close to the minimum that can sustain you."

"Sustain me! That's all it can do. I can't even get out of bed. I merely exist. If I lose blood, I die; if I don't, I may as well be dead. To be or not to be? That is indeed the question."

"Don't even ask that question, Patrick. We can only pray to God to give us guidance."

"That's the only question worth asking. But don't worry, Corinne. I'm not going to kill myself. I choose to be. We must always choose life. It's our nature."

We sat silently for a while. All that could be said had been said. The room took on a depressing tone in spite of the beam of sunlight streaming through the window. Hopelessness slowly overtook me. I wondered if Corinne felt it too. I think she must have since she decided that it was lunchtime when it was only eleven o'clock. She left me with my uncertainties.

I ordered a big lunch. A sliced turkey sandwich with all the trimmings, French fries, a large chocolate milk, and a fruit plate with slices of papaya, cantaloupe, honeydew, and watermelon soon arrived. I felt like I could eat an elephant; my body was crying out for food, yet I could not eat. I drank some of the milk, ate a slice of cantaloupe, and nibbled at the edge of the turkey sandwich. I munched on some saltine crackers, which didn't take much energy. I wondered if this was another manifestation of my blood problem. I needed the nutrition, but my stomach was still full from breakfast. My digestion had become sluggish, perhaps from insufficient blood supply to carry the nutrients throughout my body. Or perhaps I was just too tired to eat. Perhaps my blood issue was becoming the catch all for everything that was not going right in my life.

When Corinne returned from lunch, she brought a vase full of winter roses. She placed them on my side table and arranged them so they spread evenly above the vase in a hemisphere of red and green, dotted with white baby's breath. They brightened up the room but not my mood.

"These flowers are from Daddy," she said. "He wanted me to tell you that he hopes you're feeling better."

"I suppose he picked them himself," I said.

I knew that Dad had not sent the roses. That was not his style. Corinne was hoping I would take it as a forward move toward reconciliation and make a move myself. But things just weren't that simple. There was more water under that bridge than a hundred dozen roses could absorb.

Dr. Blumenthal came in and questioned me about the blood drives in high school and my freshman year at IUPUI but had no new information about my condition or about any plan of action. I began to think there would never be news for me. What could they possibly do for me now?

"I'll be back to see you tomorrow, *Nessa*," Dr. Blumenthal said, moving toward the door. "I have something else we need to talk about, but I need to check on several things first."

I rolled over and turned my back to him without saying goodbye. He had something else to talk about? What else was there? We could discuss my last will and testament, or we could chat about moving me to a corner room in the cancer ward with windows all around. Joan Gray was willing to pay my medical bills, so why not do it right?

The nurse did not check my vital signs and no lab boys showed up to prick my fingers throughout the night, but I slept fitfully all the same. I could not face the future, and I did not relish the present. I could only live in the past.

Chapter Eighty-One

MORNING FINALLY ARRIVED. It was another bright and sunny January day. What happened to all those blustery winter days that I remember from my childhood? The winters of old were cold and full of snow. I recall drifts as deep as three or four feet along the red brick walls at Braeburn Village and even higher along the grassy banks on Wallace Avenue. It seemed that global warming was taking over and winter would never be the same.

What did it matter to me? I would never go sledding again. I would never again spend a winter day skating on the pond or huddling by the bonfire at the pond's edge. Never again would I fall into a snowdrift with Toby Rosen. What did I care?

Corinne arrived at the same time as Dr. Blumenthal. He was anxious to get to his point of the day, so our cordials were short. He wasn't smiling when he introduced his new idea, but he spoke in hopeful tones.

"There is something else we can try, *Nessa*," he began. "My staff and I have been discussing this since we brought you in a couple of days ago. It is potentially dangerous, but it may be the only option we have, given the fact that you are not producing blood to replace what you have lost."

Corinne's eyes brightened as she looked hopefully across the bed at Dr. Blumenthal. "What is that, Doctor?"

"Blood transfusion," he said. "If we can fill you up with fresh blood, perhaps it will resolve your deficiencies."

"I didn't realize that a blood transfusion is dangerous," I said. "Isn't it just like giving blood but in reverse?"

"Not at all," he responded. "Your body will have to accept the new blood for the transfusion to be successful. It's similar to a heart transplant in that the body may accept or reject the new blood. To maximize the chance of acceptance, the blood needs to match your blood type as closely as possible, and we need to consider other factors such as the presence of antigens and antibodies. Some blood types are more widely accepted by the body than others. You may have heard that type O negative is a universal donor. That isn't exactly true but it is commonly accepted by other blood types. Sadly, people with O negative blood usually cannot accept other blood types and may also have issues with antigens and antibodies."

"I have O negative blood, right?"

"We're not sure of that. Originally, we thought you did because your blood screened like type O negative, but with the other unique qualities of your blood that we have discovered recently, we have to wonder what effect those qualities have on your typing. We have assigned a new type designation to your blood: type C positive."

"I never heard of that blood type," Corinne said. "Is that a new type just for Paddy?"

"Yes, it is. Patrick's blood is so different from any other blood we know we have to give it a new type designation, and we don't really know how it will react to the introduction of a foreign blood to his circulatory system. We have done all the normal prescreening, and we have a blood donation that has not reacted negatively in that prescreening. So it may be possible that your system will accept this new blood."

"So the concern is that my body may not accept the new blood?"

"That's right."

"Well, there's one way to find out—try it."

"It's not that simple. Blood transfusion rejection is fatal in almost all cases. We only use transfusion when a patient has lost so much blood that it's absolutely necessary to replace that blood or the patient will die, like in a car accident. I will tell you that blood rejection itself is rare, but that's because we take great pains to match blood types and control the other factors. In your case, we're not sure what other factors may be involved since we know so little about your blood."

"So if this doesn't work, I'll die."

"That would be my presumption."

"And if it works, I may be able to resume a normal life."

"That's a possibility, but we don't know for sure what your body will do with the new blood."

"And if I don't do it, I may as well be dead."

"I need to add that if your body rejects this blood, it will be an excruciatingly painful death. It's not a decision that you want to take lightly."

"I always did well on binary tests, Dr. Blumenthal," I said. "Give me two choices and I usually make the right one. I want you to proceed with this transfusion as soon as you possibly can. That's my final answer."

He looked to Corinne for confirmation. She nodded.

"As long as you're sure," he said, "we can proceed this morning. As I said, we have the blood donation identified and in the cooler. We have already completed the prescreening tests and have no coagulants and no adverse reads. We just need to do the required paperwork. You will need to sign consent forms, and we have blood tracking and matching forms that need to be completed on our part. If it's okay with you, I will get started on that right away."

"The sooner the better," I said.

The moment he left the room, the sunbeam disappeared from the window, winter clouds crowded out the blue sky, and the branches of the oak tree traced darkly against a gray background. The sudden change in the weather cast a shadow on the day but not on my mood. I was as bright as a day in May and had hope in my life for the first time in years. The thought of a blood transfusion had never entered my mind, but now it seemed so obvious, like Medicine 101.

With new blood I could regain the stamina of my former years. I could get a job and hold it. I could go back to school part-time and get that degree in engineering that Mother said was in God's plan. A whole world of opportunities opened up before me, and I could clearly see my potential for the first time in years. I might actually be able to make things right.

"Corinne," I said, "may I borrow your cell phone? I need to call Dad."

Chapter Eighty-Two

"Merry Christmas, Dad."

That was what Corinne had told me to say on Christmas Day back on Temple Avenue. I couldn't think of anything better. At least it got things started.

"Patrick…son, is that you?"

"Yes, Dad, it's me."

"Patrick, I'm so glad you called." I thought I detected a sniffle in his voice, but I hadn't spoken to him since last summer, and he might have developed a sinus problem, so I could have been wrong. "How are you? What I mean is, Corinne told me about your problems with your blood, and I understand that your situation is quite serious, but how are you holding up?"

"I'm doing well, Dad. Really."

I briefly reiterated the cancer cure capability, the aplastic anemia, and my recent loss of blood just to be sure he was up to date on all of that. Then I told him about the transfusion that was at the moment being scheduled.

"This could finally be the solution, Dad. This could restore me to my former self. I am so sorry for all the torment I have put you through. I know you have no reason to believe that I can change, that I can be a better man, a responsible man, but I tell you I'm no longer that person that took your money and lied to you. I'm so sorry that I did that, and I promise I will make it up to you. I'm no longer that person that couldn't keep a job and failed at everything I tried. I really am a better man than that inside. With this blood transfusion, I can become the man you wanted me to be. I won't have this anemia holding me back. I'll have nothing holding me back. I'll go back to school part-time and get that degree in engineering. Mother said it was in God's plan, and I'll make sure it happens. I just need you to say you'll be able to forgive me when I show you that I've truly changed and I make things right with you and with Brian."

"I forgive you now, Patrick." Yes, there was a sniffle in his voice—I heard it quite clearly that time. "I forgave you at 'Merry Christmas,' son."

So Corinne was right as always. "Merry Christmas" was all I had to say after all. Dad was as forgiving as Corinne, and all I had to do all along was reach out to him just as she said.

But that didn't change my need to make things right. I had done a lot of stupid things and created a bunch of hurt. I had a ton of making up to do. But that was not going to be a problem. As soon as I have a full complement of blood in my body, I will have the energy that I had back in high school. With Dad's acceptance, I will be able to conquer the world.

"I'll be over to see you later this morning, if it's okay with you, Patrick."

"Of course, it's okay with me. Thank you, Dad. Thank you for being there for me, in spite of all I've done."

"I love you, son."

"I love you too, Dad." Now I had the sniffle in my voice.

After I signed off, Corinne bent over the bed and hugged me. She held on long after I let go and squeezed me robustly. When she lifted her head, she had a tear on her cheek and a familiar sniffle in her voice.

"I love you, too, Paddy. I'm so proud of you. You made the move, you reached out, and now you've saved the family. Now I know that you will be fine no matter how the blood transfusion works out. I know it was hard for you to do, but you did the right thing. I love you."

"I love you too, Corinne. I should have listened to you sooner. You were right all along. Dad is just as forgiving as you are. All I needed to say was 'Merry Christmas,' and he accepted me even before my apology. All was forgiven."

She took a tissue from the box on my side table and dabbed at her eyes. She was doing that a lot lately.

A new nurse entered my room carrying a folder full of papers. She appeared to be about Corinne's age, but when I looked into her eyes, she reminded me of Toby Rosen. Those eyes were as green as the sea, and the blush in her cheeks was like a bed of coral. Her jet-black hair fell around her face just as Toby's had, and her smile was every bit as bright.

"Hello, Mr. Maloney," she said. Her voice was cheerful and tinkled like Toby's did when she was happy. "My name is Sandi Slavin, and I am going to be the nurse in charge of your blood transfusion. I have a consent form that you will need to sign before we can set you up."

Corinne touched Sandi on the shoulder and said, "Hello, Sandi. Do you remember me? Corinne Maloney, from nursing school."

Recognition crossed her face, and her smile spread and brightened. She stepped to Corinne's side and gave her a hug.

"Of course, I remember you. You were the smartest girl in the class, Corinne. I think you were the only one to get an A in Dr. Blumenthal's class on cancer and cancer patients. Do you remember?"

"I remember his class, but I don't think I got the only A."

"I think you did. I didn't make the connection in your last name. Is this your husband?"

"No, he's my big brother."

"Her not-so-big brother," I said.

"Well, if this transfusion is successful, we may be able to put some meat back on your bones, Mr. Maloney."

"Please, call me Patrick."

The paperwork didn't take long. My consent form was just a one-page document requiring only one signature and a date. Sandi verified the name and numbers on my wristband and cross-checked them with the plethora of papers in her folder. I didn't need to see any of the myriad of other papers.

Later Dr. Blumenthal explained the process.

"We will start with a one-unit transfusion of whole blood. That's approximately one pint. We'll give you a couple of days to assimilate the new blood. If all goes well, we will repeat the procedure as many times as necessary to get your circulatory system up to full capacity. It may take four or more transfusions depending on how well you receive the new blood and how rapidly we feel we can move. We can do multiple units in a transfusion once we know your system is accepting the blood without problems."

I was surprised that the procedure took place right at my bedside. I expected them to wheel me into an operating room, make me count backward from ten, and put me to sleep. I was actually awake for the whole thing. From my perspective, my initial intuitive mental picture was accurate. It was just like giving blood but in reverse and in slow motion. They hooked up the unit bag with clean, clear tubing to the IV that was already in place. The blood dripped, dripped, dripped slowly from the bag into the tube and flowed surely into my bloodstream. The difference was there were always two nurses in constant attendance, continuously measuring my vital signs, repeatedly checking and double-checking the apparatus, and generally monitoring me for any signs of irregularity.

Corinne went to the family lounge to allow Sandi Slavin and her assisting nurse plenty of room to do their work. Dr. Blumenthal also left to see other patients during the procedure. I had the full attention of both nurses for the entire two hours.

All went smoothly, and there were no irregularities. I had been lying in this bed for just two days, yet my calves and thighs had already begun to atrophy from lack of stimulation. But now I could actually feel the oxygen being delivered to my muscles. With renewed energy, I bent my right knee and pulled my leg up to a tent position. I then did the same with my left leg. Silently, I rejoiced that I was able to accomplish this simple task. This was not much of an achievement in the universal scheme of things, but it was a monumental triumph in the miserable failure that my life had become.

Chapter Eighty-Three

"Your blood pressure and pulse are still low, but your body temperature has risen to 98.3," Sandi Slavin informed me. "We don't expect your blood pressure to fully recover until you have a full complement of blood, so this is fine so far. I'm surprised that your temperature is recovering so quickly. Dr. Blumenthal will be able to give you more details after we are able to do some lab tests, but I don't think he wants to poke you too soon after the transfusion. How do you feel?"

"I feel great. I can lift my legs. I have more energy than I've had since I first woke up in this hospital two days ago. I think I might even be able to get out of bed. I'd like to look out the window."

"You don't want to rush things, but you may be able to do that later. We will need to wait for Dr. Blumenthal to check you out and give the go-ahead. There's nothing to see out there but snow anyway."

"It's snowing? I can't tell from this angle. All I can see is the gray sky and the top of that white oak tree."

"Hello, *Nessa*. How are you feeling?" Dr. Blumenthal said as he entered the room.

"I'm feeling great. Nurse Slavin and I were just discussing whether I should be allowed to get up and look out the window. I understand we have some winter weather happening."

"Do you feel like you can get up?"

"Sure, this is the best I've felt since I got here."

"I see no problem in trying. Just make sure that every time you do, someone is here to help you. When you stand up, you could lose blood circulation in your head, become dizzy, and fall. You don't want to have to deal with that. Let me check your heart, and then we'll give it a try."

I rose slowly to avoid the dizziness issue. It didn't happen. With help I was able to get out of bed. I only needed an arm for balance as I walked to the window, and once there, I leaned on the sill.

The view was spectacular. Snowflakes as big as Ping-Pong balls floated gently out of the sky, resisting the pull of gravity. I felt like I was inside a snow globe that someone had just shook to get the snowflakes swirling. The ground, the street, and the houses were covered by a blanket of white as though a bedsheet had been thrown over the city. The great white oak and the other trees were dark and bare like streaks of charcoal on an artist's sketch pad. It was an undisturbed winter scene in black and white. So much for global warming.

I stepped back from the window, turned, and without aid, stood with my arms open wide. Dr. Blumenthal beamed like a proud father witnessing his son's first steps. Encouraged, I decided to push the schedule.

"We can do another transfusion today," I said. "I feel great, and I see no reason to delay. The sooner, the better."

"Your positive response so far has made me optimistic, *Nessa*, but we need to proceed with caution. It can take days for the new blood to be fully assimilated, and negative reactions don't necessarily manifest themselves immediately. There will be plenty of time for you to enjoy life if all goes well, but we need to protect against the possibility that things may not go as well as planned."

I walked back to the bed unassisted to show how much I had improved. Dr. Blumenthal was impressed but unmoved. I resigned myself to follow the original schedule and impatiently await the okay for a second life-changing transfusion.

Once I was safely tucked into bed, Dr. Blumenthal and the assisting nurse left. Sandi Slavin checked my vital signs again, instructed me to use the call button if anything changed, and then she also left me alone.

I didn't realize how tired I was until everyone was gone. I had only received one pint of blood, and although a pint made a world of difference, I was still critically short of essential supply. I no longer had to put on a show of strength, and I quickly fell into a deep sleep.

When I awoke, the room was filled with people. The first person I saw was Corinne, fully smiling for the first time in days. Her cheeks glowed rosy pink, and her eyes shone with happiness. She had obviously heard the good news of my positive reaction to the blood transfusion, and she was doubly pleased by the presence of others in the room. Dad and Brian flanked her, and Aunt Mary sat in a chair by the window.

"Dad," I said. "Thank you for coming to see me, and thank you for taking me back into the family. And, Brian, I'm so glad you came. It's so good to see you. I need to apologize for what I did to you. I am so sorry I messed up your credit. I stole your driver's license. I can't believe I did that. But I promise I'll never hurt you again, and I'll make up for everything as best as I can once I'm out of here and on my feet again."

"Everything's okay, brother," Brian said. "We didn't know about your blood problem. I thought you were a derelict or a lazy freeloader, but now I know better."

"I was a derelict, and I was a freeloader. My blood disorder was a poor excuse for my bad behavior. I ran away from my problems rather than face them. I chose the easy way. But I will change all of that. The blood transfusion has worked, and just as it did for Joan Gray, it has given me a new lease on life. I intend to make the most of it."

"Just get better, Paddy," Brian said. "Everything else will work out. Not to worry."

"Aren't you going to apologize to me too, Patrick?" Aunt Mary chimed in. "You seem to be giving apologies out freely, and I demand to have one of my own."

"Aunt Mary," I laughed. "Thank you so much for coming, and I apologize for anything and everything I may have ever done to offend you."

"That's better," she said, "and I forgive you too."

Sandi Slavin came into the room to check my vital signs.

"I see that you have lots of visitors this morning, Patrick. I hope you're still feeling good after your nap."

"I'm tired of lying in this bed. I've been on my back so long it's starting to ache. Can I get up and stretch it out?"

"You have back pain? Where exactly is the pain?" She attached a blood pressure cuff to my bicep as she spoke.

"In the small of my back."

"Do you mean your lower back?" She took my pulse and placed a thermometer in my mouth.

"Yes," I said around the thermometer.

She didn't respond until she finished her measurements.

"Your temperature is elevated. It's 100.2 degrees. We'll need to see what Dr. Blumenthal thinks before you get out of bed again. I'll call him right away." She hurried out.

I didn't need Dr. Blumenthal to tell me that things were taking a turn for the worse. In spite of the high temperature, I began to shiver. It was a painful shudder that started in both forearms and moved up to my shoulders, across my chest, and down to my lower back where it joined with the ache there and intensified it. Another painful chill started in my ankles, moved up my legs, and connected with the first in my back, amplifying the already severe pain. I felt a strong hand clutching my chest, and I became short of breath. I pressed the nurse call button and cried out for help.

Corinne rushed to my side while Dad dashed out for the nurse. I squeezed Corinne's hand roughly as bolts of pain shot through my body. I let go and pushed her away for fear I would crush her hand in my torment as another blast racked me. I curled into the fetal position, which seemed to help. The pain began to subside as I broke out into a cold sweat.

Nurse Sandi Slavin came in followed closely by Dad. There was nothing any of them could do except try to comfort me. Sandi wet a washcloth with warm water and placed it across my forehead. She set about checking my vital signs, but that was to keep busy more than anything else.

Dr. Blumenthal arrived moments later, checked Sandi's notations of my vital signs, and listened to my heart. He said he'd order antibiotics and a morphine pump, but that was about all he could do. It was up to my body, my circulatory system, to handle things from here. I thought my system was not handling it very well, but at least the intense pain had stopped, for now.

The IV location in my right arm began to swell and rash over. They removed that IV, cleaned the spot with alcohol, and applied an antiseptic salve. Then they had to insert a new IV in my other arm for the antibiotic drip and morphine pump. I didn't need the morphine pump at that moment, but it wasn't long before I was glad I had it.

The pain returned in the same fashion as before. It started as a chill, moved through my body, and centered in my lower back, repeating the cycle over and over. It was excruciating. Even though the pain emanated from a chill, I was sweating profusely. I pushed the morphine button as soon as the pain started, but it took a minute or so for the drug to make it into my bloodstream and another minute to take effect. Those were the longest two minutes of my life. The morphine pump allowed me to take a dose every six minutes, and I took full advantage of that, watching the clock, ticking off the seconds, and popping the button as soon as time permitted. Morphine didn't eliminate the pain, but it eased it enough to take the edge off. It made it close to tolerable. Even with the drug in full effect, the clutching of my chest made me scream out.

In one of the milder minutes, while drug-dulled spasms moved through my legs, I thought of my statement yesterday to Corinne. I chose then "to be," but with the knowledge that I was probably soon to die anyway, I thought now that I might choose "not to be" and would end this torment. And the worst was yet to come.

Dad brought me a bedpan when I asked for it. The pain had momentarily subsided, but my stomach was queasy and I began salivating. Memories of Pleasant Run Parkway, whiskey, beer, and Mary Kelly flooded back from my high school days. I knew I was about to throw up my breakfast.

As it turned out, I threw up more than that. My breakfast was generously mixed with blood. Strangely, I wondered how I was going to replace that loss. I continued to dry-heave with only a small additional amount of blood loss. Amazingly, I was glad to dry-heave in spite of the pain. At least I wasn't losing more precious blood.

I continued to sweat throughout the ordeal, but after I vomited, I noticed the sweat on my forearms had a reddish tint. The color deepened, and great pain accompanied the change. I clenched my fists as my arms were compressed as though each was caught in a vise that squeezed tighter and tighter. That agonizing pain spread throughout my body, and I thought I could no longer endure. My face was drenched, and I saw that a drop of sweat hung on the end of my nose, red as the winter roses in the vase on my side table.

With all the pain and all the vomit and all the chills and fever and spasms and all the suffering and anguish, I still worried about the blood. I didn't want to lose it. I wanted to live. Even while racked in agony with no hope that the torture would ever end short of death, I chose "to be."

Chapter Eighty-Four

NOW, NOT ONLY my arms but my whole body was in a vise that was crushing me with enormous pressure, squeezing me like an anaconda wrapped around my torso, constricting and constricting until my insides gave out. My bladder released, and fluid flooded my groin area and soaked the sheets around me. I wet the bed.

The pressure eased and the weight lifted. There was still pain, but the morphine was able to dull that. I cried, but then I had been crying all along. These tears, though, were tears of relief. I knew that the worst was over. I had reached the crest, gone over, and the rest was downhill.

Corinne removed a blood-soaked washcloth, rinsed it in a pan of warm water, and returned it to my forehead. The warmth of the water penetrated my skin for the first time even though she and Sandi had been rinsing my face the whole time. I was coming out. The pain was receding, and life was returning. I pushed the morphine button just to be safe.

It took another hour for all the pain to go away. All that was left was soreness: soreness in my calves, my thighs, my back, my stomach, my biceps, my forearms, even my forehead. My whole body ached, but I did not have sharp pain. Thank you, morphine.

"I'm alive!" I said after giving it much thought and to no one in particular. "Why am I still alive? Rejection of a blood transfusion is fatal, I was told."

"You are truly a unique individual, *Nessa*."

"You know, I'm getting a little bit tired of being so unique, Dr. Blumenthal. But I guess this time it's for the better."

"Yes, apparently your old blood rejected the new blood, but instead of killing you, your system purged the blood from your body while retaining the old blood to keep you alive. A small amount was expurgated when you vomited, some was actually removed in your perspiration, but the bulk of the new blood was eliminated through your urinary tract. Don't ask me how this worked. I know what happened, not how it happened."

I was not the only one to suffer that day. My family went through hell. Corinne, Dad, Brian, and Aunt Mary had to watch while I writhed and screamed and moaned and cried. They could only stand by helplessly while I rushed headlong to my inevitable death. Corinne tried to help by spelling Sandi with the warm washcloth, but this only brought her closer to the reality of my misery. My miraculous survival merely heightened the tension. There was visible relief when Dr. Blumenthal said that he thought I should be left alone to rest this night.

Dad, Brian, and Aunt Mary wished me well and promised to return tomorrow. Corinne lingered after the rest left.

"So I'm back to square one," I said. "I have enough blood to stay alive, but not enough blood to live. To be or not to be? I keep asking myself that question."

Corinne stood silently by the shelf with her back to me. She was staring at the crucifix. I knew she was praying, so I said no more until she made the sign of the cross and turned around to me.

"Paddy, have you asked yourself why you keep surviving these fatal events? You contracted aplastic anemia—normally 100 percent deadly—but you survived for over seven years; you had a serious and potentially deadly fall onto a solid concrete floor, but you survived; you lay on that cold concrete floor in the dead of winter suffering significant loss of blood and a high risk of hypothermia for nearly twenty-four hours, but you survived; and you experienced rejection of a blood transfusion, also 100 percent deadly, but you survived. Have you wondered why?"

I knew where this line of thinking was going, and I didn't have any answers. I already knew Corinne's answer, but hers was not an answer that I could accept.

"Of course, I've wondered why, but I don't know the answer to that one. And neither do you, Corinne. I know you want me to ask God. Well, I'm sorry, but God doesn't talk to me. Maybe you should ask Him to tell you what the deal is, then you could relay His answer to me."

"I have done that, Paddy. He told me that you have to ask Him yourself. Just ask Him, Paddy. You know how. Reach out to Him. Just say 'God help me,' and He will. He'll tell you what you need to know."

"I thought I had the answer in the blood transfusion, but that turned out wrong just like everything else. To be or not to be? That is the only question left."

"No. God didn't tell you the blood transfusion was the answer. Dr. Blumenthal thought it might be, and it was worth a try. It didn't work, but God still saved you for some purpose. Ask Him what that purpose is."

"When I was at the worst of it today, Corinne, when I was sweating blood from every pore and blood was dripping off my nose and running in my eyes, and I was sure that the only relief from the pain was death, I still wanted to live."

"Ask God why He wants you to live, Paddy. He'll tell you."

"To be or not to be? That is the question. I choose to be."

"I'm going to leave you now. Think about it. Then ask God for guidance. I love you."

"I love you too."

Chapter Eighty-Five

THE MORNING BROUGHT no pain. What a welcome relief. I didn't know what to expect. Things turned on a dime in this hospital. One minute you're full of energy with new blood that your body has seemingly accepted, the next minute you're doubled up with pain and sweating blood. I thought this all might have been a bad dream, but bad dreams don't receive get-well cards.

There was a pile of cards in the morning mail. I didn't realize how many people knew I was in the hospital. As I sorted through them, I noted that most of them were from family. Being Irish Catholic, I have a lot of aunts and uncles and cousins. Our family loves to send get-well cards. We think they help, and they probably do.

But some of the cards were from others. There was one from Joan Gray's husband wishing me well and reiterating his desire to pay all the medical bills. There was one from Michael Jones of Bolton Avenue with no written message other than six names listed at the bottom (apparently Latisha had another baby since I saw them last). How had he heard? Why did he care? There was one from the employees at Jackson Hewitt Tax Service. The manager had called to see if I wanted to work this year and got the news of my illness from Dad. But the one that surprised me the most was from Mary Kelly. Her note said she was living in Columbus, Indiana, working as an administrative assistant at Cummins Engines, and she would love for me to come to Columbus to see her new apartment when I got well.

Everyone assumes I'm going to get well. I'm not going to get well. Do I write Mary Kelly a letter and tell her not to hold her breath waiting for me to come to see her new apartment in Columbus? Do I explain to her that I can't leave this hospital because I don't have enough energy to sit up in bed for more than ten minutes at a time? Do I give her details like the fact that I'm going to die in this hospital but it may not be for another twenty years or so? I don't have the energy to write that letter. I don't have the energy to send her a text, even if I had a cell phone.

I didn't read the rest of the cards. I didn't have the energy.

Corinne showed up reliable as always and stood all the cards on the shelf next to the crucifix. She plucked several dead leaves from the roses, added some water to the vase, and cleaned up my breakfast tray.

"Daddy said he'll be over to see you this afternoon. He was very tired when he came home from work this morning. He must have worried about you all night."

"Good morning," proclaimed Sandi Slavin, bouncing into the room with the vigor and enthusiasm of Janie Hodge from the *Popeye and Janie* morning cartoon show. "I've come to check your vital numbers again."

She popped a thermometer into my mouth before I could respond, and she had the blood pressure cuff wrapped around my bicep and pumping up before my temperature registered. How do nurses learn to be so efficient? It's as though they have four arms like a Hindu goddess.

"It's no wonder that Dr. Blumenthal calls you *Nessa*," she said. "It's a miracle that you survived that ordeal yesterday."

"What's the word for cursed?" I asked.

Sandi became totally serious. "Mr. Maloney, I understand that you have severe problems. I don't take your infirmity lightly, and you have reason to be dejected, but I don't think you understand the meaning of the word *cursed*. You are here in the cancer ward, but you do not have cancer. I wish you could walk down this hall and talk to each of these patients and come to know the suffering they endure. And most of them endure it with greater dignity and optimism than you will find anywhere outside of this hospital. Dr. Blumenthal is a great example of that dignity and optimism. He continues to work trying to save the lives of his cancer patients even as his own lung cancer has recently moved into stage two. You might take a cue from him when you think of yourself as cursed."

I was astonished by the revelation of Dr. Blumenthal's cancer. He had not said a word. There was no indication of any problem of that sort. Corinne must have been stunned as well. She said nothing while Sandi finished recording my numbers and left with tears in her eyes.

"Dr. Blumenthal never said anything about having cancer to me," Corinne said once we were alone.

"Not to me either. I didn't know."

"Well, now we know."

"I don't see that it makes much difference. His cancer has nothing to do with me."

"It probably doesn't have anything to do with you."

"I can't be expected to give my blood to cure his cancer. It would kill me."

"Did he ask you to do that?"

"No. He never mentioned that he had cancer."

"Then I don't think he expects you to do it."

"Even though he saved my life by finding me after I fell down the stairs, there was no risk to his life. I can't be expected to give up my life for him."

Corinne stood silently gazing at the crucifix. She clearly was asking God for guidance. I didn't need to ask for His help in this decision. This was a no-brainer. I choose to be.

"He is a good friend and he has tried his best to treat my condition, but I don't owe him that much. I don't owe him my life. I hope he can find a cure through other means, because I am not his answer."

"You're right, Paddy. You don't owe him that much. You have an obligation to yourself and to God. It's an obligation that God has given to everyone. You must choose life. We must always choose life."

Chapter Eighty-Six

A FEW MINUTES LATER, Sandi Slavin returned. She surprised me by sitting next to Corinne beside my bed.

"Aren't you going to take my pulse or plug a thermometer in my mouth?" I asked.

"No," she answered, "I'm on my break. I need to talk with both of you. It's personal."

She fidgeted apprehensively in her seat. She was not the nervous type, so she got my attention.

"First of all, I want to apologize for sounding off a little while ago. I had no business speaking to you that way. I'm truly sorry. I have my reasons, but there is no excuse for acting so unprofessionally. I hope you can accept that."

"There's no problem, Sandi," I said. "You have a tough job, and you do it well. You've been very professional as far as I'm concerned."

"Thank you."

"That goes for me too," Corinne said. "There's something else bothering you, though, isn't there?"

"Yes, there is another thing." She gathered herself again before proceeding. "I told you that Dr. Blumenthal has lung cancer. I was out of line. He has given me strict orders not to tell any patient that he has cancer. He feels that his time with his patients needs to be about them, not about him. He thinks that if a patient knows that he has cancer, it may adversely affect his relationship with that patient. I'm sorry that I told you, and I don't know what can be done about it."

Corinne made the pragmatic statement. "Well, it can't be taken back. We now know, and we can't undo that. Why did you tell us?"

"I blurted it out without thinking. I just learned last night that his cancer has developed further. Things are not going in the right direction, and I know all too well how lung cancer advances." She took a tissue from my box and dabbed at her eyes. "He still has time and he may beat this eventually, but his prospects are not good. The odds are against him."

"You're very close to him, aren't you?" Corinne asked. "You have more than just a working relationship."

"Yes, we do. I met him the same time you did, in the class we took on cancer in nursing school. That class draws students not only from the IU School of Nursing, but medical students from the IU School of Medicine and Medical Technicians from both Bloomington and IUPUI. He teaches nearly all of the new doctors in Indiana, as well as most of the new lab and medical technicians and a great many of the nurses in this state. He not only impressed me with his knowledge but also with his enthusiasm for his work and his commitment to his patients."

"Is that why you came to work at Community East?"

"Yes, and the cancer ward in particular. I've worked here since we were graduated in May of 2009. I got to know Amit and his wife, Toby, a lot better since we go to the same temple. The three of us spent time together during Rosh Hashanah that fall and have had dinner together many times since then. We sat together at the Seder Dinner last year, and I hope we will again this year. They are such a pleasure to be with because they are such a loving couple."

"Did you say her name is Toby?" I asked. Could there be two Tobys in Indianapolis?

"Yes. Amit and Toby Blumenthal."

"How old is she? What does she look like?" There could not possibly be two women named Toby. The name is not that common. It has to be her.

"She's probably seven or eight years older than I am. She may be around thirty. Why do you ask? Do you know her?"

"Does she look like you?"

"Actually, some people have said we could be sisters. You do know her."

"Toby is married to Dr. Blumenthal." I had a hard time getting my mind around that.

"Yes. She met him when she took the cancer class just as Corinne and I did. She was a medical technology student in the School of Medicine at IUPUI. She's a lab tech at Wishard Memorial Hospital now. How do you know her?"

"She taught me Spanish."

"Oh, that's right. She taught Spanish in high school for a while. We are talking about the same person."

"Is she doing well?"

"As well as can be expected. She is healthy, but Amit's health is weighing heavily on her. They are so committed to each other that it's as though they both have the cancer."

"She loves him deeply, then?"

"Very deeply."

"She's happy?"

"What an odd question. She's not happy about the cancer, but she's happily married to Amit if that's what you mean."

"That's what I meant. I'm glad for her for that."

"My break is over, and I need to get back to work. I'll be by to check on you soon."

I closed my eyes. *God help me,* I thought, and it all became clear.

Corinne sat silently through the last of that conversation. Now she moved her chair closer to me.

"Paddy?" she said.

I opened my eyes and saw expectation in hers.

"I've spoken with God," I said.

"Did He tell you what to do?"

"God doesn't work that way, Corinne. Mother told me that, and she was right. You told me to ask for guidance, and you were right. Two days ago, I said, 'If only I had the smartest girl in the class sitting next to me right now, I would know what to do. But I don't.' I was wrong about that. I do have the smartest girl in the class sitting next to me. I just wasn't listening to her."

"What are you going to do?"

"I'm going to give a pint of my blood to Dr. Blumenthal. His cancer must be destroyed. Toby's happiness is the most important thing. I'll also give a pint to you, Dad, Brian, and Toby to protect each of you. The rest of my blood, however much there is, will go to Dr. Blumenthal to be used for cancer research. This will be done tomorrow on the seventh anniversary of Mother's death and will be done in her honor."

Corinne began to cry. "Oh, Paddy! Are you sure you want to do this? This will kill you. Is this what God told you to do?"

"God doesn't work that way, Corinne. God merely showed me that I was asking the wrong question all along."

"What do you mean?" she cried.

I wiped her tear from her face, and with a satisfied smile, I said,

> To be or not to be? That is not the question.
> To be or to greater be? To love or to greater love?
> These are our choices.
> And I always did well on binary tests.

Author's Notes

YOU MAY BE aware that in 2003, Hanukah began at sunset on Saturday, December 20. It did not begin on Friday, December 12[t], as stated in this text. I needed to change the calendar in that one respect, so I exercised my literary license. I hope you will forgive me that one discretion and do not petition for the revocation of that license.

In chapter 47, I mentioned that *The Invisible Hand* and *Run and Gun*, two suspense thrillers by John W. Fosnaught, were among the books on Professor Lutz's bookshelf. This is, of course, an anachronism since the scene mentioned takes place in December of 2003 and *Run and Gun* was not published until 2010. I would be forever grateful if the reader will permit me this small dose of shameless self-promotion. I hope I have made up for it with interesting and exciting writing of a high quality.

Thomas Carr Howe High School was built in 1937–1938 and opened its doors in September 1938. The first graduating class was in 1941. The school was closed in 1995 and was reopened as a middle school in 2000. There was no graduating class in 2003, and the students and teachers in this book were the only high school students and teachers during that time. I'm delighted that Patrick Maloney and his fellow students were able to keep the school alive during its slumber. It is now a high school once again. Welcome back.

The Rootie Kazootie Club was a children's television show in the 1950s that featured Rootie Kazootie, his girlfriend Polka Dottie, their dog Gala Poochie Pup, and villainous adversary Poison Zoomack, among other puppet characters. Rootie and his troop were also featured in comic books.

Chloramphenicol is a bacteriostatic antimicrobial. It is considered a broad-spectrum antibiotic. It has been effectively used against typhoid, cholera, and meningitis but has fallen out of favor due to some serious side effects, including aplastic anemia. Chloramphenicol used in eyedrops rarely causes aplastic anemia, but when it does, only a small dose is necessary for the reaction. Some studies of the drug suggest that the link between chloramphenicol eyedrops and aplastic anemia is "not well founded." In any case, it is no longer an ingredient used in eyedrops in this country, although it is still widely used in Mexico.

Cancer is the second leading cause of death in the United States, behind heart disease. It is estimated that 577,000 people will die from cancer in 2012 and over 160,000 (nearly 28 percent) of those deaths will be due to lung cancer. More people die of lung cancer than of colon, breast, pancreas, and prostate cancers combined. Yet according to figures from the National Cancer Institute, less money is spent on lung cancer research than on research for any of those other cancers. Breast cancer research gets more than twice the funding that lung cancer research gets even though lung cancer kills more than four times as many Americans. I am all for supporting research for cures, early detection, and improved treatments for all types of cancer. I only wish the funds were more equitably distributed without regard for the political correctness of the disease.

If you can, please give generously to the American Lung Association and to your local blood bank.

Thank you very much for reading my book. I hope you enjoyed it.

John W. Fosnaught

About the Author

JOHN W. FOSNAUGHT was born and reared in Ellwood City, Pennsylvania. He attended Penn State University, Slippery Rock State College, and Indiana University. He received a BA in English and an MBA. This is his third published novel.

John now lives in Indianapolis with his wife, Ellen. His two sons, one daughter-in-law, two granddaughters, and two great-grandsons live entirely too far away to suit him.

CPSIA information can be obtained
at www.ICGtesting.com
Printed in the USA
FFHW020702121019
55526822-61328FF